THE EDEN PRESCRIPTION

—

Ethan Evers

www.edenprescription.com

ISBN 1439276552
ISBN-13 9781439276556

Library of Congress Control Number: 2010910071

DISCLAIMER

—

This work is, above all, a work of fiction. Names, characters, business establishments, institutions, and the like are either the product of the author's imagination, or, if real, are used fictitiously without any intent to describe their actual conduct. Any resemblance of fictitious entities to actual persons, living or dead, business establishments, events, or locales is entirely coincidental, notwithstanding any fictitious accounts of interactions with real entities, events, or locales. The story takes place in a fictitious future, and any reference to people, places, incidents, institutions, business establishments, or the like is made with respect to a future, fictitious version of said entities. Some historical accounts have likewise been fictionalized. The author is not a licensed medical practitioner and is not engaged in rendering advice to the individual reader. All of the information and ideas in this book are provided for entertainment purposes only, and are not meant as a substitute for consulting a physician. All matters regarding one's health require supervision by an appropriately licensed medical professional. No guarantee can be made for the completeness or accuracy of any information provided in this work. This disclaimer applies to all front and back matter as well as the novel itself.

DEDICATION

———

To my wise, beautiful, patient, and wonderful wife. Thank you for supporting this at every stage. You are truly a gift from God.

To my mentor and best friend, C., who helped me so much on this from the very beginning. Halfway through this work, C. was diagnosed with liver cancer and lost his life to it just six months later. I'll see you again in Glory, my friend.

He is no fool who gives what he cannot keep
to gain that which he cannot lose.

—Jim Elliot

FOREWORD

Since pen first hit paper for this novel, the science of natural medicine has progressed far faster than I ever hoped, let alone expected. Basic research at the university and institutional level has advanced our understanding of the anti-cancer potential and mechanisms of action for vitamin D, intravenous vitamin C, green tea, curcumin, pomegranates, conjugated linoleic acid, and many others. Vitamin D has gone from being hotly contested to largely acknowledged as the most important nutrient for general health, cancer prevention, and cancer treatment today. Vitamin D from sunlight enjoyed such a reputation in the past, over one hundred years ago. Sadly, it lost credibility for much of the intervening time—time which can never be regained. Likewise, vitamin C therapy as a treatment for cancer was discredited over thirty-five years ago, but now has gained a firm scientific foundation. The story is similar for green tea. Much more impressive than this, however, is how rapidly natural medicine has advanced beyond lab experiments and into clinical trials, and on a scale never seen before. A surge of clinical trials has been recently initiated for various cancers and registered under the National Institutes of Health (www.clinicaltrials.gov), all still active at the time of this writing:

- 47 trials with vitamin D or (less commonly) analogs thereof
- 26 trials with green tea extracts
- 11 trials with curcumin
- 9 trials with pomegranate juice or extracts
- 9 trials with vitamin E (including tocotrienol)
- 6 trials with high-dose, intravenous vitamin C
- 4 trials with sulforaphane (broccoli sprout extract)
- 2 trials with conjugated linoleic acid
- 1 trial (Phase III) with a cysteine-rich whey protein isolate

These trials have the potential to dramatically shift our approach to cancer treatment in the next years, and lend great plausibility to the development of all-natural cancer treatments in the future. And when we get there, we won't be looking back. But this battle is far from over. The cancer industry is worth fifty billion dollars per year in revenues, is highly profitable, and is growing quickly. There are those who are unlikely to watch their cash flow dwindle without taking action. If we don't understand their tactics, we cannot defend ourselves or the science of natural medicine. And many years could be lost again.

All warfare is based on deception.
—Sun Tzu, *The Art of War*

FALL

CHAPTER ONE

Friday, September 18
Front Page of *The Vancouver Tribune*

Landmark Cancer Trial with Plant Extracts Delayed
After Principal Researcher Disappears
Computer hard drives missing after bizarre 6-day lock-in

On the eastern edge of Vancouver's UBC campus, rain was mixed with tears yesterday as terminal cancer patients were turned away from the Center for Natural Medicine. They were coming to receive experimental "cocktails" of nutritional supplements and plant extracts together with Mitaxinyl, a late-stage cancer drug by Vancouver-based biotech firm Mitogenica. The all-natural cocktail is expected to boost the effectiveness of Mitaxinyl and may significantly extend patients' lives. For most, this trial is their last hope.

"I was supposed to get my first dose of medication today," said Jim Caldicott, a prostate cancer patient. "Every week counts for me now. Maybe every day."

Jim was one of several terminally ill patients being turned away this week because the principal trial researcher, Dr. Elliot Lindell, has been missing since Monday. Dr. Lindell formulates the cocktails for Mitogenica using several plant extracts and other supplements. Mitogenica declined to comment on the matter. But Lindell's disappearance is bad news for Mitogenica, which is hoping for a much-needed boost in sales of Mitaxinyl—its only approved drug. In the meantime, Mitogenica is currently in lockstep with rival biotech firm Chromogen in launching its next generation cancer drug.

The only lead the Center has so far on Lindell is a possible sighting by one of his colleagues just yesterday at Kloten International Airport in Zurich, Switzerland. Dr. Lindell's disappearance follows a bizarre episode in which he locked himself in his office for nearly a week. "At this time I can offer no explanation of why Dr. Lindell disappeared," said Dr. Li Wong, director of the Center for Natural Medicine. "We are doing everything we can to locate Dr. Lindell and get the trials started, for the sake of both the patients and their families."

Dr. Lindell's lab was discovered empty on Monday and all computers were missing their hard drives. Dr. Wong declined to speculate as to what Dr. Lindell had been working on and said police have found no signs of foul play. There is also no information on the whereabouts of Dr. Lindell's natural supplement cocktails, which have gone missing from storage at the University Hospital.

Besides his work on the Mitogenica trial, Lindell's largest project is a computer model of cancer cells. In development for over thirty years and still not complete, it is claimed by some experts to be the most advanced cancer model in existence. Finished or not, pharma companies worldwide have sought unsuccessfully to work with Dr. Lindell and use his computer model to speed their cancer drug development. That Mitogenica finally succeeded early last year is remarkable. Dr. Lindell has shunned drug companies his entire career, and vowed long ago that he would use the model to create an all-natural cure for cancer which he dubbed "The Eden Prescription."

Few in the industry believe Lindell will reach his goal despite his numerous breakthrough discoveries and legendary intellect. A child prodigy, Lindell graduated from Caltech magna cum laude at the age of fourteen, earning degrees in biochemistry and computer science. By nineteen, he held a PhD in both subjects and had started to program his model of cancer cells. That makes it all the more puzzling why Dr. Lindell would suddenly disappear, jeopardizing the future of his own model and Mitogenica with it. *For more, please see "Toward a Natural Cure for Cancer," page A12 column 3.*

Cleveland, Ohio

Annika Guthrie couldn't stop thinking about the online newspaper article on Dr. Lindell as she navigated her old blue Mazda Miata toward Glenville University Hospital. The same thoughts kept running through her mind: *Is it my fault that Dr. Lindell disappeared? Did someone find out what we're doing?* Lindell had gone silent and then vanished just days after she sent him last month's data. She couldn't shake the feeling that something had gone terribly wrong. But she had always known the huge risk she was running. She, working for Chromogen on its newest cancer drug, Chrotophorib. Lindell, working for Mitogenica—the competition—on its cancer drugs. Both companies racing for FDA approval. Why did she ever agree to feed Lindell data on Chromogen's patients? To prove out her theories, of course. To do that, she was walking a tightrope slung between disaster and quite possibly a miracle.

Annika drove to the far corner of the underground parking lot and barely squeezed her car in the space left between a truck and a large SUV. She rested her forehead on the steering wheel and cleared her head with a deep breath. This was turning out to be a very complicated week. A large van with darkened windows pulled in ten spaces down from her car as she got out. She walked to the hospital entrance, put on a forced smile, and started toward Trevor Wilkins's office—and the next batch of data from Chromogen's prostate cancer drug trial. The data she had to analyze for her master's thesis. The data that just might explain what had happened to Dr. Lindell. Annika always asked to get the data by email. Trevor always refused. He was paranoid about security and insisted on personal delivery. He also had a thing for redheads. Annika in particular. Which was why she had dressed in loose-fitting jeans and an extra-large sweatshirt that hid everything feminine about her. She knocked.

"It's open!" Trevor called from the other side.

Annika opened the door to find stacks of files piled high all over the office. Trevor sat at his computer looking exhausted. Two days' worth of stubble covered his face. The eyes that normally walked up and down Annika's slim body were bloodshot and tired. They held themselves fixed on her face, looking for something. Trevor forced a smile. Something seemed different about him.

"Wow. What's going on?" Annika asked, as her sky blue eyes swept the office, trying to find what she had come for.

"Can't you tell? I'm celebrating!" Trevor said, with more than a touch of irony.

"And what would that be?"

Trevor jabbed his finger toward the top file in front of him. "This. Last patient, last visit. Chromogen's trial is officially over."

"Already?" Annika asked.

"Hey, I thought you'd be counting down the days," Trevor said, trying to lighten up. "You and...what's his name?"

"Peter."

"Oh, yeah. I still don't see any evidence of this guy's existence," Trevor said, looking at Annika's ring finger. "What's he waiting for, the next ice age?"

"Global warming will hit first," Annika said with a smirk. This was Trevor's usual banter. Maybe everything was OK.

"I was assuming your master's thesis would hit first. Isn't that what you're waiting for?"

"Nothing's written in stone."

"Definitely not in this office," Trevor said, holding up a flash drive.

"Is that my data?" Annika asked, stepping forward.

"Affirmative. Now you can start writing up your master's thesis, right?"

Finally, Annika thought. She leaned forward to take it, but Trevor pulled back his hand at the last second.

"There's just one problem." He looked at her questioningly. Almost suspiciously.

"Which is?"

"Up until this summer all the results were within reason. But those anomalies from the last data set got even worse."

"What anomalies?" Annika asked with an innocent shrug. This was exactly the conversation she didn't want.

"Several people who withdrew from the trial are getting better. Much better."

"And that's worse?" Annika kept the innocent act going.

"Annika, late-stage prostate cancer patients aren't supposed to get better after they stop treatment. They're supposed to get sicker. And eventually die."

"Maybe these ones have a different opinion on that."

"Maybe they're getting help," Trevor said. His narrowed eyes beamed suspicion at her.

"Help? What does that mean?" Annika managed not to falter. Barely. She leaned back against the wall to put more distance between them.

Trevor leaned forward in his computer chair toward her. "Normally, patients who decide to withdraw from a trial just disappear and never come back."

"I know that."

"Well, these guys are coming for their follow-ups more regularly than our active patients. It's like they're expecting good news. How do you explain that?"

The conversation was taking a turn for the worse. "How could I possibly know?"

Trevor glared at her. "Because last year I saw you at the hospital cafeteria with one of these patients."

"Is it illegal to talk to a patient?"

"It might be, when you give them bottles of pills under the table."

Annika felt the floor fall away from beneath her and her heart started racing. Finally, disaster had caught up with her. "That patient had already withdrawn. I was just trying to help," she stammered.

"I know you and your fixation on natural supplements. So, how many patients are you doing this with?"

Annika closed her eyes. "Twenty-three," she said, barely above a whisper.

"Oh, God," Trevor said, as he buried his head in his hands. He looked up at the ceiling, his face even graver than before. Then he realized something. "Twenty-three? But only seven withdrew in our trial center."

Annika looked more awkward. "I know."

Trevor was now horrified. "You've dosed active trial patients with your supplements?" He glared at Annika in disbelief.

Annika grew defensive. "Most wanted to withdraw. They were pressured into staying on despite terrible side effects."

"Of course they were! That's how we get results!" Trevor said, raising his voice. "Do you realize what you've done?"

Annika stood fast. "Yes. Apparently, I helped some people live longer."

"Don't play guilt trips here. We're neck and neck with Mitogenica, and you've just thrown a wrench in the machine while nobody was looking."

Annika corrected him. "You were looking."

Trevor immediately shot back. "Don't you remember that Chrotophorib could be a billion-dollar-a-year drug for Chromogen?"

"You know I think Chrotophorib is too toxic, with or without vitamin D. Mitogenica will win this time."

Trevor raised his bushy eyebrows with indignation. "Well, Chromogen happens to pay half the research budget in this hospital. So do forgive me if I hope we hit a home run with this drug. You should be hoping, too."

"Why is that?" Annika asked.

"My grapevine tells me that you got a very nice job offer from Chromogen this week. Do you really want to ruin that?"

Annika was astounded. "How do you know about that?"

"Do you really think they'll let their fair-haired vitamin D genius walk out the door to the competition?"

Annika took a deep breath. She was at his mercy. "What are you going to do now?"

Trevor's eyes darted among the piles of folders on his desk. He was running the numbers in his head and starting to calm himself. "OK. If you did this randomly, it should balance out."

Annika felt her whole body loosen from the grip of impending calamity. "So?"

"Despite your reckless idealism, I do like you. So I'm not going to tell anyone."

Annika bowed her head slightly. "Thank you," she replied sheepishly.

"For now, that is," Trevor added. He looked at his watch. "In two hours we start unblinding the database and everything will come to light. The more of these healthier patients fall in the non-treatment group, the worse we look. And I can tell you, Chromogen will stop at nothing to get this drug through."

"And if I made Chromogen look worse?"

"You may have some tough questions to answer."

Annika resigned herself to the situation. She held out her hand. "I still have a master's thesis to write. Can I have my data, please?"

Trevor placed the memory card in her hand. "At some point, you'll have to join the real world, you know."

"How do the patients look?"

For the first time, Trevor looked at her with some understanding. "Oh, *your* patients, you mean? Five have falling PSA levels. Three might be in remission."

Annika stopped dead. "Remission?"

Trevor nodded. "I said *might be.* For now, their MRIs came back clean. No more tumors. I've never seen anything like it."

Suddenly, the disaster of the day had given way to the miracle. Annika could not help but smile. "That's wonderful!"

Trevor narrowed his eyes again and looked gravely at Annika. "I am happy for them, Annika. I really am. But if they're on the wrong side of the statistical fence, it's a disaster with nine zeroes behind it and your name on top."

"Then I'll hope for the best," Annika said, gripping the card tightly and walking out.

"And I'll prepare for the worst," Trevor called after her.

Annika started back for her car, beaming with fulfillment. For the first time this week, something had gone wonderfully right. None of Trevor's disaster scenarios mattered now. Yes, of course she had been giving them supplements. A cocktail of supplements, in fact, designed by herself and the legendary Dr. Lindell. At first she had only approached those who had withdrawn from the trial. But they had felt so much better. Soon, she couldn't help herself from offering the cocktails to everyone. She only wanted to help. Annika got into her Miata and started for her office at Glenville State University. Seconds after getting on Interstate 90, she noticed an SUV with darkened windows pull in a few cars behind her. *Isn't that the same SUV that was in the parking lot?* Her thoughts turned back to Dr. Lindell. Obviously, the new formulation he had designed in the summer was working wonders. Once she analyzed the blood work fully she might even know why. Quickly, her contentment turned to frustration. The one person on the planet she *had* to talk to about this had disappeared at precisely the wrong time. Where on earth was he?

Zurich, Switzerland

Dr. Elliott Lindell paced down Bahnhofstrasse, the street which led from Zurich's main train station southward to the Lake of Zurich. A light drizzle fell through the cool evening air as the sun set behind a veil of thick, low-lying clouds overhead. Lindell held his umbrella low and close to his head to keep raindrops off his glasses and, more importantly, to hide his face. The sidewalks were filled with bankers making their way home and last-minute shoppers rushing through Europe's most expensive shopping district. Lindell blended seamlessly into the throng of bobbing umbrellas that lined the sidewalk around him. But he couldn't help feeling nervous. Ever since he started working with Gwen Riley and Mitogenica last year, there was no doubt he had been followed on many occasions. And much more frequently leading up to the Mitogenica trial he was now delaying. *Poor Annika*, thought Lindell. For her own sake, he couldn't tell her what he was really doing with the Chromogen trial data she was sending. Nor that his computer model had already predicted some very impressive results for the next testing round on the patients—results she must be marveling over. Results that he himself had to act on without delay, under the cover of disappearing. For the model was more advanced than anyone realized. For the first time, he wasn't telling the model what to do. The model was telling him what to do, and he had to do it quickly.

Just a few blocks before Paradeplatz, Lindell turned to the left down a small side street where he was suddenly alone. A few paces more and he checked behind him. Nobody. He quickly turned left toward a small row of sixteenth-century stone buildings. Lindell placed his footsteps carefully along the narrow cobblestone street. He smiled. These streets looked exactly as they had back then. Secret. Hidden. Safe. Thirty-five years ago, the student Elliot Lindell made his first trip to Europe. His grandfather brought him here, to the nine-figure bank account he would eventually inherit and everything that went with it. Lindell arrived at a familiar wooden doorway hidden behind tall shrubs. A tarnished brass nameplate on the door read "Liechtensteiner Privatbank AG."

Lindell brought his face just inches from the security console next to the door. A bright flash of red light from the tiny lens at the center scanned his retina. He keyed in his PIN on the number pad. Within a few seconds, the thick wooden door clicked open. Inside, two armed guards stood at either side of steel elevator doors. One of them rapidly keyed a long code into the elevator and motioned Lindell to enter. The normal drill. Lindell got on and the elevator started downward.

The elevator doors soon opened to a grand antechamber that belonged more in a Victorian duke's manor house. Wood paneling and artwork were on every wall. The floor was covered with red, green, and white marble tile. Plaster busts of the bank's founding fathers stood on a dozen marble columns which lined the room and helped to mask the complete absence of windows. An attractive brunette in her late twenties stood waiting for him. She held out her hand and greeted Lindell with a flirtatious smile.

"Dr. Lindell, please follow me. Mr. Takanawa is waiting for you," she said, with only the slightest Swiss German accent. She led him out of the antechamber through a broad hallway with the same décor. Her shoes hit the marble floor with a loud tap on each step. "I hope you are having a pleasant stay in Zurich."

"Yes, as always," Lindell answered.

They approached a set of small private rooms. She gestured toward the first door, knocked, and opened it. Inside, a tired-looking Japanese man was sitting at a small desk in the middle of the room, with a laptop in front of him. He immediately stood up and smiled.

"Dr. Lindell," he said, giving a slight bow.

"Mr. Takanawa," Lindell said, extending his hand.

"Just knock on the door when you are done," the young woman said, then closed the door behind her.

Lindell removed a mini-DVD disk from his jacket pocket and handed it to Takanawa. "This is the first molecule together with the validation runs through the model."

Takanawa inserted the disk into his laptop. He intently read the data that came up, nodding several times. "Of course, we need to verify this with our own computer models in Tokyo."

"I understand," Lindell said.

"If verified, we will meet next Tuesday to collect the remaining specifications and give you full payment."

Lindell held up another disk in his hand. "I have them with me. I'll let you know where and when."

Takanawa briefly smiled at what he saw on the screen. "The initial data appears to be in order. We will make your prepayment." He stood up and knocked at the door. The young woman came back.

Takanawa spoke quickly. "I authorize the transfer of two hundred and fifty thousand Swiss Francs from the Mitsushima Pharmaceuticals corporate account to Dr. Lindell's. Here is the order, countersigned by the CFO," he said, and handed over a completed form.

The woman smiled as her eyes scanned the form with lightning efficiency. "Yes, of course. Everything looks in order. The transfer will take effect within twenty-four hours. Please come with me."

Minutes later, Lindell walked briskly along Bahnhofstrasse toward the Grand Hotel am Zurichsee. The rain had stopped, and the streets were nearly empty. He glanced at his watch. Eight thirty p.m. Time enough. He soon recognized the next watch store up ahead. He stopped at the display window and looked in. Thirty-five years ago his grandfather had taken the young Elliott Lindell here after the Liechtensteiner Bank and let him pick out a Tag Heuer in this very window. It was a combined gift for completing his master's thesis in computational biochemistry and for his recent birthday. He had just turned sixteen. It was also to be a reminder of the ever-traveling grandfather who managed to see him only once every year, at most. Lindell glanced at his own reflection in the window. The wide-eyed, vibrant youth had been replaced by a grandfatherly man in his mid-fifties, slightly overweight but otherwise in excellent physical condition. His formerly rich, brown hair was nearly all gone. Decades of chasing his dream late into every night had left their mark of wrinkles across his face, half covered by a thin white beard. But Lindell's glowing ocean blue eyes radiated perseverance and defiance.

Lindell noticed something odd reflected on the window. He snapped back to the present and looked again. There. A man, thirty paces behind, looking directly at him. The man quickly dropped his gaze. Lindell scowled. Damn! Lindell hurried back toward the hotel. He had left Vancouver undetected. He was sure of it. But that was blown yesterday when he was coming back from India and happened to cross paths with Phil Worley at the Zurich airport. He had known Phil was visiting the University of Basel that week. Stupid. Stupid. Stupid. And then the newspaper article. Someone had used that information quickly. But who? It was ironic that he had come to Zurich in order to keep operating below everyone's radar. His advisors had told him clearly just weeks before: all his other bank accounts were being monitored. Only his grandfather's Swiss account was safe to use undetected. Without looking behind him again, Lindell walked rapidly into the Hotel am Zurichsee, past the reception desk and up to his room.

Inside his room, Lindell logged on to the Internet using his own encryption program and connected a flash drive. One by one, he received confirmation that he had connected to four IP addresses around the world, in Paris, Rome, London, and Bermuda. He hated to bring Annika deeper into this, but he had no alternative now that he was being followed. A flashing green box read: "Encrypt model?" He was glad he had sent Annika the disk.

"Sorry, Annika," Lindell whispered, as he hit the Y key and then the return key. "You're the only one I can trust." The screen flashed: "Encryption in progress." Lindell sat back in his chair, impatiently. He pushed his glasses up on his nose and glanced down at his watch. Barely enough time. He had developed his own encryption algorithm. It was far more secure than commercially available systems, but also much slower. It would take about twenty minutes to encrypt the 10.8 gigabytes of information on the flash drive, parse it into four packages of information, and send these on to the four nodes. Once there, they would await the activation code to be reassembled somewhere safe. A long, empty bar on the screen showed the progress of encryption. As he watched it slowly fill, Lindell thought back to that first visit to Switzerland. It had been cut short by a frantic phone call from his biochemistry professor at Caltech. Something strange was happening in the National Cancer Institute's Plant Screening Program. Certain plant extracts appeared to be killing cancer cells, but everyone considered them "false positives" and ignored them. Everyone but his professor. He noticed peculiar reactions occurring in the cancer cells' mitochondria just before they imploded. It would be perfect for Lindell's PhD. So Lindell had cut his vacation short to fly back and investigate. He had had no idea that what he was going to see would become the focus of his life's work. Despite his many attempts to inform the world over the last thirty-five years, they all were still looking in the wrong direction.

The bar on the screen read: "Encrypted file transfer successful. Waiting for activation code." Lindell erased the contents on the flash drive. He took a second flash drive from his pocket and copied its contents onto the first one. He shut down the laptop and packed it away. He went to the balcony overlooking the water of Lake Zurich for a breath of fresh air. The sun had just set and countless lights around the shoreline shimmered over the dark waters. The phone inside rang. Lindell glanced at his watch. That would be the taxi to take him to his Bangkok flight. Lindell thought about the man following him. He ran his hand over his bald head. The information on his flash drive was safe. But how safe was he?

Vancouver, B.C., Canada

Gwen Riley frowned as she looked over Mitogenica's latest revenue streams from Mitaxynil sales. As CEO of Mitogenica, it was her job to keep sales increasing. But for the first time since she had founded the company, she felt nearly powerless. Once more, Mitogenica would post declining sales and slipping profits. Gwen ignored the sparkling Vancouver skyline that spread itself behind the wall of windows opposite her desk. Digging her heels into the plush wool carpeting under her chair, she clenched her right hand tightly around the mouse. This was why Lindell's computer model of cancer was becoming so important. And urgent. Gwen knew more than anyone else what it would be ultimately capable of. For a moment, her frown disappeared. With Lindell tied to Mitogenica, the model was as good as hers. When it was complete, "competition" would be a thing of the past. Mitogenica just had to stay solvent in the meantime, if only by a gossamer thread. Gwen's eyes were drawn back to those terrible numbers on her screen. If this kept up, Mitogenica wouldn't be able to fund its next set of trials. She clicked the article on Dr. Lindell and shook her head. And now, of all times, Lindell had pulled a stunt like this. And she is left looking like the village idiot. Her frustration peaked.

Enough was enough. As usual, she would finish work at home. Tonight especially. She glanced at her cell, waiting for the all-important call that still hadn't come. Gwen stood up and started packing documents into her briefcase. A very youngish forty years old, at five foot two and with a slight build Gwen was the definition of "petite"—and to many she seemed out of place behind such a large desk in the CEO's office. But anyone who crossed paths with her quickly learned otherwise. Gwen hated the word petite. Until she overheard someone at the water cooler describe her as "petite like a wolverine." That version she liked. Except this wolverine had a pack of hungry hyenas nipping at her heels. The hyenas were Chromogen.

Chromogen was like a mirror image of Mitogenica—both companies developed cancer drugs, both had one approved drug out, and both were targeting prostate cancer with the next generation drug. Both had uncertain futures. It was no coincidence that Chromogen would put its New Drug Application for Chrotophorib into the FDA in about two months; precisely when Mitogenica would do the same for Mitasmolin. The similarities stopped there. Everyone in the business knew Mitogenica's approved drug Mitaxynil was superior to Chromogen's Cyrozetix. By a significant margin. Despite that, Chromogen was slowly stealing market share from Mitogenica. Gwen sneered at the numbers in her head again and nearly slammed her fist down, but restrained herself on the off chance that her assistant was still at her desk so late on a Friday evening.

The rumors were that Chromogen was adding generously to research budgets in hospitals with large oncology wards and bribing the doctors who decided which chemo drugs to buy. But where did they get their damn money from? Gwen picked up her case and walked to the elevator, jamming her finger on the down button. The worst part of it all was that Chromogen owed its very existence to a colossal mistake that Gwen herself had made ten years ago—the single biggest mistake of her life. The mistake which haunted her as much as the rumors did. For, as hard as she tried, she could find no hard evidence to back the rumors. Until, perhaps, now. A few weeks ago, Gwen's security consultants had detected a major leak in Mitogenica. The elevator doors opened and Gwen hit the parking level button. She started down, wondering when the call would come.

Gwen looked up as the elevator stopped on the third floor, where the research labs were. The doors opened to reveal Henry Cheung, appearing quite dumbfounded to see the CEO looking back at him. Gwen smiled. Speak of the devil. He stood there, paralyzed, as if torn between taking a step forward or bolting in the opposite direction.

"Hello, Henry," Gwen said politely. "Are you getting on?" She dared not act out of the ordinary.

"I'm sorry. Of course, Dr. Riley," Henry replied. He stepped in, clutching his briefcase closely to his chest.

"You can call me Gwen, Henry."

"Yes, Dr. Riley."

"Taking work home with you?" Gwen said, smiling.

At that, Henry's face flushed a deep crimson and beads of sweat popped out all over his forehead. His eyes started dancing nervously in all directions around the elevator—any direction but her.

"Yes, for the Eden Project," he stammered with a forced smile. The elevator doors opened at the garage level and seemed to give Henry the ability to breathe again.

"Well, have a nice weekend, Henry," Gwen said.

"You too," Henry replied, looking at the ground. He dashed to his car.

Gwen strolled toward hers in the reserved spot next to the elevator. She packed her things slowly in the passenger seat, waiting until Henry's car left the garage. Immediately, she called a number on her cell phone.

"He's just left now."

A male voice answered, "We're on him."

"I've already lost two batches of data to someone out there. I can't lose another one," Gwen said sternly.

"Don't worry. The data looks real, but it isn't."

"And your trace program?"

"That's very real."

"Fine. Where will the exchange take place?"

"We don't know yet."

"Why not?" Gwen asked impatiently.

"They set that up within an hour of the event."

"Then I want updates, real time."

"Yes, sir. I mean, ma'am."

Gwen frowned and hung up. She started driving home.

Henry Cheung was the leak. Had he only been selling data from the Eden Project, they never would have caught him. But he had used a data mining program provided by his backers to dig out the latest trial data on Mitasmolin. And Gwen's security team was at the ready after Cheung's colleague, Paul Hammond, reported several large offers made to him by a woman named Sydney a few months ago. Because of that, Gwen's security caught it—just in time. Mitogenica's trial had just reached end-point in lockstep with Chromogen, so all the data was in but the unblinding was yet to start. Perversely, this leak was the break Gwen had been hoping for. Chromogen was getting far too cozy with big pharma giant Avarus Pharmaceuticals. Rumors of a buyout were circulating. Avarus had friends in high places at the FDA. Conflicts of interest were legion within the FDA, and everyone knew it. That would give Chromogen the upper hand. But a cross-border industrial espionage case complete with proven bribes would put the matter into the hands of the FBI. Politics would turn to Mitogenica's side. The FBI would just need to dig a little deeper into Chromogen to find data manipulation, bribing of hospitals and doctors—everything it would need to hang Chromogen out to dry. Avarus Pharmaceuticals would have no choice but to leave them hanging.

Gwen scowled as she remembered the stinging words of an old nemesis: "Being a successful drug maker has far more to do with business than with science." Success had required Gwen to bend many rules to the breaking point along the way, but she would never believe that statement. Partly because it was made by a longtime enemy from her previous career, before she founded Mitogenica. Partly because she prided herself on picking out the drugs that were superior. But her longtime enemy would have his chance to vet his little theory. After all, he was the CEO of Chromogen.

Cleveland, Ohio

The letter from Chromogen's CEO was the first thing Annika saw when she entered her modest student's apartment. In her rush out the door that morning, she had forgotten where she left it. The thought of discussing it with Peter was unbearable because it was going to change everything they had planned for. And today's good news from Trevor wouldn't matter. Peter was so far away from that. Annika quickly walked over and set her pile of mail on top of the letter, moving it to the back corner of her desk. Peter Grafton closed her door behind him. This was their usual chat time after a date night. He always drove straight in from Alameda Alloys, picked up Annika, then came back for a coffee. As usual, he eyed the computer desk in Annika's living room where the TV should have been.

"I've got to get you a TV for your birthday," Peter said, plopping himself down on the cheap sofa. His hand lifted by reflex to reach for a remote that wasn't there.

"No, you won't," Annika said, putting her hands firmly on her hips.

"Why not?"

"Because you'd spend your time here watching financial news and streaming stock quotes."

"Can I at least get online real fast?" Peter smiled and winked one of his hazel eyes.

Annika sighed. "Can't you wait till you get home?"

"Not tonight. I fly out first thing tomorrow, remember?"

Annika shook her head in frustration. "I totally forgot."

"Since when do you forget my MBA weekends?"

"It's been a complicated week," Annika said.

Peter came closer and put his arms around her. "What's up?"

"We need to talk. Do you need a coffee?"

Peter glanced at his watch. It was past one thirty a.m. "Yes, please."

Annika walked into her tiny kitchen which adjoined the living room, and plugged in the kettle. Peter turned back to her computer and put his hand down where the mouse normally was, only to find a half-inch-thick, flat, white square device.

"Hey, what is this?"

"Part of what we should talk about." Annika reached for the wireless mouse, hidden under some papers. At the first shake, her computer whirred to life. Seconds later, a chain of black and white spheres appeared in midair, floating above the flat white device. They were organized into a curved row of hexagonal rings with a single red sphere at the top. Peter grasped at the spheres in fascination as his fingers passed through the solid-looking objects.

"Hey, nice toy!" Peter said in awe. "But what is it?"

"It's a three-D projection device from Chromogen," Annika said solemnly as she gazed down at it.

"They must like you a lot. What's it for?"

Annika pointed to the spheres. "That's a molecule of twenty-five-hydroxy vitamin D. It helps me visualize in three-D how it fits into the cancer picture."

"It doesn't look *that* complex."

"The vitamin D molecule isn't," Annika said. She clicked the mouse several times. "But where it fits is."

Suddenly, the simple orbs disappeared and a mass of fine, multicolored ribbon-like structures appeared in amazing detail and clarity. Some were twisted into helixes; others curved into loops and attached the helixes. Again, Peter let his fingers pass through the solid-looking mass that floated above Annika's desktop.

"Wow. What's this one?"

"It's called 'the vitamin D nuclear receptor ligand binding domain.' There are other vitamin D receptors, too. We didn't know about them until just a few years ago."

Peter smiled mischievously. "Will it do real-time stock quotes in three-D?"

Annika sighed and rolled her eyes, but she couldn't suppress a laugh. Peter usually looked so serious: dark brown hair, straight eyebrows, solid chin, and eyes that constantly seemed full of purpose and planning. And he always wore a suit. When he did crack a joke, the contrast made it even funnier. However, in every jest there is some truth. Annika loved Peter dearly in every way except his love of money. And that would make the next conversation all the harder. It was time to tell him.

"I got the job offer from Chromogen," Annika finally managed to say.

"Fantastic! We should have celebrated that tonight! Where is it?"

Annika pointed to the pile of mail. "It's at the bottom."

Peter quickly reached for it, sending the rest of the mail falling to the floor. "Sorry!" Peter said, as he took out the letter and started reading.

"The three-D imager came with it," Annika said. *Like a bribe,* she wanted to add.

As Peter read, Annika looked up at the wall next to her loaded bookshelf. Being a straight-A student and graduating at the top of her biochemistry class, she could have hung many awards there. Only one was displayed with pride. It was the best paper award for her landmark piece on vitamin D's role in killing cancer cells. Of course, her name was placed after Professor Fallon's on the author list. She wrote it with him during the summer of her junior year. But she had put her own spin on the research project. She had proposed a novel mechanism for vitamin D to trigger programmed cell death in cancer cells—by weakening their mitochondria. Then she showed that vitamin D greatly enhanced the anti-cancer properties of high-dose vitamin C and other natural supplements through that very mechanism. The rest was luck. That winter, two years ago, at a major international cancer conference, Dr. Fallon had lost his voice. Annika filled in and presented the paper. She was an instant hit. Chromogen reps had approached her because they had noticed high-dose vitamin D enhanced the efficacy of their new chemo drug Chrotophorib in Phase I and II trials, but they didn't know how. Until they saw her paper and her theory. They made a generous offer for a master's thesis looking further into the matter. It was well-known that vitamin D boosted several chemo drugs, but this was the first case of a drug just starting Phase III trials. And Chromogen was desperate for every advantage it could get over Mitogenica. Even if it came from vitamin D. Now that the end of her master's was in sight, Chromogen wanted her to continue her work with the company directly, but not at all in the direction she wanted.

Annika could tell when Peter got to the salary figure because his jaw dropped three stories and his face went white. The unspoken understanding between them was always that she had the book smarts and he had the business smarts. Peter stopped his education after his bachelor's in mechanical engineering, but he had taken a freight elevator up the corporate ladder at Alameda Alloys in the seven years since graduation. Now he was finishing an executive MBA in Chicago. And yet, his current salary would be lower than her starting salary at Chromogen. Ouch. Peter looked up with a smile of conflicted pride on his face. He recovered surprisingly well from the body blow to his ego.

"Wow. Ninety-five thousand to start, and the offer is countersigned by the CEO, no less!"

"I'm not taking the job," Annika said in almost a whisper.

Peter was staggered. "What? But look! They're going to repay your student loans! That's over sixty grand!"

"Seventy-three thousand and counting," Annika said softly.

"And you won't take it?" Peter said incredulously.

"No."

"Why not?"

"It's not the job I wanted."

"But it is the money you wanted. And more!"

Annika turned her lips down in a frown and was about to speak when the kettle started loudly whistling in the kitchen. She nodded toward the computer. "You check your stocks. I'll get your coffee."

"OK, but—"

Annika raised her hand to silence Peter and looked him straight in the eyes. "In the meantime, you think about what kind of person I'd be if I did things just for the money."

CHAPTER TWO

Vancouver, B.C.

The dimly lit grounds of Stanley Park lay deserted and quiet under the light drizzle of an unusually cold September night. One hour before midnight, a lone black Hummer H3 sped east along Stanley Park Drive until it came to the boot-shaped piece of land known as Brockton Point. The vehicle veered northward just before a patch of thickly wooded land and came to an abrupt halt behind the small souvenir shop across from a line of totem poles.

Ken Dochlin and Matt Swanson jumped out of the Hummer and flung open the rear door. Inside, their equipment was piled high, waiting. Each fitted himself with night vision goggles and then grabbed a large bag of gear from the back. Ken slammed the rear door shut and led the way, sprinting past the totem poles and into woods ahead. Just before passing the tree line, Matt briefly looked over his shoulder. No sign of life except the distant car lights moving along Lion's Gate Bridge, which loomed high in the rainy mist above the waters of the First Narrows. Both men started running uphill into the forest, their dark fatigues getting wetter with each unavoidable brush against the trees and bushes. They reached the top of the small hill one hundred meters in. Ken stopped at a small clearing with line of sight to the parking lot and pointed down to the ground.

"Let's go. They'll be here any second," Ken said through labored breaths. He started setting up a video camera fitted with a large night scope.

Matt shook his head in disagreement. "Cheung lives in Richmond. We've got at least a ten-minute lead time." He took out a parabolic microphone and offered Ken one end of the wire connector.

Ken glared back. "It's not Cheung I'm worried about." The whites of his eyes seemed luminous against the dark green paint covering his face. He grabbed the wire and plugged it into his camera.

As if on cue, the sound of a car approaching drowned out the patter of raindrops on the tree leaves around them. Matt went into double-time to set up. He stuck an earpiece in his left ear and offered one to Ken.

"Nice call on the timing," Matt admitted.

"Watch and learn, my young apprentice," Ken said with his usual grin.

Matt was, after all, new to civilian corporate security. And freshly retired from Special Forces duty after his last mission in Pakistan's Toba and Kakar Mountains went terribly wrong and half his unit was destroyed. His military friends in Canada's special forces JTF2 unit had all assured him that corporate security was a well-paid cakewalk into old age. He aimed the parabolic microphone down toward the far tip of Brockton Point. With his naked eye, Matt could still make out the silhouette of the old lighthouse against the waters of the Burrard Inlet, which lay due east. The faint, hazy lights of North Vancouver lay to the north across the Burrard Inlet. On the other side, the lights of downtown Vancouver were mostly obscured by the thick plumage of the surrounding trees. Matt now heard the amplified sound of the car as it pulled to a stop in the U-shaped parking area next to the lighthouse. A man and a woman got out and headed under the large oak tree in the middle of the U. Matt looked through his light-amplified binoculars. The two appeared grainy and tinged with green, but he could make out their features. She had light hair, a beautiful face, and a very shapely body revealed by a raincoat pulled tight at her waist. The man was tall and heavily built. Matt turned to Ken.

Ken smiled with satisfaction and adjusted his camera carefully. "So, we finally meet our agents of biotech espionage."

"I thought you've been following them for a couple of months already," Matt said.

"We tried to. This is my first visual."

"They're that good?" Matt asked. Out of the corner of his eye, he could see Ken nod.

"Way beyond any corporate spooks I've ever seen."

"As in?"

"Untraceable emails. Encrypted satellite phones."

"What about Cheung's last meeting?"

"Missed it."

"How?"

"It was arranged at the last minute over a disposable cell phone they gave Cheung."

"And they're from tiny little Chromogen?"

Ken nodded. "Who else would pay Cheung six figures for Mitogenica's data?"

"I guess we'll find out if Ping's trace program works."

"It will. It always does," Ken assured him.

The sound of another vehicle approaching cut Ken off.

Matt watched a white Toyota Camry cautiously park next to the first car. An Asian man in his early fifties got out of his car, looking nervously around him.

"It's Cheung," Ken whispered, looking through the camera. "This is it."

Matt continued to look through his light-amplified binoculars. He listened as Dr. Cheung approached the two slowly and cautiously.

"Ms. Vale," Cheung said loudly, "I thought we were to meet alone!"

She smiled back. "This is Owen, an associate of mine. And please call me Sydney."

Matt could see Ken smile. Now he had names to go with faces. The conversation continued down below.

Cheung held out a flash drive. "This is the last of Mitogenica's trial results."

"And the data you gave to Dr. Lindell before he disappeared?" Sydney asked.

Henry nodded vigorously. "All our work from the Eden Project."

Sydney gestured to Owen. He took out a satellite phone and dialed while Sydney removed a laptop from of her bag and opened it. Her face shone brilliantly in the dark night as the laptop screen lit up.

"Why did this take so long?"

"Like I said on Monday, a virus got into the network and there was a total shutdown. It wasn't restored until this morning."

Ken whispered in a low voice, "No, that's how long it took us to plant our trace program and dummy data on your computer, you sellout."

Matt quietly chuckled and looked on through his binoculars.

Sydney dug into her pocket with her left hand and pulled out her own satellite phone. She connected it to the laptop and then hooked it to the top of her screen. She plugged in the flash drive from Cheung and watched the screen closely.

"Do you know what Lindell did with your data?" she asked Cheung, her eyes still on the screen.

Cheung shrugged and shook his head. "He's calibrating his computer model of cancer cells like always, I guess."

"Does it help him?"

"It must. Otherwise he would never help us—I mean, Mitogenica—develop cancer drugs."

"Does he ever talk to you about his work?"

"Never."

"Do you know anybody in Switzerland?"

Cheung took a step back and shook his head again, harder. "No."

"Does Lindell?"

"How would I know?" Suddenly, Cheung's face shifted expression. His mouth partially opened in realization. "You mean, you don't know where Lindell is either?"

"Don't make assumptions, Dr. Cheung," Sydney said. Something she saw on the screen made her turn to Owen.

"We're connected. Are they ready for the transfer?"

Owen spoke into his phone and immediately nodded. Sydney hit a key on the laptop and waited.

Cheung watched with a puzzled look. "Why don't you just copy the data like usual?"

"Because you're already five days late and Lindell disappeared for a reason."

Up on the hill, concealed among the dark foliage, Matt looked over to Ken with his hand raised in a question.

Ken shrugged in return. "This is happening fast, and Chromogen's written all over it," he whispered.

Matt missed something. When he looked back toward Sydney, she had stepped back from Cheung and was looking frantically at Owen. Matt struggled to understand what was happening. For a split second the laptop screen was twisted in Matt's direction. It was flashing bright red.

"Something's wrong! What's wrong?" Sydney yelled at Owen.

He listened to the phone. His eyes widened. "There's a trace program! Disconnect! Disconnect!"

Sydney grabbed her satellite phone off the laptop screen and violently flung her arm out, yanking the cord out of the laptop. She frowned at Cheung with fierce, narrowed eyes. "What are you trying to do?" she yelled.

Matt and Ken winced at the painful volume in their earpieces.

"Nothing, I swear! I'm just doing this for the money!"

Sydney barked back at him, "Did you do anything different this time?"

"No! I used your program like always to get the data!"

Owen stepped in. "It's OK. It never got past the firewall. But the data's bogus."

The last words from Owen made Sydney silent and motionless. She spun around to Cheung. "Did you come alone?"

"Of course!"

She nodded toward Owen. "Make sure."

Owen ran to their car and disappeared behind the opening trunk. Matt watched in horror as Owen emerged carrying an automatic assault rifle mounted with a large scope. Matt couldn't make out the model, but did recognize the large military grade silencer at the end of the weapon. He prayed that the view scope was not infrared, or they were sitting ducks. As Owen walked back to Sydney, she pulled a small handgun from her purse and aimed it at Cheung's head. Cheung raised both hands, waving frantically. Owen aimed the scope toward the hill near Matt and Ken's position. They both hit the ground.

"Damn it!" Ken said under his breath.

Matt's heart thumped wildly in his chest. "Let's get out of here!" he whispered to Ken.

Ken frowned back. "Not without our evidence."

"But our guns are back in the Hummer!" Matt protested.

Ken fingered the ground below Matt. "Just stay down!" He gingerly took his camera off the tripod and laid it on the ground. A single shot rang out from below.

Matt started to raise himself to see what was happening, but stopped dead when he saw a red laser dot wavering in the branches above him. The streak of bright red light piercing the misty air slowly made its way down until it rested on his left shoulder, flickering through the windswept tree branches in front of him. His heart was pounding furiously.

"Run!" Ken shouted.

Just as both men jolted upward, a spray of bullets hit the trees, ricocheting and sending wood splinters in all directions. Ignoring the scrapes and scratches of running through the woods, both sprinted at top speed down the hill for the Hummer. Seconds later they cleared the tree line below and dashed toward their vehicle.

"Weapons are in the back!" Ken shouted.

They both ran to the rear door of the Hummer. As Ken hit the unlock button on his remote, a volley of bullets slammed into the vehicle and shattered the rear side window. Matt and Ken dove behind the Hummer, each taking shelter behind a tire.

"You're sure this guy's a corporate spook?" Matt yelled.

Ken was busy figuring out his next move.

Matt heard more bullets hitting sheet metal and glass on the other side. The passenger side window above him burst into a spray of broken glass. By reflex, his eyes shut and he turned his head downward just before being showered with pieces of window. He felt multiple stings on the back of his neck. He wiped it with his hand, which came back smeared with blood.

Infuriated, Matt looked over at Ken. "OK, let's see what he does in a real fight."

Matt opened the back passenger side door and reclined the seat all the way back. With bullets flying, he crawled low through the Hummer H3 into the back, lay down next to the weapons case and flung it open to reveal two Glock .45 autoloaders. He cursed himself for not thinking to take a rifle. He quickly loaded a magazine into one and tossed it through the window to Ken. The next for himself, and an extra clip. His foot then latched onto the rear door of the Hummer and flung it open, and he lifted his head up at the window just enough to look out. The opening rear door was too obvious a target for the shooter. Another flurry of bullets hit the door. Through his night vision goggles, Matt saw the almost blinding flashes coming from the silenced machine gun behind one of the totem poles.

"Third pole from the left!" Matt yelled to Ken.

At the next pause in fire, Matt and Ken returned fire with both guns blazing at the totem pole. This was answered by another two short salvos of automatic fire. Then— silence.

Matt glanced out the window to see a dark figure disappear into the woods.

"He's running!" Matt shouted.

Matt and Ken ran back into the woods in pursuit. Matt was the faster runner and quickly gained the lead. He could just make out a figure up ahead as he crested the top and started down. But as he ran over the spot where they had been staked out, he stopped dead. All their equipment was gone. Ken caught up with him and saw it.

"Damn!" Ken yelled. "We've got nothing now!"

Both men sprinted with new urgency down the hill, guns at the fore, ready to shoot anything that moved. Halfway down the hill, Matt saw a figure emerge from the tree line down below. Incredibly, the figure holding the automatic rifle was Sydney, not Owen. Owen stood by the car, waiting. She yelled to him; in response, Owen tossed her a clip for the rifle. In one fluid motion, Sydney caught the clip and rammed it into the rifle while turning back to Matt and Ken. Both men took immediate cover behind the nearest tree as volleys of bullets sprayed the forest around them. Just after the last bullets went flying, the car door slammed and the screeching of tires sounded below.

Without a word, Ken took off after the car. Matt decided to head them off at the pass. He gritted his teeth and launched himself off his tree to the north at top speed. In a few seconds, sporadic gunshots went off in Ken's direction. Matt could hear the car's engine roaring through the trees. It was getting closer, to the left up ahead. Time was short. Matt's adrenaline surged as he ran through the forest, ignoring the tree branches that tore at his face and body. Matt emerged from the trees to see the car speeding toward him. But it was on the road dug below in the hillside. No good shot. Still running, Matt tucked his gun under his belt, drew his knife and leapt into the air. Like a hawk in flight, he never took his eyes off his prey. His hand streaked through the air in a wide arc, plunging the thick blade of his knife deeply into the car's metal roof. Matt's large, muscular body impacted the car with such force that the muffler skidded against the ground in a shower of sparks and the car lurched to the side. After regaining control, the car started to violently veer left and right to shake him. Matt's left arm shot out to grab the side of the roof. His knife carved out a long, jagged slice in the rooftop as his body whipped back and forth. The veering stopped and the engine bellowed at full power, heaving the car forward at top speed. The tires then screeched to a sudden halt, sending Matt flying in front of the car. Matt yelped in pain as he hit the ground with bone-breaking force and his night vision goggles were ripped from his face. He quickly regained his footing, every joint and muscle seared with pain. He faced the car defiantly, his bruised arms at the ready for attack, his heaving breath a stream of fog against the wide beams of the car's blinding headlights. The car leapt at him with surprising power and speed. At the last second, Matt pulled his gun from under his belt and fired shot after shot at the driver. The car simply ignored his bullets. Just as it was about to hit him, Matt leapt as high as his battered, soaked legs would take him. The car's windshield hit his lower body with agonizing force. He spun in the air, holding on to the gun at all costs. With a painful thud, Matt hit the ground and rolled. The car sped away. He emptied his clip at the rear window, the tires, the gas tank. Nothing but ricochets. Running footsteps came up behind Matt.

"It's all bulletproof!" Ken shouted, exhausted and out of breath.

"No kidding!" Matt yelled back in frustration. The sound of the car faded, and darkness once again surrounded them. Except for the small raindrops hitting the ground and the trees, they were in silence. Blood and sweat mixed with the rain and ran down his face. "What about Cheung?"

Ken shook his head, looking sullenly to the ground. "Gone." He flicked on a flashlight and cursed.

"Back to square one," said Matt.

"Now we have to tell Riley." Ken motioned to the trees, in the direction of the Hummer.

Matt started walking, limping slightly. "Tell her what? We got our asses kicked by a couple of corporate spies who happen to carry military grade hardware?"

"I don't know who they are anymore."

"If they were so willing to kill, they must be covering far more than just Chromogen," Matt said.

That stopped Ken in his tracks. He whipped out his cell and dialed, looking grimly at Matt. "You're right, and covering their tracks means covering their only other contact in Mitogenica, and our only other lead."

"Who—"

Ken cut Matt off, speaking rapidly into the phone. "Ping, we lost Cheung and the evidence. Get me a location on Paul Hammond and send him a warning. His life is in danger."

Ken started running for the Hummer. "We have to move! Now!"

Cleveland, Ohio

Peter still sat at Annika's computer, looking at the day's news and checking the movements of his meager stock holdings while carrying on their conversation.

"I just don't get what's so bad about Chromogen," Peter said.

"They want me to research their next chemo drug and not vitamin D."

"Won't their chemo drug help people too?"

"Maybe, but with terrible side effects."

"Aren't all chemo drugs like that?"

"That's the point. Vitamin D isn't like that, and we already know it's active against several major cancers."

Peter sat back, flabbergasted. He held up the job offer. "I just thought this was our dream for the last few months."

"So did I," Annika said.

"I finish my MBA in December. You get a job after your master's next spring," Peter said. He never quite finished that thought with "and then we'll get married." But Annika knew he meant it. Eventually.

"One out of three isn't bad," Annika said.

"Why not take this job and then move into something you do like at Chromogen?"

"Right now, I doubt there's any job I would like at Chromogen."

"Is there a job you'd like at any drug company?" Peter retorted, still eyeing the screen.

"If we're going to talk seriously, will you shut that off and look at me?"

Peter begrudgingly closed his trading screen, only to reveal the underlying window with the story of Dr. Lindell's disappearance. He narrowed his eyes as he skimmed over the story.

"Why do I know this guy?"

"I told you about him. I'm the one that knows him."

Peter nodded. "Right. He's that nutritional cancer guru you met a while back."

"He's a world-class scientist and I met him at that cancer conference two years ago," Annika said, standing up and coming over to Peter. For the first time, she realized something. "And the very next week when I came back, you showed up all sweaty and flirtatious in my gym."

Peter shrugged off the comment and kept skimming. He couldn't hold back a snicker. "Yeah, nutritional cocktail against cancer. I'd line up for that."

"Mitogenica fought hard to get Lindell's help. Maybe they know more than you," Annika shot back. This was going in the same direction as it always did. It was so frustrating.

"I'm sure his natural stuff helps a little," Peter admitted.

"But—"

"I just don't think it can compete with *real* chemo drugs."

"You don't know Dr. Lindell very well."

"Apparently neither do you. He's really disappeared?"

Annika nodded. "That's the other complication of the week."

Peter turned and looked at Annika. "You have no idea where he is?"

"Why should I?"

"I thought you were in contact."

"Well, uh, rarely," Annika said, looking away. That part was a lie.

Peter shook his head, as if putting two and two together. "Ah, don't tell me he's the reason you won't work for Chromogen."

Annika stood back and crossed her arms. "I do have independent thought, you know."

Peter eyed her guardedly. "Are you thinking of working with him, way out in Vancouver?"

"No!"

"You're sure?"

"He hasn't taken a grad student in fifteen years!" Annika said, her face reddening.

Peter sat back in relief. "Good to hear. What kind of a quack is this guy, just disappearing like that?"

Annika flicked back her long red hair and snapped angrily at Peter. "He's a quack that gets better results than your beloved Chromogen." She immediately regretted her outburst.

"What's that supposed to mean?" Peter asked, intrigued.

The only sore spot between Peter and Annika was his near-complete disbelief in the usefulness of nutritional supplements. Even after many hours of discussion with Annika on her vitamin D research, he was only half convinced. And Peter insisted on getting his D at the beach, not from supplements. Besides that, his diet was appalling. He seemed to live for fast food, fast coffee, and fast stock trading. And got very little sleep. He thrived on it for now, but Annika assured him that he would crash hard one day. She had pledged to reform him once they were together. Really together. But finally, now, she might convince him.

"It means that Dr. Lindell and I designed a nutritional cocktail for the patients in Chromogen's trial."

"You did what?" Peter bolted off his chair.

"Some of them are in total remission," Annika said excitedly.

"But Lindell is working for your competition!"

Annika shook her head. "Not my competition. Chromogen's."

"Don't you think Lindell is using you to practice for this other trial he has now with Mitogenica?"

Annika shook her head adamantly. "He's using me to calibrate his model."

"So where's the difference?"

"Don't you get it, Peter? We may have saved lives."

Peter started pacing around the room, thinking. "Who else knows?"

"One of the research staff at the hospital," Annika admitted.

Peter scowled in frustration and grunted. "Honey, you could get yourself into real trouble here." He looked concerned.

"The only thing I care about is that this worked. We helped people."

"You won't help people if you destroy your career before it starts!" Peter said almost angrily.

"I don't need a career if I can help Dr. Lindell perfect his formula."

"What?"

"It's enough just for our voices to be heard."

"And what would that do?"

"Change cancer treatment forever."

"Great! Why not let someone else do that?"

Annika frowned deeply and spoke with an intensity that made Peter freeze. "Because way back in the 1970s a few researchers showed that vitamin D hugely reduced cancer risk, but their voices weren't heard. If the establishment had listened, and even just raised the stupidly low RDA for vitamin D back then, it could have saved thousands if not millions. Including my—" Annika cut herself short.

"I get it. This is about your father."

That one hurt. Annika's father had passed away years ago from prostate cancer, when she was a young teenager. "I think you should go now."

Peter came over and put his arms around her. "I know it still hurts to have lost your father. I just don't want to see you throw away a brilliant future. I care about you."

"Please," Annika said weakly. She wouldn't look at him.

Peter picked up his things and went to the door. "I'm sorry."

"I'll see you in the morning," Annika said, speaking to the floor.

"OK. Good night." He gently closed the door.

Annika couldn't hold back the tears any longer. She wiped her eyes and started crying in short, uncontrollable sobs. That was a much greater disaster than she had anticipated. Peter was such a wonderful man in so many ways, but she wondered if they would ever see eye to eye on what was so important to her. She walked over to the pile of mail on the floor and started picking it up, one piece at a time. Her sobbing stopped short when she picked up a particularly thick envelope which was postmarked on September fifteenth from Zurich, Switzerland. The place Dr. Lindell had been spotted. Annika quickly ripped it open to find a DVD inside. She inserted it into her computer. A small window appeared in the center of her screen. A movie started. It was Dr. Lindell, with very tired-looking eyes behind his wire-rimmed glasses. The background looked like he was at home. He started speaking.

"Hello, Annika. By now, you must have seen some very impressive results on your patients from our last cocktail formulation. That's part of the reason why I had to disappear. I can assure you I'm perfectly safe."

Annika noticed that her hard drive was spinning furiously as Lindell spoke.

"Right now, I need to temporarily download some software on your computer via the Internet. It's the only place that's secure. In a couple of months I can explain everything to you. But only in person, here in Vancouver. For now, you have to trust me. And trust that we could soon be changing the face of modern medicine."

Downtown Vancouver, B.C.

I know that face, thought Paul Hammond, as he glanced away from the striking blonde woman who had suddenly appeared at the back of O'Malley's. *Funny, I don't remember seeing her come in.* And he could see everyone from his stool at the bar. Paul turned back to his gin and rubbed his fingers in the cool drops of condensation on the side of the thick glass while keeping Ms. Déjà Vu at the edge of his vision. A friend of his ex-wife? No, he would remember that one. With a flick of the wrist, he finished off the remaining gin and set the glass down on the bar. He glanced at his watch and quietly sighed. Once again, he had outlasted the rest of his colleagues from Mitogenica, and it wasn't even midnight. What can you expect from a bunch of lab geeks with PhDs? Only because of Paul had O'Malley's become their favorite watering hole on Friday nights. But sports and girls were not the topics of conversation. The large portions of beer and hot chicken wings only brought out the latest rumors of how Mitogenica was doing on the trial against Chromogen, and who would survive in the end. Of course, big pharma conspiracy theories abounded. Who the insiders in the FDA were secretly supporting. Or were supported by. Who would get crushed. Who would get bought out and by whom. Those last thoughts stirred in the back of his mind as Paul raised his hand to order another gin, but he pulled it back at the last second. He could feel the numbness of the evening's drinking kicking in. The thick brain fog setting in told him he was already well past his limit. Just as that thought was completing, a warm, feminine hand gently draped itself over his wrist. Paul turned.

"Allow me." It was Ms. Déjà Vu herself, suddenly sitting next to him.

Paul nearly jumped off his stool. Before he could say anything, she had already ordered two double Tanquerays on the rocks. His gin of choice. She smiled at him. Her intoxicating scent permeated the air.

Through the thick haze of alcohol, Paul's memories of her began to crystallize. The gins arrived.

"Cheers," she said. With unladylike speed, she downed the double in a second.

Paul followed suit. But as he put his glass down, it stopped in midair when he finally placed her. He looked at her through narrowed eyes, slowly nodding to himself.

"Sydney, isn't it?"

"I'm touched you remember me."

"You offered me money for data from Mitogenica."

"What if I offered my body instead?" Sydney returned, looking dead serious.

Paul snickered. "What if I offered you mine?"

Sydney didn't laugh. "Why don't we discuss this outside?" she said, with a flirtatious nod toward the exit.

Before starting work on the very secret Eden Project, Paul had been thoroughly briefed by Mitogenica's security on corporate espionage techniques. This was a classic. Of course he had refused Sydney all those months ago, and reported her. This was the first time he'd seen her since then. But maybe this time he could take some candy from the baby and get away with it.

"Sure," he said, getting up.

As soon as he planted his foot, he could feel the room slightly spin around him. That last drink had been a major mistake. Sydney gracefully slipped her arm around his waist and steadied him. Paul started feeling warm and very relaxed. His brain oozed with desire, and that inner voice reassuringly told him there was no problem here at all. As they left the noisy bar for the much quieter outside, Paul heard his cell phone beeping. He pulled it out. Ten missed calls. And twenty text messages, all saying the same thing: GET OUT OF THERE NOW, PAUL! YOUR LIFE IS IN DANGER!

"Damn it!" said Paul, reading the message in shock. His adrenaline kicked in, and he looked all around for any signs of danger.

"What is it?" Sydney asked. She leaned up against his body and took his hand in hers so she could see the message. "Oh, that's some kind of sick advertising campaign. I got those today, too."

Paul kept walking with her, but the shock of the phone message and the cool night air brought him a little ways back to the land of the sober. He finally realized he could be trashing his career with one stupid move.

"Sorry, this is a mistake. I need to go."

Sydney tightened her grip and slid her hips up against Paul. "Perhaps another time, then. But could you be a gentleman and walk me to my car?"

Paul started looking around. "Where is it?"

"It's just in the lot right up ahead. I'm nervous this time of night."

"OK," Paul said hesitantly. He wondered if he would still have enough willpower by the time they got that far. He struggled to keep his feet walking in a straight line to the entrance of the parking lot, but finally they reached it.

Sydney pointed to a lone red car in the back, just past the darkest corner.

Paul proceeded with her. But as they walked to the car, a large man jumped out from around the corner and punched Paul solidly in the solar plexus. Paul's dulled reflexes were far too slow to do anything in return. With the wind knocked out of him, Paul immediately fell to his knees. Sydney grabbed his hair and yanked his head back with surprising force. In a blur of motion, the tall man shot his hand out in front of Paul's face and sprayed something into his open mouth, just as Paul's lungs were refilling by reflex. Sydney pushed Paul forward and let him crumple onto the ground. She and the man left, running.

Trying to find some meaning in what had just happened, a dazed Paul Hammond stood up and started walking in the direction of his home. But soon after leaving the parking area he felt a sudden tightness grip his chest. His breathing became labored and shallow. The tightness quickly turned into a crushing, icy paralysis. He stopped to catch his breath, putting his hand on the nearest utility pole to steady himself. Soon, he was struggling just for the smallest gulp of air. Paul looked around frantically for an explanation that wasn't there. His heart and mind were racing, and he fell into full-blown panic. Paul gasped in terror and madly clutched his throat, falling to the ground. His lungs had completely shut down. He began writhing uncontrollably in the terrified knowledge that his life was about to end. A few seconds more, with his oxygen finally depleted, his writhing stopped. His head turned to the side and everything started to go blurry. Nearby, a dark vehicle came to a screeching halt. Two feet ran swiftly toward him. Through the fog of approaching unconsciousness, he heard his name called.

"Paul! Paul Hammond! You're going to be OK!"

Those were the last words Paul Hammond ever heard.

CHAPTER THREE

———

Saturday, September 19
Cleveland, Ohio

Fifteen minutes before dawn, Peter stood in front of his apartment building, reading his case studies by the light of the entrance lamps. As Annika drove up, he looked up with a humble smile. Annika wondered how much sleep he had gotten. The tiredness on his face was visible from a distance. Annika wondered how that would play into his mood. Any time they'd argued before, which was rare, Peter usually softened up the next day. She also couldn't help but replay the message from Dr. Lindell in her head over and over, wondering what it meant. But now was not the time to tell Peter. He loaded his suitcase into the trunk and hopped in.

"Get much sleep?" Annika asked. Tension was in the air.

"No," Peter said, holding up his wad of reading materials. He turned to her. "Look, I'm sorry about last night."

"Don't worry about it."

"I'm just really stressed right now."

"I understand," Annika said, with a quick nod.

"I know we can make this work. OK?" He looked at her with raised eyebrows and his classic "I've been a jerk" look. The tension was gone.

Annika smiled. "I know we can, too." She looked down toward the full cup of coffee sitting in the holder between them. "There's your latte, with two extra shots of espresso. The cranberry scone is in the glove compartment."

Peter smiled widely. "You're the best, honey," he said, and started gulping down the coffee.

"No, I'm just the best for you. And don't you forget it," Annika said, as she gently kissed Peter on the cheek.

"I know that."

"So, are you going to read your case studies all the way to the airport or are we going to finish our conversation from yesterday?"

"We can do both."

"Huh?"

"I forgot to tell you. One of my modules for the MBA this time is intellectual property. Mainly patents."

"How interesting," Annika said, raising her eyebrows in a doubtful glance.

"All the case studies are on drug companies. You can help me!"

"Can I really?"

"Sure! And I can understand where you're coming from." Peter shuffled through some papers and pulled out one.

"For starters, the drug companies make way too much money," Annika said.

"Wait a sec. Listen to this. Global sales of the pharmaceutical industry topped seven hundred billion dollars last year! Cancer drug sales were about fifty billion of that and growing fast. See, don't you want to be part of that?"

The car came to a red stop light, and Annika rested her head on the steering wheel. She let out a slow, calming breath.

"No, I don't."

"Why not?"

"Like I said last night, it's not about the money."

"Then what's it about?" Peter asked.

"It's about helping people with cancer treatments that can't be patented. Natural treatments. Cheap treatments."

Peter rolled his eyes. "I know you and your friend Lindell believe in that stuff—"

"Chromogen does, too."

"What? I doubt that highly."

Annika bit her lip in frustration. "What I'm about to tell you is really, really confidential information, OK?" She looked around them as if someone in another car might be listening.

"Understood." Peter leaned in.

"Do you want to know why I'm working on vitamin D for Chromogen?"

"Sure!" Peter said with a sly grin.

Annika kept her eyes on the road. "They need vitamin D because they're having some major toxicity problems."

"Toxicity?"

"Yes. Like liver failure, kidney failure, bone marrow damage. A couple of patients died within twenty-four hours of the infusion."

"Wow."

"Vitamin D is such a potent accelerator of Chromogen's drug that they can cut their dose nearly in half and get the same results with fewer side effects. That's what they're doing in their second treatment arm. Without it, they wouldn't stand a chance against Mitogenica's drug Mitasmolin. If that ever got out..."

"Very interesting," Peter said, with a dangerous look.

"Peter, don't you dare trade stocks on that information."

He shook his head. "Cross my heart. Seriously."

"Did you get the point?"

"OK, OK, vitamin D really works. For Chromogen."

"Today, with chemo drugs. Tomorrow, with other natural supplements."

Peter shook his head. "Can't be tomorrow. That stuff takes years of testing."

"Not with Dr. Lindell's computer model of cancer cells."

"Ah, the famed computer model. Which is still unfinished."

Annika's mouth turned down in a disappointed frowned. "You don't believe it will work, do you?"

"Now there you're wrong. I think it will work."

"Really?"

"Sure. Just not in our lifetimes," Peter said confidently. He knocked back another long gulp of coffee.

"Oh, I guess that's why a large Swiss pharma company recently offered Dr. Lindell twenty million dollars for the model, as is."

Peter's last swig of coffee got stuck in his throat, and he fought hard to stop from coughing it all over the windshield. He finally recovered.

"Twenty million! Why?"

Annika smiled. "Read through your papers and you'll see how much it costs to develop a new drug."

"Hundreds of millions. Maybe a billion," Peter said.

"They have to start testing drugs *in vitro*—in a test tube. Then *in vivo*—in animals—and then humans. But Dr. Lindell's model does all that testing *in silico*. He can compress many months of research into days or hours at a tiny fraction of the cost."

"I guess that's why Mitogenica likes him so much," Peter said. "If the model works, they could leapfrog everyone else and grab a big slice of the fifty-billion-dollar cancer market for years!"

Annika smirked. "That's not going to happen."

They arrived at the airport. Annika drove into the drop-off zone and Peter pulled on the door handle. He looked back to Annika. "Thanks for the lift, honey."

Annika nodded. "It was nice to talk."

Peter leaned over and kissed Annika, then jumped out and grabbed his suitcase from the back. He stopped by her open window for one last kiss. "See you tomorrow night."

Annika watched Peter disappear into the domestic departures terminal. She pulled out and started driving home with a sense of guarded relief. That had gone much better than last night. But soon, she would have to start looking for a job or a PhD thesis. And staying local was a necessity. Peter loved his job at Alameda Alloys. He wasn't likely to give that up just for…Annika shook off the thought. At least now she knew Dr. Lindell was safe, and soon she would be able to tell Peter everything. But then Peter's words came to mind. Was Lindell just using her to help his cause with Mitogenica?

Somewhere Over Chiang Mai Province, Thailand

If only Gwen Riley knew what I am going to do to her drug trials, thought Elliot Lindell as he stared out the window of the ATR-72. And not just the trials with Mitaxynil and his own natural cocktails, but also to the trials on Mitogenica's second generation drug Mitasmolin. And Chromogen's new drug Chrotophorib. But it wasn't for the sake of malice. The small cabin aircraft hummed loudly from the turboprops spinning outside in a blur of motion. Far below, rolling hills of dense tropical vegetation moved past in a gently flowing haze of green as the plane flew north toward the mountainous regions of northern Thailand. Lindell looked due west. There it was. Thailand's tallest peak. The Doi Inthenon. His next destination. *I've seen it too many times before*, he thought. Promising new natural and cheap treatments for any kind of ailment had been routinely squashed into oblivion in the past. This time, it would not happen again. Even if it meant bringing Gwen and her beloved Mitogenica to the brink of collapse. There was not time to do it any other way. That much became clear in Zurich, when he saw that he was being followed again. Lindell frowned and shook his head in frustration. At this point, it could be anybody following him. Chromogen.

Mitogenica. One of the big pharma companies that had offered millions for his model. Or one that hadn't yet. Did it really matter? His advisors had been right. At the first sign of trouble two years ago he should have taken action. Now it was almost too late. Lindell ran his hand over his nearly bare scalp. His eyes squinted slightly as he thought about the events leading up to now. He refused to feel guilty for what he was about to do. If the blame was to lie with anyone, it should be with Mitogenica's CEO, Gwen Riley herself.

For years, Gwen Riley had been his tormentor-in-chief. She would publish little bits of experimental data he needed so badly for his model of cancer cells and then offer to share it only if he collaborated with Mitogenica. He always refused. Until she unveiled the Eden Project. It was a new technology that could directly measure key intracellular parameters of cancer cells as they were being attacked by experimental new chemo drugs—or plant extracts of Lindell's own choosing. While the Eden Project would tell *what* a molecule would do to cancer cells, Lindell's model would tell *why*—and then suggest how to do it better. The two technologies together would be a drug development juggernaut. Gwen Riley knew it, of course. Lindell detested the thought of bringing that much power within her grasp. But using the Eden Project, she proved undeniably to Lindell that he needed her drug Mitaxynil to reactivate cancer cells' mitochondria before he could successfully challenge them with his own formulations. When he ran the combinations in his computer model, he realized how much he needed Gwen Riley and the technology of her Eden Project to complete his model. And so he had collaborated, with the goal of one day finding natural supplements that could replicate what Gwen's drug accomplished.

From that point on, it was a constant exercise in negotiation with Gwen: for every scrap of data she gave Lindell on his plant extracts, she demanded more runs of his model on Mitogenica's newest third generation drugs. But most of all, Gwen wanted to see what the model told about her competitor Chromogen's new drug, Chrotophorib. Lindell had held back as far as possible, using that as his ultimate bargaining chip to squeeze more and more data from her. His model couldn't yet properly generate Chrotophorib's active metabolites, he claimed. As Mitogenica's trial had progressed, Gwen had grown more desperate for that data. Of course, he had already run Chromogen's drug in his model. Mitogenica's Mitasmolin would trounce it. Less toxicity. Greater effectiveness. But he wouldn't give Gwen the satisfaction. He would make her suffer first, just as she had made him suffer. And two weeks ago, his brinkmanship had paid off. Far greater, in fact, than he had ever hoped.

When Henry Cheung sent him the last batch of data, it held everything he had ever requested of Gwen, and more. Lindell felt a surge of adrenaline as he thought again about that night. Cheung's data plugged so many holes and plowed through so many brick walls after over twenty hours of nonstop programming. Surely Gwen had no idea of what she had given him. And after he programmed in Annika's data from the Chromogen trial, the model started running with stunning accuracy. What was a week behind locked doors when the completion of his life's work was in sight? After several runs over the next days behind closed doors, he realized what he was now capable of. Gwen wanted to boost sales of her old drug Mitaxynil, in its fight against Chromogen's old drug Cyrozetix for prostate, colon, and breast cancers before her new drug could cover all those bases. With his new formula, he would boost Mitaxynil so much it would outperform both companies' second generation drugs by a wide margin, rendering them nearly worthless. Just as Mitaxynil's patent was about to expire. Everyone would be able to use the formula at the cost of generic drugs. Mitogenica and Chromogen would both crumble, as would others. And with his model validated, he would get all the funding he needed for a trial on a purely natural cocktail of ingredients against cancer.

The PA system on the plane came to life. First in Thai, then English. Chiang Mai was only twenty minutes away, and his next ingredient not long after that. Lindell looked constantly around as he hurried off the plane, through baggage, and into the waiting area. A Thai man stood in the public area holding a small sign with Kiet's name on it. Lindell looked behind him as they left the airport. Nobody he recognized. Nobody suspicious. Perhaps he was safe after all.

Lindell fought his tiredness as they drove south down Route 108 toward Chom Thong. He was never able to sleep well on airplanes. With every mile driven, the towns and settlements grew more and more sparse and his exhaustion greater. When they turned onto Route 1009, Lindell watched attentively through the back window of the old Toyota pickup truck. The lights of Chom Thong fell behind the last hill, leaving only a hazy orange glow hanging above in the dark night sky. No other headlights were in sight behind them. Ahead of the truck loomed Thailand's tallest mountain, the 2,575-meter-high Doi Inthanon, with a climate more like Canada than Thailand. The surrounding hills and mountains were alive with sparsely dotted lights marking the hill tribe settlements and, somewhere among them, Lindell's destination. The driver was concentrating on the road, but periodically turned and smiled. He couldn't speak a word of English. No matter. Lindell's drowsiness grew heavier as the truck wound its way up into the hills along narrow dirt roads. His eyes followed the headlights as they illuminated endless palm, teak, and other trees until they blurred together into a flowing sea of green.

Eventually, Lindell felt a tug on his shoulder and opened his eyes. The truck had stopped at a deserted clearing in the forest and the driver held Lindell's door open. He pointed to a handful of large bamboo huts with thatch roofs. The compound was dimly lit by a single line of old, dirty light bulbs dangling on a lone wire strung between two thick wooden poles. Each light bulb was surrounded by a swarm of flies, furiously diving to and from the bright, hot light which promised sustenance but yielded only death.

The driver concentrated and then forced out, "Please to wait!" in a thick Thai accent. He pointed again to the wooden buildings. Lindell grabbed his leather briefcase and got out. The driver got back in the truck and continued up into the dense mountain forest. Soon, even the faintest remnant of the truck's sound was lost in the perfect silence of the thick foliage. Only the faint, distant calls of unknown creatures echoed through the chilly night air.

Lindell looked around the dark forest. Where was Kiet? Years ago he had met Kiet, a botanist and herb grower, at a conference on the phytopharmacology of native Asian plants. When the model demanded a certain strain of ginger from Southeast Asia, Lindell knew Kiet could deliver. Or so he thought. Lindell wrapped his arms around himself to stay warm, wondering if something had gone wrong. He was glad he no longer carried the model. It wouldn't be safe here. A tinge of guilt swept through him, knowing that Annika's computer now held the only complete copy of his cancer model. And she didn't even know it.

Cleveland, Ohio

Annika's stomach grumbled with hunger as she skimmed once again through the data Trevor Wilkins had given her. The numbers were amazing. And he was right. Changes as dramatic as this were going to be hard to ignore once Chromogen's database was unblinded. And that would be soon. Her stomach rumbled again and she quickly pressed her hand onto her midsection to stifle the sound. She had skipped breakfast in her rush to pick up Peter and it would soon be lunchtime. But the excitement of what she and Dr. Lindell had done was still pumping adrenaline through her system. She wondered when she could talk about this with Dr. Lindell and begin the next step. She had to finish her master's first, of course. That would take six months. She thought about Peter and how much he loved his job at Alameda Alloys. He would never move. So many problems. But the data. The amazing data. Another growl. Finally, she went to the fridge and quickly threw together a sandwich and took out a chilled green tea. Several patients stood out from the rest—the patients in full remission. She hoped one of them was Mitch Purcell. He had struggled so terribly with his advancing prostate cancer. But two months ago he suddenly began to improve. That was shortly after she had started him on the latest formula. She liked Mitch. He reminded her so much of her father. She stopped at that thought. Was Peter right? Was this all about her father?

It had begun thirteen years before, just after Annika's tenth birthday. Her father had started making frequent visits to the doctor and came back each time looking very depressed. Finally, her parents told her: he had prostate cancer, but he was getting treatments and it seemed to be stabilizing. She was furious that they had kept it secret for so long. She was even more furious when the cancer came back three years later, and this time the doctors said there was nothing more they could do.

Annika's father was a janitor and her mother a hospital orderly. Neither had made it beyond high school. But both were fighters to the end and were not about to give up, even when the doctors did. So they started looking around for anything that might help. And since Annika was a straight-A student in high school with top marks in science, her parents depended on her to guide them. First came Hoxsey and several different formulations of Essiac Tea. They sounded wonderful at first. Even scientific. But the miracle stories of "so many" nameless cured patients in faraway places proved too good to be true. And what about the patients who were treated but didn't recover? Nobody mentioned them. Were there hundreds? Thousands? More? Then, when Annika could not duplicate the miracle cures on her father, the excuses started. You used the wrong version. You didn't make it properly. Use more.

Hope quickly grew more distant. And the further hope was, the faster Annika's father chased after it. As her parents grew more desperate, so grew the strangeness of the new approaches. Magnetic therapy. Bracelets. Energy waves. Magic ions. Ozone. Everything short of snake oil. In some cases, the shady salesmen wouldn't tell what was in their cure or how it was made. They simply "cleansed." They "balanced energy levels." Annika's patience grew thin. One man claimed his pet rabbit was cured from a

tumor on its foot by eating a special mixture of herbs from a secret corner in his backyard. Annika told the man he should sell his cure to rabbits. Another claimed to impart
his mystery solution with special "cosmic energy." Annika asked if the cosmic energy
could be measured, detected, or reproduced. Blank. No answer. Annika remembered
watching the man bring a bottle of the thick brown sludge out from his briefcase. She
immediately shouted, "Oh no! Your cosmic energy just escaped!" She then challenged
him to prove that it hadn't. He left within seconds. Annika's family was at the end of
hope, and her father had just a few months to live. Then something quite unexpected
happened.

Through some friends at church, Annika met Dr. Baumgartner—a semi-retired
doctor and herbologist from Switzerland. Dr. Baumgartner agreed to see Annika's
father, and brought his Chinese wife of thirty-five years. Dr. Baumgartner's family
had been practicing herbal medicine for four generations in Europe. He had met his
wife in China, while he was on tour in a little-known cooperative program for sharing
herbal medicine knowledge. Her family had been practicing traditional Chinese herbal
medicine for at least ten generations. She claimed to be able to trace her ancestry back
to Shen Nung, who started traditional Chinese herbal medicine around 3450 BC. The
two of them worked together on Annika's father using the full arsenal of traditional
medicine from two cultures. They were also the first to look at X-rays and take blood
samples.

Annika became fascinated by it all. According to the Baumgartners, there were
small portions of the truth floating out there even among the snake oil vendors. The
miracle cures really had helped *some people*. But it was futile to sort through a thousand cures when you only had time to try twenty. Or ten. Generations of experience
told them which herbal formulations would work against which cancer, and for which
stage of that cancer. They documented everything about their extracts down to the last
detail—because it mattered what part of the plant was used, what time of year it was
harvested, even what part of the forest it was taken from. Each herb was then carefully dosed out according to the active ingredients. The Baumgartners formulated their
own combinations according to traditional Chinese practice; anywhere from eight to
twelve different plants were used at once. In China, over 150 different herbs have been
used for centuries for treating cancer, and the Baumgartners knew all of them. Annika
could see the logic and the wisdom in that. But one part of the treatment struck her
as highly odd. Her father was to walk outside in the early afternoon sun for twenty to
thirty minutes at least three times per week, daily if possible. He should wear a light
shirt with short sleeves, and short pants as well if weather permitted. Sunblock was
forbidden, as was getting a sunburn. Lying out under the sun was encouraged in the
heat of summer. None of it was needed during the winter months. Annika did not find
this part of the treatment odd at all. She had figured it was for her father's mental well-
being. What was so odd about it was how important the Baumgartners said the walks
were. The more short walks he took in the sun, the longer he was likely to live. And
live longer he did.

But one day, the Baumgartners informed Annika that even their herbal cures had
limits, and nature eventually had to run its course. Annika's father finally passed away
four years and eight months later than the doctors had given him. Although baffled and

fascinated by the herbal treatments and how they well they had worked for Annika's father, none of his doctors took the time to find out about it, or even took it seriously. They had all the excuses. It was all in their heads. It was determination that made him live longer. It was luck. It was anything but real.

It was also the summer before Annika was to start university. By that point, she had determined to spend her life turning the Baumgartners' art into science and showing just how real it could be. She enrolled in a biochemistry and botany double major at Ohio's Glenville State University. But even where scientists believed in the power of plants to cure cancer, they hadn't yet figured out what the Chinese had known for thousands of years: a single herb or drug would never provide a complete cure. Only the right combination would work. But there were so many possibilities. When Annika heard of Dr. Lindell and his computer model, she knew that was the only way to compress generations of wisdom and testing into just a few years. That was why she couldn't resist helping him with Chromogen's data. With the results she got from Trevor yesterday, she knew they were so close. And behind it all, Annika had made herself the promise that someday she would bring to someone else the same gift of prolonged life that the Baumgartner's had brought to her father. Perhaps Peter was right. Maybe it did all stem from her father. But there was nothing wrong with that. And many things very right about it.

Hill Country of the Doi Inthenon, Northern Thailand

Cold and exhausted, Elliott Lindell kept his arms wrapped tightly around himself and started walking around to stay warm. He walked to the furthest bamboo hut to put some distance between himself and the bug-surrounded lights. He was getting worried. He wondered if this trip had been a mistake after discovering he was being followed in Zurich. He walked around the back of the last hut, seeing if there was a place he could look inside. The hut bordered on dense forest. Lindell jumped back when something rustled in the trees. A small bird flew away. He suddenly realized how alone and exposed he was. Up here there was no public, no police, nowhere to run for help. But unless he verified in person the quality of the key ingredients for his new formula, the trials with Mitogenica would be worthless. The single compounds like sulforaphane, cholecalciferol, ascorbic acid, or the tocopherol succinates were easy to obtain. But others were not. That's why he had to disappear. First to Beijing, because six ingredients the model called for were Chinese herbs, three of which were exceedingly rare. Next had been Kuala Lumpur for a steam distillation extract of Malaysian palm oil, rich in full-spectrum tocotrienols. Then two stops in India. To Tamil Nadu for a strain of *azairachta indica,* or neem tree, that was particularly rich in limonoids and triterpenoids. And to Andhra Pradesh for *curcuma longa,* or turmeric. The model called for a strain particularly rich in diphenylheptanoids and the carabrane sesquiterpenes. And now here to the foothills of the Doi Inthenon for *Zingiber zerumbet* Smith—a strain of Southeast Asian ginger rich in a key sesquiterpene that killed cancer cells from the inside out. For most of the ingredients, it was peak harvest time. It would be years before he had another chance like this. Too many years. He could restart Gwen's trials with the new formula the week he got back. Unless, of course, anyone figured out what he was doing.

Suddenly, the sound of a vehicle approaching broke the silence of the night. Lindell walked back toward the road, hopeful that his friend Kiet was finally arriving. A black Land Rover sprang out of the forest and came to an abrupt halt forty paces from Lindell, its blinding headlights aimed directly at him. Lindell put up his hand to shield his eyes from the bright light. With the motor still running, two figures jumped out. Lindell started backing away slowly. He strained to see their faces against the headlights.

"Kiet, is that you?" Lindell asked. He backed up another step.

"I'm afraid not," the passenger said loudly as he advanced.

Lindell felt his adrenaline surge. "Who are you?"

"Call me Ben."

"Why are you here?"

Ben smiled. "I was about to ask you that, too," he said, looking around. "Of course, I'm most interested to know why you disappeared in the first place."

"Disappeared from where?" Lindell asked, taking a further step back. He could feel the rear corner of the hut with his left hand.

"Don't insult me. You left your home just as bare as your office. Did you make a breakthrough in your computer model?"

"What model?"

Ben laughed. "We could talk like this all night. Or you could give me what's in the briefcase and leave here in one piece."

"The model's not here."

"Now that, I don't believe," Ben said. He reached behind his back and brought out a large handgun. In one fluid motion, he pulled back on the casing and flicked on the gun's red laser sighting. As he started raising the gun to aim, Lindell bolted behind the corner of the hut and lunged headlong into the thick foliage of the forest.

"Lindell!" The shout rang out behind him.

Lindell's heart was pounding in his chest as he ran with hands out front to push away the branches from his face. His eyes were still getting accustomed to the dark after looking down the Rover's headlights. Between heaving breaths and his own noisy steps crashing through the underbrush, Lindell could just make out the sounds of the two men struggling through the dense rain forest behind him. Gasping for every breath, Lindell sped up, ignoring the scrapes and scratches he was getting all over his legs.

Ben's voice rang out again. "You can't run forever!"

Lindell unexpectedly broke through the forest into a clearing fifty meters wide under full moonlight. Without a second thought, he sprinted across as fast as his legs would take him. His feet sank deeply into the soft, cultivated earth, but he was far faster than in the forest.

"Lindell!" he heard again, this time more distant. Lindell turned back to check for any sign of his pursuers. Then he saw it. His own footprints, like a giant arrow pointing to him. *Oh no,* he thought. He turned back and again lunged into next section of forest. An arm shot out from behind the next tree and landed squarely on Lindell's collarbone. Lindell felt himself being lifted in the air. He felt weightless for a split second, just before the ground came up from behind and knocked the wind out of his lungs. As he heaved for breath, a powerful hand covered his mouth and a Thai face appeared above, backlit by the moonlight. Lindell's body relaxed as he recognized a friend's face. The hand moved away.

"Kiet," Lindell whispered. "What's going on?"

"You were followed," Kiet whispered back. "Do you know them?"

"Of course not." Lindell shook his head.

The voices of Ben and his driver carried through the night air. Kiet looked up and made a "Shhhh!" gesture soundlessly. The voices sounded closer. The two men came out of the forest on the far side of the clearing.

"Look! Tracks!" Ben said. They both started running directly toward Lindell. Kiet's hand grasped Lindell's shirt and hauled him straight up. He pointed northward and started through the forest with amazing speed and silence. He dodged and ducked under branches like a seasoned expert, barely touching anything as he ran. He knew exactly where he was going.

"Quickly! I have a truck!" Kiet said as he ran.

Lindell tried to keep up, but the faster he went, the more resistance he met. His arms started stinging from the scrapes and scratches. To his relief, another clearing lay up ahead. This one was over one hundred meters wide and on a large hill. Kiet slowed to allow Lindell to catch up. They finally emerged from the forest and ran through the clearing up the hill.

"My truck is just over this hill!" Kiet whispered loudly, with a frantic wave of his arm. He bolted up the hill almost effortlessly. Lindell strained to catch up, pushing himself harder and harder. But halfway up the clearing, Lindell's left foot came down on a large angular rock and twisted sideways with a burst of intense pain. Lindell was thrown off balance and went sprawling face-first into the dirt, gasping as he hit the ground. Kiet immediately stopped, spun around, and sprang back to help. He grabbed Lindell's arm and pulled hard.

"Are you OK?"

"I think so," Lindell said, jumping to his feet.

Both men froze as they looked down the hill. Ben and his driver broke through the forest line at the bottom of the hill. In a split second, Ben drew his gun and had his laser pointed at Lindell's chest. Lindell stared with horror at the dot above his heart, knowing at any second the red light could be replaced with his own streaming blood. How stupid he had been to come here. Kiet stood by helplessly as Ben walked up the hill to Lindell, the dot never wavering more than an inch from its target. Lindell looked up in dread as Ben arrived and stopped one meter away. He was tired, sweating, and very angry.

"Give me the briefcase. Now," Ben said, between labored breaths.

"I don't have the model with me," Lindell said in a wavering voice as he pushed the case over.

Ben rifled through the briefcase and then dumped the entire contents onto the ground as his driver watched. A single data DVD sparkled in the moonlight. Ben smiled and motioned to the driver, who quickly grabbed it.

"What's the cipher key?" Ben asked.

"There is none," Lindell said. "It's unencrypted."

Ben shook his head angrily. "You always encrypt your work."

"Run it and you'll see—"

"How about I run this?" Ben brought his gun up to aim at Lindell's forehead with complete steadiness.

Lindell could see the beam of red laser light train itself exactly between his eyes. His heart beating furiously, he was expecting the end to arrive any time. Then, out of nowhere appeared two needle-thin beams of intense green light cutting through the cool night air. They both landed somewhere in the center of Ben's upper back. Lindell quickly traced the columns of light back to the dark forest below at the left. Just as his gaze arrived there, two bright flashes appeared almost simultaneously, followed by two thunderous blasts which ripped through the forest. Ben lurched forward as if he had been hit by a truck, immediately falling facedown into the mud. The driver watched in shock as Ben lay motionless, and then he spun around toward the forest. His eyes went wide with terror. He dropped the disk and drew his own gun, frantically waving it at the forest, looking for the enemy. But the green lasers had disappeared. He started firing off shots randomly into the trees until his clip was empty. As he grabbed another clip to reload his gun, the two green beams once again appeared, centering on his chest with lightning-fast precision. Ben's driver filled his lungs to scream, but any sound he made was overpowered by two more shots. Life drained out of the driver's body the instant the bullets impacted his chest, and his corpse jumped back several feet before landing on the ground.

Both Lindell and Kiet stood frozen in place, watching in disbelief as two figures clad in dark fatigues emerged from the forest carrying rifles with the green laser sightings still active. Both wore night vision scopes and never stopped scanning the clearing. As they drew closer, Lindell could see the night vision goggles covering most of their faces and black paint covering what was left. They approached to within several paces.

"Who are you?" Lindell asked in a shaky voice.

Neither man uttered a word. One of them picked up the DVD off the ground and pocketed it. Then, each man grabbed a body, swung it over his shoulders, and headed back to the forest. When they disappeared, Lindell started collecting the effects from his briefcase, still visibly shaking from the experience.

Kiet stared blankly. "What was so important on that disk?"

"It's not what they think," Lindell said.

"Let's get out of here," Kiet said. "My truck is still over the hill."

Lindell pulled himself together. "No. First the ginger."

Kiet reluctantly nodded. He led the way back to the first clearing, next to the huts with the lights. "We noticed you were being followed on the way in. Sometimes the mob makes raids. They're very dangerous," he said apologetically.

"Raids for what?"

"Drugs. That's the easiest cash crop here. But we only grow herbs for food and traditional medicine," Kiet said, as they emerged into the clearing.

"That was no mob," Lindell said.

Several hill people were waiting for them in the clearing. They were shorter and darker-skinned than Kiet. Kiet nodded to them. For the first time, Lindell noticed low-lying green bushes covering the ground of the clearings. One of the hill people walked over to a bush and cut into the ground with a small shovel. He brought up a large section of twisted roots. He snapped off a large piece and brought it over to Kiet.

"This is what you came for," Kiet said, handing it to Lindell. "It took me a lot of testing to track these down. Why is this strain so important?"

Lindell drove a small spiral tool into the flesh of the root. "It is very rich in a sesquiterpene called zerumbone."

"What's that?" Kiet asked.

"A very potent destabilizer of the mitochondrial transmembrane in cancer cells," Lindell said. He pulled the tool back out and ejected the specimen into a test tube. He then poured in liquid from a small plastic container, put a rubber stopper on, and started shaking vigorously. He waited, watching the test tube carefully.

"Is it good?" Kiet asked.

Lindell watched the liquid in the test tube as it changed color to a deep red. "Yes. Very good. You'll have your money by the end of the day tomorrow."

"We'll begin shipping the day after," Kiet said. "Now, where can I take you?"

Lindell glanced at his watch. "Chiang Mai Airport. I have a flight in four hours."

Kiet paced down the road toward his truck. "We have to go quickly. What is your destination?"

"As far north as you can go and still be in the land of promise."

Kiet shrugged off the comment. "What about your disk?"

"I have a copy. Somewhere safe."

CHAPTER FOUR

___

Malibu Beach, California

Austin Hayes cursed under his breath as he hauled his overnight bag, a sack of groceries, and his laptop case up the stairs into the kitchen. This was supposed to be his weekend place to get away from it all, but he never got away from anything. He craned his neck and brought his arm up to glance at his watch. Damn. He was due to call Nolan in thirty minutes. First, he had to call Gwen Riley and try selling her on Nolan's private placement proposal for Mitogenica. *But why*, Austin wondered, *was Nolan growing so desperate to get a chunk of Mitogenica and this Eden Project technology? What did he know?* Austin cursed again. He was the picture of stress. Thirty-five with a face that looked forty, prematurely gray, a paunch he constantly struggled to keep from growing. High blood pressure. Insomnia. And a real shot at retiring in five years with fifty million in the bank. But it all depended on keeping Nolan happy. That was the hard part.

Austin picked up his cell phone to call Gwen. He stared out his kitchen window at the Pacific Ocean, which lay in his backyard. That always calmed him. And he should be calm. Gwen owed him, after all. When Gwen was nothing more than a bright kid with a great idea fresh out of Genomic Pharmaceuticals, it was Austin Hayes that got his venture capital buddies on Wall Street and enough cash together for her to launch Mitogenica. Later, Mitogenica's Initial Public Offering was fifty-seven times oversubscribed, and the stock tripled from its original indicated price on the first day. *Ah, the days of easy money,* Austin thought with a smile. That win allowed him to jump out of the investment banking business and open his own hedge fund—the Hayes Biotechnology Opportunity Fund—with Mitogenica as the flagship investment. Then along came Chromogen to spoil the party. No matter, Mitogenica was still going to win. He was sure of it. So was The Street. So were all his inside sources that didn't officially exist. Personally, he liked Gwen and considered her a good friend. But there was only so far you could stretch a friendship with the likes of Gwen Riley.

Austin dialed Gwen's number. She picked up.

"Hello, Austin."

"Gwen! How are you today?"

"What can I do for you?" she said with an air of professional accommodation.

"Is there any news on Dr. Lindell?"

"Check the newspaper."

"You know what I mean."

"I don't know where he is," Gwen replied flatly.

"My investors are getting nervous, you know. And my fund does hold almost five percent of your stock." *First destabilize her*, he thought.

"Then sell your stock." Gwen's tone said she meant it.

Austin shook his head. She would kill him at poker. "You know I'm in this for the long term, Gwen."

"Then why are you calling me now?"

"That friend of mine still wants in with a private placement."

"I don't need his money."

"Come on, Gwen. I know your numbers. Chromogen is thrashing you guys."

"They won't after our new drug comes out."

"Haven't you seen how few of the small biotechs are getting their Phase Threes through the FDA these days?"

"We will. Our science is better."

Austin snickered. "Science isn't enough. It's all about being with the big boys now."

"Are you saying the FDA is corrupt?"

Austin let out a belly laugh. "Of course not. But how many FDA panel members does Mitogenica have on payroll as consultants?"

"None."

"Well, Avarus has several who will speak up for Chromogen. This friend of mine can bring the influence you need to fight that."

"Mitasmolin is going to beat Chromogen's Chrotophorib hands down," Gwen said with confidence.

"But if it doesn't, you won't have enough cash for your next Phase Three."

"I'll sell more shares to raise the cash."

"And your stock will tank overnight," Austin quickly added.

Gwen paused. He knew she considered that possibility. "But if I accept, he gets to see my technology."

"Of course that's central to the deal—"

"Forget it," Gwen said.

Austin knew that subject was closed for the day. But Gwen had come just a little closer than before. Surprisingly. "OK, OK. By the way, can you tell me why Mitogenica is spending so much on computer hardware lately? You buying some big iron?" Changeup out of nowhere. Would she swing?

That made Gwen skip a beat. "I don't know what you're talking about."

Bingo. "Really? It's mentioned in your last ten-K." That was a lie. Austin had inside sources and now he would find out how worthy they were.

"Then you can find everything else you need there, too," Gwen said impatiently. "I'm very busy today, Austin. Good-bye." Gwen hung up.

Damn. One of these days she was going to have to crack. Austin walked outside onto his balcony and breathed in the fresh sea air. He liked Gwen. He hoped she would see reason and know when to sell out and cash in. So many others didn't and lived to regret it—in the poorhouse. But then again, maybe Gwen Riley did have something up her sleeve. Including one tidbit he didn't fully grasp yet.

Of all the possible sources of "gray information" at Austin's fingertips, one of the best had always been inside a company's purchasing department. Lab equipment. Manufacturing lines. Chemicals. Computers. How much, from where, when, and to which specs. They all told a story. And Austin's source inside Mitogenica's purchasing department had flagged a major new development. Austin had speculated it could be a massive supercomputer. But for what? Millions of dollars' worth of purchases had been made through offshore shell companies. No official requisitions. No specs. No end manufacturer. His source in purchasing had no idea what was being bought, or even if it was twenty pieces of small equipment or a single, massive, multi-million-dollar piece. The first portions were arriving in locked crates and went straight to the large secured space in the basement, to be assembled by outsiders. A handful of Mitogenica staff knew what was going on, but they wouldn't talk for fear of Gwen Riley. Something big was brewing at Mitogenica.

Chiang Mai International Airport

The bright red laser light was still there every time he closed his eyes, hitting him in the middle of the forehead. Or over the heart. It had kept him from sleeping during the whole road trip back from the Doi Inthenon. Elliott Lindell tried to block the scenes out of mind. He stared out the window at the planes lined up at their gates, ready for the first morning flights out of Chiang Mai. Out to safety. He couldn't stop thinking just how close to death he had come in those hills. He frowned that this was necessary at all. He shouldn't have to be doing this now. Because the world had already had its first real chance at an all-natural cure for cancer those thirty-five years ago. It had come that close.

Lindell had first seen the great promise when he flew back from Europe at the bequest of his master's advisor. Something groundbreaking was happening at the National Cancer Institute—the NCI. They were screening tens of thousands of plants from around the world in the hunt for a natural cure for cancer. The so-called Plant Screening Program was initiated in July 1960 by Dr. Jonathan Hartwell, a Harvard-educated organic chemist with a keen respect for the use of plants in medicine. He seriously considered each of the numerous letters he received from the public with accounts of using plants successfully against their own cancers. The Plant Screening Program couldn't have had a better leader.

But when certain plant extracts started showing positive results against cancer, others in the NCI dismissed the results as "false positives"—and then changed the cancer screen used in order to avoid any more. So many false positives appeared, in fact, that the cancer screen had to be changed repeatedly. Those very plant extracts—polyphenols and phytosterols—were proven decades later to be highly active against cancer. Back then, Lindell's thesis advisor was outraged. He had obtained several samples himself and showed the young Lindell. These were certainly not false positives. They were the real thing. Lindell observed a new form of cell death in which the cancer cells digested themselves from the inside out while healthy cells were left perfectly unharmed. And the process always started at the mitochondria. Nobody believed it. Nobody wanted it. Then they fought against it. What Lindell had observed that day came to be known as programmed cell death, or *apoptosis*. Thirty years later, it was accepted that apoptosis was controlled and initiated by the mitochondria. While big pharma was busy attacking the cancer cell's nucleus, the battle lines were drawn at a different part of the cancer cell altogether. It mystified Lindell and his professor that nobody seemed to get it, until Dr. von Bösewissen showed up.

For weeks, Lindell made queries to the NCI about his findings. One day, the German biochemist, Dr. Maxim von Bösewissen, paid Lindell and his professor a visit. Later, Lindell learned that Dr. von Bösewissen was a consultant paid by several international pharmaceutical firms. He was a brilliant scientist and just as brilliant a politician. That combination made him dangerous. He was dead set against Lindell's theories about what was happening in the "false positives" and wanted to shut down that line of research altogether. Lindell still remembered the heated exchange in his own student's lab.

"These extracts are inert. Stop wasting your time and mine," von Bösewissen said heatedly.

"How can you call them inert if they kill cancer cells?"

Von Bösewissen waved his hands. "The cancer screen was un-optimized. It was simply a false result."

"It seems many of your screens were un-optimized."

"It can't be replicated in a living being."

"Have you tried it?"

"I don't have to."

"Why not?"

"Cancer cells can only be attacked at the nucleus, where they divide uncontrollably. All successful chemotherapies are based on this. And everyone knows it."

"Everyone but the cancer cells."

"You're just a stupid American teenager! What do you know?" von Bösewissen sputtered loudly, his face reddening.

"I know there's another mechanism at work here," Lindell said.

"Like what?" von Bösewissen sneered back.

"Something starting at the mitochondria."

Von Bösewissen laughed. "And what could possibly start at the mitochondria?"

"Something never seen before. A death program."

Von Bösewissen laughed harder. "A death program?"

"Yes. I think these substances are like a chemical key, triggering a death program in the cancer cells."

"And how will you ever prove that ridiculous theory?"

"I think I can model it with a computer program. In fact, I know I can."

At that statement, von Bösewissen's laughter abruptly halted. For a split second, he looked uncertain. Even worried. His eyes then darkened and pierced Lindell like daggers. "Your research will go nowhere, I'm afraid. So don't waste your time."

The next day, Lindell and his professor were called to the dean's office. Overnight, several large private and corporate donors to the university had called to expressly forbid the pursuit of computer-based research on cancer with their grants. They threatened to pull their funding outright. For the first time in his life, Elliott Lindell had been blocked in his tracks. That was a terrible summer. It was the same summer that both his parents died. If it hadn't been for his grandfather, everything would have stopped there. The same way that everything stopped so inexplicably at the NCI.

Soon after, Jonathan Hartwell retired from the NCI in 1975. Without his leadership, the program deteriorated rapidly after that. On October 2, 1981, the NCI's Plant

Screening Program was officially abolished in its entirety, despite a massive outcry from the scientific community. During its twenty years the program had screened thirty-five thousand plant samples, representing perhaps only 6 percent of all the world's species. All the dozens of false positives that Lindell had urged them to reconsider were ignored. In fact, only a single plant-based cancer drug came out of it all: Taxol. Curiously enough, Taxol was the only natural drug on the NCI's roster that was actually patentable, since it was so rare in nature that it was only feasible to make semi-synthetically via a patented manufacturing process. Because it was patented, the price could be set without limit. Taxol became the best-selling cancer drug of all time, making two billion dollars per year for its owner in its best years.

An announcement came over the PA. Lindell's plane to Bangkok was ready for boarding. Then on to Tel Aviv. His final destination was almost twenty-four hours away. He got up and started walking. He smiled to himself. That would not be the last time nature would trump man's invention in the fight against cancer. But the next time, the natural solution wouldn't be handcuffed with patents or high prices. Lindell would make sure of that. He was still troubled, however. There had been more to Dr. von Bösewissen than just a few pharma companies paying him a consultant fee. There was something bigger. Something organized. And something that he had severely underestimated. Lindell never before imagined that they would try to kill him, but they had. And somebody else had protected him. Someone even better equipped than his enemy. But who? And who were they protecting him from?

Malibu Beach, California

Austin Hayes stared at the waves rhythmically pounding the beach below his deck and breathed in the clean ocean air. He always had to center himself before calling Nolan. He had to figure out how best to parse the good news with the bad news. Above all, he had to keep Nolan happy. It was Nolan's amazing track record of predicting FDA decisions and surprise company takeovers that had kept the Hayes Biotechnology Opportunity hedge fund far above the rest. Especially during the crash of 2008 and 2009. But even Nolan's reach had its limits. Especially over the last couple of weeks. He was on a rampage for all information possible on Mitogenica and the researcher Elliott Lindell. In fact, Austin realized, Mitogenica had been a leading concern of Nolan's almost from the start. It was just getting very hot now. That was good for him. Austin was better placed than anyone to dig up information on Mitogenica. Could that be why Nolan had recruited him in the first place?

Austin first met Nolan quite by accident five years ago in New York's Regency-Excelsior Hotel. He was at the Next Generation Health Sciences Investment Conference, pitching his fledgling biotech hedge fund. He had spent the evening in the hotel's smoking bar chumming with potential investors over drinks and Cuban cigars, bragging about his recent big gains and exchanging business cards. He left sometime past one a.m., drunk on his own recent success and large amounts of single malt. As Austin waited for the elevator to arrive, two men suddenly appeared from a dark corner and got in behind him. One was tall, very well dressed, and smelled of the old-money pedigree Austin was used to catering to. The other looked to be recently retired from the NFL and was obviously the bodyguard of the first man. Both got in after Austin and turned to face the door. Neither pushed a button. The doors closed. The elevator started going up to Austin's floor. Without looking back, the well-dressed man spoke clearly and slowly.

"Mr. Hayes, do you wish to take your career to the next level?"

In his drunken stupor, Austin blathered, "Uh, what does that mean?"

The elevator arrived at Austin's floor. The doors opened. The two men in front of him didn't move. Both continued looking straight ahead. From behind, Austin could see the shorter man tighten his jaw muscles.

"Yes or no?" The shorter man asked, clearly for the last time.

The next three seconds seemed to tick by like months for Austin. At first, it had seemed amusing to be caught up in a surreal scene usually reserved for spy movies. But the sudden realization that this was truly happening made him nervous. The next level. Hmm. Despite his recent success, his take last year had been considerably less than several of his Harvard MBA classmates. Who was to say they didn't have a similar boost? As they say, if you're not on the inside, you're on the outside.

Without a second thought, Austin spoke. "Yes."

The bodyguard jammed his finger on the Door Close button, inserted a key into the top position of the elevator key pad, and up they went toward the penthouse suite. Austin could accept what happened next as reality only because he was stone drunk and buzzed on nicotine at the same time. The bodyguard took out a small cell, dialed, and mumbled something inaudibly.

When the elevator doors opened into the opulent presidential suite, a small team of people was waiting for him. Several computers and scanning machines had been set up.

"Who are you?" Austin asked the short man.

"Nolan."

"Nolan who?"

"Just Nolan. And I have a proposal."

Austin eyed all the hardware around him. "I'm listening."

"We'll give you the benefit of our…internal research."

Austin grinned. He knew what that meant. "In return for?"

"Your own research. And your willingness."

"To do what?"

"Buy or sell whatever we tell you."

Hmm. Buying power. That's how all the big boys on The Street moved stocks as they wanted—often counter to everyone's expectations. It always drove his traders nuts.

"Of course," Austin said.

Nolan nodded to the rest and walked over to a sofa at the far end of the room. Immediately, the group of five sprang into action.

"Stand there and don't move," said one of the team.

A camera mounted on a robot arm swung in a smooth arc around Austin's head, taking pictures continuously. Austin was then walked to a scanning device.

"Put your hands flat on the screens firmly. Press your fingertips down."

Austin did so. A bright green bar of light scanned up and down several times.

Another came with a long cotton swab. "Please open your mouth."

"DNA? You've got to be kidding."

The man nodded condescendingly. "Now, please."

A woman approached. "Read this clearly into the microphone, please," she said, as she handed Nolan a paper with text on it.

It was all over within minutes. Nolan came back.

"What was that for?" Austin asked.

"We need to know where you are at all times."

"Whether I want you to or not?"

"Precisely. Fingerprints. DNA. We also have access to security cameras around the world. In airports, and out. Don't ever forget it."

A man arrived with a cell phone sporting a thick, large antenna.

"Satellite phone?" Austin asked.

"Not just any. It's encrypted and will only work with your voice. Keep it with you always."

Austin was shown to the elevator.

"We'll be in touch," Nolan said.

Austin turned back to face Nolan. "Who do you work for?"

"Don't ever ask that again," said Nolan flatly.

The doors closed, and that was the last time he ever saw Nolan face-to-face. When he woke up hungover the next morning, he wasn't sure if it had all been a dream or reality. Then, he saw the satellite phone, and knew he had graduated to the big league at last. But strangely enough, he was no longer sure he wanted to be there. Until, of course, the following week. Five new accounts came in out of nowhere worth a total of seventy-eight million dollars. Welcome indeed.

Austin came back to the present and dialed Nolan's number. The reply came almost immediately.

"Central Operations. Voice check." It was always the same drill.

"Austin Hayes."

A rush of beeps and clicks followed as normal, and then after a couple of seconds a ring signal.

"Austin, tell me you have something." The connection was so clear Nolan sounded like he was in the same room. And more impatient than usual.

"Gwen Riley is still a no."

"You have to try harder."

"Do you really expect her to just roll over and play ball?"

"Actually, I don't."

Austin was stupefied. "Then why do I keep calling her for you?"

"Because when the game changes, she'll know what to do."

That one threw Austin. Sure, Nolan had the inside track on FDA decisions. But this was going a level beyond that. This sounded like he was actually in control. Austin shrugged off the thought. That was impossible.

"Well, in the game I'm playing everyone thinks Mitogenica is going to beat Chromogen hands down with their second generation drug."

"Good. Let them think that."

Austin was intrigued. "What do you know that everyone doesn't?"

"To start with, Mitogenica lost a couple of key research staff yesterday."

Austin's jaw dropped at that and the phone nearly fell from his hand. He replayed the words several times to make sure he heard right.

"Lost?" Austin repeated.

"You'll read about it in the papers," Nolan said with no emotion.

"Read about what?"

"Do you have anything else?" Nolan demanded.

Austin tried to put that behind him for the moment and sound upbeat. It was time for the good news. "I've got the data set that Dr. Lindell received from Mitogenica just before he disappeared." There was silence for a few seconds. But as usual, Nolan didn't flinch. Not audibly, anyway.

"Where is it?"

"On the way to you direct from Vancouver. You'll get it tomorrow morning."

More silence. "Very good, Austin."

Wow. That was rare.

"Wait, there's more. But it might not be exactly relevant."

"Why not?"

"It has more to do with Mitogenica's competitor, Chromogen."

"Tell me," Nolan said, with greater interest. That was odd.

"Chromogen just finished their Phase Three trials on Chrotophorib."

"Something new, please."

"Someone has been slipping a mix of plant extracts to some of Chromogen's patients."

"What?" Nolan reacted with real surprise. That was a first.

"The initial data says this mix is working wonders on several of them."

"How many?" Worry was in Nolan's voice. That was a first, too.

"A dozen or two. It may seriously botch Chromogen's results."

"Who is doing this?"

"Some student named Annika Guthrie."

"Who is she?"

"A master's student. She's paid by Chromogen."

"How did you discover this?"

"So was that relevant?"

"I asked you a question."

"That's one you're not supposed to ask, Nolan."

"I'm asking now!" Nolan shot back, nearly yelling.

"No way. That's my only leverage to keep my information flowing from you." Austin nearly bit his own tongue after those words. But giving up his source was just too much.

"Do you have any hard data?"

"You'll get it Monday. Once the database is fully unblinded I can—"

Nolan cut him off. "Fine." His tone said things were not fine.

Austin waited for more demands or insults. Nothing. The silence meant Nolan was thinking. That was bad. Austin finally broke the silence. "So do you have anything for me?"

"Morpheonic Pharmaceuticals is going to have their new sleeping pill drug approved by the FDA at month's end."

"Morpheonic? What about the psychotic episodes?"

"There were none."

"Understood—"

The connection was abruptly severed as per usual. Austin bit his lip and shook his head. For several months, very credible rumors had been flying that Morpheonic's Phase III trials were plagued by several episodes of patients waking up in psychotic states. In one case, apparently, a patient under observation had trashed his room at the clinic and attacked the staff. Morpheonic's stock had taken a pounding. But if the rumors were false... Austin quickly ran the numbers through his head. An FDA approval could double the stock price overnight. This was going to be a great way to finish the quarter. And of course he would dip in tax-free from his private accounts on Grand Cayman and the Isle of Man. As he picked up his cell phone to make the necessary calls, Nolan's words about Mitogenica losing researchers rushed back into his head. Austin shrugged it off. Must have been a misunderstanding.

CHAPTER FIVE

Monday, September 21
Northern Israel

"Dr. Lindell! Dr. Lindell?" The voice outside the car grew louder, as did the rapping on the window.

Lindell struggled to wake from his sleep. He found himself half drenched in sweat, groggy, and disoriented. He realized he had arrived at his destination. The driver was looking back at him, waiting for instructions. The car door Lindell was leaning on opened. He looked up, shielding his eyes against the glaring sunlight.

"Welcome to the Ya'ara pomegranate orchards!" said a large, bearded man in his forties with a thunderous voice. He was dressed in tattered jeans and a T-shirt.

Lindell looked at the man, puzzled. "Who are you?"

"Jeremiah Moses Epstein, at your service," said the man, extending his hand.

"I was supposed to meet Isaiah."

"My brother sends his apologies. He was called away on urgent family business."

Lindell frowned. That was not good. With a late afternoon flight back to Zurich, Lindell had precious little time to bring Jeremiah up to speed on what he needed. Lindell had met Dr. Isaiah Epstein years ago at the International Conference on Phytopharmaceuticals for Cancer Prevention. Pomegranates had just ripped onto the cancer scene after several small clinical trials showed they significantly improved prostate cancer markers. Isaiah had presented the results of one of the studies. Only recently had Lindell realized Isaiah's family ran the largest pomegranate plantation in Israel. And only last week had he realized that they could be uniquely positioned to supply him with what his cancer model was now requiring. Perhaps.

"Do you understand what I'm looking for?" Lindell asked.

"But of course! My brother only researches the health benefits of pomegranates. I'm the one who grows them. Come! You need fresh air." He grabbed Lindell's hand so hard it felt like it might break. Lindell let himself be pulled out of the car. He turned back to the driver.

"Stay here."

Lindell's stiff body complained sorely as he followed Jeremiah, who moved with the vigor of an adolescent shopping for a sports car. Jeremiah took him through row after row of pomegranate trees. They stood nearly three meters tall and offered welcome shade from the midday sun. But for speed's sake Jeremiah walked under the sun between the rows. It was just before lunch and the sun was beating down harshly. Lindell broke into a sweat immediately. Down one row, several trucks were parked between trees and pickers stood on ladders, plucking the fruit and filling boxes for the trucks. Harvest season was full on, and Jeremiah watched all the activity with an observant and approving eye. It energized him. He turned back to Lindell as he walked.

"My father started these orchards when I was a child, thirty-five years ago. But first, we had to choose the best variety out of the five hundred that are available of *Punica granatum*."

"How did you do that?"

"We scoured the regions from Egypt and Iran to India and the Himalayas, then back down through Iraq. We went everywhere pomegranates were known to grow at the dawn of civilization." Jeremiah waved both hands toward the rows of trees he walked between. "We found the most productive and hardy cultivar of all, and that's what you see growing here today. That is the foundation of our success."

"But this isn't the variety Isaiah told me about," Lindell said.

"No. That one is over here," Jeremiah said.

Finally, they stopped at the back corner of the orchard, where a small clutch of about twenty rather humble-looking trees stood, isolated from the rest. They were filled with fruit, which was smaller than the others but deep crimson in color. Jeremiah looked proudly at them.

"Which of the five hundred varieties is this?" Lindell asked.

"This, my dear Dr. Lindell, is variety number five hundred and one."

Lindell stood there for a moment, perplexed. "What do you mean?"

"I mean it doesn't fit any variety anybody has ever heard of."

"Then where did you get it?" Lindell asked.

Jeremiah looked wistful. "We had been traveling many days by jeep in Iraq, far into the uninhabited reaches of the Tigris and Euphrates river valley. We stumbled into a small, hidden valley that appeared on no maps and was spoken of by no one. It must have been fed by an aquifer because we saw no river or streams, but there was lush vegetation everywhere."

"Including these?" Lindell said, looking at the trees.

Jeremiah smiled. "I wish! These were growing halfway up a small cliff. My father made me climb up and take some samples. I nearly fell to my death! Look!" Jeremiah flexed his right arm to reveal a long, deep scar that ran from his elbow to his wrist.

"Why not grow these commercially?" Lindell asked.

Jeremiah plucked a fruit off the tree. "It's our private stock. They don't yield the large fruit of the other trees." He sliced the fruit open with a knife. "But they make up for it in taste and richness." Inside, the seeds were covered by fat and fleshy fruit so dark crimson that it almost appeared black. The pulp surrounding the seeds was a deep golden yellow. "Don't get the juice on your clothes. The stain will never come out!" Jeremiah dug his knife into a large pocket of fleshy arils, scooped up about ten, and deposited them on the cut surface of the fruit. "Try it!"

Lindell took a few and ate them. Instantly, his salivary glands went into overdrive at the intense tartness. "Excellent."

"We never thought to chemically test them until your special request came in to Isaiah."

"Do you have it?" Lindell asked eagerly.

"Come. I'm expecting the email any minute now at the house."

They walked back a different way, along the northernmost border. Large tractors were leveling the land and the fence was being extended.

"What is going on?" Lindell asked.

"We've purchased more land bordering the orchard and in another five years we will double our capacity. Ever since those first trials of pomegranates against cancer, we can't keep up with demand. Shipments to Europe have gone through the roof. Last week, I was in Brazil setting up another plantation. Do you know the growing season they have there?"

"Impressive," said Lindell, looking at the large tractors.

"Now that science is behind us, our future success is guaranteed," Jeremiah said, sweeping his arm toward his new land.

"I'm afraid science guarantees nothing."

Jeremiah was taken aback. Almost insulted. "But of course it does!"

Lindell shook his head. "Only science that makes money can guarantee success."

Jeremiah frowned adamantly. "You of all people! How can you say that?"

"Because I've already watched the two cheapest anti-cancer drugs in history rise up with far more science behind them than pomegranates, only to be crushed into the ranks of quackery for decades."

Jeremiah was dumbfounded. "Tell me! I've never heard of them."

"Yes, you have, but only a very one-sided account."

Lindell recounted the stories of vitamins C and D. The science of vitamin C against cancer started in Germany in the 1950s, when Dr. E. Schneider gave mega-doses to his cancer patients. Then in the 1970s, Linus Pauling and Ewan Cameron proved the science. They ran trials in which they extended the lives of many terminal cancer patients with injected and oral vitamin C, in doses of ten grams per day. But the establishment rejected that science. Then the Mayo Clinic performed two of its own trials on vitamin C and found it did nothing for cancer patients. But they did not inject the vitamin, which was critical to the treatment's success, according to Pauling. Did the Mayo Clinic trials fail by design? It didn't matter. The media heard only the negative news and blasted it out to the public with such ferocity that the credibility of vitamin C was lost for a generation. But a quarter century later, science fought back. Researchers proved that injecting vitamin C results in blood levels fifty times higher than achieved with the same dose taken by mouth. They also showed that such high levels of vitamin C achieved in the blood do indeed selectively kill cancer cells—by flooding them with hydrogen peroxide. And incredibly, not one but several clinical trials for intravenous vitamin C were being started again. But the media was keeping quiet about it. Very quiet.

The science of sunlight and vitamin D started much earlier, at the turn of the century. Photobiology and heliotherapy were major scientific pursuits in Europe. In 1903, the Danish physician Niels Finsen won the Nobel Prize for successfully treating *lupus vulgaris*, or tuberculosis of the skin, with sunlight. Rickets, psoriasis, tuberculosis, and many other illnesses responded so well to sunlight that hospitals across the USA and Europe built solaria and balconies for their patients to get into the sun. Many food manufacturers started fortifying their products with vitamin D, including milk, soda, bread, hot dogs, and even beer. But then something happened. Penicillin was discovered in 1928. The sulfonamides were discovered in the 1930s. As helpful as they were, the new and very profitable wonder drugs ushered in a new definition of medical science—science that makes money. Since free and un-patentable vitamin D from the sun profited nobody but the patients, heliotherapy was promptly forgotten as an old fool's cure-all. Half a century later, science fought back. The American researchers Cedric and Frank Garland published a landmark analysis in 1980, showing that Americans in the Northeast had an incredible 67 percent higher death rate from colon cancer than those in the sunny South. The establishment would still have none of it. Even worse, the five-billion-dollar-a-year sunblock industry soon launched a media campaign to terrify the public of any exposure to the sun without first covering up with its products. Apparently, sunlight was highly dangerous at any dose.

Science kept fighting. By the early 2000s, large-scale population studies proved that vitamin D could dramatically reduce the risk of many cancers: breast, ovarian, uterus, colon, bladder, prostate, rectum, lung, and stomach. It could also help against asthma, heart disease, stroke, both types of diabetes, multiple sclerosis, rheumatoid arthritis, Crohn's disease, and even dementia. Vitamin D was back—and yes, it really was a cure-all. Dozens of clinical trials testing vitamin D against cancer have been started. Curiously, years after the science was proven, no country has yet raised its official recommended daily allowance of vitamin D. Gross vitamin D deficiency remains commonplace throughout North America and Europe. And the big news that vitamin D can boost some chemo drugs has been kept surprisingly quiet—because companies like Avarus Pharmaceuticals and Chromogen don't want to depend on a cheap vitamin. Instead, they spend their time and money searching for patentable, man-made versions of vitamin D so they can turn a greater profit. Science for the people becomes science for the money.

The stories seemed to ease Jeremiah. "You see? Science will win in the end."

"I hope it does. But the delays have cost countless people their lives."

They arrived at Jeremiah's house. He went inside and came back a minute later with a printout. "This is my science. And I won't stop fighting for it."

Lindell looked over the numbers in wonder. "I've never seen anything like this."

Jeremiah nodded. "Normal pomegranate juice has nine times the antioxidant power of orange juice. This one has twenty times."

Lindell read the numbers aloud. "More than double the normal amount of catechin and procyanidins. Triple the amount of flavonols, anthocyanins, ellagic acid, and tannins. It's off the charts on all counts."

Jeremiah quickly added, "More importantly, it is particularly rich in the rarer gallotannin fractions and ellagic acid derivatives you wanted so badly."

"Yes," Lindell mumbled as he scanned the paper. "The seed oil is eighty-five percent punicic acid. And the terpenoid content is very high."

"So? What do you think?" Jeremiah asked proudly.

"I'll need fifty kilograms."

"Done!"

Lindell handed a sheet of paper to Jeremiah. "Here's how to process them."

Jeremiah nodded as he read. "You want the seed oil separately cold pressed?"

"Can you do it?"

"Of course. But why is that so important?"

"It contains a rare conjugated linoleic acid with three double carbon bonds. It accumulates within the mitochondria of cancer cells and destabilizes them, triggering programmed cell death."

Jeremiah grinned broadly. "You see? Science will prevail in the end."

"Others know that, too, and will try to stop it."

"What others? Who are they?"

Lindell looked up into the hills in the distance. A glint of reflected sunlight caught his eye. "I don't know. But they're out there. I've felt them for decades."

"Someone trying to stop you?" Jeremiah asked.

Lindell turned to him. "Yes. But I'm also trying to stop them."

Jeremiah took a step back in surprise. "I wish you success, my friend."

Lindell glanced at his watch and then back in the direction of the driver. "I need to leave soon. I have a plane to catch this evening."

Jeremiah smiled graciously. "Won't you stay for some lunch? My wife made a wonderful pomegranate sorbet just this morning."

For a moment, Lindell let himself relax and smiled. "For that, I can take five minutes."

Malibu Beach, California

The clear morning sky brightened quickly in the last minutes before the sun thrust above the horizon. On a good morning, Austin could clearly see the beaches of Las Flores, Castellammare, and even Santa Monica from his raised deck. Today would be such a morning. And with the tide low, he would enjoy the view during an extra-long run. Austin stretched his muscles in the chilly morning air. The small table next to him held his laptop and a steaming mug of coffee. Austin had one of the rare houses on the strip of Malibu beach that ran due east-west, meaning he watched the sun set and rise over water. But for the moment, his eye was on the screen in front of him. New York had just opened for trading. He watched his Level II screen as ever more bids started piling up for Morpheonic Pharmaceuticals, taking large chunks of stock off the market. Most of those, he knew, were being bought by his own traders. Some from his offshore private accounts. That was going to be a great trade. Ah, there was the sun. What a perfect way to start the week. He glanced three houses down to see if there was any sign of activity. Two local girls had spent a few good years on the international model circuit and pooled their money to buy that house just a couple of months back. Both were apparently still unattached. And they liked their morning beach jogs, too.

Austin took another gulp of coffee. He zipped up his windbreaker, tightened his running shoes, and ran down the stairs to the sand. The tide was still going out, leaving a large swath of firm, dense sand behind. Wonderful for running. He planted his feet on the hard beach and quickly found his pace, breathing evenly every three paces. He did everything to avoid looking inside the models' house when he ran past. They weren't on the beach this morning, but he would have his day. Even if it meant strolling down from the mega-mansion he would eventually own further up the hill. And that day was not far off as long as Nolan kept the information flowing. With Nolan, that meant life on the edge, but it was a far better life than what his father had. He could pass on that wisdom to his kids once he started a family. Austin gazed at his twenty-foot-long shadow on the beach in front of him. His mind wandered to the life of his father, the mistakes he made, the mistakes Austin would never make himself.

Austin's father had carved out his career the old-fashioned way—up a very long ladder of working late nights, working weekends, and working the politics at Drexel Pharmaceuticals. Austin hardly remembered spending time as a child with his father. But eventually, all those years away from the family paid off when his father was made head of Drexel's most important business unit: oncology. Austin still remembered his father's big promotion party, just days after his own twelfth birthday. Mother was so happy. They moved into a much larger, new house with a swimming pool. Austin started in the best private school in the state. And for the next few years life was great. That is, until his father's brainchild development—a new drug for childhood acute lymphoblastic leukemia—didn't live up to expectations. The disease was the most common form of leukemia in children—a niche market, but a lucrative one with little competition. Drexel had been depending on that drug to bolster its shrinking pipeline. But the Phase III trials were faltering. Drexel was running its drug directly against the standard of care at the time which used vincristine, a natural alkaloid extracted from the Madagascar periwinkle. Vincristine was winning. Father looked depressed. Mother looked depressed. She told Austin that his father might lose his job if he didn't make it work. Then the house would go. And private school. And forget about an Ivy League university. The despair grew worse for many weeks, until it exploded one night. Austin still vividly remembered waking up to the sound of his parents in a heated argument. It was rare enough to see them together and talking. But yelling at each other—that was a first. His door creaked open, and he went into the hallway, just around the corner from their majestic curved staircase. Down the stairs, he could hear the sickening sound of fists pounding against flesh. That sound unleashed such adrenaline in his body, the moment was burned into his mind forever. And what happened next.

His father yelled out, "Stop it! That hurts!"

Then Austin heard the sounds of a struggle. Two bodies fell against the wooden banister and onto the stairs down below. He dared not look. His heart was pounding in his chest as he wondered was what happening.

"You're a monster! You're a monster!" yelled his sobbing mother.

"I am not!" his father yelled back defensively, his voice soaked with guilt.

"But they're only children! They're just little children!"

"Look at all this!" shouted his father.

"Look at what?"

"Do you want to keep this? This house? This life? Do you?"

For several seconds there was silence. His mother started crying again.

"Yes," she said weakly.

"Then let me do what I have to do."

His father left through the front door, slamming it so hard Austin thought the adjacent windows would shatter. He heard his mother fall down, weeping bitterly. He crept back to his room shaking with fear and in a cold sweat. He never got back to sleep that night. Only much later did he find out what was behind that fight. In order to make Drexel's leukemia drug look better against vincristine, they had started decreasing the vincristine dose to the absolute minimum. It was a trick known to the drug industry in the quest for FDA approvals, but in this case the casualties were children. Drexel's leukemia drug was later resoundingly approved by the FDA. Drexel advertised its new drug by inviting doctors from around the country to weekend "leukemia education seminars" in Florida, Mexico, and the Caribbean—all expenses paid, of course. Soon after, Drexel shocked the industry when it sold all rights for the drug to a competitor, saying leukemia was no longer part of its core business. Drexel got a very nice price for the drug, and the deal launched the career of Austin's father skyward.

At the time, Austin didn't know those details. He only knew that they did keep the house. He did stay in private school. He did get accepted to Harvard. He still remembered that morning, just days before leaving for college, when his father drove up in the convertible BMW and proudly handed him the keys. It was Austin's dream car. And that smell; the smell of the new leather. The power of the engine. How women looked at him as he drove by. And looks were just the start. Austin was so thrilled with his life that he barely noticed how his parents had both started drinking. How they no longer looked at each other in the same loving way. His father no longer talked about work with the same delight in his eye. His mother no longer looked at her house with the same pride. All those hints fell horribly into place when he got the news in his last year at the university. Austin's tearful mother called and told him his father had taken his own life. She told him all about the leukemia trials, and how his father had been on heavy anti-depressants ever since then, and never recovered. He had left a note saying: "There is no other way out. I'm so sorry." Drexel Pharmaceuticals, however, had been very kind in waiving the suicide clause in the corporate life insurance policy, so they would be taken care of financially.

Austin winced at those memories. He slowed his pace as his run ended. He liked to cool down and walk those last hundred meters to his house. He remembered the deep depression he had gone into for weeks after his father's death. And the therapy. When he emerged, he thanked God he hadn't gone into the sciences to follow in his father's footsteps. He despised Drexel Pharmaceuticals for having destroyed his father's integrity and then life—and for profiting handsomely from it. He determined that he would one day profit from Drexel and all companies like it. So far, he had done just that, and with Nolan's help he would do it better than anyone else in the industry.

Austin climbed the steps to his deck and between breaths gulped the last of his coffee. He opened the sliding glass door to walk in for a refill, but leapt back at what he saw. A strange man was sitting at his laptop, downloading its contents onto an external hard drive. Another was scanning Austin's cell phone. Yet another was searching through his stacks of papers on the kitchen table. Instantly, Austin thought they were spies from a rival fund or investment house.

"Hey! Hey!" Austin yelled. "I'm calling the police!"

"No, you're not," a fourth man said, walking around the corner.

Emerging from the kitchen was the one man Austin was never supposed to see again. Ever. Austin's mind started spinning with all the implications of this surprise visit.

"Nolan! What are you doing here?" Austin asked in shock.

"Your information on the Chromogen trials has caused a stir."

"What? That student Annika Guthrie and her little experiment?"

"It's anything but little."

"Well, I'm glad I could help. But why are you here?"

"I need to know your source."

Austin put both hands up. "Give me time. I'll get everything you need."

Nolan walked closer, raising his voice. "There is no time. I need to know now."

Cleveland Hopkins International Airport

As usual on Peter's MBA weekends, Annika spent her Monday morning picking him up from the airport and dropping him off at home. It saved Peter a lot of money in airport parking fees since Alameda Alloys would only cover his MBA tuition. It also gave them a small sliver of quality time that was otherwise nonexistent while he was gone, save for a few text messages or a quick phone call. Annika watched as Peter walked out of the security zone in Concourse C, trailing his small suitcase behind him. He looked exhausted. But there was something different. A strikingly attractive blonde woman walked next to Peter. In fact, she seemed to be walking *with* Peter more than just next to him. She wore a short, tight-fitting skirt with a loose, nearly transparent silk blouse that did nothing to hide a dark crimson lace bra. Peter briefly turned to her and gave a nonchalant smile good-bye. She waved her fingers one by one and pursed her lips as if about to kiss him. She walked off in the other direction without acknowledging Annika in the slightest. As Peter approached, Annika caught a whiff of the woman's perfume, which was nothing short of exquisite. She looked down at her own scruffy jeans and sweater that hung loosely on her athletic curves, but dismissed any feeling of inferiority.

Annika raised her eyebrows at Peter and tossed a glance toward the other woman. "Hard at work on the flight?" she asked tersely.

A twinge of guilt flashed over Peter's face. "What, her? I never met her before."

"Before what?"

"Before she sat next to me on this flight!"

"Should I be jealous?" Annika asked, arms crossed.

"Of course not! She just wouldn't stop talking the whole flight."

"I'm sure talking isn't her most practiced skill," Annika sneered.

Peter motioned to the exit. "Hey, relax. Any news on Dr. Lindell?"

"Since when do you care about him?"

Peter grabbed Annika's arm and gently pulled her back. "Hey, I missed you." He planted a soft kiss on her lips.

"I missed you, too," Annika said. Peter the sweetheart was back. She hoped.

"How was your weekend?" he asked.

"I got a good start on writing up the thesis." Oops. That brought back the topic of where to go once it was over. Annika didn't want to go there just now. And she saw Peter sensed it, too.

"You won't believe what our biggest case study was on," Peter said.

"What?" Annika asked, relieved that he had changed the topic.

"Mitogenica and Gwen Riley."

"A whole case study just on her?" They walked out the exit toward the hourly parking lot.

"Yeah, how she started Mitogenica from nothing. She's a genius!"

Annika shook her head. "She's a genius snake."

Peter chuckled. "Well, that snake made vice president of Genomic Pharmaceuticals by the age of thirty!"

"I guess I still have a shot if I hurry," Annika said. They arrived at her car and Peter threw his suitcase into her trunk. They got in and she started driving.

Peter continued. "She had some ingenious master plan. And a new theory of how to attack cancer. She quit her job to—"

Annika cut Peter off. "I know all about it."

Peter turned to her, surprised. "You do?"

"And it *wasn't* her own theory to attack the mitochondria of cancer cells."

"Whose was it?"

"Dr. Lindell started that over thirty years ago. Some started listening a few years ago, but before Gwen Riley."

Peter was intrigued. "What happened?"

"Some doctors started looking at DCA-dichloroacetate."

"What's that?"

"It's a drug used to treat lactic acidosis resulting from inherited defects in the mitochondria. They saw that it killed cancer cells in a test tube by activating the mitochondria. Then they started testing on people."

Peter squinted and lowered his eyebrows. "But that's not the drug Gwen Riley used."

"Of course not. DCA is unpatented so she couldn't charge a lot of money for it. But Mitsushima Pharmaceuticals had a newer, patented version of DCA that they were selling to treat lactic acidosis."

"Right! The Mitaxynil molecule!"

Annika rolled her eyes. "Gwen only called it Mitaxynil after stealing it from Mitsushima."

Peter became defensive. "No way. What she did was perfectly legal."

"What your case study probably didn't divulge was that Mitsushima started looking carefully at their patients after the news broke about DCA. They were about to figure out that their patients' cancer rates were far lower than the general population."

Peter was astonished. "Then how did Gwen Riley beat them to it?"

"She bribed a few of Mitsushima's researchers to hush up the real data."

Peter fell silent for a moment. "What? I just read that she bought the marketing rights for Mitaxynil from Mitsushima and then ran over to Wall Street to round up enough venture capital to start Mitogenica."

Annika shook her head and sighed. "How often do you think we get real story?"

Peter frowned. "The real story was that she brought a new cancer drug to market and helped a lot of people."

"And helped herself to a fast hundred million dollars while doing it."

"Why not? She made many friends on Wall Street," Peter said, almost proudly.

"And lifelong enemies at Mitsushima," Annika added.

"Yeah, and another one right in this car, apparently!"

Annika ran out of patience. "Fine! She's smart!" she blurted out, almost yelling. "Why do you like her so much anyway?"

"I don't know. She's really a woman on a mission."

"A mission to make money!" Annika said.

Peter smiled. "Hey, you could work at Mitogenica!"

Annika gasped with shock. "I will never...Peter, look at me...I will *never* work for Gwen Riley!"

"Can I ask why you hate her so much?" Peter asked.

"Because she is manipulating Dr. Lindell to gain access to his model."

"Surely he knows what he's doing."

"Sometimes I wonder," Annika said, looking off into the distance. "When she gets what she wants, she'll just throw him out like the garbage."

"So then back to square one. We still don't know where you'll go after your master's."

Annika's eyes reddened at those words. "Don't you mean where we'll go?"

Peter grew silent. "I didn't mean it like that. I'm sorry." He looked in the rearview mirror, then turned around and gazed out the back window with a slight squint.

"What is it?" Annika asked.

"I think that's the same car I saw behind us back at the airport."

"Are you sure?"

"Positive," Peter said. He looked concerned. "We're almost back to my place now."

"Why would someone follow us?"

"I don't know."

"Keep watching then," Annika said. She turned off the highway and did a full loop around Peter's neighborhood before driving to his garage. Peter looked back the whole time.

"Still there?" Annika asked.

Peter's worry deflated. "No. Maybe you're right."

"Maybe you watch too many spy movies."

Peter grinned. "Maybe you don't watch enough." With a kiss he was off in his own car to work.

Annika's smile disappeared the moment she started her drive to Glenville University. She hadn't forgotten Peter's words about her and the direction they were headed. She was at a loss for what to do. Thank God she had a walk scheduled with the Purcells in a couple of days. Mr. Purcell was one of her star patients and was like a father to her. He always had good advice.

CHAPTER SIX

—

Tuesday, September 22
Vancouver, B.C.

Gwen Riley sat at her desk and glared pure rage. "Do you know why I hired you six months ago?" Sitting across from her was John Rhoades, fresh off a plane from Israel. He looked exhausted. Unsettled. Maybe even worried. All the better.

"I came highly recommended," John said, obviously fighting his fatigue.

Gwen nodded. "By my friend Will Conleth at Cypress Turbines."

"Yes. Cypress," John said flatly. His normally boyish face suddenly lacked any emotion, as if it was chiseled out of cold stone. Gwen hated that. People who weren't read easily weren't controlled easily, either.

"Now, two of my people are dead because of you," Gwen hissed. She picked up the phone and held it in the air in front of John. "Shall I call up Will and tell him?"

"I didn't pull the trigger on Cheung," John said calmly.

"No, your damn trace program did. Nice work."

"The trace program didn't murder him, either."

"Well, apparently Cheung wasn't even murdered," retorted Gwen.

John nodded in partial defeat. "Cheung was found in his car. Perfect suicide shot through the temple. No other prints in the vehicle."

"That's what the police told me this morning," Gwen said. "Suicide."

"We have no evidence to prove otherwise. They took it all."

Gwen shook her head in disgust. "And Paul Hammond had a heart attack."

"Ventricular fibrillation. That's the official story."

"And unofficially?"

"There were traces of chemicals on his face."

"What chemicals?"

"We're looking into it. This was professional work."

"I thought you were the professionals," Gwen said, glowering at John as she leaned forward. "Oh, that's right, you can kill, too."

John didn't budge. "One was about to shoot Lindell in the head. The other emptied his magazine at us. I made the right call."

"Your call could bring me down instead of Chromogen!"

"Nobody is going to find the bodies."

Gwen thrust her hand to her forehead, gasping in repulsion. "I don't want to know about it!" She looked up at John, steaming with anger. "No more killing."

"OK, the next time I'll let Lindell get his brains blown out. We can discuss it later by conference call."

Gwen realized he was right. The simple game she thought she was playing had quickly escalated far beyond her worst expectations. Later for that one. She changed the subject. "Do you have the disk?"

"Lindell's?"

"Yes."

John handed it over. Gwen immediately put it into her computer and waited. She puzzled over the data that came up.

"It's not even encrypted. That's not like Lindell."

"Maybe he didn't have time."

"He always has time," Gwen said, studying the data carefully. She frowned deeply. "You're sure this is the disk you retrieved in Thailand?"

"Of course. What's wrong?"

"It's far too small to be his model."

"Then what is it?"

Gwen ran the executable file. The three-dimensional image of a molecule appeared on her screen. A familiar-looking molecule. Gwen slammed her hand down on her keyboard in frustration. "It's an analog version of the Mitaxynil molecule."

"Analog?"

"Lindell has slightly altered the molecular structure."

"To treat cancer?"

"No. Mitochondrial disease."

"What? Why?"

Gwen frowned. "Only one company could be interested in this. Mitsushima."

"What does Lindell have to do with them?" John asked.

"That's now your job to find out," Gwen said, with a new level of frustration building in her voice.

"OK. What's next?"

Gwen looked down to the floor. "Where's the other data?"

John put a flash memory card on her desk. "Chromogen's latest trial data."

Gwen took it without looking at him. "If this ever gets back to me—"

"It won't."

"If it does, your head will roll with mine."

"There's something else."

"What?"

"Lindell is dealing with a student doing her master's for Chromogen."

Lindell and Chromogen? Gwen thought. *What is he doing?* "Dealing with what?"

"We don't know yet."

"Find out everything about her, and what she's doing."

John stood up to leave. "Is there anything else?"

"Yes. No more guns while working for me."

"But—"

"Or I'll find someone else."

John conceded. "For now."

Gwen looked up at John. "I still don't get it."

"Get what?"

"In this business everyone spies on the others. Getting caught just labels you as stupid, not criminal. Why would they kill?"

"I've been in corporate security for forty years. Never, not a single time before, have I seen corporate spies so willing to kill and so well equipped to do it."

"Then who are they?"

"I don't know. I've never seen anything like it." He turned and left.

Gwen sat back in her chair, bitterly disappointed. That was probably her last shot at taking down Chromogen before it made its new drug application for Chrotophorib. And she had nothing. Even worse, a new enemy had emerged out of nowhere and she didn't even know what they wanted. She looked at the data on Lindell's disk again with a sneer. What was Lindell playing at? Whatever it was, it was costing her time, money, and God knows what else. And if it was costing her, it damn well was going to cost Lindell, too.

* * *

John Rhoades left via the freight elevator, as always, looking down at all times so that security cameras would not record his face. His jet-black hair, gentle chin, and youthful blue eyes belied his age of just under sixty, and he certainly did not look the part of an ex-Special Forces, twice-decorated war hero. Medium build. Average height. He had a disarming, almost tranquil appearance. One would never guess that his hands had killed dozens of men while on duty…and off. Daily training had given him a physique which was the envy of men thirty years his junior. There was not an ounce of wasted flesh on his body. As he rode down the elevator, Gwen's last question ran over and over in his mind: who are they? His answer to her also replayed over and over. Because it was a lie.

The elevator doors opened, and he walked out into the garage, quickly scanning in all directions. He had a very good idea of who they were. And for the first time in over twenty-eight years, he was worried. John walked hurriedly through the parking garage to his Hummer H2, fresh out of the repair shop. The bullets he had pulled out of it were military-spec hollow-tip 7.62-mm NATO rounds manufactured by Lapua— a favorite of agencies and military forces around the world. And mercenaries. From Matt's description, the automatic rifle with suppressor and IR scope had been custom manufactured. And there was the encrypted communications gear. Their willingness to kill. Those all pointed in the same dangerous direction. That reminded John unmistakably of those he had encountered twenty-eight years before. And had been hiding from ever since.

Zurich, Switzerland

Elliot Lindell paced around his room at the Dresdener Grand Hotel, hoping his visitor would soon arrive. It was the last thing he had to do before he could return to Vancouver and restart the trials with Mitogenica. He walked over to the room service trolley. Freshly baked breakfast pastries filled a basket sitting on top, and their sweet buttery smell reached every corner of his room. He took a bite and went to the balcony. He didn't like being back in Zurich, but the Dresdener was the safest place by far. It was private. And discreet. The hotel lay due east of Zurich, nestled in the heavily wooded hills between the lakes Zurichsee and Greifensee. That side of the Zurichsee was known as the "Gold Coast," partly because the setting sun bathed those hills in golden sunlight every evening, and partly because it was home to the rich and the ultra rich. The properties far up the hill and close to the Dresdener were the most sought after, which seemed odd due to their poor view of the Zurichsee. But the rich moved there not out of concern for their view of the surroundings, but for what their surroundings could see of them—which in that neighborhood was almost nothing. Lindell's grandparents had taken him to the Dresdener on that visit thirty-five years ago. It was one of the few places where they felt "at home." Home to the rich. He felt at home there, too, Lindell realized.

But despite the many millions in his account, Elliot Lindell had never really felt rich. His mother, Dr. Isabelle Cooke Lindell, had made sure of that from the start. A strict Baptist from the dairy farms of Iowa, she had a keen disregard for riches or anyone rich. It was through his father, Dr. Francis Harvey Lindell II, that Elliot inherited his money. But growing up, the only evidence Elliot had seen of money was the occasional Christmas visit from his mysterious grandparents bearing opulent gifts. His mother disallowed any other form of material generosity. Except education. The young Elliot received the best schooling and tutors that his grandparents' money could buy, and he quickly showed his academic potential. Not that he wasn't genetically predestined. Isabelle was an associate professor of biochemistry at the California Institute of Technology and a world expert on mitochondrial structure and function. Francis was associate professor of computer sciences and programming. Elliot learned from them both every chance he got. For his master's thesis, he married his parents' two disciplines into one: computational biochemistry. And with it, he modeled the functioning of human mitochondria with a computer program. Finally, when Elliott reached sixteen and with his Master of Science freshly under his belt, his mother felt he was finally ready to travel the world and see his grandparents. And the money.

Lindell arrived first in Paris. His grandparents had an apartment near Place Victor Hugo, in the Sixteenth Arrondissement. After several days in Paris it was off to Amsterdam, then London, Rome, and finally Zurich. In each city except Zurich, they owned a well-appointed apartment in the city center. Every visit was quick and low-key. Almost secretive. As if they didn't want to be noticed. Or found. Strangely, none of their apartments had the Lindell name on them, but rather the name of some owning company. Lindell remembered only the one on the London apartment: the Sea Venture Trading Company. According to his grandfather, it was the name of the tax haven company that he had established in Bermuda. That Grandfather came from a long line of bankers in London was already known to the young Elliot. During that trip, Grandfather let him in on a family secret—that he had made his own fortune in New York just before the great crash in 1929, and got out just in time. Since then, they were perpetual travelers. Or perpetual tax evaders, as Lindell's mother called them. But they weren't greedy cheaters of society like his mother had claimed. In fact, Lindell's grandfather obsessed over "giving something back." When Lindell had called them a month later from the USA to explain the research funding roadblock at his university, they were overjoyed to hear that he was pursuing cancer research and promised full support. In the millions. That was where things went terribly wrong. Because Lindell's mother strictly forbade such "flamboyant" generosity. Lindell never understood if his parents were afraid of him being spoiled or didn't want to upset the political apple cart and their chances for tenure. Their motivation mattered little because days later, they both died.

The door buzzer rang. Lindell snapped back to the present and glanced at his watch. Exactly eight thirty a.m. Right on time. Lindell peered through the peephole, then opened the door to a small delegation of three middle-aged Japanese men. They had just stepped off the plane from Tokyo and their faces were drooping with fatigue. They made their introductions. Takanawa, the man Lindell met only days before, was in the lead. He stepped forward.

"Dr. Lindell, this is Dr. Hakiro Izumo, senior researcher in the mitochondrial diseases division of Mitsushima Pharmaceuticals. He will verify your source code and the other new molecule designs." Takanawa pointed to the third man. "Mr. Hashimoto will assist us." Business cards were presented, and Lindell accepted them in exchange for his.

Lindell handed them his flash drive, with information from Annika's computer. They crowded around their laptop and studied the data, with nonstop Japanese conversation running the whole time. After several minutes, Izumo glanced up to Takanawa and nodded, adding a few sentences that seemed to surprise Takanawa.

Takanawa turned to Lindell. "Thank you. We accept your results and will deposit the remaining five hundred thousand Swiss Francs to your account here." He then hesitated, and glanced back to Izumo, who urged him on. "If you are interested in selling a copy of your model, we would be most interested in negotiating a price. Any price." He looked downward with embarrassment after asking the question.

Lindell politely declined. "I am sorry. I'm not interested."

Lindell wasn't just sitting on the world's most advanced computer model of cancer cells. The core of that program was the world's most advanced model of mitochondria and their interaction with the rest of the cell, whether healthy or cancerous. And that model could churn out very interesting drugs targeting mitochondrial diseases—something Mitsushima was willing to pay liberally for. But the model itself was not for sale. The delegation left minutes later. Lindell relaxed and poured himself some tea from the trolley. Mitsushima's money would be secretly funneled to complete his construction project. Then he could continue his work unobserved by anyone else, and the model would be safe no matter where he went.

After so much time, it was difficult to fathom that the fulfillment of his life's work was within reach. His only regret was that he had carried it out alone. Lindell took his tea to the balcony and watched the rising sun light up the waters of the Zurichsee. A brisk wind whipped up small waves, which glistened in the morning sun like a thousand brilliant diamonds. It was on a day just like this that he had lost the only woman he had ever loved. In this very hotel.

Twenty years ago, he had been a visiting professor at MIT. Emily Hargraves was an exceptionally gifted and strikingly beautiful student working on her master's. Full of energy and life. And full of rebellion against her father, a highly placed executive in the pharmaceutical industry. As a result, Emily was intensely interested in Lindell's work on natural treatments. He loved teaching her and was always surprised by how quickly she learned. Soon, they were spending every spare minute with each other, discussing her work, his work, and the model. She was the only one he had ever trusted to see the source code of his cancer model. Emily was so gifted that she had even started programming some parts herself. He found himself dreaming of the two of them completing the model together. The dream started to become reality. After one year together, they both realized they were deeply in love. When Emily earner her master's, they stole away to Europe for a month. They toured the very cities Lindell had as a student, using the apartments he had inherited from his grandparents. The tour ended in Zurich at the Dresdener Grand Hotel. There, he presented Emily a diamond ring and proposed marriage. They spent the day planning, talking, drinking champagne, and watching the sailboats on the lake. He finally divulged to her that he was drawing on his own family fortune to fund his research, and would likely exhaust it to complete the model. If it even could be completed in his lifetime. But they could still lead a comfortable life. The next morning when he woke up, Emily was gone. She had left his ring on top of a note which only read: "I can't." Lindell never stopped hating himself for falling in love with a student more than fifteen years his junior. She was immature. Volatile. Capricious. But he knew she had loved him. So why did she leave?

Lindell jumped when the phone rang. He picked up.

"Sir, your taxi for the airport is here. Shall we send up the bellboy to collect your bags?"

"Yes, of course. You can come now," he answered. He gazed back out the window.

Why Emily left was a mystery he had never resolved. Perhaps something he had told her that day. Perhaps the fear of commitment at such a young age. Or the bitter divorce her mother was going through with her workaholic, absentee father. Only months later did Lindell find out that Emily had moved to London with her newly divorced mother. When he called, he found her a different person. Cold. Impersonal. Uncaring. Like he had never known her. Emily was starting her PhD in biochemistry at Oxford, and with it a new life. She took on her mother's maiden name. And reordered her own. Emily Gwendolyn Hargraves was gone forever. In her place was born Gwen Emily Riley.

Downtown Vancouver, B.C.

Will Conleth was right, John Rhoades thought as he waited at the stoplight on Granville and Robson. *Mitogenica's CEO was nicknamed Wolverine Riley for a reason.* But Gwen had her reasons to be on edge. Mitogenica's future was hanging by a thread and it was up to him to deliver the evidence on Chromogen. So far he had failed. He couldn't even prove Henry Cheung and Paul Hammond had been murdered. And that made him nervous. The last time he tried to fight those people, he barely escaped with his life. He might not be so lucky the next time.

John Rhoades grew up in a military family in Fairfax County, Virginia. Three generations of decorated war heroes preceded him. His father was a Marine serving in Force Recon, and specialized in deep reconnaissance. From the time the young John Rhoades could hold a knife in his hand, his father taught him everything he knew, starting with his Force's motto: *Celer, Silens, Mortalis*—Silent, Swift, Deadly. John volunteered for active duty fresh out of high school and got to Vietnam for his first tour in 1971. He quickly became a legend at navigating through the jungle, evading and tracking the enemy. Soon, he was taken unofficially on low-level covert operations. He dreamed of serving alongside his father, who was then in the 3rd Force Reconnaissance Company, running intelligence-gathering missions deep into the strongholds of the Viet Cong. He proudly traded war stories with his father every chance he got. Until that final meeting, just eight weeks before his tour of duty was up. When they sat at the bar that night, there was something about what his father said and the way he said it. As if it could be his last chance to see his son. Something was clearly wrong. But he wouldn't say what. Two weeks later, John got the news that his father and his whole recon team had been wiped out during their last mission. John's tour of duty was cut short by a few days so he could catch the next flight home for the funeral. At the time, he was stationed in one of the 3rd Marine Division's fire support bases along the northern border area near Khe Sanh. Unable to sleep, he gladly took the midnight shift on guard duty that night at the south guard bunker. He spent the hour trying to think of how to tell his mother. On his way back to the barracks, in a daze, another marine slammed into him running at top speed.

"Sorry, soldier," were the only words spoken. John never saw the face.

When he got back to his sleeping quarters, John felt something in his jacket pocket. It was an envelope addressed to him from his father. The letter inside made his guts churn. His father had stumbled across some top-secret U.S. military documents in a Viet Cong command and control post. But the papers had not been stolen, captured, or bought by the enemy. They had been sent there by high-level military insiders to coordinate staged battles. It was nothing short of treason. If anything happened, John's mother would know what to do. But that was only the beginning. En route to his home for the funeral, John received a radio message that his mother's house had been burned to the ground, with her in it.

That day was seared into his memory with the glowing red iron of loss, rage, and vengeance. He drove his car up to the former site of his parents' house, just south of Huntley Meadows Park in Fairfax County, Virginia, to see the smoldering ruins. It had been so thoroughly burned that nothing more than bones was left of his mother. He burst through the police lines to see the coroner examining her still-smoldering remains. Nightmare turned to horror when he saw the fractures of her collarbones, wrists, leg, and facial bones. She had been subjected to the most brutal of tortures before she died. But for what information?

"Mother! Mother!" John had screamed uncontrollably. He was, after all, still a teenager. He was escorted by police back to the street to compose himself. Through swollen, tear-blurred eyes he saw Doris Scripps standing just outside her front door in housecoat and curlers. Doris had been their longtime neighbor across the street, famous in the neighborhood for her nosiness. She raised a trembling hand to motion him closer. Ashamed of his tears, he put on his sunglasses and walked over.

"I'm so sorry for you," she forced through trembling sobs.

"It's not your fault," he said numbly.

"Your mother wanted you to have something. She asked me to keep it, in case anything happened to her."

"What?"

"I'll be right back." Doris went inside and quickly re-emerged with a small brown paper envelope. But when she looked up to hand it to him, she looked horrified, as if fearing for her own life.

"What's wrong?" John asked her.

"I think I know who did this."

"Who?"

"Two men. I saw them going inside yesterday evening."

"What did they look like?"

"They're standing behind you, across the street."

John removed his sunglasses and angled them to see the reflection of the two men. They were staring right at him and Doris. "Mrs. Scripps, you're going to be OK. Go inside."

She held her trembling hand in front of her mouth to stop herself from crying. A single tear ran down her face as she nodded. "God help you."

John walked past the two men in their car, visibly pulling out and inspecting the envelope Doris had handed to him. Bait for the fish.

He made sure he could be easily followed in his car as he drove north in the direction of Alexandria, stopping in the seediest part of town along the way. He parked and walked into a back alley which lined a row of bars and strip clubs. The hot, sweaty jungles of Vietnam were an easy trade for an alley filled with garbage, perfect hiding places, and dozens of possibilities for makeshift weapons. Waiting for his prey with supreme patience, John lay motionless and silent in a dumpster among the putrid spoils of the previous night's food service. Slowly, their quiet footsteps came closer. They were becoming more cautious, less sure, with each pace toward a quarry that had inexplicably vanished. Maybe they sensed something was wrong. Too late. When one of them opened the dumpster, John met his surprised gaze with a crushing blow to the Adam's apple. Before his victim could fall backward, John grabbed his head with both hands and slammed it down so hard on the thick steel lip of the dumpster he could hear the neck snap in two. The body fell limp. John sprang out of the dumpster like a coiled viper at the terrified second man. Before a weapon could be drawn, John was on top of him. A battering of powerful blows left the man's nose broken and cracked ribs on each side. Another brutal shot to just below the sternum snapped off his zyphoid process and drove it deep into his lungs. John slammed his body down on the asphalt and muffled the man's screams of pain with an iron grip over his face. He brought his own face within a hairsbreadth.

"I've killed dozens in Vietnam," he whispered to the man. "Just imagine what I'm going to do to you if you don't tell me who you work for."

The man laughed sickly. "You're already dead."

With that, he whipped out a pistol and tried to take aim. John pushed the muzzle away just as it went off, sending the bullet ricocheting off the alleyway walls. With ears ringing painfully, John saw a drunken bum down at the far end of the alley running for help.

With eyes full of spite, the man on the ground laughed at him. "You've got nothing."

"No. I have this," John said, waving the envelope from Doris in the air.

John then gave him a crushing blow to the skull. With heart pounding and breath heaving, he ran to their car and drove it into the alley. He piled their bodies in the trunk and drove off just as police sirens could be heard in the distance. Four hours later, deep in woods of West Virginia, John unloaded their bodies. The man's dying statement had been quite wrong. Both murderers were carrying ID. But it still made no sense at all. Until John read the letter he got from Doris.

As he read it, John realized that before his eyes in black and white was the summation of all the fears behind the anti-war movement. High-level military contractors and suppliers knew the end of the Vietnam conflict was nearing. In order to maximize their profits before the war ended, they were conspiring with the Viet Cong to stage battles and air strikes in which large amounts of armaments would be deployed. In return, small bunkers of arms and munitions would be "abandoned" in various locations to be used by the Viet Cong after U.S. involvement ended. It would make millions for the war industry, but at the cost of many young American soldiers fighting for a free world. Several suppliers of heavy equipment, munitions, explosives, and defoliating agents were involved. John's mother had worked in logistics for fifteen years and had already tracked down and noted two dozen names. The names of those who had killed his father. But before he could strike back, he knew he must patiently bide his time. John started the intense training program for serving in the Marine's Force Reconnaissance company with the intent to return to Vietnam as a bona fide Special Forces operative. His career in Special Forces was assured, and his vengeance about to begin.

Cleveland, Ohio

Annika squinted as she looked at the waters of Lake Erie, sparkling brightly under the midday sun. She pushed down her visor and drove off the Grand Army of the Republic Highway, exiting for Edgewater Park. She quickly found a parking spot near the water. The air was fresh, cool, and smelled like the water. Up ahead, an elderly couple waved to Annika from the foot of a large pier that jutted out into the water. Annika smiled back and started walking toward them. Mitch and Sarah Purcell had become good friends with Annika over the last year. They were both in their early sixties. Their three children had moved away years ago and visited rarely with their own families. Especially now, when the visits produced only tears. Mitch was the first patient from Chromogen's Chrotophorib trial who started taking the cocktail of natural supplements that Annika designed with Dr. Lindell. He was eager to try it since he saw no improvement at all during Chromogen's trial, and was starting to count the days he had left for Sarah and his family. Annika had always suspected he had been randomized into the treatment arm that did not get Chromogen's drug. When he began taking the supplement cocktail, Mitch started to stabilize, then slowly to improve. With the latest formulation he began two months back, he had made astounding improvements on all fronts. His PSA levels didn't just stop increasing, they started going down. Quickly. Then his latest scans from last week came back clear of metastases. Trevor didn't need to unblind any data points to tell Annika that. Mitch told her himself. He was Annika's star patient. As Annika walked up to the Purcells, she could see the remarkable impact of the recent good news. They smiled. They laughed. They held on to each other tightly, with love. Hope was in their eyes.

Sarah hugged Annika. "Thank you," she said. She pulled away with reddened, moist eyes and wiped a tear with her hand. "Thank you so much."

Annika smiled back. "I'm very glad I could help." Looking at both of them, Annika knew there was nothing else she would rather be doing with her life than this.

Mitch grasped Sarah's hand and gave her a kiss. He smiled warmly at Annika. "Let's take a walk."

Annika was all the happier to be helping the Purcells because she was so reminded of her father when she saw Mitch. Helping him was like reaching back through time and giving her father those few extra moments of life. He would be proud. Annika started walking with them. It was a perfect day. Children were playing the field. Mothers pushed their babies in strollers. Joggers were out enjoying the weather. The Purcells' traditional hour-long stroll took them several times along the path that curved around the large green field next to the water's edge. As usual, they asked about Annika's studies, her mother, Peter, and what she would do next. They told her about their upcoming trip to see the grandchildren, the visit Mitch thought he would never have again just three months ago. They continued down the path as it curved between the edge of the large parking lot and a thick swath of beach.

Mitch was about to say something when a jogger passing by yelled in his direction. When Mitch turned, the jogger sprayed him in the face with an inhaler bottle. A loud hiss of mist erupted out of such a small bottle.

"Hey!" yelled Mitch in surprise.

The jogger broke into a full sprint, heading for the parking lot.

"What happened?" Sarah asked.

"He sprayed something at me!" Mitch said.

"Maybe it was just an accident," Sarah said.

Annika did not see the jogger's face, but watched as he sprinted to a convertible, which was already moving toward him in the parking lot. A woman sat in the driver's seat, wearing a scarf tied around her head and large sunglasses that concealed most of her face. She looked familiar. Before Annika could place the face, the jogger leapt into the convertible and it screeched out of the exit.

"Are you OK?" Annika asked, turning back to Mitch.

Mitch tried to talk but no words came. His eyes went wide in confusion.

"Darling, are you alright?" Sarah asked, coming closer.

Mitch grunted heavily, and suddenly grasped at his chest and then his throat. He fell to his knees and then on to the ground, still clutching his throat.

"Oh, Mitch!" Sarah cried out loudly.

Annika took her phone from her purse, dialed 911, and handed it to Sarah. "Tell them we're in Edgewater Park, at the northwest corner of the main parking lot. Mitch is having a heart attack."

Sarah nodded, her face ghastly white as she looked helplessly at her husband of thirty-four years. Mitch was going into shock and spending every ounce of his strength just to fill his lungs with air.

Annika looked down at Mitch. "It's going to be OK." Her CPR training from her lifeguard days came surging back in an instant. She placed her hands on the center of his chest and started pumping in short, rapid compressions. Sarah was frantically explaining the situation over the phone. Help would be minutes away, Annika knew. Hospitals were numerous in this area. She pinched Mitch's nose and firmly breathed into his lungs, watched them deflate, breathed again, then resumed the pumping. She paid no attention to the small droplets on Mitch's face and around his mouth. Soon, however, Annika noticed a strange tingling sensation in her mouth. When the tingling turned to a cold numbness, Annika figured it was from pressing her mouth against Mitch's for the CPR. She started to feel strangely weak, but the sound of an ambulance siren in the distance gave her the strength to keep going. The numbness started to spread rapidly to her face and down her throat. Her vision started to blur. Suddenly, she found that she could barely force air into her own lungs, let alone into Mitch's. The siren was close. Very close. Annika wouldn't give up pumping Mitch's chest no matter how weak she felt. Wheels screeched nearby and the siren stopped. She glanced in the direction of the sound. Two blurry figures were running toward her. Everything started spinning around her, and suddenly it all went black.

Vancouver, B.C.

John Rhoades drove down the Oak Street Bridge, recalling his conversation with Gwen Riley and, quite involuntarily, the darkest days of his life. He had spent those days training for black operations in Force Recon—waiting for the chance to go back to Vietnam and track down those who had killed his parents. Their methods back then were so similar to what he now saw. By the time he returned to Vietnam, the U.S. was quickly reducing its military presence, and the staged battles were occurring more frequently. On his first leave in Saigon, John located one of the people on his mother's list—the senior vice president of Blackworth Inc., a major munitions supplier. He spent the night at a strip club and staggered back to his hotel. John made a quick end to him with a slice through his neck. One by one, John found the others on the list. They too, turned up dead, or disappeared completely. He also found coded letters, which he never could decipher, and several miniature listening devices with radio receivers. And with every kill, he found further connections to others, often high in the ranks of the military or the government and far beyond his own reach. John kept himself hidden from the others, and was confident that only he knew the common connection between his parents' death and those he was killing in vengeance. Or so he thought, until one night he awoke in his bed to the feel of cold steel against his jugular. The holder of the knife came close enough for John to smell his acrid breath. His face was silhouetted against the moonlight pouring in through the open window. And he wore the unmistakable dark fatigues of a black ops marine on night mission.

"I couldn't save your father. But I can save you," he whispered hoarsely.

"What are you talking about?" John asked.

"I made a promise to your father."

That voice. He knew that voice. It was the man who'd passed him the letter from his father back in the fire support base near Khe Sanh.

"You knew my father?"

The silhouette nodded. "And he would never take vengeance like you have."

"That's my business," John said bitterly.

"Not anymore. They know who you are now."

"How?" He was always so careful to leave no trace of himself.

"You don't get how far they reach, do you?"

"A little bit less now, thanks to me."

"You haven't touched them. They're in the government. The military. The banks. Industry. Everywhere there's money and power. You can't hide from them."

"Why don't you help me fight them?" John asked.

"I have two young children back home."

A noise outside the window startled the stranger. The blade suddenly pressed so hard into John's neck he was sure it was about to slice into his flesh. The stranger turned his head to look at the window; in that moment, John caught a glimpse of his face. Strong, deeply bitter stress lines crisscrossed a face well acquainted with pain. And a grotesque, jagged scar stretched from his left eye down to his chin.

"What do I do?" John asked.

"You disappear. Tomorrow is your last chance." At those words, the man slipped out the window and vanished into the night.

John never saw the stranger again. But, as before, his visit was perfectly timed. The next day, John flew out as planned on a black ops mission to the northwest of Tây Ninh, where the Vam Co Dông River crosses the Vietnamese-Cambodian border. As darkness was setting in, he fell behind the rest of the group and quietly disappeared into the jungle. During the next few days, he crossed one hundred miles over land and water to Phnom Penh, where he had papers forged and changed his name from Henry Tucker to John Rhoades. He then flew to Vancouver via Singapore and Australia. Henry Tucker was listed as MIA and John Rhoades started his new life in the fall of 1974. He had to lay vengeance aside in order to remain hidden. Over the years he presumed that the rest of them had simply passed away from old age. And with their passing, so he hoped passed any searching or memories of him. He had started to feel comfortable and safe. Now he was looking at plots of land in Kelowna for his retirement. A small hobby farm with an orchard. The last thing he ever wanted was to run into them again, so many years later. But it was too late. They were back. They were already planning their next move. He couldn't do anything to stop them.

Cleveland, Ohio

Annika winced as her eye was forced open by someone's fingers and an incredibly bright light was shone directly into her eyeball. She twisted her head to get away from it.

"Ouch!" she yelped in protest.

"She's coming to. She's going to be fine," an unknown voice said.

In a few seconds her eyes were accustomed to the light and she opened them. She looked around. She was in a hospital room. A doctor she had never seen before stood next to her bed. Standing just inside the doorway were Peter and Arthur Cormack, the CEO of Chromogen. As if he had been waiting for an introduction, a very nervous-looking Trevor Wilkins stepped in from the hallway.

"Where am I?" Annika asked them.

The doctor smiled. "You're in Glenville, of course. I'm Dr. Hennings."

"What happened?" Annika asked. The memories were still foggy.

"Your friend Mitch Purcell had a heart attack," Hennings said.

"Mitch! How is he?" Annika asked.

"I'm very sorry. It was just too late."

Tears started to run down Annika's cheeks. "Mitch! No!"

"You did everything correctly, Annika. Mitch was too far gone."

"But some man in the park...a jogger..." Annika struggled to remember.

"What about the jogger?"

She could see it again in her mind. "He sprayed something in Mitch's face!"

Hennings nodded. "Sarah Purcell told us. An asthma inhalator."

"Yes, that's right!"

"Annika, Mitch was likely hypersensitive to that jogger's asthma spray. One accidental dose in the wrong direction could have sent Mitch over the edge."

"I want to go." Annika tried to sit up. The room started spinning around her.

The doctor put his hand on Annika's shoulder. "You went into heavy shock trying to save Mitch. You need to take it slowly."

"But...," Annika protested. She noticed a small bandage over a vein on her left arm with a spot of blood in the middle. She looked at the doctor questioningly.

"Just routine blood work," he said.

"I feel something strange in my mouth, too."

The doctor glanced at the CEO of Chromogen before answering. "Sarah Purcell said you complained of numbness in your mouth. We did a scraping just to make sure everything was in order."

Annika's memories came flooding back. Dr. Hennings was lying. She knew she had said nothing of the sort to Sarah. But she nodded in agreement. "OK."

Arthur Cormack stepped toward Annika. "You're fine to go anytime you want. Why don't you rest a little while, then Peter can bring you home. OK?"

"OK, thank you," Annika answered weakly.

"There is just one more thing," the CEO said.

"Yes?"

"It turns out that Mitch Purcell was one of the patients in our trial on Chrotophorib. I can't stress to you how critical this trial is to Chromogen's future."

"Yes, I understand."

"Good. Then I hope you understand when I ask you to stop any personal contact you may have with other patients in the trial."

"Yes, of course," Annika said. Inside, her guts were twisting in knots at the thought that Cormack might know everything. She glanced over at Trevor. His face told her the worst case scenario had indeed occurred.

"Good. I need to get back to work on our trial results." Arthur Cormack and Dr. Hennings walked out. Trevor looked at Annika with a mixture of pity and shame on his face, then quickly followed the others.

"That was Chromogen's CEO?" Peter asked.

Annika nodded slowly. "Yes."

"He knows, Annika. Oh, God, he knows everything!"

"I wasn't going to take the job anyway."

Peter walked over. "What happened to you? Are you OK?"

"I'm OK. Mitch isn't."

When she saw Peter's face up close, Annika remembered the woman driving the convertible at Edgewater Park—and where she had seen her before. The one walking with Peter at the airport, who had sat next to him on the flight. Annika tried hard to conjure the face. Blonde hair instead of jet-black. No hat. No eyeglasses. Revealing clothes. Maybe. But she couldn't be sure.

"Hey! Are you with me?" Peter grabbed her hand.

She pulled her hand away for a split second, but then relaxed it. "Yeah. I'm here."

"You're sure you're alright?"

"Yes, I'm sure. Let's go." But Annika knew she wasn't sure. About anything.

WINTER

Chapter Seven

—

Two months later, Annika still had nightmares of poor Mitch Purcell lying helpless on the ground in front of her. She had long given up trying to explain the numbness in her mouth and passing out. Or what happened afterward. Later, Sarah called to tell her that when she got home on the day Mitch died, there had been a break-in. Only minor damage. But all the supplements they'd gotten from Annika were missing. Every last pill. Annika missed Mitch terribly. And she missed the others. Of the twenty-three patients she had given Dr. Lindell's supplement cocktail to, she had contact with only three in the last eight weeks. To attend their funerals. But none died of their cancer. One had been killed during a drugstore robbery. Another was mistakenly prescribed penicillin to which he was fatally allergic. Another drove off the road into a concrete barrier, apparently asleep at the wheel. It felt like a curse. The strangest part was that the same story had emerged from all the families. All the deceased had been cremated hastily after examination. Three of them due to "administrative error" at the hospital. Two families were filing lawsuits. It then occurred to Annika that she might be the only common thread among those four families.

Annika wondered what good she had really done for those patients. For Mitch Purcell. For anyone. At least the data she had collected for Dr. Lindell had helped him. That much she knew. Because Dr. Lindell had invited her to visit Vancouver and get the latest data. He even paid for her plane ticket. Annika didn't really care what the visit was about. She was happy to escape from Cleveland. Especially with Peter. Especially now. Chromogen had been pressuring her about the job offer, wondering why she wouldn't accept. Trevor was giving her no more information at all. She felt totally alone. Thank God for Peter.

Annika sat back in her seat on the Airbus A320 and watched Peter work furiously on his laptop before he had to shut it down. He looked more exhausted than usual. And stressed. Annika could see the attendant down the aisle eyeing Peter disapprovingly. The plane's engines revved up and it left the gate. She held Peter's double latte in one hand and her green tea in the other—the only breakfast they managed in the rush for the early flight. She needed to meet with Dr. Lindell before lunch.

"Honey, I think you need to shut down now," Annika said.

"Just a second. I really need to finish this group assignment by tomorrow."

The end of his MBA was a little over a month away, and he was more motivated than ever to finish it well. He had talked about getting promoted once the MBA was finished, but things at the office weren't going well. And he wouldn't say why. He looked nervous. His right eyebrow always twitched when he got nervous and he blinked in rapid spurts. Annika remembered he was like that the last time they had visited his family. Peter spent his childhood years growing up in Cleveland but had moved to Vancouver in his early teens. In fact, when Annika first met Peter two years ago at her gym, they talked about Vancouver at length. It was their first connection. She had visited Dr. Lindell there after her cancer conference and loved it. Then, she visited with Peter last Christmas to meet his family. Peter finally switched off and closed his laptop just as the flight attendant was approaching him. She noticed, cracked a half smile, half frown, and turned back.

"Thanks for taking a day off work to come with me. It means a lot to spend this time with you," Annika said.

Peter smiled and put his hand over hers. "I know I've been really busy lately. It's going to change, I promise." He said it like he wanted it to be true, but knew it probably wouldn't be.

Annika restrained herself from going further down that path. "And it's a great chance to see your family again!"

There was the eyebrow twitch again. "Yeah."

"How are they doing?"

"Oh, the normal stress."

Annika knew the story. Peter's father Joseph grew up in a factory worker's home. He worked every summer he could to help pay bills, then started apprenticing as an electrician the day after high school graduation. His younger, smarter brother Alex had it better. No summer jobs. He got into college. His career took off. Ever since then, it was payback to his brother Joseph. Back in the early '90s, Alex moved to Vancouver for some great executive-level job. Joe was struggling to find work in the recession of those days. Alex quickly got him a job in Vancouver, in the same company. Then, he helped put both Peter and his brother through college. But Joseph deeply resented the situation. To complicate matters further, Peter idolized Alex.

"Stress like what?"

"Uncle Alex is retired now at sixty. My dad's still grinding away at sixty-five and just scraping by."

"Doesn't Alex still help out?"

"I'm not sure he can anymore."

"Why not? I thought he was well off."

"He lost a bundle in the crash of 2008."

"I'm sorry to hear that."

"It's so strange."

"What is?"

"He was like this trading genius before. Every stock he touched turned golden, even during the crash of 2000. But it's like he just lost it completely the last couple of years."

"Everyone makes mistakes sometimes."

Peter chuckled. "Not Uncle Alex. At least never before." He stared out the window. Something else was bothering him.

"Are you OK?"

Peter shook his head. "Not really."

"What's wrong?"

"Do you remember that friend of mine, Stuart Gannet? He works in Alameda's finance department."

"Sure. Nice guy," Annika said.

"He's leaving the company."

"I'm sorry. He's a good friend, isn't he?"

"Yes, but there's more to it than that."

"Such as?"

"The reason he's leaving. He told me yesterday over lunch that Alameda Alloys is in deep trouble over a bunch of commodity derivatives they bought a few years back."

"What kind of trouble?"

Peter gripped his closed laptop so tight his knuckles were going white. "It could bankrupt the company."

"Are you serious?" Annika exclaimed.

"Management is already looking at bringing in a cleanup crew."

"What does that mean?"

Peter looked out the window again and spoke. "Downsizing. Layoffs."

Annika put her hand on his shoulder. It was stiff and unyielding. "I'm so sorry."

Peter looked back with a forced smile. "Maybe we'll both be looking for work by the time you finish your master's."

Annika changed topics. "So, are you looking forward to meeting Dr. Lindell?"

"I am, actually. I still can't figure out why you need to fly out to see him, though."

"He doesn't want me to give him any more data via the Internet. It's not safe anymore."

Peter grimaced. "I thought you were done with that!"

"I will be once Dr. Lindell has the data."

"Why does he need it so badly?"

"To calibrate his model. He's so close."

"And then?"

"We'll talk. He's very well connected in the research community."

"Yeah, until he gets caught with Chromogen's trial data."

"I'm serious here. He can help me find work. Or a PhD placement."

Peter raised his eyebrows in doubt. "I hope he's worth the risks you're taking."

"He is. You'll see that."

The Center for Natural Medicine
Vancouver, B.C.

Elliot Lindell's ocean blue eyes swept over the screen in front of him, reading the latest batch of data from the Eden Project. Whenever he concentrated he invariably squinted, accentuating the two vertical creases emanating upward from the bridge his nose. He gently rubbed the hairless top of his head. The data looked perfect. By themselves, every plant extract he collected on his emergency trip in September was performing as expected. Gwen Riley had been furious, of course, at his last-minute reformulations for the trial when he reappeared after two weeks. Perhaps that was why she was stalling on the results of the complete formulations combined with Mitaxynil. Or perhaps losing those two employees of hers had slowed her down that much. But, at some point, Gwen would see that the new formulations worked—better than her new drug. She would start to get nervous and might react in an unpleasant way. He had to be ready. The credibility he would earn on this trial would set the foundation for the last trial he would ever need to run. Two junior technicians scurried busily in the other corner of the lab, carrying multiple test tube samples of plant extracts from the ultracentrifuge to the gas chromatograph. Lindell looked back at his data.

The lab door banged open as Carter Feldman, his lab technician, walked in with his bike. Lindell glanced up at the clock on the wall. It was ten o'clock.

"You're late, Carter."

"I get my work done, don't I?" Carter lifted his bicycle high in the air with one arm to remind everyone it was made of titanium. Lindell always wondered how Carter could afford such an extravagance.

"Barely," Lindell said. But Carter was right. When he *did* work, he did it well.

"Any new developments?" Carter asked, peering around to get a view of the data on the screen.

"Just rearranging some files."

"Oh." Carter looked disappointed at seeing only file names scrolling by. He had never actually seen the source code of the model, nor any results.

"We're running low on the IV bags from Mitogenica. Can you check on that?"

"Oh, yeah, they had a box downstairs for you this morning."

"Are you going to pick it up?"

Carter logged on to his computer. "Sure. When I go get my coffee."

"Do inventory and then run it over to University Hospital."

"Got it, boss." Carter was busy typing. And by the smile on his face it obviously wasn't work-related.

"I've put the latest MRI scans onto the data folder. Process the volumetric scans and correlate back to baseline, please. And cross-correlate with the blood work."

Carter glanced up for a second. "Sure. By the way, are you doing any runs today of the model?"

"Yes, I am. The Gen-Silico will be full tasked."

"Oh." Carter looked disappointed.

"So no gaming today. You can tell that to your friends," Lindell said, nodding toward Carter's computer.

Carter grinned. "You think I would use a multi-million-dollar supercomputer to play games with my buddies?"

"So the rumors that you're the star on campus with the Gen-Silico are unfounded?" Lindell asked, as he walked toward the door.

"Of course they are," Carter said. He looked down and typed something in the computer. "But if they were, they won't be true for today."

"Glad to hear it." Lindell usually turned a blind eye to Carter playing multi-player games as long as he got his work done on time and didn't play when Lindell was running batch-jobs for his model. One time last year, Carter had ten users on the CPU at the same time, and a glitch in the system crashed the computer and Lindell's calculations along with it. Lindell made it clear that was a mistake Carter would only make once in his career there.

Carter edged toward the door to go get his coffee. "Hey, did you know there's a blog all about you on the Internet?"

"I don't have time for that sort of thing, Carter," Lindell said.

"It's done by a guy right here in Vancouver!"

That piqued Lindell's interest. "By whom?"

"I'll send you the link. They're talking about your trials with Mitogenica."

That's not good, thought Lindell. He didn't let Carter see his concern.

"They're making a patient support group."

"What?"

"Yeah, they're even meeting tonight. You should go!"

Lindell shook his head. "I can't discuss the trial with patients."

"Oh, I guess not." Carter opened the door to leave. "I'll be gone a bit longer for lunch today, by the way."

"You just got here!"

"Uh, I'm lunching with a special friend." Carter flushed a depth of red Lindell had never seen before on him.

"Just get your work done."

"Promise. And I'll bring Mitogenica's shipment in a minute."

* * *

Carter Feldman sailed down the hallway to grab his coffee and a muffin for breakfast. He often amazed people with how quickly he could move for someone who looked so pudgy and out of shape. His thin, wispy black hair flew around, accentuating his every movement. His dark eyes always looked disinterested, but they weren't. They were very interested—in obtaining the good life. Carter loved the Vancouver lifestyle, in particular the on-campus version. Mountains, parks, bike trails, ocean. It would be a crime to actually put in forty-hour weeks and miss out. Some of his classmates had decidedly taken a lower pay to stay in the area and enjoy the West Coast life. Carter simply hadn't been able to find another offer in such a bad economy. But it wasn't a bad life. University lab technicians are, after all, a breed apart. Most of Carter's lab tech friends had specialized skills that were needed desperately by the faculty, such as how to calibrate and operate a scanning electron microscope. Some were mechanical geniuses, able to construct whatever experimental apparatus was desired—from high-temperature metallurgical vacuum furnaces to biochemical reactors. But all shared the same peaceful university existence, which was punctuated only briefly with a frenzy of long, desperate hours brought on by a new research grant or the dreaded new grad student. For Carter, it was a one-way ticket to a relaxed career with a relaxed salary. Except for the little nagging realization that at twenty-eight he was already getting locked into that system. Controlled by the system. Never to escape to the "real world" even if he wanted. It was all quite unjust. Unless, of course, you used the system to your advantage. And that's exactly what his lunch date was all about.

Los Angeles

Austin Hayes slammed his office door behind him and tried to calm himself as he stared out his twentieth-story window on Wilshire Boulevard into the business district of LA. His heart was still thumping loudly in his ears and he could feel heat in his face. He stared at his blood pressure monitor on his desk, not daring to take a reading now. Wait half an hour. Rarely did he break down into outright yelling at his people. But in today's Friday morning staff meeting he had completely lost it. He stared briefly at the satellite phone Nolan had given him, wondering when he would hear from Nolan again. All his attempts to call Nolan in the last weeks were answered with static. That was exactly what had led to this morning's breakdown. Austin's traders had been caught so wrong-footed for the last month that they had swung the Hayes Biotechnology Opportunity Fund from a 27 percent profit to a 3 percent loss for the year. And they had the gall to blame him. He wasn't giving guidance, they said. Austin gritted his teeth and squeezed the pen in his hand. They were probably right. Ever since Nolan broke into his Malibu house back in September, there hadn't been a single call. Not a single tip. Nothing. The Morpheonic Pharmaceuticals trade had tacked on half the year's profits. And now those had been vaporized. Austin stared in the window at his reflection, which unnervingly seemed to resemble his father's more every day. He nearly jumped a foot in the air when the satellite phone rang. He leapt for it and picked up. He had to play this one cool.

"This is central. Voice check."

Austin spoke clearly and loudly. "Austin Hayes."

"Please hold." The typical series of clicks and buzzes ensued. Nolan's voice came on.

"Austin, how are you?" From Nolan's tone, it was clear he didn't really care.

"Not good."

"I know. I leave you alone for two months and your fund falls to pieces." His usual tone of condescension. Austin could hear the sound of wind rushing by. And traffic in the distance.

"So it was a rough month. Where were you?"

"Busy. How is Gwen Riley?"

"She's great. Mitogenica is one of the few bright spots in my holdings."

"That's not what I mean."

"She's still not going to take your offer. You know that."

"Then you have to get more serious."

"How?"

"Tell her you're going to sell all your Mitogenica stock. Then really do it."

"What? That stock's got nowhere to go but up! Everybody knows it."

"Up until about April."

"Then what?"

"Avarus will buy out Chromogen."

"What?" Austin stopped dead. No matter who Nolan's source was, that made no sense at all. "Impossible. Chromogen's new drug is no match for Mitogenica's."

"Chromogen will get their drug approved. Mitogenica won't."

"No way. Not on the data I've seen."

"You didn't see the final version."

Austin fell back a step in his office. He quickly glanced at his door to make sure it was really shut. This was the kind of conversation that got jail time. He lowered his voice. "What are you talking about? Data manipulation?"

"Just an adjustment."

"To what?"

"Where it should have been in the first place."

Austin ran through the whole situation with Chromogen in his head. One big red flag came up. "This doesn't have anything to do with that student Annika Guthrie, does it?"

Nolan ignored the question. "Make your trades gradually. You have until April. So does Gwen."

"Just how far inside Chromogen and Avarus are you?"

"Call up Gwen Riley and let her know the timing."

"What good does that do?"

"Because when it happens she'll finally realize she has no choice."

"Gwen Riley always has a choice."

Nolan laughed. "That's true. Either we take Mitogenica intact, or we buy it in pieces after she goes bankrupt."

Austin realized that Nolan was playing a far larger game than insider trading. This was about taking a major position in an entire industry. It was empire building. How many other takeovers had Nolan orchestrated? He had to ask the forbidden question one more time. "Who are you people?"

"I told you never to ask that again."

"That was before you dragged me into defrauding the FDA. I want to know who I'm working with on this."

"Working for, don't you mean?"

Austin didn't like the sound of that. But he didn't have much choice. "Fine. Working for."

Several long seconds ticked by. "We call ourselves The Trust."

"What does that mean?"

"You'll find out soon enough." The connection ended abruptly.

New York

Nolan Ponticas Vasquez pocketed his satellite phone and leaned forward on the carved limestone railing of his terrace. He never relished the dramatics that his position required, but they did have their effect. Nolan enjoyed watching New York's rush-hour traffic some thirty stories below. He loved the feeling of power he had as he looked down on the ant-sized people. He thought about what trades he should send to Austin to keep him happy for the next few weeks. And how to bring him one step closer. It was surprising, actually, that Austin had not been more demanding much earlier. But now, if there was any hope of taking Mitogenica smoothly in one piece, Austin would have to come up to the next level in The Trust. Timing was always the issue. A chilling breeze swept through his close-cropped black hair. The sound of motors roaring and horns honking below became distracting. Nolan walked around the terrace to the quiet side, where his favorite table stood. It was hewn from a solid lump of granite. The table sat close enough to the edge to see the full splendor of Central Park while sitting comfortably and enjoying an afternoon coffee.

Nolan sat down and picked up a sterling silver espresso pitcher. At least he called it that in his head. It was actually a teapot. And nearly empty. As he tilted it high to pour out the last of the espresso, the hallmarks on the bottom glinted in the afternoon sun. The same hallmarks were on all the pieces of the tea set—the Imperial Warrant mark of Fabergé and the 1901 mark of the Moscow assay office. It was his prized possession. A glance to the butler standing just inside the glass doors was all that was needed to have him rush out and gingerly take the teapot away to refill the espresso. Nolan sometimes amused himself at how Fabergé would react to someone using his teapot for coffee—a beverage almost unknown to nineteenth-century Russia. But, after all, he could do as he pleased. Nolan watched the butler disappear behind the glass doors leading inside. He looked at his own reflection on the glass. Unlike many of his colleagues in The Trust, he actually looked like he belonged in this setting. Tall, slim, with the darker skin of southern Europe, a high forehead, and a Roman nose; he looked like a proud Spanish aristocrat, his mother had always told him. But being born into a long line of steelworkers in Pittsburgh, that look had caused him endless fights growing up. Fights he eventually always won.

Nolan had decided early on not to follow in his father's footsteps at the steel mill. But trying to get through college with only mediocre marks left him little choice but to work the summers on the floor of the No. 1 Melt Shop of Anacott Steel. The union wages were too good to pass up. Nolan's father had warned him that the foreman had it in for all college boys. Him especially. On his first day, he was sweeping the floors in the ladle re-bricking shop when a loud siren went off. The foreman, an ugly and enormous man, stood there smiling at him as he continued to sweep. Nolan was oblivious to the meaning of the siren. Nobody had told him that small explosive charges were routinely used on ladles to dislodge large pieces of solidified steel and the glass-like slag left over from a botched pour. Nobody told him the siren meant that the next blast was ten seconds away. The explosion knocked him flat and sent a small shard of razor-sharp slag straight at his forehead, opening a wide gash an inch above his right eye.

Afterward, the foreman walked up to him with a big smile and said, "Now you know what the siren is for."

The ringing in Nolan's ears finally went away after a few days, but the scar on his otherwise perfect face would be there for life. It took Nolan a month to grow his hair long enough to cover the scar. Until then, the foreman stared at the scar with a pleased look of accomplishment each time he saw Nolan. And doubly so when he hauled Nolan into his office to yell at him for a quarter of an hour for doing something wrong. Every time he sat in that office, Nolan stared not at the foreman but at the big cast-iron horseshoe hanging on his wall. It was painted a bright blue and hung several feet above the foreman's head. His good luck piece, the foreman claimed. It was not good luck for Nolan. Anacott Steel was his worst nightmare.

But Nolan's resolve to excel at school was cemented forever after that first summer. He had majored in biochemistry, targeting big pharma companies—the next big place to be, apparently. He taught himself to get by on four hours of sleep a night and gave himself no life beyond his textbooks. In his sophomore and junior years he scored second highest in the class. But he still needed the money from the steel mill. And during each of the next two summers, the foreman at Anacott reached new levels of cruelty. During his final weeks of work at Anacott, Nolan found out when his tormentor foreman was on night shift. Two days before his last summer work ended, Nolan slipped into Anacott Steel in the middle of that shift. He removed the blue horseshoe from the foreman's office and waited in the tundish preparation room. The foreman never knew what hit him. He fell unconscious into one of the massive pouring tundishes—big enough to hold two cars—just before the preheat gas burners fired up. Only ashes were left of him when the liquid steel was poured through that tundish. There wasn't enough left even to show up as an impurity in that heat of steel. Before slipping out of the No. 1 Melt Shop that night, Nolan dropped the cast-iron blue horseshoe into a ladle of white-hot liquid steel fresh from oxygen blow-down. He watched it melt to nothing in seconds. Nobody ever suspected his role in the foreman's death. He never got a single call or question. It was then that he realized the power of being able to break the rules and get away with it. In his senior year, Nolan graduated at the top of his biochemistry class. His former competitor was found hanging in his dorm room after spring break, a perfectly scripted suicide note neatly typed and laying on his bed.

For Nolan, being inducted into The Trust was a logical extension of his career path. Others like Austin had to be brought in slowly, with the truth given in measured doses. It always started with the same history lesson. Since civilization began, man's existence has been kept orderly by two governments: the one he sees, and the one he does not. The unseen government is the invisible thread which holds together the chaotic fabric of human history. It is ever evolving and reinventing itself to remain the guiding force of reason and order. The Trust is the latest incarnation of that invisible thread, born out of U.S. money trusts of the late nineteenth century. Over the last hundred years, The Trust has administered markets and made whole industries more efficient, putting an end to destructive competition. Both world wars were shortened by The Trust, as were the Great Depression and the crash of 2008. The Trust always made sure that the best means of production fell into the most productive and creative hands. That meant the hands of The Trust itself. It was all to establish a superior world order. For Nolan, bringing Gwen Riley's technology into the fold of The Trust was an essential part of that. Gwen had no idea of the real potential of the Eden Project. Only The Trust could properly control it, and eventually it would. No matter what rules had to broken along the way.

CHAPTER EIGHT

Mitogenica, Inc.
Vancouver, B.C.

Gwen Riley was at the edge of physical and mental exhaustion as she walked out of Mitogenica's executive conference room just before noon. Her tired, puffy eyes and roughly pulled back hair were an odd combination with her immaculately pressed suit and shiny new shoes. But there was little time for sleep when Mitogenica was in the final stages of preparing the NDA—New Drug Application—for approval of Mitasmolin by the FDA. It was a massive document of over five hundred thousand pages. And it had been prepared in record time since last patient, last visit, and the unblinding of the database. Gwen had just spent all morning in the final review meeting. Mitogenica would hand it over to the FDA on Monday. Chromogen would submit its own NDA for Chrotophorib the very same day, according to Gwen's intelligence from John Rhoades. That didn't bother her. The intelligence also told her that Chromogen's toxicity problem had worsened. The rumors in the biotech community confirmed it. So did Chromogen's steadily dropping stock price. There was just one problem. Gwen's gut was screaming that something wasn't right. Chromogen's CEO, Arthur Cormack, always had an ace up his sleeve. Obviously, he hadn't played it yet. John Rhoades had delivered nothing on who killed Henry Cheung and Paul Hammond. Whoever was trying to infiltrate Mitogenica was still out there, and she had no idea who it was. Gwen walked briskly toward her office but almost lost her balance when a wave of dizziness came over her. She realized she had eaten nothing so far today. She walked up to her assistant Nadine's desk. Nadine immediately stopped typing and looked up.

"Coffee, please," Gwen said in a tired voice.

"Right away, ma'am." Nadine dropped everything and flew off her chair.

Gwen walked in her office and let herself fall onto her well-cushioned leather chair. She pulled up the latest version of Mitogenica's press release for the filing of the NDA. The smell of a freshly brewed double espresso with cream and sugar wafted in as Nadine entered with the cup. She set it gingerly on Gwen's desk.

"Get me a sashimi bento box from Shikama Sushi, please. No squid this time," Gwen said. That was the normal routine. Nadine went out to sushi lunch every Friday and brought back take-out for Gwen.

Nadine nodded. "Of course." She turned to leave, but then spun back around. "Ma'am, I forgot to tell you, Mr. Hayes has called several times this morning for you. He says it's urgent."

Gwen sighed and rolled her eyes upward. "Of course it is."

"If he calls again—"

"Put him through."

"Yes, ma'am."

As the door shut, Gwen recalled that she'd turned her cell phone off for the NDA review. She flicked it back on, and the missed call messages started rolling down her screen. Nearly all of them were from Austin. Gwen shook her head. She brought her coffee cup up to her lips and went back to reading the press release. Perhaps two minutes had passed when the phone rang. She gulped the rest of her coffee before answering. She kept reading the text on her screen as she spoke.

"Hello, Austin. What could possibly be so urgent today?"

"Sorry, Gwen. I know today of all days—"

"Make it fast, Austin."

"Is there something about Mitasmolin you haven't told me? Something bad?"

"You should know better."

"Somebody else does know better."

Gwen took her eyes off the screen and sat up in her chair. "Who?"

"I can't say. But I need to unload all my holdings of Mitogenica." This time, Austin's voice said he really meant it. Gwen took that seriously. Had Chromogen's ace been put into play?

Gwen tried to remain calm. "What have you heard, Austin?"

"That Chromogen will get approval. And you won't."

"Austin, we haven't even filed our NDAs yet!" Gwen said impatiently.

"I know."

"Then how can anyone know the outcome?"

"You really need to meet these friends of mine. Quickly." Austin sounded scared. That was a first.

"I don't need your friends' help!" Gwen said sharply.

"You will by April."

"April will come and go. Nobody's getting Mitogenica's technology."

"If you reconsider, just call me anytime."

"Can't you tell me who these people are?"

"No."

"Austin, what the hell is going on with you?"

"I have to go now, Gwen. Sorry."

"Austin!" Gwen shouted. The line went dead. "Damn it!" She slammed the phone down on her desk. The possibility that Austin had connections with Chromogen had gone through her mind before. But he was smarter than that. He was playing at something, and it might be important. Gwen pulled her desk drawer open and reached for the disposable cell phone John Rhoades gave her to contact him. As her finger hit the first button, Nadine buzzed through.

"Yes, Nadine?"

"Ma'am, it's Jeff Lowe."

"I can't take the call."

"No, he's standing right here. He says it's important."

Gwen bowed her head in momentary resignation. She hid the disposable cell. "Come in."

Jeff Lowe, Gwen's head of research, came in the room. He was normally high-strung, but today he was a nervous wreck. Gwen had noticed that in the NDA meeting.

Gwen glanced down at her watch. "This has to be fast. What's so urgent?"

"It's your trials with Lindell," Jeff said, nearly out of breath. As if he had run there.

Gwen opened both hands and raised them in the air. "What about them?"

"I thought you wanted to go in baby steps with this."

Gwen closed her eyes for a second. Jeff was always hyper-cautious about combining natural ingredients with Mitaxynil. He had warned of the dangers of being too good with something that couldn't be patented. "What makes you think otherwise?"

"Lindell's cocktails are working far better than we thought."

"It's too early in the trial to tell that. Let's talk in four months."

"That might be too late."

"Why?"

"I just got the latest results from the Eden Project on his three new formulations." He held out a thick wad of printouts. "I've never seen anything like it."

Gwen stood up to read through the data. "Seen anything like what?"

"Lindell's now helping Mitaxynil reactivate dormant mitochondria in cancer cells. His cocktails never did that before."

"So what?"

"So before, we had seventy percent of cancer cells dying in the test tube. Now it's ninety-five percent."

"That's good, isn't it?"

Jeff shook his head vigorously. His jaw muscles tightened. "It's too good. It's better than our new drug Mitasmolin."

"In a test tube, maybe. But the trial has barely started."

"But once he gets this data he'll reformulate and do even better."

Gwen struggled to maintain her composure. Austin's words kept echoing in the back of her mind. Chromogen was a wild card. She had another meeting in two minutes. And her head of communications urgently needed her sign-off on the press release. "Relax. It's just too early."

"But what if his model is fully functional now?"

"It's not."

"Something changed since the first formulations. Hugely," Jeff said, still holding out the printouts. He was becoming insistent.

"I hope so. That's why I'm working with him." Gwen's voice was gradually rising.

Jeff shook his head. "No. There's something else going on here."

"What?"

"I don't know yet. I haven't figured him out." He stared at the printouts.

"I have."

"But what if he doesn't even need Mitaxynil in his next formulation?"

"He will."

"I don't think so. I think he's playing us for the Eden Project."

"He isn't. I'm playing him for his model. His *unfinished* model."

"Gwen, if he improves on this, he could outdo Mitasmolin."

"He won't. You need to relax, Jeff."

"He could outdo all chemo drugs on the market!"

"Then let him!" Gwen shouted at the top of her lungs. A smashing sound in the next room told Gwen that Nadine had just dropped her coffee mug on the floor. Gwen could feel the blood rush to her face and felt her pulse pounding heavily in her neck. She gripped her cell phone so hard the plastic casing made a cracking sound. Jeff stood there, wide-eyed and speechless. Gwen breathed slowly and evenly to calm herself down. She spoke in a firm but quieter voice. "Try testing Mitasmolin with Lindell's latest formulas."

Jeff gazed blankly at Gwen, still shocked by her outburst. "Why?"

"Because then you'll understand what I'm doing."

"With Paul Hammond and Henry Cheung gone, we're backed up for months."

"Then do it when you have time."

Jeff looked highly doubtful. "OK. First results in April."

Gwen took a step closer with a deep frown and narrowed eyes. "I do know what I'm doing, Jeff."

"I hope to God you do. Because I sure don't." Jeff turned and walked out.

University of British Columbia Campus
Vancouver, B.C.

Peter Grafton looked at his watch as he drove the rental car along Lower Mall on the UBC Campus.

"Hey, we're way early. Is that OK?"

"Sure," said Annika. "Why not?"

"I just figured Dr. Lindell would be a very busy person."

"I'm sure it will be fine," Annika said.

Peter turned into the West Parkade, which lay halfway up the campus on the west side, next to the Marine Drive residence. They walked down Lower Mall and crossed over Agronomy Road. The Center for Natural Medicine stood directly in front of them. Annika opened the door.

"It looks ancient," Peter said, looking around the interior of the building.

"It's an old government research station," Annika said, leading the way. "They just rent it. They're not even officially part of the university."

"What, a separate research institute?"

"Mm-hmm," Annika said. She walked up to the reception desk. "I'm here to see Dr. Lindell, please. Annika Guthrie."

The woman behind the desk was busily typing, and after several seconds finally looked up for an instant. "You're early," she said without emotion as she continued typing. "But he's in his office." She jabbed her finger toward the hallway on the right. "Go down the hall, turn left. Dr. Lindell's office is the last door on the left."

Annika and Peter continued down the hall. As they approached Dr. Lindell's office, they both noticed a strange green light coming from behind the frosted glass of the door's window. The hues and shapes constantly shifted. It was as if the entire lab was filled with green lights, and they were moving. A soft, mechanical-sounding female voice was speaking. Then another one. As Annika and Peter drew closer, they realized that there was actually an entire chorus of female voices gently and rhythmically talking. There must have been hundreds of them. But a few of them seemed louder than the rest.

"Shh!" Annika said softly, holding her finger to her lips.

The voices grew quiet, except for one. They could hear soft, mechanically enunciated words.

"Mitochondrial reactivation complete. Inhibition of aerobic glycolysis at ninety-seven percent, oxidative phosphorylation restored. Apoptosis at twenty-seven percent of sample population. Commencing challenge with therapeutic agent XDR-341."

Several seconds passed and there was a marked shift in colors and the light patterns. The voice continued. "Down-regulation of Bcl-2 proteins at eighty percent. Warning: critical dissipation of mitochondrial membrane potential. Membrane pore formation at ten times normal. Release of caspase activators into cytosol has commenced. Apoptosis at seventy percent."

Annika looked back at Peter with awe on her face.

He shrugged. "What does that mean?"

"I think he's running his cancer model!" Annika softly uttered, and pressed her ear to the door. A sound like an alarm went off and the female voice continued.

"Endoplasmic reticula and lysosomal signaling at ninety-two percent. Concentration of caspase activators in cytosol at critical levels. Warning! Mitochondrial membrane has been breached. Permeabilization is complete. Irreversible cytochrome-C cascade initiated. Apoptosis at eighty-five percent. Executioner caspases released. Intracellular protein cleavage at fifty percent and rising. DNA fragmentation initiated. Apoptosis at one hundred percent of the sample population. Expression of macrophage activators is complete." The voice faded into silence.

Peter was impressed. "I thought the model wasn't finished yet," he whispered.

"Me too!" Annika said. She turned back to the door, only to bump her head with a loud thud on the glass. The green lights disappeared. Annika immediately pushed on the door but found it locked. She knocked.

"Dr. Lindell? Hello?" she asked loudly.

After a few long seconds, the thick deadbolt lock was turned and the door opened. A tall man in his fifties opened the door. He was bald on the top of his head only, with a crown of light gray hair around the sides. He raised his eyebrows in a look of surprise, which instantly turned into a smile.

"Annika! You're quite early!" he said, with more than a hint of surprise.

"Yes, there was less of a headwind than normal. Sorry!"

Lindell turned to Peter to shake hands. "You must be Peter! Annika has told me so much about you! Please come in, both of you."

Annika was nearly overwhelmed by emotion as she fought hard not to explode with questions for Dr. Lindell. Where had he been during those weeks in September? Why did he have to disappear? What had he stored on her computer? And she had so much to tell him. But she couldn't in front of Peter. Those patients in Chromogen's Phase III trial that had died. All of them on Dr. Lindell's latest supplement cocktail. All of them doing wonderfully. All of them dead for every reason but their cancer. Dr. Lindell had to know. But it would have to wait for the visit tomorrow, when Peter would spend time with his family. Annika came back to the moment and realized there was no obvious source of the green lights she and Peter had seen through the frosted window. Or those voices.

"Were there people talking in here?" Annika asked, still scanning the room.

"Yes. I was just watching some research updates on streaming video." Lindell's ocean blue eyes said that no matter how many ways Annika asked, she would get that same answer.

Annika couldn't help but notice a large, black semi-cylindrical apparatus sitting on the edge of Lindell's desk. It was about a foot high and ran along the entire six-foot length of the desk. It was studded all over with clusters of three small lenses. The end of the device had a large sticker with the international insignia for laser radiation, a danger sign, and several lines of Japanese text organized in vertical columns. "What does this do?" Annika asked.

"Just an experimental I/O device." Lindell came over and politely slid a sectioned plastic lid over the entire half-rounded top of the device. It locked shut with a loud click. A wire ran from the device along a small wire tray bolted to the ceiling. It ended at a small room in the back corner of the lab. The room was dark, except for an eerie blue backlighting with the odd flashes of green. A constant humming noise came through the partially closed doorway.

Peter was instantly impressed. "You have your own mainframe right here?"

"Ah, Carter! Always leaving the door open," Lindell said with annoyance. He turned the light on. Annika and Peter followed. Inside, the air was cool. The little room vibrated with the humming of the air-conditioning unit in the ceiling.

"The air-conditioning gives it away," Peter said. "We had one just like this in our Comp Sci lab. But not this big. Wow."

Both Annika and Peter stood looking in awe at the two massive computer frames, which towered over two meters high, a meter deep, and a meter wide. Small green LED lights were flashing all over them.

"What kind is it?" asked Peter.

"It's a Gen-Silico 5300 GX2 supercomputer," Lindell said proudly. "This is what I run the model on."

"Wow!" Peter said, truly impressed. "What's the spec?"

"Eighteen terabytes of global shared memory and twenty-two teraflops in performance." Lindell led them out of the little room. "Sorry, we have to keep the door shut when it's fully tasked; otherwise, it will overheat."

"Peter would love to hear more about your research," Annika said to Lindell.

"Of course," Lindell said. "What are you interested in?"

Peter looked around the room. "Everything. Like why your method is right and the whole cancer industry is wrong."

Lindell started explaining. "The science of cancer started back in the 1920s, when it was understood to be due to uncontrolled cell division. Since cells divide at the nucleus first, the pharmaceutical industry targeted the nucleus. But progress was slow. By 1960, the FDA had approved only six anti-cancer drugs—all of them artificial chemicals, either anti-metabolites or alkylating agents. But they were aiming at the wrong target and fighting the wrong war. Only decades later did we discover that all cells carry a death program. Trigger the death program, and the cell digests itself from the inside out and dies. This process was called apoptosis. But that discovery helped little, because nobody knew how to trigger apoptosis in cancer cells. Fast-forward to the late 1990s, when it was finally confirmed what part of the cell triggered apoptosis: the mitochondria. Not the nucleus. And all along, nature has provided us with multitudes of chemicals in plants that specialize in attacking the mitochondria of cancer cells, triggering the death program. Everybody missed that until now because they were looking in the wrong direction."

Peter broke in. "If it was that simple, then why don't you already have a cure for cancer?"

Lindell continued. "Because it's not that simple. Cancer cells are programmed to survive. That is why they actually suppress their mitochondria, shrinking them in size and altering their function. This was first observed back in 1923 by the Nobel laureate Otto Warburg. Now, back to the late '90s, when mitochondria took center stage. Gwen Riley realized that medications used to activate defective mitochondria in people with hereditary diseases might also reactivate the suppressed mitochondria of cancer cells. In particular, she targeted medications to treat lactic acidosis. She was right. In fact, the re-activation process alone can kill off quite a few of the cancer cells."

"Mitaxynil!" Peter said. He looked at Annika. "See, I told you she was a genius." Annika rolled her eyes.

"A greedy genius," Lindell said. "Dichloroacetate does the same thing, maybe even better. But it wasn't under patent protection. Mitaxynil was patented, so Gwen used that so she could charge a hundred times what it costs to make. But I must admit that my plant extracts are much more effective on cancer cells' mitochondria once they are reactivated with Mitaxynil."

"So you aren't aiming for a totally natural cure after all?" Peter asked.

Lindell glanced at Annika. "It just may be possible to reactivate mitochondria with certain plant extracts as well."

"That's fascinating. I just don't get why you need such a complicated model and large computer," Peter said.

"Think of it this way: the death program of the cancer cell needs a password to activate it. I am looking for that password. I have thousands of possible natural chemicals to choose from, each representing a single letter or digit in that password. The model runs through all possible combinations, predicting if they will work or not by reconstructing actual living cancer cells in mathematical models. The data I get from Gwen Riley and Annika helps me to calibrate the model."

That jogged Annika's memory. She dug her cell phone out of her purse. "I almost forgot! All the data is here."

"Wonderful." Lindell took the phone and connected it to his workstation.

"By the way, whatever happened to that data you stored on my computer in September? I couldn't find anything when I looked." Annika noticed that Peter perked up with curiosity. She glanced back at him, realizing she hadn't told him that detail.

"Don't worry, I took it off as soon as I got back," Lindell said.

"What data was that? Didn't you disappear in September?" Peter asked.

"I urgently had to fix a major glitch in the model," Lindell said.

Annika nodded.

Lindell typed a few commands into his terminal. "Annika, I'm downloading my latest results for you to look at in detail."

"Of course! I'd love to!"

Peter interrupted. "Um, excuse me, is there a toilet here?"

"I thought you went in the airport," Annika said.

Peter smiled sheepishly. "Too much coffee, I guess."

Lindell pointed to the door. "Just on the other side of reception, on the right."

"Thanks!" Peter left in a hurry.

Annika waited in silence for what seemed like forever as Lindell's data was transferred to her cell phone. She didn't know how to broach the subject, so she spoke directly. "I decided not to take the job Chromogen offered me."

"I certainly hope not."

Annika stalled again, feeling awkward. "Do you know anyone looking for a PhD student?"

Peter came back.

"Just in time, Peter," Lindell said.

"For what?"

"I would like to offer Annika a position here as my PhD student."

Peter stood there in shock.

Annika's mouth dropped open. "But I thought you normally didn't take grad students."

"You're not a normal grad student," Lindell replied, smiling.

"I...I don't know what to say."

"There's no rush. Think about it." Lindell glanced at the clock on the wall. "I need to run now. Why don't you and Peter come as my guests to the life sciences faculty reception tonight at seven o'clock? It's right here on campus at Cecil Green Park House."

"Are we free tonight?" Annika asked Peter.

He stood there, still stunned. "My dad is on late shift tonight anyway. Sure."

Lindell added, "Gwen Riley will be there."

"Great! Peter can get her autograph," Annika said with a smile.

Peter wasn't laughing.

"Very well. I'll see you there," Lindell said. He walked them to the door. "I'll look at your data later and we can discuss it tomorrow."

Outside, a cold wind was blowing as Annika and Peter left the Center for Natural Medicine. They turned onto Agronomy Road and started walking past the Ritsumeikan House toward the center of campus. Annika held Peter's arm tightly and huddled in closely for warmth, but she couldn't help feeling like he was a million miles away. She knew what he was thinking.

"So much for Lindell not taking grad students anymore," Peter said in a monotone.

"Peter, I had no idea."

A few painful seconds passed. "What are you going to do?"

Annika knew she had to admit it sometime. "I want to take it."

Peter looked down at his feet and held back a frown. "How badly?"

"More than anything."

"More than me?"

Annika felt almost numb at the words and what they might lead to. "Does it have to be like that?"

"You tell me." Peter gestured to turn left onto West Mall.

Annika's mind was spinning. She paid no attention to where they were going until Peter turned right up Stores Road. The wind whipped Annika's hair across her face. She pulled it away and tried to put it back into place. "Where are we going? Isn't your car over there?" She pointed to the left. She was glad to have anything to talk about other than their future. Or the lack of it.

"I need a coffee badly. There's a place at the Student Union Building."

On their right, they passed a large brick building and beside it a small green wooden building with white trim. They emerged onto Main Mall, a wide avenue of grass which divided the UBC campus almost exactly in half down its length. Main Mall was bounded on each side by a row of red oaks with leafless branches that swayed in the cold wind. Classes were in mid-session, and only a smattering of students walked by on the two broad sidewalks which spanned the grassy boulevard.

"That was a strange shortcut," Annika said, looking back at their path.

Peter nodded back toward the tall brick building. "That's where I did my metal-lurgy degree. I always walked this way from my place at Totem Park residence."

"Oh, really!" Annika said. She watched as the front door of the green wooden building opened and two people walked out holding sandwiches and coffee. "Hey, that place has coffee."

Peter shook his head. "That's the Barn. I don't like their coffee."

"What's wrong with—"

Annika was cut off when a hefty skateboarder dressed in a loose-hanging green jacket slammed headlong into Peter at top speed. The collision was no accident. As Peter tumbled to the ground, the skateboarder reached out and grabbed Annika's purse with one hand while shoving her back powerfully with the other. Annika saw his face only for a blurred instant, just long enough to realize he was at least ten years too old to be a student. Annika yelped in pain and hit the ground next to Peter. She watched the skateboarder take off eastward down Main Mall with her purse in hand, picking up speed incredibly fast. The handful of students who noticed the incident watched in surprised fascination. Peter lay beside her, still stunned.

"My purse!" Annika shouted. Her cell phone was in the purse, with all the data she had given to Dr. Lindell.

Peter shook himself out of his daze and jumped up with a look of anger Annika had never seen before. Without even looking down at her, his feet hit the ground with a loud thump and he sprinted toward the skateboarder with everything he had. But Peter didn't have a hope of catching the skateboarder, who was whizzing down Main Mall at top speed. Until a stranger on the sidewalk swept his arm up to neck height and violently clipped the skateboarder as he whipped by. The board went sailing onto the grass and the skateboarder rotated in midair. The stranger gripped the skateboarder's neck and shoved downward with brutal force, until the boarder's body hit the ground like a slab of meat. Instantly, the skateboarder tucked in his legs and kicked the stranger up in the air several feet. They both tumbled onto the grass between the Main Mall and the small green house, and started trading kicks and punches faster than Annika could follow. The skateboarder quickly got the upper hand. After several well-placed punches put the stranger on the ground, the skateboarder took his board and raised it to strike the stranger's head. From out of nowhere, a second stranger appeared and lunged at the skateboarder, who answered him with powerful blows all over his body with the wooden board. Soon, the skateboarder was engaging both men with a speed and ferocity that Annika had seen only in one of Peter's martial arts movies. In the midst of it all, Annika's purse was flung to the ground several meters from the action. Peter, who had been standing and watching the entire incident at a distance, sprinted to the back of the green building in order to grab the purse from behind. But just as Peter rounded the corner of the house, the skateboarder extracted a large gun from his jacket and fired round after round at the strangers. Both strangers jolted violently as the bullets impacted their bodies. In seconds, they both fell to the ground, motionless. Students everywhere fled the scene in all directions, screaming. The skateboarder picked up the purse and sprinted behind the green house. Exactly where Peter was headed.

"Peter!" Annika screamed at the top of her lungs. "Peter!"

She kept calling him as she ran behind the green house to find him. When she arrived, Peter was standing there, wide-eyed and in a stupor, holding her purse.

"Oh my God! Are you OK?" Annika looked everywhere on Peter's body to see if he had been shot.

"Yeah. I think so."

"What happened?"

"He just dropped it and ran."

"Just dropped it?"

"Yeah. I don't get it."

Annika froze in shock when she saw the two fallen strangers emerge from the back corner of the green house, both walking stiffly, clearly in pain.

"You were shot! Both of you!"

"It's OK, ma'am. We're campus cops," said the first one. He opened his leather coat and revealed a bulletproof jacket underneath. Three flattened slugs lay embedded in the thick black material. "Any idea why he wanted your purse so badly?"

I can't tell them the truth, Annika thought. "I don't know. Money, I guess." She quickly looked through her purse and found her cell phone. She was so relieved it was still there. She pulled her wallet out and flipped through the contents.

"All my money is here. And credit cards, too." Annika surprised herself at her own words. *Then why did he take my purse? Nothing is missing!*

Peter came forward suspiciously. "Do you two have any ID?"

"No. We're under cover."

"Undercover campus cops? With body armor?"

"That's right."

"Do you have names?"

"I'm Matt. He's Ken."

"Well, Matt, nothing was taken, so I guess we're done here," Peter said. He took Annika's arm, turned, and walked away.

"Peter! What are you doing?" Annika said, resisting the urge to pull her arm away.
"Those aren't campus cowboys."

"What? How do you know?"

"Body armor? Fighting like they did? No way."

"But they helped us!"

"With no ID? Campus cowboys never go under cover. They just crash drunken parties at night and break up fights."

"Then who were they?"

"I don't want to find out."

Annika was putting her phone back in her purse when she noticed something. "Oh God, Peter! This isn't my phone!"

Peter looked at it. "Of course it is. It even has our picture as the background."

"No! Do you see this scratch?"

"Yeah, it's always been there."

"Not on the left side of your face. The scratch was always on the right side."

Peter stopped and raised his thick eyebrows. "Are you sure?" He looked concerned.

"Yes."

"Well, check if everything is there."

Annika ran through the entire contents of the phone's memory.

"That's odd," she said.

"What?"

"Everything is there except Dr. Lindell's data."

Peter shrugged. "Maybe he didn't download it correctly."

"Dr. Lindell? He's an expert programmer." Annika couldn't take her eyes off the scratch that was in the wrong place. She ran her finger down its length.

"It's just a little scratch," Peter said.

"But it doesn't feel right." *I know this isn't my phone!* she thought.

Peter cupped his hands on her cheeks and got that sweetheart look again. "What doesn't feel right is the whole situation that just happened. Let's go get something warm to drink and sit down for a bit. Then we can grab Uncle Alex for lunch. OK?"

Annika was shaken. She realized for the first time that her whole body was trembling with shock from the episode. She didn't want to argue any further. "OK," she said.

But it wasn't OK. The scenes of the robber pushing her down on the ground and taking her purse kept playing over and over in her head. Something didn't fit with the situation. She just couldn't tell what.

Granville Island Market
Vancouver, B.C.

Carter Feldman was late for many things, but never for his lunch dates with Sydney. He parked his rusty, ten-year-old Tercel in the lot bordering Bridge and Johnston Streets. The thick wooden post in front of his car was marked in large green letters with "2 Hours Maximum," the same sign that was scattered throughout the lots at Granville Island Market. He grabbed the flash memory card sitting on the passenger seat and walked briskly through the chilly, damp air over to the main building. He glanced back at his old wreck. It was pathetic, but on the salary he got from Dr. Lindell as his lab technician, this car fit the bill. His titanium bike, however, did raise eyebrows. But it wasn't odd to a bike aficionado when two wheels cost far more than four.

Carter entered the market in the middle of the fruit and vegetable stalls. Workers were stocking the stands with fresh produce for the surge of weekend shoppers that always began early on Friday afternoons. They smiled at Carter as he walked by. It made him feel uncomfortable. If they could see him, others could too, couldn't they? But Sam wouldn't be here. Never. Carter picked up his pace and sped by the European cheese store, past the China Tea Importing Co., and on to the small food court section at the far end. He bought a large coffee and a doughnut, and walked upstairs to the small, discreet sitting area and tried to keep calm. But his nervousness grew. He looked at his watch and tried to tell himself that Sam would never show up here.

Sam had provided Carter with his first apprenticeship into the world of industrial espionage. He had started chatting with him at the Barn cafeteria on campus last year, shortly after Lindell's involvement with Mitogenica became public. Sam had told him how he was worth so much more than his salary as a lab tech. That he should use his knowledge to the fullest. That people would pay for that knowledge because it would help them keep a little ahead of the investment crowd. Just to make a little more money. And that wouldn't hurt anyone, would it? Sam had been right. Nobody got hurt. Carter made money. It was that simple. Until Sydney showed up at the end of September. She offered more money than Sam. She wanted to know exactly what information Carter gave to Sam and when. Carter didn't mind that. Nor that Sydney demanded far more information on Lindell's trials than Sam ever had. It was just so easy working with her. Carter looked up from his coffee. There she was, walking up the stairs and speaking on the phone. Her face broke into a wide smile.

Carter stood up. "Hello, Sydney!"

She thrust her hand down and gently shook her head. "You're not supposed to say my name out loud," she said softly.

Carter sat down. "Sorry!"

"That's OK, Carter." As she sat down, her magnificent perfume surrounded Carter in a cloud of hungry desire.

"How are you doing?" He nodded at her phone. "Got some good news?"

She shrugged it off. "A friend of mine just picked up a phone for me."

"Oh." Carter gazed at Sydney's fine features and flawless long blonde hair. Her body was as taut as a violin string. Obviously she worked out. She was simply the most beautiful woman he had ever laid eyes on.

"The important thing is, how are you doing?" Sydney asked. She leaned in toward him and put her hand on his. At the moment of contact, waves of tingles drenched Carter's body and his nervousness melted away.

"I'm fine," Carter heard himself say. He was floating in the numbness of pure pleasure.

"How is the trial going?" Sydney asked, as she caressed her long blonde hair with her hand.

"Just fine. Oh!" He reached into his pocket and produced the flash drive. It was coated with pocket fuzz. He cleaned it off and handed it over. "It's all here."

Sydney put it in her purse. "So, did you get his latest formulations?"

"You mean after he came back from Europe?"

"Exactly."

Carter frowned and hung his head. "Sorry. He keeps that totally secret."

Sydney slid imperceptibly on her chair until her knee touched Carter's leg. For a few wonderful seconds, Carter froze, in a state of pure ecstasy. "Are you sure there's no way you can get them?"

"Not until the trial ends."

Sydney looked disappointed. "That's such a long time." Her knee pressed harder against Carter's leg, and she stroked the center of her chest, just above her breasts. Carter's eyes went wide and his face flushed.

"I don't even know if he keeps that on the computer at the center."

"There's no way at all you can find out?" Sydney bit her lower lip and raised her eyebrows in a helpless look.

Small beads of sweat started appearing on Carter's forehead. "I'll do my best," he stammered breathlessly.

Sydney smiled. It was like fresh rays of sunshine breaking into the room. "That means a lot to me. What about the specifications of the Gen-Silico?"

"I had a tech buddy help me. It's all on the stick, right down to the memory configuration."

"That's wonderful!" Sydney said. "And that strange black object on Dr. Lindell's desk you told me about?"

"Nothing. No requisition. No invoice. Not even a shipping record. Nobody in purchasing ever heard of it."

"So Dr. Lindell hauled that thing in himself?"

Carter nodded. "Apparently."

"Can I get some pictures of the lab next time?"

"Pictures of what?" Carter asked.

"Everything. Especially that big black thing on Dr. Lindell's desk."

"Sure, no problem."

"I knew I could count on you," replied a beaming Sydney. She pulled an envelope out of her purse and slid it across the table to Carter. "Your help means a lot to us."

Carter looked around and tucked the envelope into his jacket. "Thanks," he said awkwardly.

"You can count it if you like," she said.

"I trust you," Carter said, starry-eyed. "When will I see you again?"

"I'll call you. But if anything urgent comes up, you've got my number. For emergencies only, OK?" Sydney said, winking. She walked down the stairs from the upper-level sitting area, put on her large sunglasses, and disappeared into the growing crowd of shoppers.

Carter felt the thick wad of cash in his envelope. Five thousand dollars monthly. Tax free. That would make a nice nest egg. Of course he knew how to get Lindell's secret formulations. His buddy Dan could hack into any mainframe on campus. But this was a waiting game. The more Sydney waited, the more she paid. He glanced down at his watch and gulped the rest of his coffee. He had an hour to get over to the Skywalk Café at Pacific Center Mall to meet Sam. Today was a double payday. And it was so easy. Carter got up and started walking. He felt more confident in his new reality. The spy movies he loved so much had obviously piled the normal Hollywood hype onto the espionage business. These were just normal people doing a different kind of job. And Sydney was so nice. She would never hurt anyone.

UBC Campus
Vancouver, B.C.

Annika sat staring at her purse. She couldn't get the image of that skateboarder out of her head. Especially the look of intent on his face when he grabbed her purse... apparently to take nothing.

"Are you OK?" Peter asked.

"Yeah. Still a little shaken up. How about you?"

Peter drove out of the West Parkade into a light drizzle falling from the overcast skies. He looked straight ahead at the road for a few seconds before talking.

"Just a few bumps here and there."

"I've never seen you like that."

"Like what?" Peter turned right onto Northwest Marine Drive.

"That look of anger. And how fast you ran."

"Well, I've never seen you knocked down and robbed before."

Annika still couldn't shake the feeling that, for those few seconds after her purse was stolen, Peter had become a different man. He turned onto Chancellor Boulevard, in the direction of his Uncle Alex's house.

"Are you still upset at me?"

Peter sagged in his seat for a moment and sighed. "No. I'm upset at the whole situation."

"Your job at Alameda?"

"Yeah. Can we talk about it later?" Peter looked distant as they left the campus grounds and passed a large sign reading "Pacific Spirit Regional Park." Leafless maple and birch trees mingled with evergreens along each side of the wide double boulevard.

Annika sat in silence and watched the windshield wipers streak back and forth across the rain-spattered windshield for several moments. They left the park and merged onto Fourth Avenue. Peter stopped at a red light. A young couple crossed the street in front, huddling together under an umbrella. The silence was no longer bearable.

"So how is Uncle Alex enjoying retirement?" Annika asked.

"Not much, I think. He actually had to retire."

"Why?"

"Something with his heart. I think my aunt Julia's death put him over the edge." Peter kept driving for several blocks along Fourth Avenue, which bordered Jericho Beach Park and the waters of the Burrard Inlet. Annika could see several large ships out on the water.

"It's beautiful!"

"This neighborhood is Point Grey. You never saw Alex's house before, did you?"

"No, last Christmas he was out somewhere for work."

"Oh, yeah. I think he was in China."

Peter navigated the car to a side street off Fourth Avenue. He parked alongside a tall stone fence overgrown with ivy and moss. The front of the house was completely concealed by tall evergreen trees behind the fence, except for the clearing at the heavy wrought iron gate in the middle. Peter pointed through the gate at the forest green house behind. "There it is."

"Wow, this is my dream house!" Annika said.

"Keep dreaming," Peter said with a smile. "It's worth over two million." He got out and led the way through the gate, which was heavily decorated by gold trim.

"So he's doing well then, I guess."

Peter shrugged in doubt. He spoke quietly as they approached the house. "He got a good retirement package from his company. I just don't know how much he lost on the stock market."

They walked up to the front door which was set back in the deep veranda. The top floor had large dormer windows, and the roof extended in all directions to make a portico over the veranda supported by massive wooden columns. Peter rang the doorbell.

"Which company did he work for again?" Annika asked.

"Cypress Turbines."

The door was opened by a slim, shorter man with thick salt-and-pepper gray hair and the prominent laugh lines one gets from a lifetime of smiling. The deep crow's-feet around his dark hazel eyes made them smile, too.

"Hey, kid! You look great!" Alex said, beaming at Peter. He turned to Annika. "And you must be Annika! You're even more beautiful than Peter told us! Come in, both of you!"

Alex motioned them inside to the living room. Peter and Annika were both taken by surprise by the ad-hoc-looking office on a large table in the center of the room. A big tower computer sat in the middle, with two twenty-one-inch flat panel computer monitors—one positioned on either side. Real-time stock prices and forex rates streamed across the left screen while a live trading screen was buzzing with information on the right. At the back of the living room, a massive LCD TV was showing business news. Alex immediately grabbed the remote and muted the TV.

"Sorry! New York is just about to close and I wanted to get a couple more trades in."

"Well, now I know where you get your love of business news," Annika said to Peter. He grinned sheepishly.

"And sorry about the mess here," Alex said. "I'm renovating half the upstairs right now, including my office."

"No problem," Peter said.

Alex eyed something on his trading screen. "Just a second." He walked to his computer and started typing. He looked puzzled and frowned as if bothered by the same thing for the hundredth time.

Peter started to look seriously worried. "Are you trading stocks again?"

"What do you mean by 'again,' Pete? I never stopped!"

Peter grimaced. "So that's your hobby in retirement?"

"That and many others, kid." Alex watched his trading screen with full concentration. A large vein popped out on Alex's left temple, and his face went red.

"Isn't that kind of stressful?" Peter asked.

Alex chuckled. "I'd rather die of stress than boredom, kid."

"Alex—"

"There!" Alex slammed his finger down on his mouse. "These biotech stocks are strange little guys. They just jump all over the place."

"They sound risky," Peter said.

"You bet! There's a huge risk of not making money if you don't trade them."

Peter rolled his eyes. "What about big pharma stocks? They're nice and stable."

"More like a dead horse lying in its stable. They've gone nowhere for ten years, kid! Lawsuits. Empty pipelines. Generic makers lining up at the gates. Forget it, kid. Little biotechs are where it's at." Alex still eyed his trading screen. He shook his head. "Weird, weird, weird."

Peter couldn't suppress his curiosity. "What is?"

"There are two really hot stocks now, just about to put in their New Drug Applications. Mitogenica and Chromogen."

Peter threw a cautious glance at Annika. "What about them?"

"Well, Mitogenica appears to have the better drug again..."

"But what?"

"Even though Mitogenica stock is up on the good rumors, someone is slowly taking a sizeable short position on it, betting that it's going to get clobbered. And to boot, Chromogen stock is lying wounded in the ditch, but somebody is slowly accumulating large positions," Alex said, with growing uncertainty in his voice.

"What does that mean?" Annika asked.

Alex nodded toward his screens. "The big boys are playing this. They know something."

"Like what?" Peter asked innocently.

"I have no idea. Impending good news for Chromogen, maybe?"

Annika noticed Alex was carefully studying her face. She shrugged. "No idea."

"Oh, I'm so stupid!" Alex said. "I totally forgot you actually work for Chromogen, don't you, Annika?"

Annika smiled. "Don't worry about it."

Alex sighed. "Looks like the big boys win another round." He switched his screens off.

"And who are these big boys?" Annika asked.

"The ones that break all the rules and get away with it. And generally, they wrote the rules in the first place—to their advantage. Come on, I'll give you the grand tour."

The smell of fresh paint was thick in the air upstairs. Alex walked them into the master bedroom. Annika looked out through the large dormer windows. North Vancouver lay in the distance across the waters of English Bay. To the right, Stanley Park and downtown Vancouver looked close enough to touch.

Annika fell in love with the view. "It's breathtaking!"

"So, I hear Alameda Alloys is about to go belly-up," Alex said, as if in passing.

Peter spun around in horror. "How did you hear that?"

"Relax, kid. Alameda's a major supplier of alloy to Cypress Turbines. I know half the guys on the board. So, is it true?"

Peter bowed his head in resignation. "Probably."

"Kid, if you need a job, just say the word."

"It's OK, really."

"It's not OK. I'm still buddies with the CEO, Will Conleth."

"I don't doubt it."

"I'll get you any job you want. Heck, it'd be a promotion from where you are now."

Peter nodded. "Thanks. But I'm going to hang on as long as I can."

Alex lowered his thick gray eyebrows in confusion. "Why?"

"I don't want to lose my career there."

"News flash, kid! Alameda's head of finance already lost it for you with his stupid bet on derivatives."

"Maybe. But he'll jump ship with a golden parachute," Peter said.

"Welcome to reality, kid. There are only two kinds of people on this planet, you know. Those that make things and those that take things. Those that take generally have a lot more fun. Well, right up until they spark a revolution and get lined up against a wall," Alex said with a wide smile.

Peter laughed. "I won't forget your offer."

"So, what's your next move after your master's?" Alex asked Annika.

Annika looked at Peter before answering. "I don't know yet."

"Will Conleth happens to be best buds with Gwen Riley, head of Mitogenica. We could fix you up there in a jiffy."

Annika froze for a second, running all the connections through her mind. "I don't think Mitogenica is really my style."

Alex shrugged. "OK. Oops!" He glanced at his watch and got that same worried look Annika saw so often on Peter's face when he was pressed for time. "Look at the time! Let's go grab some lunch, shall we? I have a doc appointment at three I really can't miss."

Peter looked concerned. "Is everything OK?"

"Relax, kid. It's just nutritional counseling for my cholesterol."

"That's great! I can make a list of recommendations for you," Annika said.

"Sure!" Alex said. "That's sweet. Let's do it over burgers, shall we?"

CHAPTER NINE

Collingwood Apartment Building
Vancouver, B.C,

More than a score of cargo ships and tankers lay anchored for the night in the Burrard Inlet as a cold drizzle put its mist over Vancouver's seaboard. It was well after sunset. As usual, Ian Ponce liked to watch the lights of the ships shine out like beacons in the dark night. As on most winter nights, he watched through beaded raindrops trickling down his living room window. He remembered decades ago driving down there, to Jericho Beach with his girlfriend Betty. He sat her down on one of the massive logs lying on the beach and proposed to her as the ships went sailing by. He swore one day he would get that view every day from their place. The door buzzer sounded and jolted him out of his momentary daydream. He turned and nodded to several people who were standing near the door buzzer. One of them hit the button. He looked at his watch and walked to the center of the room with the slight limp he never got rid of from his car accident ten years back. He held his hands up slightly to silence the chatter that was going on. People started sitting down on his sofas, armchairs, and several rows of folding chairs he had set up in his large living room.

"Thanks, everyone, for coming tonight to my house in sunny Kitsilano."

There was some laughter in the crowd.

Ian stroked his thick, well-groomed beard and went on. "Welcome to the first real-life meeting of our chat group. I'm glad you've all found my cancer blog so helpful. I've got a big stake in this. I lost my father and older brother to prostate cancer, and I had it myself two years ago. I beat it back with standard therapy combined with some complementary treatments suggested by Dr. Elliot Lindell in his research papers." He smiled and looked down at himself, patting his flabby body with his hands as if to make sure he was still real. "And, well, so far it looks like I'm still here!"

Several in the room laughed. They started to look at ease.

Ian laughed himself, his belly heaving up and down with each chuckle. "OK, so let's talk about Dr. Lindell's trial with Mitogenica. That's what we're here for, right?"

The buzzer rang again. Ian motioned to the people next to it. "Just buzz them in, it's fine."

The woman standing next to the console reached over and hit the button.

* * *

At the buzzing sound, a casually dressed Sydney Vale pulled open the glass entrance door to the Collingwood Apartment Building. Owen followed closely behind into the large entranceway and pushed the up button on the elevator. Both eyed the outside, looking for anyone who might be approaching. The elevator arrived. Before

Owen turned away from the window, a foot came flying through the opening elevator doors and landed on his rib cage, sending him backward into the wall.

"Remember me?" Matt said, as he lunged after Owen.

John Rhoades walked out of the elevator eyeing Sydney.

"You have some cameras that belong to me, Sydney."

As Owen and Matt sprawled on the floor, Sydney stood motionless, her face giving away no shock at the mention of her name. She fixed her gaze steadfastly on John, sizing him up from every angle. In the blink of an eye, her right leg became a blur of motion as it swept through the air toward John's head. He leapt back, feeling the rush of air on his face as the bottom of her shoe came within an inch. She lunged forward, swinging her fists in precisely aimed shots for his chin, eyes, and face. John blocked and deflected blow after blow until she dug her nails into the flesh of his cheek. He grabbed her wrist tightly and twisted hard while pulling and turning his body. Sydney yelped in pain as she was helplessly pulled through the air over John's shoulder. But John could feel her curl her legs inward tightly as she fell to the ground. She snapped her arm back so hard he lost his grip. Like a falling cat, she regained her bearings in mid-flight and hit the floor with both arms first. Instantly, her leg shot out with lightning speed, right into John's stomach. He fell backward hard, impacting the elevator doors with a loud thud.

Matt and Owen were still busy trading punches and kicks. John saw Sydney roll on the floor to grab her purse. John launched himself off the elevator doors straight at her. She pulled out a fist-sized metal canister just as he was on top of her. With a scream of defiance, she struck the can viciously across his face. He ignored the searing pain and grabbed her hand, pulling at her fingers to pry out the canister. She gritted her teeth, digging her nails into his hands. Just as John was about take the canister, Owen fell flat on top of him. Sydney pulled back the canister and retreated to the corner as Matt leapt back on Owen and they resumed their fight. John jumped upright, only to have Sydney pounce on him, aiming the canister at his face. His arm thrust out and pushed hers just as she released a long puff of mist. The spray shot out beside his head, hitting the wall behind him. Sydney scowled and aimed again, but John deflected the spray. Losing patience, Sydney jumped for him with canister in hand, swinging wildly at his head. He grabbed her wrist with an iron grip, twisting her tendons to the breaking point to force her palm open. As Sydney screamed in pain, John smacked the canister out of her grasp with his other hand. It flew straight for the entranceway, hitting the corner of the steel door frame at high speed. The tip of the canister broke off, and a loud hissing noise filled the room as the canister spun around in circles, venting its contents rapidly in all directions.

"Owen!" Sydney screamed.

One look was enough for Owen to disengage. He and Sydney bolted down the hallway for the exit at the other end.

"Don't breathe!" John yelled at Matt. He yanked him out the door next to them. They stood outside panting.

Matt looked inside, pointing to the canister. "That was it, wasn't it?"

John nodded. "That's what killed Hammond."

"But the residue on his face. It was harmless."

"Exposed to the air, some chemicals break down quickly. But there's still something left in the canister."

"Damn, they fight well," Matt said between breaths. "Military or terrorists." His face was starting to swell up from the fierce pounding it had taken.

"Or both," John said. He ignored the blood oozing from his facial wounds.

Matt pounded the window and cursed.

"What's wrong?" John asked.

"We got nothing again."

John smiled and shook his head. "I got this." He held out a satellite phone.

Matt cracked a painful smile. "Now we're getting somewhere."

Both men were startled when the phone let out a loud, shrill ring. John shrugged and hit the answer button. He put it to his ear.

"Who is it?" Matt asked.

"Nobody." John looked at the small LCD display on the phone. It was filling with digits and letters.

"That's just random noise," Matt said.

Before the characters filled the entire screen, John suddenly vaulted the phone as high as he could in the air.

"Hey, why did you—"

An explosion sent small bits of phone flying in all directions. The acrid smell of burning plastic filled the air. They could hear the screech of tires in the distance as a car sped away.

"Damn! Like I said, we still have nothing," Matt said, hanging his head.

"No." John walked to the window of the entranceway. He pointed to the long smudges made by Owen's face when Matt had him pinned against the glass. Beside these was a large, clear handprint. Lying on the ground just below the print was the empty canister. "Let's move."

* * *

Ian watched his front door a few more seconds, expecting someone to enter, then shrugged it off. "Well, I guess that was a wrong number. Anyway, I'm not a doctor, but I do have a master's in chemistry, and I've done a lot of background work on this. As far as I'm concerned, Dr. Lindell is the best in the business for alternative medicine. I'm glad you decided to be a part of it. Can I get a show of hands of all those already enrolled in the Mitogenica trial?"

Of the twenty-six people in the room, nineteen hands went up. A man at the back said loudly, "I'm going in next week to enroll. My doc's all for it."

"Great! Now put your hands down if you have not started treatment yet."

Three hands went down.

"OK. If your hand is still up, I think we are all interested in what you've experienced so far."

A tall, gaunt man in the second row spoke first. "The daily pills are fine. But when I go in for the IV bag once a week, I get real bad heartburn and just about lose my lunch." Nearly all the others nodded.

"And hand tremors, too," said one from the back. More nods.

"Well, all that's pretty normal with Mitaxinyl," Ian said.

"And memory loss!" said another.

"Oh, I forgot that one," Ian quickly added. There was more laughter.

"I thought you said this was the trial to be in," said a Chinese woman in the middle of the room. "But it feels exactly like my first chemo treatment. When will I feel better?"

Ian put up a cautionary hand. "With Mitaxinyl, results don't normally show for at least two to three months. We have to be patient, patients."

"I think I feel worse than with my other chemo treatments," another said.

"You do know that some of you are the control group. That means you get only the chemo drug Mitaxynil and none of the natural cocktails. That's the only way we really know what treatment works best," Ian said. He looked at two men sitting in the front who still had their hands up. "What about you?"

One of them, dressed in jeans and a T-shirt, stood up. He was one of the few in the room with a smile on his face. "I'm Jim Caldicott. The doc told me yesterday I'm all clear."

The chatter in the room came to screeching halt. Ian lost his humorous smile. "What do you mean, exactly, by 'all clear'?"

"No more tumors. That's what the MRI scans showed."

Gasps sounded. Another man in the room stood up and said, "Me too!"

Ian ignored the second person for a moment. "What kind of cancer did you have?" he asked Jim.

"Prostate."

Ian looked at the man in the back. "And you?"

"Colon cancer," said the older man.

"Breast cancer," said a middle-aged woman sitting at the side.

"And you both had scans?"

Both nodded vigorously.

Ian was at a complete loss for words. "How…how many others here have had their first MRIs?" he asked the group. Fifteen hands showed. The looks on their faces told the rest. Jim and the other two were alone.

The chatter level rose to a furor. Ian stepped forward and tried to calm everyone down.

"Folks, this is great news."

"It's not great for me. I've still got my cancer," said the tall, gaunt man.

"Can we switch treatments and take what they're taking?" the Chinese woman asked.

Ian shook his head. "No, I'm afraid you can't. You all agreed to take a treatment and stick with it. That's how we can make reliable statistics in the end and know which treatment really works," Ian said.

"Screw the statistics," said the tall, gaunt man. "I want to know what they're taking."

"Yeah!" echoed about ten voices from the room.

"Everybody! Please!" Ian said loudly. "This is great news. Something is working very well. When the trial ends we'll find out and we can use it!"

"Sure," said the gaunt man. "By that time, you'll need a real long IV tube to reach six feet under."

"Damn right," someone else said.

A tall, athletic, and well-groomed man dressed in a suit calmly came from the back and stood beside Ian. His thick black hair was slicked back. "Hi, everyone, I'm Tyler Evans. I can help you find out what these three are taking."

Ian was dumbfounded. "What kind of cancer do you have?"

"I'm actually not in the trial," Tyler said. "I'm a medical doctor."

At that moment, the only thing audible in the room was the gentle pelting of raindrops on the window.

"What are you doing here, then?" Ian asked.

"I run a complementary and alternative medicine clinic with some partners. I'm just keeping up on the latest, and it looks like you have a winner here."

"How can you help us?" someone asked.

"Look, we all know Lindell is trying just three different cocktails of natural supplements. I'm willing to bet our three lucky friends here all took the same winning formula."

"So how can you help us, then?" the same person asked. "Ask Mitogenica for free samples?"

A few nervous laughs sounded.

"No. I'll give you all a syringe. You take it with you during your chemo session and take a sample from your IV drip line. And ten of the pills you have to take daily. That's it. My clinic will do the analysis."

Ian started becoming alarmed. "Are you trying to steal Dr. Lindell's formula to make money at your clinic?"

Tyler raised his hand and turned to the group. "Hey, we all know the list of possibilities, don't we? Vitamin D, ginger, pomegranate extract, lycopene, grape seed extract, ginkgo biloba, green tea polyphenols, a bunch of different Chinese herbs, tocopherol succinates, tocotrienols, and a few dozen others."

"So what's your point?" Ian asked.

"Most of this stuff you can pick up at the corner drugstore. It's all safe. So if you take part in our little experiment, I'll give you the winning formula for free at my clinic."

The group was abuzz with excited chatter again.

"And the Mitaxynil for free, too?" someone asked.

"Absolutely!" Tyler said. "We've already been treating patients with Mitaxynil for years."

"And just where is your clinic?" Ian asked.

Tyler hesitated for a few seconds. "Tijuana."

"*Tijuana?*" a woman exclaimed. "Will I get a free boob job, too?" Everyone laughed.

Tyler didn't lose face. "We treat cancer patients every day in that clinic." He turned to the woman. "And we don't do boob jobs."

"Didn't I see you on an infomercial?" another asked.

"No, but you can see me presenting my review paper at the International Conference for Complementary and Alternative Medicine this June. It was accepted by the review committee three months ago."

The room fell silent at that. Tyler went on. "Do you want results like them, or not?" He gestured toward the three who were in full remission. "Who is in?"

Every hand in the room except Ian's shot up.

Ian spoke up. "This has gone far enough. You are going to destroy this trial!"

Tyler shook his head. "Not at all. Everyone has the right to withdraw whenever they want to. Let Mitogenica get guinea pigs from somewhere else."

"And you make your money selling the treatment to others."

"I'll be saving lives. Starting with theirs," Tyler said, looking at the group.

Ian closed his eyes for a half minute. He knew it was just a matter of time until his own prostate cancer came back. Just like it had for his father and brother. Damn. Was this his only hope? The choice was obvious, no matter how much he hated it.

Ian continued meekly, "OK. Go ahead."

Tyler addressed the crowd. "This only works one way. Nobody says a word. Not to anyone. And nothing by email. Got it?" Every face in the room radiated agreement. And hope. Ian's stomach tightened when he saw it. He felt Tyler's gaze upon him.

"Got it," he said.

"Now, everyone, give me your phone number and address."

"When do we meet again?" the tall, gaunt man asked.

Tyler shook his head. "We don't. Not until we have all the results in. Ian will post a special notice on the blog for a second meeting when that happens. But remember, if anything leaks out, I disappear and you never see me again."

CHAPTER TEN

—

University of British Columbia
Vancouver, B.C.

"I'm glad I finally met Uncle Alex," said Annika, as she walked out of the Rose Garden parking area with Peter.

"Why is that?"

"It explains a lot about you."

Peter laughed. "That's what a lot of people say."

They walked out from the cover of the parking lot and into a constant drizzling rain. Darkness had already fallen and the night air was cool enough to see one's breath. Annika shivered slightly, wrapped her coat tightly around herself and huddled next to Peter under his umbrella. "Which way?"

Peter motioned to cross the street. "Are you sure you want to move here, with all this rain? It's like this all winter here." They turned down Cecil Green Park Road.

Annika didn't want to start anything. "I'm not sure about anything right now."

They walked down Cecil Green Park Road until they could see a large, magnificent Tudor-revival-style house lit up on all sides by bright floodlights. The first floor was entirely of stonework. Above it, the white exterior of the second floor inlaid with olive green planks seemed to glow in the night air. Peter and Annika walked down the driveway, which looped around at the front of the house. A black limousine drove past them and came to a stop at the entrance, under the cover of a grand porte cochere. The driver jumped out and opened the passenger door.

Peter smiled. "Like I said. This business has money."

A petite woman dressed in an immaculate silk evening gown got out of the limousine, followed by an older man in a tuxedo. Annika noticed Peter was staring at the two. She tightened her grip on Peter's arm. "You can stop gawking any time. She's already got her sugar daddy."

"No, she doesn't," Peter said, as if certain.

"How do you know?"

"That's Gwen Riley."

Annika turned back in disbelief. But the two had already disappeared inside and the limousine was driving off. "You know what she looks like?"

"Sure. Her picture was in the case study we did at the business school."

Peter and Annika arrived at the massive entrance. The porte cochere was supported by thick stonemasonry columns and underlit by multiple small gold-colored lamps.

"Your names, please?" a man standing at the entrance asked.

"Annika Guthrie. We're guests of Dr. Lindell."

He scanned down his list and nodded his head. "Enjoy your evening."

The first room they entered was no less resplendent than the guests, with inlaid hardwood floors, oak beams criss-crossing the ceiling, and solid wood trim throughout. Glass-covered bookcases line one wall, while the others were appointed with rich wood paneling. The loud chatter of two dozen mingling guests nearly drowned out the man playing a grand piano in the back corner of the room. Several uniformed servers walked around with trays of champagne glasses, the bubbles still streaming to the top in each. Others carried platters of freshly baked hors d'oeuvres, which smelled wonderful and overpowered the constant undertones of fine perfume. And wealth. Peter grabbed two champagne glasses and handed one to Annika.

"Here's to Dr. Lindell. He really knows how to party."

Annika took a sip and smiled. "I know of one way we can go to these more often."

Peter was about to speak when he felt a hand on his shoulder.

"Peter, Annika, I'm so glad you could make it," Lindell said.

"This is a beautiful house," Annika said.

"When it was built in 1912, it was the crowning jewel of the lower mainland. The paneling in this room is a rare Australian walnut. The leaded glass windows are all original. You two really have to look around."

"You seem to know a lot about it," Annika said with surprise.

"It reminds me of my grandfather's house," Lindell said.

The purse snatching earlier in the day suddenly came rushing back into Annika's mind. And the phone that might—or might not—be hers. She started feeling responsible for the lost data, and struggled to find the words she needed. "Dr. Lindell, I can't seem to find the data you put on my phone this morning."

"That's odd. I'm sure the transfer was fine. But I can give it to you tomorrow when you come by."

"If by some chance somebody got it, how bad would that be?"

Lindell shrugged. "It would be quite serious…in about twenty years."

"Twenty years?"

"That's how long it would take them to break my encryption. And please remind me tomorrow to give you the cipher key."

Annika was relieved and nodded. "So who are all these people?"

"All the major financial donors to the university's life sciences programs and the faculty that brought them in."

"I thought the Center for Natural Medicine wasn't part of UBC."

"It isn't. But Gwen Riley funds the faculty of medicine as part of her work with me for the trials. Ah!" Lindell motioned for two Japanese men to approach.

"Annika, Peter, this is Dr. Tatsuro Takahashi. He is visiting from Osaka for the week, from Mitsushima Pharmaceuticals. They have kindly opened a grant for mitochondrial disease research at the faculty of medicine."

After brief introductions and some small talk, Lindell and Takahashi went on their way to find the dean of medicine. Annika and Peter took refuge in the glass-encased conservatory.

"Honey, I've got to find the washroom. I'll be right back," Peter said.

Annika followed him with her eyes as he left the room, and then she turned her face to the floor when she saw Gwen Riley enter the room. Then, Annika realized that Gwen Riley probably didn't even know who she was. Annika watched as Gwen strutted around the room with supreme confidence, greeting everyone who looked important, going from target to target. She was unexpectedly attractive. There was something about Gwen's manner that was familiar, but Annika couldn't put her finger on it. Gwen turned toward Annika with a smile, as if she had been observing Annika from out of the corner of her eye the entire time. Annika was thrown off as Gwen approached. She looked for any possible escape route out of the room, but Gwen was approaching from the center. Annika had no choice but to stand still.

"Annika Guthrie, isn't it?" Gwen said. Her dark hazel eyes seemed to look at, through, and past Annika all at the same time, sizing her up in every way possible.

"Yes. And you must be Dr. Riley," Annika said politely, as she struggled to maintain her composure. Looking into Gwen's eyes was like looking down a very deep, waterless well. There was nothing at the bottom except darkness.

"Oh, please, call me Gwen. All my friends do," Gwen said, friendly and disarming. She put her hand gently on Annika's arm. "And by the way, you made a very good choice."

Annika resisted the urge to pull away. "What do you mean?"

"Not taking Chromogen's job offer, of course."

Annika could feel her mouth gape open for several seconds. She would have taken a step back except for the presence of a wall behind her. "How did you know that?"

"I knew Arthur Cormack, you know. Well before he took the helm at Chromogen."

"Really?" *She didn't answer my question,* thought Annika.

"Arthur is ninety percent politician and ten percent scientist. And if he had any real brains for the science at all, he certainly never brought them to the office."

"He seems to be holding his own against Mitogenica."

"Not for long, with Elliot Lindell's help. By the way, are you going to take his offer?"

Annika was becoming completely unnerved. *What else does she know about me?* "I guess that depends on my boyfriend."

"Oh, I see," Gwen answered with a slight sneer. "Well, I never let any man get in the way of what I wanted."

"Even if he was the right one?"

Gwen laughed. "If he was the right one, he would have known not to bother me in the first place. But I can respect your priorities."

Annika had the strangest feeling that during their entire conversation Gwen was mentally keeping tabs on every person in the room, and at the same time running a dozen trains of thought through her head. The New Drug Application they were about to file with the FDA. The ongoing lawsuit with Mitsushima Pharmaceuticals. The latest complications at the U.S. patent office. Dr. Lindell's trials with her drug. Dr. Lindell himself, perhaps? Definitely.

Annika suddenly remembered what she recognized in the way Gwen talked, looked, and moved. The summer before starting her master's, Annika had traveled to Tibet on a service project with some friends from church. During a visit to a Buddhist monastery, she was highly impressed by a Buddhist monk she spoke with for over an hour. During their entire conversation, he held a small string of prayer beads in his hand and rhythmically thumbed his way through them, over and over. He later explained that he was repeating the name of God in the back of his mind the entire time, and keeping count with the beads. Only twice during the conversation did he need to stop the bead counting and concentrate on the question he was being asked. Back then, it seemed easy to accept that forty years of monastic life could train incredible levels of disciplined concentration into the monks. But Gwen Riley showed exactly this level of concentration and focus. Annika marveled at how someone like Gwen could achieve such an ability. The critical difference was that the name of God was the monk's central underlying thought. What occupied that place in the mind of Gwen Riley? Power? Money?

"Speaking of men, how did your work go on Chromogen's Phase III trial?" Gwen asked. Her other thoughts still running. Or calculating.

"You know I can't talk about that."

"Of course. Still, Chromogen's Chrotophorib is no match for our drug. It's a pity, though," Gwen said in a leading tone. The carrot was dangling.

Annika couldn't resist. "What is?"

"I heard there were quite a few patient deaths that had nothing to do with the trial."

"What?" Annika asked, nearly in shock.

"We call those Extreme Adverse Events. Very frustrating," Gwen said coldly.

"I call them people."

"Well, you know what they say, ashes to ashes," Gwen said.

Annika's knees nearly buckled at those words. "What are you talking about?"

"Nothing, really. But we seem to have far fewer Extreme Adverse Events than Chromogen. Why not come and work for Mitogenica?"

"The only way I'll wind up in your labs is if I die and come back as a Wistar rat."

"Somehow, I doubt the members of Glenville Baptist Church believe in reincarnation."

Annika fell back against the wall. "How do you know that about me?"

"I check out all my potential recruits before making an offer. And I'll offer you five times what you'll make as a PhD student with Dr. Lindell."

"I'm not motivated by money," Annika said.

"Then what does motivate you?"

"Helping people."

"Because of me, Mitaxynil is making thousands of cancer patients live longer. And I'm about to get even better with Mitasmolin. Isn't that helping people?" Gwen asked.

"And you made a hundred million in profit."

"If I didn't make money at it, nobody would invest in Mitogenica to develop those drugs in the first place." Gwen gazed into Annika's eyes. "If you want to find greed, don't look at me, Annika. My boss is the people on the street who invest money in Mitogenica. And I have a very, very greedy boss. If you're fighting me, then you're fighting the wrong battle."

Gwen glanced up at the window next to Annika and suddenly lost that look of being in a thousand places at once. Every thought came to a single focal point, directly behind her. She turned around with a smile.

"Dr. Lindell, what a pleasure."

Annika cringed at the thought of Lindell helping someone like Gwen Riley.

"Gwen, I see you've met Annika," Lindell replied.

Gwen remained focused on Lindell. "A very intelligent young woman. By the way, my head of research tells me your latest formulations are working beyond all expectations."

"Or at least his expectations," Lindell said.

"In any case, I assume that means your model is running well enough to finally get results on the Chrotophorib molecule?"

"I can't promise anything."

"Good. Then I won't feel bad not promising any more data from the Eden Project until you can."

Just then, Peter returned from the toilet. Annika watched his eyes go wide when he saw Gwen Riley standing next to her. Peter walked up and joined the circle.

"You must be Annika's boyfriend, Peter," Gwen said.

"Uh...yes," Peter replied.

"That man you saw me enter the house with was William Conleth, CEO of Cypress Turbines. Unfortunately, he had to leave on urgent business; otherwise, I would introduce you."

"Well...thanks." Peter stood there, dumbfounded.

Gwen's small handbag let out a high-pitched ring tone. With the speed of a practiced expert, she took out her cell phone and flipped the screen on. "And now it seems I have some urgent business to attend to myself. If you'll excuse me." She walked toward the back exit and onto the covered terrace outside.

Annika turned to Lindell. "She knew everything about me!"

Lindell scowled and swiped his bald head with his hand. "It's OK."

"But I think she knows about the Chromogen trial!"

"Don't assume anything. And don't tell her anything."

"I won't."

Lindell gazed out the window at Gwen, who was busily talking on her cell. "Whatever you decide to do in the future, just remember one thing, Annika."

"What's that?"

"No matter what, don't ever trust Gwen Riley."

New York

Nolan Vasquez sat inside his penthouse, watching the first snow of the season settle on the granite table and shrubs outside on the terrace. The snowflakes appeared out of an empty night sky, glittering for a few seconds in the beams of the bright lights outside, then hit the ground and melted away. Nolan felt comfortable inside the drawing room which was warmly lit by three grand chandeliers made of the finest nineteenth-century French crystal. Ceiling roses decorated the base of each chandelier. Victorian-style frescoes and moldings richly decorated the rest of the paneled ceiling. As usual in the late hours before midnight, Nolan calmly sipped decaf espresso from his favorite silver tea server. He took his cup into the gallery, which adjoined the drawing room. The walls were paneled in natural walnut and oak. Oil paintings hung throughout, most of them originals. Rodin, Sisley, Couture, and his two signed Cézannes. For the first time since Ben had disappeared in Thailand while following Lindell, Nolan started to feel like things were coming back under control. Chromogen's Phase III trials on Chrotophorib were set to be a grand success. He had a firm grip on Austin's information flows from the source. And even better, he would soon get an account directly from the participants in Mitogenica's trial with Lindell. He almost felt relaxed, were it not for the continued problem of Gwen Riley. He glanced at his watch and took another sip of espresso as he toured his collection of art. Nolan stopped at his prize piece: a perfect late-nineteenth-century reproduction of Jacques-Louis David's *Marat Assassinated*. He liked it so much because it was a lie. It depicted one of the most horrific and murderous leaders of the French Revolution as a righteous and innocent victim of violence against the people. And it did so with such skilled artistic endeavor that it became as much a driver of the revolution as Marat himself ever had been. The killer of the people became the friend of the people. It was the perfect political weapon of its day. Perfect because of its deceit.

The phone rang. Nolan hit the speaker phone button. The familiar voice sounded.

"This is Central. Voice print verification for Sydney Vale."

"Put her through." A brief flurry of clicks sounded. "Report!" Nolan said.

"I have the specifications on Lindell's computer from Carter. You'll get it by tomorrow."

"I have no doubt of that. What about Ian Ponce's group meeting tonight?"

Sydney hesitated. "There was a problem."

Nolan frowned. "I pay you not to have problems. Who was it?"

"The same ones that were in Stanley Park. And at UBC today."

"They didn't stop you there."

"They were better prepared this time."

"Really? It always seems to be three steps forward, two steps back with you," Nolan snapped back.

"They knew about the spray. Enough to avoid it."

Nolan closed his eyes. His feeling of control was quickly evaporating. "I told you Lindell had help. That's why Ben disappeared," he said, his voice quickly rising.

"If Lindell has help, he doesn't know it," Sydney said. "I'm certain of it."

"How can Lindell not know who's helping Lindell?" Nolan yelled.

"Because somebody else is helping him."

"Then find out who. And why!"

"Of course. I'm sorry, Nolan."

"Don't be sorry. Be better!" Nolan slammed his hand on the disconnect button. The only thing he hated more than loose ends was having to report them to those above him. In particular, reporting them to Smoke. And that was exactly what he would have to do in five minutes. Nolan sat down on his Victorian armchair and cradled his head in his hands for a moment. He laughed to himself as Austin's last question ran through his mind. He couldn't tell Austin who he worked for. Not out of secrecy. But because he didn't know himself. That was the way The Trust worked. Nobody knew the inner circle. Nobody knew Smoke. They only knew the history of The Trust.

Nolan looked around at his prized possessions, all from late-nineteenth-century continental Europe with a splash of Victorian England. That was no accident. It was during that time when the Illuminated Ones—the architects of The Trust—moved from Europe to the United States. They were following the massive inflows of European old money brought by J. Pierpont Morgan to finance the building of a new world power from a nation of farmers. Together they shifted the financial center of the world from London to New York in just a few short decades. They became owners of steel mills, railroads, mines, oil companies—all manner of heavy industry. They mercilessly crushed their competitors and built themselves into industrial trusts which dominated their markets. Little did Morgan realize he was also building the foundation for the most powerful new elite the world had ever known. When he did find out, it was already too late. The first rift happened when Morgan stepped in to stabilize the global stock markets during the panic of 1907. He found himself trading against his onetime partners, who were trying to crash the markets. When Morgan died in 1913, there was nobody of consequence left to fight against, not even the U.S. government. The government made the unwise choice of trying to destroy the industrial trusts under the Pujo Commission. In response, the architects of The Trust drove the stock market into a speculative frenzy, took massive short positions against it, and then spun the market into the ground in 1929. They made their greatest fortune ever in the process. And they conveyed a message of supreme arrogance to the government: back off. That, it turned out, was the mistake of the century.

In the Great Depression that followed, many members of The Trust were hunted down and assassinated. Their fortunes were quietly assimilated by the government and fed back into works programs for the unemployed. Some claimed that J. P. Morgan himself had a hand in it; that he left in his legacy those who tracked The Trust and gave them up to the government. It didn't matter. The Trust moved underground. They hid in holding companies, then shell companies and offshore accounts. They evolved into an untraceable network of interests connected by nothing more than radio waves traveling through the air, all managed by Central Operations. Nolan knew nothing about Central Operations except that it was a mobile unit and hopped around the world as regularly as the sun rises and sets. The architects of The Trust reformed themselves after the Great Depression with a new vision of their place in the world.

That was where the beginner's version of history met the real version. New inductees were brought in to "put productive capacity into the right hands and help make the world a better place." Once the seduction by power and money was complete, the full version made perfect sense. A perfect world order could only be established after the reign of perfect chaos. Good can only be defined by evil. Truth, by lies. Mercy, by terror. The Trust orchestrated World War II, Korea, Vietnam, and most others since then. They ran the oil crisis of the 1970s, the crash of 1987, the housing bust, and the crash of 2008.

"Let us do evil, that good may come," was the mantra of the architects of The Trust. Their rightful commission for bringing order to the world was the spoils of their war on the free markets. The Trust didn't just follow economic super cycles—it created them and used them to strip the working masses of their loosely held money. And it was so easy because nobody cared. Military-industrial complexes, bubbles in the international bond markets, manipulation of the funding currencies. What makes people yawn at a dinner party is likely to be controlling their lives. Because, in their state of deception, the public is fighting the wrong battles while The Trust collects its hundreds of billions and makes its hold on power absolute.

A ringing sound in the next room broke Nolan out of his thoughts. He bowed his head and got up. Money and power had its price, and he was about to pay it. He walked into his office to find his large screen automatically lighting up. The familiar mechanical voice sounded.

"Incoming video signal. Please stand by."

The screen went dark again, except for a slightly blurred image of a lone man sitting in a chair. As always, the backlighting was so strong that nothing was visible but his silhouette. And the smoke that rose in the air above him. Whether he actually smoked or not was the subject of great speculation, which was why he was simply referred to as "Smoke" by those in The Trust who had seen his image—or hoped one day they would. Nobody, of course, had ever met him in person or seen his face. There was a rumor that during one video conference the backlighting failed and Smoke's face was broadcast to two members of The Trust. They were instructed to stay put for twenty-four hours. They were dead in twelve. Why he insisted on videoconferencing was a mystery. It did have its effect, though.

The raspy old voice thundered through the speakers. "What is the status of Mitogenica?"

"Resisting, as usual. Gwen Riley will have to be broken."

"As I always suspected," Smoke said hoarsely. There was pleasure in his voice. "And Lindell's trial with Mitogenica?"

Nolan leaned back from the monitor. "It's too early to tell."

"I meant the patient meeting! Tonight!" Smoke said half shouting.

This part would be painful. "We had some opposition."

"What?" Smoke's raspiness got worse when he yelled. He cleared his throat.

"We'll fix it."

"At your level, nobody fails twice and survives it. Do you understand?"

"Yes, sir." Nolan knew that was no empty threat.

"Is Muratte still a problem?"

Gian Muratte was CEO of Avarus Pharmaceuticals. He had risen through the ranks in Avarus's Italian operations with lightning speed, apparently aided by his connections with the mob. Those same connections helped form a quick alliance with The Trust, but in true mob style he was becoming more demanding as he realized the value of his operation to The Trust. Lately, he had threatened exposure if he didn't get more money. A lot more.

"Yes, he is," Nolan said.

"Fine. Cormack will replace Muratte after the buyout," Smoke said, with the slightest hint of pleasure in his voice.

Nolan knew that meant Muratte would die. That could be dangerous. "But Muratte has connections with the Dostinelli family."

"We can handle the Dostinellis."

"And Cormack is an idiot."

"He's a controllable idiot."

"But—"

"Don't question me!" Smoke bellowed. He went into a fit of coughing, the signal was cut, and the screen went quiet and black. Nolan gritted his teeth in anger. He didn't dare remind Smoke that it was he who had sent Sydney and Owen in the first place. Once again, something about dealing with Smoke bothered Nolan. Smoke was, after all, part of the inner circle. Everyone in The Trust envied him and aspired to take his place one day. He had untold wealth, limitless power, and unfettered access to all the pleasures of man. And yet, for all that, there was something profoundly disturbing about him. Even while Smoke held the invisible reigns to an entire global industry in his hands and at will threw parties to rival the mythical pleasure-dome of Kubla Khan, his was a joyless pleasure.

Downtown Vancouver, B.C.

"I have a word of warning about my Uncle Alex," Peter said to Annika, as they walked down Granville Street in the thick Saturday evening crowd.

"What's that?"

"Alex is usually pretty cool when he's just around me. But get him in front of my dad and he can get embarrassing."

"As in?"

"He flaunts his success and connections. You know, sibling rivalry."

"That's OK."

"I'm sure he'll pressure me about the job at Cypress Turbines."

"I don't understand why you won't look into it."

Peter turned to look at Annika, but his eyes were fixed on something else. "Look, Alex always has the life-saving offer. My father came here because of Alex, and found himself stuck in a job he's hated for over twenty years."

"At least he has a job," Annika said.

Peter glanced down. "Yeah. That's more than I can say about my brother Thomas."

"I thought he was in the ministry! What's wrong with that?"

"Nothing. Just the way he got there."

"And how was that?"

For the first time, Annika heard the story of Thomas, Peter's older brother by two years. Like Peter, he had started out in engineering school with top marks. Better marks than Peter ever had. He chose geological engineering and made top of the class. In the summer after Thomas's sophomore year, Uncle Alex fixed him up with a dream job at Pericline Opal, a major international mining company with operations in northern British Columbia. Everything went fine during the summer, until two weeks before the school was to start again. Then, Thomas showed up in Vancouver General Hospital via emergency evacuation from the mining site up past Kitsault. Thomas came in with a serious concussion, heavy bruising and abrasions all over his face and body, a broken nose, sprained ankle, and three cracked ribs. He remembered nothing of the industrial accident that had put him there. Pericline Opal claimed that Thomas's truck fell off the road on an open-pit mine and rolled down five levels to the bottom. Somehow, his seat belt became unbuckled during the process. Thomas lay in a coma for three days.

When he woke up, he was never the same again. Before the school year started he dropped engineering forever and went into the seminary. It shocked the whole family, but Uncle Alex was there for him and funded the whole degree.

"Wow. I'm so sorry for Thomas," Annika said. "But how can you blame Alex for that?"

"I don't. But not everything Alex gives away comes out perfect."

"Alex is just trying to help. He's family."

"Just trying to help? During my engineering degree all of my co-op work placements were arranged by Alex."

"There, you see?"

Peter stopped walking and looked impatiently at Annika. "No! For two of them I didn't even know it until I got there! Sometimes I didn't even know what I was doing at those places."

"What do you mean?"

Peter looked away and started walking again. "Nothing, nothing. It just feels more like control. Or being kept like a pet."

"I don't think he means it like that."

"But that's how it feels. Alameda Alloys was the first place I ever worked without any help from Alex."

"And you succeeded brilliantly!"

"That's the point, honey. I want this to be my career. My efforts. My mistakes. My life."

"There's one problem. If you were serious about us, you'd realize it's not just your life anymore." Annika could feel tears welling up in her eyes and fought hard to keep them back.

Peter frowned at himself and took a deep breath. "I'm sorry. I didn't mean it like that."

"But you keep talking like that."

A brief rush of wind in her face was a welcome distraction. Peter stopped. They had arrived. Annika cleared her throat and sniffed back the congestion that had started. He opened the door to Shikama Sushi. The smell of miso soup and jasmine green tea filled the air. Annika forced a smile when she saw Alex waving at them from a large boat-shaped table on the upper deck of the restaurant. As they walked to the table, Peter's brother Thomas stood up with a grin. He had Peter's same dark hair, steel blue eyes, and well-muscled physique, but looked much more like their father than Peter did. Comparing the two, Annika realized for the first time just how much Peter looked like his uncle Alex. Peter approached Thomas, and without warning launched a dozen short and surprisingly rapid play punches at his brother, who blocked every one of them with movements so fast that his hands made a whipping sound through the air. As they stood side by side, it became clear how much taller, bigger, and faster Thomas was compared to Peter. And, dare Annika admit to herself, better-looking. Annika and Peter gave their greetings to all and sat down next to Thomas and across from Peter's parents. Alex sat at the head of the table.

"So what was that all about?" Annika asked, eyeing Peter's still half-clenched fists.

"Just boys being boys," Alex said, giving Peter a slap on the back.

"I'm starved!" Peter said. He turned around to find a server.

"It's already done, kid. Miso soup and tea are on the way," Alex said.

"Great!"

"So how was last night's party at Cecil Green Park House?" Alex asked.

"Very interesting," Peter said.

"Great place to get married. Two of my friends did," Alex said in a leading tone. Peter rolled his eyes. "I'll keep it in mind."

"For when, kid? We're all wondering when you're going to pop the question."

Peter's mother cast a chiding glare at Alex. But only for a moment. The question was clearly on her mind, too.

Alex continued. "Just remember, kid, until she's off the market, she's on the market."

Joseph never moved his face from its slightly downward-looking angle, and his hands stayed cupped around the empty teacup. Only his eyes darted up to meet Alex. "Just leave the kid alone, Alex. He's got his timing."

Peter exchanged a look of thanks with his father. In the silence that followed, Annika noticed the striking difference between Joseph, Peter's father, and Uncle Alex. Joseph was gaunt, with drawn-in cheeks, dry skin that hung on his face, and rapidly thinning hair on top. Dark bags hung under his eyes and he sat with a slight slouch. Life was wearing him down, but he was fighting it every step of the way. Alex looked youthful and energetic next to Joseph.

Thomas broke the silence. "So, when are you two headed off tomorrow?"

"First thing. That's why we can't make church with you. Sorry."

Thomas looked a little disappointed. "It's the first time I'll be preaching as assistant pastor. Well, maybe next time."

"What are you preaching on?" Annika asked.

"Genesis. Creation."

"What about it?" Peter's mother asked.

"God only speaks the truth, and He spoke creation into existence. Therefore, everything in His creation is truth."

"Everything?" Alex chuckled cynically with raised eyebrows. "Annika might have something to say about that, with all the cancer patients she's seen."

Thomas looked to Peter, but his words were for Alex. "A man's own folly ruins his life, yet his heart rages against the Lord. That's Proverbs nineteen verse three."

Alex's mouth turned down into a frown. His normally smiling eyes narrowed. "And what does that mean?"

Annika sensed the tension between Alex and Thomas, and spoke. "I think he means that, on a global level we've polluted the land, sea, and air so much and we grow our food with so many chemicals that cancer is just an unnatural consequence of our own unnatural actions."

Thomas eased off and leaned back in his chair. "Yeah," he said. "There wasn't any cancer back in Eden."

Everyone was relieved when the server arrived with the bowls Miso soup and green tea. Annika grasped her thick, heavy ceramic teacup as the steam wafted up, carrying the rich smell of dark green Sencha tea laced with the sweet overtones of jasmine. Peter put his hand on her arm and smiled as Alex barked out orders for everyone. When he finished, he turned to Peter's parents with a relaxed smile.

"So, Pete might be losing his job," Alex announced to the table.

Peter almost dropped his teacup. Both parents glared at him. His father, who always held Peter as the success of the family, was shocked.

"What's going on, son?" Joseph asked.

Peter's defenses immediately went up. "Nothing! The company is just having some financial problems."

"They're in a financial sinkhole and going down fast, kid."

"It's not that bad and we're still very much afloat," Peter said.

Alex laughed. "That's what they said on the *Titanic*."

"Well, what's the truth?" Joseph asked, getting slightly annoyed.

Alex broke in before Peter could reply. "The truth is, I can get Pete a great foot in the door at Cypress Turbines, but he'd rather tour soup kitchens in Cleveland."

"See? I told you," Peter said under his breath to Annika. He turned to Alex. "At year-end I'll finish my executive MBA. If I leave Alameda now, I'll have to pay them back for it. That's boatloads of money."

"Well, that's a coincidence," Alex said, his normal smile back.

"What is?" Peter asked.

"I can get you the kind of job where you make boatloads of money."

Peter sighed in resignation. "I'm sure you can."

"Why don't you look into it, honey?" Peter's mother asked. "It would be wonderful to have you move back here to Vancouver!"

"Look, kid, my friendship with Will Conleth, the CEO, only goes so far these days. I can get you face time with him. But the rest is entirely up to you."

At those words, Peter sat back. Annika could see the thought working its way through his mind. Peter's defenses went down and he looked a little more at ease. Peter looked at his parents and then Alex. "OK. If I lose my job, I'll look into it."

"Perfect, kid! Then Annika could move out here, too, and work for her Dr. Lindell."

Annika stopped sipping her green tea. She thought back to their time with Alex yesterday. She was sure she hadn't told him about that possibility. She looked at Alex. "How did you—"

"Hey, you know what? You were right!" Alex said, interrupting her.

"About what?"

"My doc loved your list of supplements for me. Well, everything except the vitamin E."

Annika perked up immediately. "Oh, are you on blood thinners?"

"Nope! He just told me about some mega-study or something that came out a few years back. Proved that vitamin E can be dangerous."

"Vitamin E is *not* dangerous for most healthy people," Annika insisted.

"Well, that's what the mega-study said."

"Don't you mean meta-study?"

"Whatever! My doc told me it was back in 2005, I think."

"Oh, that one," Annika said. "That study was incredibly faulted."

Alex laughed. "My late wife always told me I was faulted whenever we had disagreements."

Annika could feel her adrenaline kick in even more. "When that study came out it caused an outcry in the scientific community because of how lopsided it was. But the press only blasted out the apparent dangers, and many people stopped taking their vitamin E."

"Well, isn't that a good thing?" Alex said.

"No, it's terrible!" Annika said. She explained further that the meta-study was nothing more than an analysis of many other doctors' original studies grouped together into one big data pool. And while the press made that meta-study appear relevant to normal, healthy people, most of the patients in the data pool were profoundly sick with cardiovascular disease. Even worse, rather than examining all available data, the meta-study excluded several key trials in which there was a low death rate of the patients. But the most serious problem had to do with something called compliance. Patients are called "compliant" if they actually take their vitamin E pill when they are in the vitamin E treatment group. The problem comes in during statistical analysis. Doctors will statistically compare death rates between the vitamin E group and the group getting nothing, but rarely verify that the vitamin E patients actually complied and took their vitamin E pills. Some call this the "intent to treat methodology." Others call it laziness. But the effects can be highly misleading. And that was exactly the case with the meta-study. One of the key trials included was called the Cambridge Heart Antioxidant Study. In the vitamin E group of that study, thirty-eight people died. But only six of those were known to be compliant, actually taking their vitamin E. A whopping twenty-one of the patients who died in that group were known *not to be compliant, and had not taken their vitamin E.* But that didn't matter. Those twenty-one deaths were counted as part of the vitamin E group anyway, due to the "intent to treat methodology," and made vitamin E look bad. But it should have been just the opposite.

And while everyone was getting unjustly frightened by the statistical confusion of the meta-study, they forgot about the history of vitamin E. They forgot that Drs. Wilfred and Evan Shute used massive doses in treating over thirty-five thousand patients at the Shute clinic in London, Ontario, starting in the 1950s. They forgot the two landmark studies in 1993 showing that men and women taking vitamin E supplements for at least two years had about 40 percent less risk of heart attack. They forgot that alpha tocopherol succinates, a form of vitamin E that needs to be injected, has been shown to be highly aggressive in killing cancer cells in a laboratory setting. But no proper trials have ever been done to test it beyond that. Even when another study came out later, in 2005, showing vitamin E was safe for the general population, the press ignored it. And of course they never mentioned that high-dose vitamin E is routinely used in clinical trials with the FDA even today.

"That meta-study is just another example of how the media blasts out negative news on natural supplements and underreports all the good news that's out there. It makes me sick," Annika said.

The server arrived with a large tray filled with sushi, sashimi, and rolls, and started dishing it out on the table. Annika realized that she had been giving a monologue for several minutes while the others had finished their miso soup. She looked down at her own full bowl. She sat back in her chair and calmed herself, smiling meekly at Peter. "I guess that was bit heavy on detail. Sorry."

"It's OK. I actually like that about you," Peter said. He had also enjoyed watching Alex be on the receiving end for a while. Everyone dug in to dinner.

Annika felt compelled to complete her thought. "It's just that nobody realizes where the true battle lies here." She grabbed a B.C. roll, her favorite, with crispy fried salmon skin inside. Sushi was one of Peter's indulgences that she wholeheartedly supported. But there was still an unfinished thought circulating at the back of her head. She draped a piece of ginger over her roll, dipped the whole thing in soy sauce and took a bite. She still couldn't remember what it was. Out of the corner of her eye, she caught Alex looking at her.

"Cheers, kid," he said with a smile. "Here's to you and Pete."

CHAPTER ELEVEN

Gwen Riley couldn't help but wince when she saw the large gashes across John Rhoades's bruised face.

"Close the door," she said quietly. It was late Saturday afternoon but she took no chances. John entered and took the seat on the other side of her desk. "Tell me you've got something."

John nodded. "We recovered a canister of what we think was used to kill Hammond."

"Why do you think that?"

"The woman tried to spray it in my face."

"I thought the chemicals on Hammond's face came back as harmless."

"We'll soon find out. It's in for analysis right now."

Gwen tapped her hand impatiently on her desk. "Don't tell me that's all."

"We also lifted fingerprints off the canister and the window."

"And?"

"Here's the good news." John tossed two large color photos on her desk.

"A man and a woman. Who are they?"

"The woman is your connection to Henry Cheung, the one going by the name Sydney Vale."

"Real name?"

"Stalina Rzymski. Ex-Russian secret service. Her partner is Andrei Petrova."

"So what's the bad news?"

"Officially they're both dead. Training accident six years ago."

Gwen rubbed her temples and sighed in frustration. "And that's it?"

"It's a big step forward."

"Into what? You still have nothing on Chromogen!" Gwen's impatience was growing.

"With all due respect, this may be out of your league."

Gwen leaned forward and glared at John. "Tread carefully."

"These people don't come cheap or easy. I doubt it's Chromogen pulling the strings."

"Then find out who is."

Gwen's cell went off. She briefly glanced at the screen. "We're done here. Come back when you have something real."

Cleveland, Ohio

Not once during the journey back to Cleveland had Annika raised the issue of the future. For some reason, Peter suddenly seemed more open to the idea of moving back to Vancouver. She didn't want to press it. She just wanted to enjoy spending time with him. Peter lugged her large suitcase behind him down the hall to her apartment.

"Forget the TV. I'm getting you a suitcase with wheels for Christmas," Peter grunted.

They arrived at her door and Annika fumbled in her purse to find her keys. She stuck her key in the door, only to have it freely push open before she turned the key in the lock. She quickly stepped back. She knew exactly what it meant.

Annika gasped. "Oh no!" She never thought it would happen to her.

Peter jumped in front of her. "Get back!"

Annika's hand tightened into a fist around her keys. First the mugging in Vancouver. Now a break-in. She started wondering why she was having so much bad luck. Peter pushed the door open and yelled into the room. He stood motionless and held his hand up, signaling Annika to keep back. For several seconds he waited. Not a sound.

"Let's just call the police!" Annika whispered.

"It's OK. We can in a minute," Peter said. He led the way around the corner to Annika's tiny living room, which doubled as her office. It was ripped apart. The sofas were overturned; every cushion was slashed to pieces. Every drawer had been ripped out of her desk and the contents dumped on the floor. Her computer was gone altogether.

"Oh no!" Annika cried. "My thesis! My work!"

Peter angrily shook his head. "Sorry, honey."

Annika got down on the floor, searching frantically through the drawers. "My backups! Everything! It's gone!"

Peter put his arm on her to calm her down. "Let's call the police now."

"But who would do this?"

"The police will find out."

"No, wait. We have to get to my office at Glenville!"

"Why?" Peter asked, dumbfounded.

"That's my only other backup!"

"OK. Let's take my car."

They ran outside and Peter went at top speed through the light Sunday afternoon traffic. Annika tried to clear her head and remember the last time she had backed up her data. She couldn't help but think of all the horror stories of other students who lost multiple months of work to a virus or a defective hard drive. She desperately hoped that she hadn't just lost two months of backbreaking analysis work.

Peter looked at her. "I thought you back up data on your phone."

"Only a few data files. It would never all fit on my phone."

"And your thesis document?"

"Yes, but I've barely started writing! I've been analyzing the data coming from the Chromogen trial."

Twelve minutes later, they arrived at Glenville State University. Annika ran inside the biochemistry building with Peter just paces behind. Down the hall, where her office was, the lights were on. People were there. Annika and Peter found two technicians in her office. Her computer was running. All the computers in the office were on.

Annika stopped in the doorway. "What's going on?"

One of the technicians spoke. "Virus. A grad student came in this morning and found his hard drive wiped clean."

Annika stared at her computer. "And mine?"

"Gone, like the rest. You do have backups, don't you?"

Annika looked frantically over her desk. She again tried to remember backing up here the last time, but her mind went blank in panic. She yanked open her bottom drawer, where she kept all her files. She closed her eyes and breathed deeply with immense relief when she saw the top data DVD on the pile. It was dated November, in her own handwriting. She calmly held it up to Peter with a smile.

"This will put me just a few days behind." She slid it into the drive and waited for the disk to be read.

"What are you doing?" Peter asked.

"Just checking it reads OK." The data folders appeared on the screen. Annika scanned all of them. They all looked exactly as they should. Her whole body relaxed. She opened the last folder and pulled up her most recent graphs on the screen. That's when everything changed.

Annika shook her head. "No! This can't be!"

"What? What's wrong?" Peter asked, looking closer.

"This isn't right."

"What isn't?"

"These graphs of liver enzymes. Chromogen had way more liver toxicity than this. I know it!"

"You're sure it's the right graph?"

Annika started looking at graph after graph. She looked at the root data, shaking her head all the time. The data was different. There were eight patients missing. "Somebody changed the data, Peter!"

"Are you sure?"

"I know what the data looks like!" Annika snapped back. She remembered her phone. She dug it out of her purse and connected it to her computer. She pulled up the few data files she had. They looked the same as the modified ones on her data DVD. They were changed, too. Annika was horrified as she realized what had happened. This really *wasn't* her phone. Somebody had known exactly what files to put on the replacement. Annika looked at the computers around her. All of them were wiped out. She felt her pulse quicken as she started to understand the scale of what was transpiring. She turned to Peter.

"I have to get to Glenville University Hospital. Right now!"

Annika bolted out of her office. Peter followed and drove her there at top speed. A few minutes later, Annika ran down the hallway of the hospital's administrative wing, up to Trevor Wilkins's office. He was always there on Saturdays. She flung the door open. "I need to see the trial data!"

"What? Why?" Trevor asked, perplexed.

"My computer at home was stolen and a virus wiped out everything at the office."

Trevor's normally pallid face went white as a sheet. He glanced at Peter and then back to Annika.

"I'm sorry to hear that. Go ahead and look." He pushed his keyboard up on his desk.

Annika called up several data files. "No! This is wrong, Trevor!" She spun around and looked Trevor in the eyes. "You know this isn't the right data. Don't you?"

Trevor pushed his glasses up on his nose. There was a slight tremor in his hand and his lower lip was twitching. But he spoke calmly. "Nothing has changed since you left Friday."

Annika kept searching. "Wait. Where's the data file on Mitch Purcell?"

"Who?"

"Mitch Purcell. He was in the trial."

Trevor stared back blankly. "That name doesn't ring a bell. Sorry."

"He's the man who died in Edgewater Park in September, remember? I passed out and was admitted here with him."

Trevor looked stupefied. "I honestly don't know what you're talking about."

A horrible realization hit Annika, and she madly searched for the names of the other men who had died. The ones she had given Dr. Lindell's formula to. Annika felt herself breaking into a cold, clammy sweat as she realized one by one they simply didn't exist in Chromogen's data pool anymore.

"You made them disappear!" Annika stammered, as she realized the enormity of her error. She stared at the screen, struggling to breathe slowly. She felt weak, and her knees started to give way. A wave of dizziness overtook her, and she started to fall. Peter caught her just in time.

"Honey, we should be going now," Peter said. He gently took Annika's arm.

"But this can't be happening!"

"Let's go get some fresh air. We'll figure it out."

They left Trevor's office, and Annika leaned up against the wall, catching her breath. She saw Peter looking at her with deep concern on his face.

"I'm OK now. Sorry."

"Are you sure?" Pete asked. He came close and looked her face over carefully.

Annika looked down the hallway and saw the main administration desk. "Just wait a minute," she said to Peter. She pushed herself off the wall and walked up to the desk. She smiled at the woman who was sitting there.

"I was admitted here for emergency treatment on September twenty-second. It was a Tuesday," Annika told her.

"Yes?"

"I need to know the exact time I came in. Can you please tell me that?"

"Sure. Name, please?"

"Annika Guthrie."

The woman typed it into her console and searched for several seconds. Her eyes narrowed and she looked puzzled. "I'm sorry, I have no record of you ever being admitted."

"What about Mitch Purcell? We came together in the same ambulance."

More typing. More puzzlement. "Sorry. Nothing on a Mitch Purcell. Where were you picked up?"

"Edgewater Park. By one of this hospital's ambulances."

"Just a second. I'll check dispatch." Several seconds went by. "I'm sorry, Ms. Guthrie, we've had no dispatches to Edgewater Park since last summer. Are you sure you have the right hospital?"

"Of course I'm sure. I work here!" Annika said.

The woman at the desk suddenly looked behind Annika with wide eyes. Annika spun around and gasped when she saw Arthur Cormack, CEO of Chromogen, standing behind her. Next to him stood a thin older man she had never seen before.

Cormack pointed at Annika and Peter. "You two, come with me. Now." He led them into an empty office down the hall from the administration desk. The thin man entered last and closed the door. Arthur nodded to him. He handed his card to Annika and Peter as he spoke.

"I'm James Geltzer, from the law firm Geltzer, Murphy, and Greenbaum. I represent Arthur Cormack and Chromogen. I suggest you find legal representation of your own."

Annika was dumbfounded. "Why?"

Geltzer held up a plastic bag. Annika immediately recognized her cell phone inside it. "Officially, we will be sent this tomorrow by someone who recovered it from a dumpster near your apartment, Annika. They recognized the Chromogen name when they looked at the data records on the phone."

Annika quickly dug out her phone from her purse. She looked closely at the one in the bag. It had the crack on the right side of Peter's face. There was no doubt it was hers. Annika felt the walls cave in around her when she remembered what was on the phone.

Geltzer continued. "We were shocked that you would give our trial data to Dr. Lindell, but the proof on this phone is rock solid. Your fingerprints are on it. So are Lindell's." Geltzer took out a large brown envelope and handed it to Annika. There were photos of her with Lindell in his lab, taken through the windows from a neighboring building. Lindell was holding that phone in his hand, and it was visibly attached to his computer.

"This doesn't leave much room for doubt, does it?" Geltzer said.

Annika went pale. She felt herself getting dizzy again. "No."

"You had such a bright future with Chromogen. Now you're facing a felony conviction." Geltzer spoke with a grin, as if enjoying the moment. Cormack had a frown of disgust on his face the whole time.

Annika was barely able to speak. "What are you going to do?"

Cormack spoke up. "No, it's what you are going to do."

Annika closed her eyes. "What?"

"Write your thesis, using the data on your backups. And agree with the very positive results," Cormack said.

"If not?"

Geltzer jumped in. "You go to jail. Lindell is ruined. And you're both discredited for life."

Tears streamed down Annika's face. "You killed them, didn't you?"

Geltzer raised his voice. "You don't listen very well, do you? I can have you in a holding cell by next week with this evidence. Do you understand that?"

Annika started sobbing. "Yes."

"You're a common thief. Get out of here," Geltzer hissed at Annika.

The drive home was the longest fifteen minutes Annika had ever experienced in her life. She was on the verge of tears the whole way. Peter pulled into the apartment complex. When she remembered the terrible mess that awaited her there, she burst into tears again.

"I'm sorry, Peter. I should have listened to you."

"Hey! It's OK! I'm going to be here for you."

"I really need you right now," Annika said between sobs.

"Come on. Let's go inside."

Peter wrapped his arm around her and brought her up the stairs. Inside, he put one of Annika's slashed cushions back on her sofa.

Annika sat down and looked up at Peter through swollen eyes. "I don't know what I'm going to do. I can't write a thesis that's a lie!"

Peter knelt down in front of her and cupped his hands around hers. "For once in your life, you need to play by their dirty rules."

"What do you mean?"

"Write your thesis. Get your credibility from Chromogen's sign-off."

"And then?"

"Then we get out of here. Both of us."

Annika forced a smile and nodded. "I need to clean up, OK?"

"Fine. I'll call the police."

Annika went into the bathroom. She could still smell the hospital and the lab on her clothes. In her hair. It sickened her. She ripped her clothes off and stood in the shower, turning the water hotter and hotter until it nearly scalded her skin. She dunked her head into the hot spray and fell against the side of the shower sobbing. All of the names missing from Trevor's list had been patients she'd treated with Dr. Lindell's cocktail. They were dead because of her, and she couldn't even tell the families she was sorry. Annika stared at the water droplets hitting the shower floor, streaming in little rivers and running down the drain. She had just jeopardized all of Dr. Lindell's work, and ruined her own life. All by her own foolishness. Now she had to figure out what to do.

Sunday, November 22
Belcarra, British Columbia

At first, it had seemed like such an odd suggestion to Lindell. The law firm in Bermuda that administered his grandfather's estate had presented him over five years ago with two parcels of land for purchase, both beachfront. One was in the isolated community of Belcarra, over an hour's drive away from UBC and Vancouver. The other was far up the coast of Indian Arm, accessible only by boat. They were getting concerned about the lack of security on Lindell's main residence, which lay near the middle of the UBC campus. They were far more than just lawyers, of course. They specialized in hiding money in safe locations around the world, but they also offered counterintelligence and security services to the ultra-rich who called Bermuda home. Even if it was home for just a small part of the year, as with Lindell. Within weeks of the purchase, they had architects draft plans for an ultramodern house in Belcarra, complete with state-of-the-art security systems and a private boathouse. Lindell constructed that one almost immediately. He saw no reason to rush on the cabin far up Indian Arm. Until he started working with Gwen Riley two years ago. The cabin was completed last summer.

Lindell came to spend many of his weekends at his secluded Belcarra house, which lay right on the border of Belcarra Regional Park. He slung a small overnight bag over his shoulder as he closed the back door behind him. The electronic lock automatically engaged. Only a ten-digit code could open it. Lindell picked up his small bag of groceries and started down the path to the water. His backyard was surrounded on three sides by thick forest and a tall concrete fence that marked off his property. Motion detectors, pressure sensors, and hidden cameras secured every square inch of the property. At the waterfront, the path ran onto a small private pier leading to his boathouse. A light breeze blew over the waters of Indian Arm. They were exceptionally calm this morning.

Lindell entered the digital code to his boathouse, and the steel door popped open. He sat down in the boat and powered it up. A minute later, his boat silently thrust out into the waters of Indian Arm. He looked back at his shrinking house in Belcarra. Not a soul to be seen along the entire visible coastline. He pulled out his PDA and sent a coded instruction over the Internet. The signal bounced several times around the planet, flung at random by four dedicated nodes in Bermuda, London, Paris, and Rome. Eventually the encrypted signal was broadcast up into space to a satellite and re-broadcast down to the entire northern hemisphere. Far up the coast in a remote corner of Indian Arm, a five-kilowatt diesel generator sprang to life. Lights came on. A heating system fired up. Lindell huddled in his parka, ramped up the boat's speed and engaged the autopilot. The chilling, damp wind seemed to find its way into every possible gap in his coat. He was looking forward to a hot breakfast at the cabin.

The boat rides to the cabin were the most boring. In the numbing cold, Lindell let his mind drift to his grandparents' house in ever-warm Bermuda. That place would always be his sanctuary. It was there that he flew after the sudden death of his parents. They had been driving from Los Angeles up to Monterey for an extended weekend when their car had fallen off a cliff on the Cabrillo Highway, where it bordered the Las Padres National Forest. That was strange, because they usually drove Highway 5 and Route 101 to get to Monterey, but the young Lindell was too devastated to ask questions. His grandparents came for a speedy funeral and invited him back to Bermuda to recover there for as long as he needed.

For a few days, Lindell forgot all about his studies, the skilled political opposition of Dr. von Bösewissen, and his desperate need for funding to continue his research. Bermuda was its own world. His grandparents' villa had been built in the eighteenth century by a wealthy shipbuilder, hidden away in the quiet reaches of Southampton Parish. Lindell still remembered playing chess with his grandfather on the heavy, solid marble table in the backyard. From their seats they watched the blue-green waters of

Little Sound sparkle in the sunlight. A cooling breeze blew past constantly, bringing the scent of ocean with it. Sailboats drifted lazily by. They played their game while drinking fresh lemonade under the shade of palmetto and Bermudian cedar trees. It took thirty minutes to clear out more than half the chess pieces and corner the remainders in one small section of the board. For the young Lindell, it was calming. Until Grandfather had to broach the subject.

"My dear Elliot, now you are the only thing I have left in this world with any meaning. You are so very gifted," Grandfather said.

Elliot could only nod, holding back the tears.

"We both know your parents didn't want me to help you financially," he said.

"I know," Elliot nodded, looking at the ground.

"In my life as a banker I have taken so very much from others. Now it is time to give something back. Through you."

"How?"

"I'm going to give you everything."

"What do you want me to do?" Elliot asked his grandfather.

"Continue your love of science. Don't ever be seduced by greed."

"OK." The young Lindell took those words too lightly.

"Listen to me, Elliot. When I was younger, I thought the more I got, the more I would be satisfied. But the more I got, the more I wanted."

"More of what?"

"Money, power, everything. Pretty soon, getting wasn't enough. I started taking. I craved. Like a common, wild animal I devoured one kill after the next. And the world calls this state success."

"What do you call success?"

"Success is to understand the joy of giving. And you can give so very much, my dear Elliot."

Grandfather picked up his lemonade, took a long sip, and moved his queen out into the open. Elliot quickly captured the queen with his bishop.

"I think I understand."

"Of course, there will be those who oppose you," Grandfather said. He took Elliot's bishop with his pawn.

"What kind of people?"

"Powerful people. Greedy people. People like me, my dear Elliot."

Elliot winced at that statement. His eyes wandered to the rook that threatened his king. "I'm being opposed already." He moved his queen to block.

His grandfather moved his king out into the fray. "Checkmate," he said, with a triumphant smile.

"No!" Elliot gasped at the sudden and unexpected defeat.

"Now, why did you not see that coming?"

"I never thought you would expose your king that way."

"Exactly. Everybody sees the advancing pawn who would be king. Nobody sees the king who would become a pawn for the sake of the kingdom." He picked up Elliot's king. "Never forget, my dear boy. You are born of kings."

Those words never made sense to the young Lindell. But his grandfather had a reputation for telling some amazing tales and stretching the truth to do it. Some truths were not stretched. When Lindell came back to college weeks later, he was summoned to the chancellor's office. The dean of science was waiting for him there as well. An anonymous donation of five million dollars had come in specifically earmarked for Lindell's research. It was enough to buy the supercomputer he needed, and on top of that, pay out a generous stipend for his PhD. In the meantime, some rather disturbing news on Dr. von Bösewissen had recently become public. Apparently, he had been having an affair with the wrong woman—one who was married to the president of his main sponsoring pharmaceutical company in the U.S. Shortly thereafter, Dr. von Bösewissen left the country in disgrace and never resurfaced. But Lindell knew that would not be the end of his opposition.

SPRING

CHAPTER TWELVE

Friday, April 26
Glenville University Hospital
Cleveland, Ohio

For Annika, the last five months had felt like the time leading up to her father's death. But this time, rather than trying to help her father fight cancer, she was forced into helping Chromogen get away with murder. She looked down at the hundred-and-eighty-page master's thesis she carried down the hallway of Glenville University Hospital. A thesis based on lies. The new data from the Phase III trial that appeared on her computer and her phone had made Chromogen's drug look far more effective than it really was. The liver toxicity was almost gone. And she knew that wasn't true. But that wasn't the worst of it. During her analysis, Annika had discovered just how profoundly she had helped Chromogen. Eleven of the patients she had given Dr. Lindell's formula to were in the treatment arm getting Chromogen's drug. They had improved remarkably once they took Dr. Lindell's cocktail of supplements. And that made Chromogen's drug look all the better. As for the other patients Annika had helped, the ones not on Chromogen's drug, they all died. Their improved health would have made Chromogen's drug look bad in comparison. And so, in the greatest possible perversion of the truth, Annika's help had made Chromogen's bad drug look good. And there was nothing she could do about it.

Annika stopped walking when she came to Trevor's office door. He was on the review committee, and would be examining her on the day of her thesis defense two months from now. Annika had spent all night making her final fixes and printing out the six copies for the review committee. This was the final delivery. The one she least wanted to make. She stood for several seconds in front of Trevor's door. At least he wouldn't gawk at her. She hadn't bathed and had barely slept in three days. Her eyes were puffy and almost impossible to keep open. Her long red hair was pulled up in a messy bun with elastic bands. She wore the same T-shirt and jeans she had put on Tuesday morning. She knocked.

"Come in, Annika." He always seemed to know when it was her.

She entered, and without a word put the thesis on Trevor's desk. It was only seven in the morning and his office already reeked of body odor and stale coffee. Trevor sat upright in his chair. His hands were busy fidgeting with a small stack of papers from a notepad. He managed a brief smile, and then quickly craned his neck to see if anyone was behind Annika. Even in her tired state, Annika could tell he was ill at ease.

Annika took no pity. "Here's the thesis."

"Why don't you have a seat?" Trevor said.

She stood back and looked at her watch. "I have to catch a flight."

"I just wanted to congratulate you."

"For what?"

"This, of course," Trevor said, gesturing toward the thesis. "You know what I think of it. And you. And Chromogen."

"No, what?" Trevor kept fidgeting with the stack of small papers.

"You manipulated data…"

Annika's tired words faded as Trevor held up the first piece of paper from the stack. Scribbled in large, jagged capital letters was: "THEY WILL KILL ME." Trevor's face went pallid, his eyes wide with fear.

For the first split second, Annika wondered if it was some sick joke. But the expression on Trevor's face and the trembling of his hands told her it wasn't. Annika's adrenaline surged, and she snapped out of her state of exhaustion. But she didn't know what to say.

Trevor put his finger to his lips. "So why don't you sit and chat a while?" He held up another paper. "THEY CAN HEAR US."

"OK. Just for a minute." Annika closed the door behind her and sat down in the chair opposite Trevor's desk.

"I just wanted to wish you well in your PhD." Trevor held up another paper. "YOU WERE RIGHT. CHROMOGEN CHANGED THE DATA."

"Well, I have to get my master's first," Annika said. A wave of relief followed by revulsion swept over her. Not only had every trace of Mitch Purcell been erased from the trials, but all the men that had died. She was so sure of what the data should have looked like, but after months of seeing the new data, Annika started to wonder if she was losing her sanity.

"I'm sure you'll breeze through it." He held up the next paper. "THEY KILLED YOUR PATIENTS." He nodded in confirmation.

Tears ran down Annika's face. She could see Trevor's eyes turn bloodshot. "Thank you. I appreciate it," Annika said, trying to keep any emotion from her voice. But she couldn't help the sick feeling that she was partly to blame for their deaths. Trevor said nothing. He recovered and raised both eyebrows, gazing at Annika. The next note was important. "I STILL HAVE THE ORIGINAL DATA." Annika nearly fell off her chair. She nodded.

"So, what will you do before your defense?" he asked. The next paper said "TELL NOBODY."

"First I'm going to go visit Peter in Vancouver."

Trevor pointed to the word "nobody" for emphasis. "Oh, I love Vancouver." Then next paper came up. "GIVE ME YOUR EMAIL ADDRESS."

Without thinking twice about it, Annika leaned forward and wrote her address on the piece of paper. "Well, maybe I'll come by after my trip and see if you have any questions on the thesis."

Trevor frowned and shook his head with eyes closed. Annika couldn't believe he was refusing her a visit. That was a first. "I'll email you any questions I have. And I'll expect quick answers," he said.

"Of course." As Annika got up to leave, Trevor was holding up one last note. "KEEP YOUR INTEGRITY. MINE IS GONE FOREVER."

Annika nodded. She stood up and walked to the door. Why he had decided to tell her all this now was far beyond her. But if he really had the original data, why didn't he turn it in to the police? Annika didn't know if she should hate him or pity him. She turned back with her hand on the doorknob. She saw a single tear well up in Trevor's eye and run down his cheek.

"Good-bye, Trevor." Annika closed his door behind her. It felt like slamming a jail cell shut. But she felt just as helpless as Trevor had appeared. Annika took a few fast paces to put some distance between her and his office. She just wanted to get to her car and go to the airport. Her bags were packed and waiting. She kept telling herself that what mattered was no longer in this city. Dr. Lindell was in Vancouver. And by some amazing twist of fate, Peter was now there as well. But she couldn't let go of that image of Chromogen's CEO, Arthur Cormack, and his lawyer, James Geltzer, when they threatened to ruin her and Dr. Lindell. Annika no longer cared so much for her own life. It was the lives of all those patients who would be affected by Cormack's lies. All for his own gain. No matter how hard she tried, Annika could not shake his face from her mind. For the first time in her life, she understood what it was to hate.

New York

Nolan Ponticus Vasquez took a sip of chilled sauvignon blanc and glanced at his watch. Arthur Cormack was late. But Nolan enjoyed every opportunity he had to reproach Cormack, even if this time it was due to the late arrival of his airplane. He lifted another slice of Ahi tuna carpaccio onto his fork and smeared it into the thin streak of white truffle oil which ran down the center of his plate. He chewed it slowly and let the taste fully develop in his mouth. The L'Eau et la Rivière restaurant was one of the few restaurants in New York to sport two Michelin stars, and claimed the truffle oil came only from the Piedmont region of Italy. But Nolan would swear this oil was Croatian, albeit of very good quality. The exact same starter and glass of wine was set at the place across the table from Nolan. The condensation on the wineglass formed a single large drop which ran down the stem and onto the base. The restaurant reminded Nolan of his own loft, which was not surprising, as it was less than a ten-minute taxi ride away and lay forty stories up in the middle of downtown New York. Original wood paneling on walls and ceilings against the polished multicolor Italian marble floor had old money written all over it. The modernity was brought in by the stone and glass bar which was as well lit as it was stocked. Nolan enjoyed the nervousness of the server who eyed the empty seat across from him, knowing the food was rapidly reaching room temperature and losing its ideal taste. Nolan watched with contained amusement as Cormack arrived and stormed past the restaurant's reception desk. He brushed off the maitre d' and walked up to the table, slamming a magazine down on the table next to Nolan's plate.

"What the hell is this?" Cormack asked, eyeing the magazine.

The people at the surrounding tables glared at him. Nolan ignored them, and calmly folded another thin slice of tuna onto his fork and rubbed it in the white truffle oil. Holding it up to his mouth, he spoke only loud enough to be heard by Arthur.

"You're late. Sit down." He slid the tuna off his fork and into his mouth. He jabbed his fork at the plate on Arthur's side. "I took the liberty of ordering for you."

Arthur reluctantly took his seat. "I thought you were in control."

"We are."

Arthur glowered at the magazine on the table. "Then what's this about?"

Nolan didn't look at the magazine. "It's the latest study showing that vitamin D dramatically reduces colon cancer risk."

"You know about it already?" Cormack said, raising his voice.

"I'm not stupid, Arthur."

Arthur leaned across the table. "Our trial results on low-dose Cyrozetix against colon cancer are due out next quarter."

"So what?"

Cormack lowered his voice. "We don't want the public to be informed that they can get the same protection with vitamin D pills at one fiftieth the price."

"Relax, Arthur."

"That's a billion-dollar market for the next twenty years!"

"Eat. We're taking care of it."

"I thought this magazine was already taken care of. What the hell happened?"

"The editor decided to get virtuous on us."

"And now?"

"They'll lose forty percent of their advertising revenues until they play it our way."

Arthur sat back with some satisfaction and sipped his wine. "What about the editor?"

"He just suffered a severe case of tropical fish poisoning."

Cormack picked up a piece of tuna on his own fork but stopped just short of his mouth, looking guardedly at it, then at Nolan. "What kind of fish?"

Nolan laughed. "Unfortunately, I need you healthy in your new role as CEO of Avarus. Congratulations, by the way. I saw the news release this morning."

Cormack grinned. "Gwen Riley must be shaking in her little high heels now."

"And you're not?" Nolan glowered at him.

"Why should I be?" Cormack asked.

"It doesn't bother you that Avarus's previous CEO died suspiciously?"

Cormack sipped more wine. "Why should it? I didn't kill him."

"No. But you're standing in his shoes now," Nolan said, narrowing his eyes.

Cormack avoided that topic. "What about the damage done by the article?"

Nolan dismissed it with a wave of his hand. "Two days ago, an eighty-seven-year-old woman in New Jersey died from vitamin D overdose."

"How lucky for us."

"Hardly. We made sure she was getting four hundred thousand IU, rather than the four hundred labeled on her bottle."

Cormack was surprised. "And that was enough?"

"She had a tumor on her parathyroid. But that will only turn up in the fine print later."

"And for now?"

"We're pushing a major press campaign about the dangers of vitamin D supplementation."

Arthur smiled and took another bite of tuna. "OK. So maybe you are in control."

Nolan frowned in return. "Yes. And if you ever make such a scene in front of me again, you'll end up sliced thinner than your tuna."

Cormack struggled to get his last bite down. "Sorry."

"If you want to worry, worry about Lindell's trials with Mitogenica."

"What? Are they still getting such good results?"

Nolan nodded. "Better."

"Better than their new drug Mitasmolin?"

"And better than ours. We don't understand what Riley is aiming at."

"Maybe Gwen Riley isn't as smart as you think."

Nolan put down his fork and knife with a thud. "If you had half the brains of Gwen Riley we wouldn't need to take over Mitogenica."

"Then why are you making me CEO over Avarus?"

Nolan looked out the window. "That wasn't my decision."

Cormack brushed off the comment. "Fine. What are you doing about Lindell's trials?"

"We're expecting a breakthrough today," Nolan said.

"What do you expect to find out?"

"The patients seem to know something about the trial."

"How do you know that?"

"They're talking about it, but nobody says what it is. They're all waiting for something."

"Waiting for what?"

"We don't know yet. But it's something big."

Mitogenica, Inc.
Vancouver, B.C.

Gwen Riley walked with a scowl on her face down the hallway of Mitogenica's third floor on her way to the labs. Her feet hit the floor with an especially heavy impact for such a petite woman, and her dark hazel eyes flashed anger in all directions. Nobody dared to look her in the face this Friday morning. The news of Avarus's take-over of Chromogen had spread at Mitogenica like fire in a tinderbox, and of course, everything that it implied for the future. To make matters worse, Gwen had just made the first quarter's earnings release that morning before the story hit the news wires. Mitogenica's earnings had actually stabilized in the first quarter, and that normally would have been greeted with a nice bump up in the share price. Instead, she had her head handed to her. But the worst insult of all was that her old nemesis, Arthur Cormack, was the new head of Avarus. Her one respite for the day was now standing directly in front of her. Jeff Lowe, her head of research. The one man who dared look her in the eye. More than that, he was studying her. Trying to figure something out. Five months before, Jeff had run Lindell's three experimental cocktails together with Mitaxynil through the Eden Project, testing to see how effectively the combinations killed real living cancer cells. To his horror, he discovered that each of the three cocktails when combined with Mitaxynil might be better than Mitogenica's newer drug Mitasmolin. And the recent data coming in from the trial on cancer patients was confirming Jeff's findings. Gwen had suggested he try running Mitasmolin itself together with Lindell's three cocktails. Five months later, those tests had just been completed.

"I take it you have good news?" Gwen asked.

"I need to know how you did it," Jeff asked, still watching her intently.

"How I did what?"

"Mitasmolin is a perfect fit with Lindell's cocktails. Whatever Mitaxynil did to kill cancer cells, Mitasmolin does five times better."

Gwen allowed herself to smile. "So it is good news."

"If we nail this science down we'll take the whole damn cancer market."

"Then start designing the trials to do that."

Jeff hauled a thick binder off his desk. "Already started. Just one question."

"Yes?"

"If you knew this stuff so well, what were you waiting for?"

"Lindell had to make his move first. He just didn't know it was exactly in the direction I wanted."

"How do you know Lindell so well?"

Gwen's eyes narrowed and her smile disappeared. "That's my business. I need a favor from you, Jeff."

"Sure."

Gwen's cell phone went off. She continued talking as she took it out and read a message on the screen. "Start going with the troops every Thursday to O'Malley's."

"What? Why?"

"Get drunk. Start talking."

"About what?"

"Your results here on Mitaxynil. The market needs to know."

Jeff looked at Gwen as if she'd gone mad, and glanced around to see if there was anyone else within earshot. "Are you sure about this?"

Gwen closed her cell phone. "Yes, I am. And I have to go now."

On the elevator up to her office, Gwen couldn't help but replay the last phone call she had with Austin a few weeks ago. He had predicted the Chromogen takeover almost to the day, courtesy of his friends in higher places. Now he was trying to call again. How predictable. She'd dodged his calls all day. Until she was ready. Until now. She walked out of the elevator and past Nadine's desk.

"Ma'am, you have a visitor."

"I know," Gwen said, without looking at her. She closed the door behind her and sat down, facing John Rhoades, who sat opposite her desk. He quickly opened a laptop on her desk. She handed her cell phone over, which he immediately hooked into his laptop.

"Tell me you finally got something on the Russians," Gwen said.

"I can't."

"Damn it! What do I pay you for?"

"We intercepted a phone call this morning to Ian Ponce."

"Who is he?"

"He writes the cancer blog on Lindell's work. He's getting an important visitor today."

"So what?"

"The Russians are likely to be there, too."

"Don't disappoint me. What about the data from Chromogen?" Gwen asked. That was the part that worried her, much more than any phone call from Austin. Because the data that John had collected through his sources had undergone a significant change recently. It looked much better than the previous data. Better for Chromogen. Devastating for Mitogenica.

"I can confirm the source. The data is good."

Gwen glared back at him. "But the data has changed."

"The new data is what was handed over to the FDA."

"Damn! This erases any advantage we ever had over Chromogen!"

"If we can nail them for this, it's fraud," John said.

Gwen snapped back, "With your stolen data? I'd go to jail, too!"

Gwen's cell phone lit up and started ringing. She cut short her thought and looked at the screen. "It's Austin."

John tapped a few keys on the laptop and nodded to Gwen. She picked up.

"Hello, Austin. What a surprise." She could hear the sound of traffic in the background. She watched John, who observed his screen with a look of surprise.

"I'm not calling to gloat, Gwen. And I liked your Q1 earnings surprise."

Gwen rolled her eyes. "The market didn't care much for it."

"I keep trying to tell you what matters. I'm on your side here."

"Get to the point, Austin."

"My friends are still willing to talk."

"I'm not."

"Everything they promised has come true."

"Including data manipulation?"

There was no response for several seconds. John glanced up at Gwen with worry on his face that the connection might be cut too early.

"Austin, are you there?" Gwen asked.

"I wouldn't know anything about that."

"It took you all that time just to come up with that answer?"

"I just need to know if you're in or out, Gwen."

"Why? Do you have to report to them today?"

"I'm meeting with them in a few minutes," Austin said.

Gwen shot a glance up to John. He nodded and waved his hand in a circle to get more time. But before Gwen could speak, Austin said, "I have to go now. Call me if you change your mind."

The connection went dead. Gwen looked at John.

"Where is he?"

"New York. En route to downtown from JFK."

"But not there yet."

John shook his head. "No. And he switched off."

"Damn," Gwen said under her breath. "What about the chemical?"

John shook his head again. After recovering the spray canister that Sydney had tried to use on him in Vancouver, Gwen had him send it to a lab in California specializing in neurotoxin analysis. The remaining contents of the canister held high concentrations of an artificial alkaloid complex that disrupted neuromuscular transmission, paralyzing any muscle it invaded. Inhalation would cause rapid paralysis and uncontrolled spasms of the respiratory muscles and the heart. But the lab found that the compound was unstable in the presence of oxygen. In the open air, it broke down in minutes. In the body, total breakdown occurred in half an hour, long after the exposed subject would be dead. After months of research, Gwen had found that the alkaloid complex was a close structural analog of Noratoprene, an experimental muscle relaxant under study by none other than Avarus Pharmaceuticals. But there was no evidence linking the chemical to anyone's death, or even to the canister it was found in.

"No police report showed any detection of the chemical, let alone analysis. It's just too unstable," John said.

"We have two months until the FDA decision is due. You have to get something by then."

John looked at his watch. "I have to go."

"I need results this time!" Gwen called out after him.

He walked out and closed the door behind him. Gwen shook her head. She was so close. But earnings had stabilized at too low a level. If she didn't get FDA approval for Mitasmolin, Mitogenica wouldn't have enough money to launch its third generation drug development that would sweep the market. Instead, Gwen would have to raise cash by issuing more stock. Shareholders would be incensed. And Mitogenica would be ripe for takeover. Austin's friends would make their move. But she wasn't going to let that happen. Gwen waited several moments after John left, then got up and walked over to a wall. She removed the original Robert Bateman painting of a wolverine from its place to reveal a small safe. Gwen punched in her code and removed a thick magnetic tape cartridge. She closed it and went to the service elevator. All things considered, she was pleased with John Rhoades's progress. But she never got results from people by letting them relax on their achievements along the way. The elevator arrived. She entered and inserted her key into the new slot, recently put into the control panel. It assured that the elevator would descend uninterrupted past the underground parking area. Three stories below ground level, the doors opened to a small space just a few meters wide. Gwen took two steps forward and pressed her hand onto a blue luminous panel, which sat next to a massive steel door. She felt the warmth of the laser light sweep past as it scanned her entire hand. The panel instantly turned bright green. The steel door opened and she walked in to the gentle humming of overhead air conditioners. On either side of her stood two-meter-tall racks loaded with the most powerful parallel processors offered by Gen-Silico Corporation. Hundreds of glowing LEDs flashed on and off rhythmically as the computer was put through its paces. Gwen didn't dare admit to Jeff Lowe, her nervous head of research, that half the molecules she had Lindell process through his computer model were nothing more than test vehicles, designed to tell her how the model worked. Where it was weak. How complete it was. Austin Hayes had been correct. She had secretly accumulated her own supercomputer over the last twelve months. One far superior to Lindell's. When she found the leak in purchasing, she had him summarily fired. Two men walked up to Gwen from the far end of the room. The two she could trust.

"Is it working?" she asked.

"All diagnostics are go," said the first.

"Well done." Gwen's rare compliment brought instant smiles.

"I just don't get one thing," he said.

"What?"

"That tape drive you made us install. Nobody uses that anymore."

Gwen held up the cartridge she had taken from the safe. "Nobody but me."

Both men gasped. "What is it?"

Gwen looked each of them in the eyes. "This goes no further than this room."

"Of course."

"It's an early version of Lindell's cancer model."

The first man gingerly took it into his hands. "How old?"

"About twenty years."

"It might take that long to break the encryption."

Gwen shook her head. "This one's unencrypted."

The man stood there with a blank look on his face. "How did you—"

Gwen cut him off. "Don't ask."

"If it's unencrypted, why do you need me?" He was one of Silicon Valley's top encryption experts that Gwen had recruited when she started buying the pieces to make her own Gen-Silico.

"Your work is still ahead of you."

The man held up the tape. "Then what do I do with this?"

"Get to know the code. And how Lindell programs." She walked out of the room, back to the elevator. "It will help you later."

"Why? What's coming later?" the man called out after her.

Gwen turned around in the elevator just as the doors were shutting. "Today's version."

CHAPTER THIRTEEN

Downtown Vancouver, B.C.

Ian Ponce walked quickly down Robson Street toward Vancouver's Central Library. The cool spring morning was warming under the cloudless sky and Ian was about to break a sweat at his current pace. His large paunch bounced almost painfully with every stride. He didn't like being rushed after patiently waiting over five months. Tyler Evans had, after all, promised the world back at Ian's cancer blog meeting in November. When three patients in Dr. Lindell's trial with Mitogenica turned up cured of their cancers, Tyler offered to sample what they were getting, find out what was in it, and make the winning formula available to everyone—free. Of course, he would also sell it to others for a profit at his cancer clinic in Tijuana, which made it more puzzling why Tyler had fallen off the face of the planet since taking his last samples back in January. No calls answered. No emails. Nothing.

Then, this morning, he called frantically at six a.m. over the Internet from the airport in San Diego. He was about to board a flight to Vancouver and had to meet in four hours in the library. Ian stopped at the crosswalk on Homer Street. The library stood just on the other side of the intersection. From half a block away, it looked more like a windowed coliseum that took up an entire city block. Closer up, the modern curve of the extra atrium on the southeast side came into view. Ian walked up the stairs and through the glass doors into the six-story-tall atrium. He looked around. To the left, a massive wall of windows displayed six stories of bookshelves and desks filled with people reading. The curve of the atrium's outer wall on the right was studded with news and fast-food stores on the ground floor. Above them, tall portals stood on three levels, opening to a wall of windows. In front of Ian was a scattering of small square tables following the curve of the atrium.

Ian glanced at the tables of the coffee shop for Tyler, not seeing him anywhere... until a lone man in a trench coat, low hat, and sunglasses gestured slightly. Ian walked over, finally recognizing Tyler when he was just a few paces away. Two large coffees sat in front of him.

"What's going on, Tyler?" Ian asked, sitting down across from him.

"Shhh," Tyler said. "Just sit down and have some coffee."

Ian sat and glared impatiently. "Why can't we call another blog meeting at my place?"

"That would be complicated."

"What's complicated is explaining to everyone that you've disappeared."

"I know. I'm sorry." Tyler stared into his coffee cup and took a long gulp.

"Sorry doesn't cut it when they're dying. You made a promise to them."

"So did Lindell. That's changed, too," Tyler said.

"What are you talking about?"

"Everyone was supposed to get one of three natural cocktails together with Mitaxynil. But the cured patients didn't get any Mitaxynil at all."

"What were they getting?"

Tyler broke out in a fake laugh as an attractive brunette and a tall, well-built man passed by. They were dressed in business attire and both wore sunglasses inside the building. Unknown to Tyler and Ian, it was Sydney and Owen. Sydney walked to a table two rows over from Ian and Tyler and sat down while Owen went to the counter to order coffee. Sydney adjusted her chair to face both men. She hoisted her purse up on the table. It held a small video camera and super-sensitive microphone on the external flap. Tyler leaned back and glared suspiciously at Sydney. She turned to face the other direction. She didn't dare reach in her purse yet to activate the camera or microphone.

Tyler turned back to Ian. "They were getting the fourth cocktail. And nothing else."

Ian sat back in disbelief. "What? Are you sure?"

Tyler nodded. "We checked it ten times over."

"So why have you been incommunicado?"

"The fourth cocktail was impossible to replicate exactly."

"But you've come close?"

Tyler nodded. "We can't match the chemical profiles of all the extracts. And there are two Chinese herbs we can't find. But we're close enough."

"For what?"

Tyler spoke quietly. "Curing prostate, colon, and breast cancer in rats."

Ian couldn't contain himself. He raised his voice. "You're testing it on rats? Why?"

Tyler held up his hand as a signal to wait. Two men in suits walked by and stood at the table precisely between him and Sydney. Ken Dochlin and Logan Helliker sat down and started to talk loudly. Sydney was incensed at the strangers' presence. Their voices masked the conversation between Tyler and Ian, which she had just begun to hear. Sydney adjusted her position several times in an attempt to regain audio. But each time the strangers seemed to move with her, their conversation getting louder.

Tyler kept one eye on them all, unaware of what was unfolding. He spoke to Ian almost inaudibly. "We're going to publish the results. Remember my paper that got accepted at the cancer conference on Grand Cayman in June?"

"Tyler, this is Lindell's formula!"

"Which he can't publish himself," Tyler whispered.

"Why not?"

"He's in gross violation of the trial protocol. Everyone was supposed to get Mitaxynil!"

"Then what's he up to?"

"Apparently he's found his Eden Prescription and he wanted to test it."

"We should go to him first," Ian said.

"Why? He's probably sold out to Mitogenica already."

"I don't want to make enemies of Lindell!"

"Why not?"

Ian looked down at the table. "My watchful waiting is over. The prostate cancer is back, and this time it's aggressive."

"Damn it, I'm sorry, Ian," Tyler said.

"Lindell's my only hope now."

"You're wrong. We have a hundred percent cure rate in over eighty rats now. I can give you the formula, too."

"And then what?" Ian said.

"Then go to Lindell. Tell him we know. You'll be the proof."

"I have to prove I have cancer first."

"Then enroll in his trial. Get scanned. Then come to me."

"And force him to go public?"

Tyler nodded. "Either that or we go public." He turned around as the loud conversation between the two men at the neighboring table came to an abrupt halt.

Owen arrived with the coffees, and at Sydney's urging confronted Ken and Logan.

"Hey, why don't you guys pick another table?" Owen said obstinately. He reached down and shoved so hard that Ken nearly fell off his chair. Tyler looked on in shock as Logan stood up and gave Owen a chop to the throat so rapid that Tyler barely saw the blur of motion through the air. Instantly, Owen fell back toward Sydney with a sick, wheezing sound as he tried to breathe. Logan stepped quickly over to Sydney, and as he sat down he drew a gun from under his jacket and rapidly brought it under the table. Nobody else in the café seemed to see the gun, but both Ian and Tyler jumped at the sight of the weapon. Tyler spilled a large splash of coffee on the floor. Unseen by Tyler and Ian, John Rhoades and Matt Swanson had been making their way from the exit during the entire scene. John spoke from behind Tyler.

"Ian and Tyler!" Both men spun around at the sound of their names. "You're in danger," John said. "Leave now. And separate when you're outside." He opened his jacket enough for Ian and Tyler to glimpse his holstered weapon.

"Damn it!" Tyler said under his breath. Both men bolted for the exit.

John Rhoades walked past Ian and Tyler to join Ken and Logan at the table. They had two Glock .45s trained on Sydney and Owen under the table. Owen was still struggling to breathe normally.

"Cell phones on the table. Now," John said. He collected them and gave them to Matt, who stood behind him. "And now the purse."

Reluctantly, Sydney slid her purse over. John pried off the large button on the flap of the purse, which held the camera and microphone. Sydney glowered at him as he pocketed it. She leaned to the side to watch in disgust as Tyler and Ian got to the exit doors. She was barely able to restrain herself from leaping up and following them.

"Don't even think about it," Logan said, jabbing the muzzle of his Glock into her ribs.

People around them started to glare and talk. They were being noticed, and it was obvious something was wrong. Some people were getting up and leaving.

At the far end of the atrium, Ian swung the exit door open and both men ran down the stairs outside.

"Who were those men?" Tyler asked between heaving, nervous breaths.

"I have no idea," Ian said. He was equally shaken and had broken into a cold sweat.

"You won't see me again in this city," Tyler said.

"Wait, Tyler, I've got a better way to do this."

"Tell me about it over this." Tyler slapped a disposable cell phone in Ian's hand.

Ian grabbed Tyler's coat at the shoulder. "Are you trying to get rich off this?"

Tyler slapped Ian's hand away. "Better me than Mitogenica. Or them." He nodded to the men still inside the library. "Which way are you going?"

Ian pointed down Robson Street. "There."

Tyler turned in the opposite direction from Ian's path and started walking. He turned back briefly. "If you want the formula, come down in a couple of weeks."

Inside the library, John Rhoades watched the exit door slowly close until he was sure the two had reached a safe distance. He turned back to face Sydney.

"You're very attractive for a woman who's been dead for six years, Stalina."

At the mention of her real name, Sydney scowled. "I'm going to find out who you are. Then I'm going to kill you."

The sound of police sirens could be heard in the distance. And they were getting closer. Logan and Ken looked at John for guidance.

"We have to go," John said calmly. He nodded to them.

Both men withdrew their weapons from under the table. But just as Logan was about to stand up, he felt the muzzle of Sydney's own gun pushed hard against his inner thigh. It was being aimed at his femoral artery. He knew one shot would give him about two minutes to live.

"Boss!" Logan said helplessly.

"The purse and our phones or he dies now," Sydney barked.

John pushed the purse over to her. Matt produced the two phones and put them on the table. Sydney hadn't budged yet. The sirens were close.

"You really want to stay that long?" John asked.

Sydney bit her lip in anger as she withdrew. She and Owen waited for a moment as John and the others took the exit furthest from the sound of the sirens, then they quickly took the nearest exit.

Outside the library, John and his group walked down the stairs calmly, saying nothing.

"You called the police just a little early, don't you think?" John said to Matt.

"Sorry, boss."

"Did you get the transponders in?"

Matt nodded. "If they stay local, we'll know where they are."

The men got into their Hummer, which was parked curbside across Robson Street. John drove off toward their office, located in the basement of the West Coast Aikido Clinic in the middle of Chinatown. Matt, Logan, and Ken were busy celebrating their small victory. This was the first big break they had had in months of tracking these people. As much as he wanted more information to start flowing, John worried about where it might lead them. So far, these people had been unpredictable. And in this business, surprises were very dangerous.

Vancouver, B.C.

Annika felt exhausted to the point of collapse as she walked off her flight into Vancouver International Airport. She had expected to sleep soundly on the plane. Instead, she had lain awake thinking about Trevor's desperate notes. She tried to put it out of her head. In two months she would defend her thesis and be done forever with Chromogen. Then she would come here. Annika found herself in a decorated section of the airport. There was a large display area with First Nations Canadian artwork, totem poles, and a dugout canoe. She followed the line of people and walked out onto a raised, glass-encased walkway with her carry-on wheeling closely behind her. Peter was waiting for her on the other side of immigration. In the last five months he had been there for her like never before, and she had fallen more in love with him than she could remember. In some ways his five months had been tougher than hers. Alameda Alloys had been brought to the brink of bankruptcy; in the restructuring that followed, Peter had indeed lost his job. He had also been saddled with nearly one hundred thousand dollars of debt from his executive MBA program. That was just three weeks ago. In desperation, Peter turned to Uncle Alex. And Alex delivered in spades. Within a few days, Peter was on a plane for an interview with William Conleth himself, the CEO of Cypress Turbines. Since then, Annika's communication with Peter had been very sporadic. If she understood correctly, he got the job on the day of the interview. She then received a few hurried phone calls from Peter on site in London, Paris, and Vancouver. One call Peter made from the Cypress company jet somewhere over the Atlantic. And then, without warning, an email arrived from Peter with an e-ticket for Vancouver for the weekend. Annika jumped at it and spent the last three sleepless nights making sure she finished her thesis in time to go.

Annika emerged into the arrivals hall. She looked behind her to see a large wall of green ceramic blocks with water flowing over them. Mounted in the center of the wall was a massive circular wood carving. In all of her visits, she had never figured out what was depicted in the carving. But it was beautiful. She went down the escalator and hurried through immigration, excited to see Peter for the first time in almost a month. But, as she came into the arrivals area, Annika nearly dropped her suitcase when she saw Peter. His left eye was slightly swollen, with a ring of faded black and blue around it. There were also large bruises and scrapes on his forehead and under his right cheekbone. Peter let himself smile, but it was quickly replaced by a grimace of pain. He raised his right arm to wave at Annika. His left arm was in a cast from elbow to wrist, and held a bunch of long-stemmed red roses. He walked toward her with a slight limp—but there was something else odd about the way he walked. It reminded Annika that all people each have their own way of carrying their weight on their feet. She brushed the thought aside and ran to him.

"Peter! Oh my God, what happened?"

"I'm OK. I got into a situation at work."

The stories about Peter's brother Thomas ran through Annika's mind. Hadn't he come back from his summer job looking like this? "Were you in an accident?"

"Something like that, yeah. How are you?"

"OK, I guess. Very short on sleep," said Annika, still looking at his injuries.

Peter smiled. "I know the feeling. Come on. I have a surprise for you." He walked with his sight limp outside into the bright, sunny spring day and to the parking lot. He walked up to the passenger side of an old rusty truck and put his key up to the door. "Do you like my new car?"

Annika couldn't stifle a laugh of surprise. "It's nice!" she lied.

Peter smirked and pressed a button on the key. Two rapid honks sounded from another car behind Peter. It was a brand-new Lexus hybrid finished in a brilliant matador red.

Annika took a step back in shock. "You can't be serious."

"I know it's your dream car. All eco-friendly and that."

"And my favorite color," Annika said, still unbelieving.

"I thought you would get a kick out of the name," Peter said. He pointed to the lettering on the side of the car, which read "RX."

Annika laughed. "But you can't afford this."

"I don't have to. It's a company car."

"Uncle Alex strikes again," Annika said. She regretted those words when she saw a grimace erupt on Peter's face. He walked her to the passenger side and let her in. Annika didn't dare mention Alex during the drive, which took them over the Arther Laing Bridge and up Granville Street. Peter told her all about his new job working as technical assistant to the CEO of Cypress Turbines. Annika listened as she got acquainted with all the features of the car. She loved the new car smell that permeated the air. She had two big weaknesses in life: high-tech hybrid cars and houses with a view. She had always figured she would end up with neither.

Annika was in awe of the magnificent downtown Vancouver skyline that stood in front of them as Peter drove over the Granville Street Bridge. He took the Seymour Street exit and drove onto Pacific Avenue.

"So, are you staying in a hotel?" Annika asked.

"Not quite." Peter turned onto Strathmore Mews and up to the gate of one of the towering new buildings. He swiped a card in the reader and drove down into the garage.

"What is this place?" Annika asked.

"You'll see."

They got out and Peter took her into the elevator. He slid a magnetic card through a reader inside and a green light went on, then he pressed button twenty-nine. The elevator surged upward into a high-speed climb.

"Welcome to the Granville One building of Strathmore Mews," Peter said.

"You have a temporary place here?" Annika asked.

"Yeah, temporarily. For about two years," Peter said. The elevator doors opened on the twenty-ninth floor. After a short walk down the hall, Peter unlocked the apartment door and they walked past an office and kitchen on the left and a master and spare bedroom on the right, emerging into a large living area with both corner walls made entirely of glass. Looking straight out, it felt like they were up in the bright blue summer sky. Annika walked up to the glass walls and was breathless at the view. The bright green expanse of David Lam Park spread out from the base of the apartment building and touched the Fraser River, which shimmered in the midday sun. Dozens of sailboats lay moored along the docks of Granville Island across the river, their masts gently swaying with the water's ebb and flow. The Granville Street Bridge stretched out to the right, and beyond it the glistening, deep blue waters of the Burrard Inlet. Far across the water, the green hills of Bowen Island were visible through the pure ocean air that constantly blew in from the west.

"This is incredible! How did you get this?"

"One of Alex's old buddies from Cypress Turbines just moved to China for the next two years to start up a manufacturing shop."

Annika couldn't help but smile. "Maybe Uncle Alex isn't so bad after all."

Peter closed his eyes for a moment. "I know, I know." He pointed over Granville Street Bridge. "UBC is just minutes away by car."

"Are you trying to sell me on this place?"

"Maybe just a little."

"Peter, you know I'm not going to just move in with you. You know I don't do that."

Peter sat down on the sofa, clasped his hands together and rested his chin on them. "You don't have to."

Annika had never seen Peter like this before. He looked nervous. Almost sad. She wondered if he was going to tell her it was all over. She could only stand there, staring at him. "What's wrong?"

"The last weeks have given me some serious pause."

Oh no. "You mean, to think about things?"

Peter nodded, looking up at Annika. "Yeah."

"And what have you thought?"

"That there's nothing in my life more important than you." He pulled out a small black box from his pocket and held it up.

Annika stood there, staggered and wide-eyed. Peter opened the box. Inside was a thick gold ring carrying a massive princess-cut diamond solitaire. It sparkled brilliantly in the sun-filled room. Annika gasped. Peter got down on his knees, and when he looked up at Annika, his steel blue eyes almost glowed in the sunlight.

"Will you be my wife, Annika Guthrie?"

Annika nearly lost her balance. For a moment she forgot about her master's thesis, Chromogen, even Dr. Lindell. She remembered how wonderful Peter had been in the last five months. How wonderful it would be to continue that. For life. Her eyes welled up with tears. "Of course I will. Of course!"

Peter got up and embraced her with a long kiss. He took the ring out of the box and slipped it on her finger.

"It fits perfectly!" Annika said.

"Your mother was very helpful in that department. Now watch this." Peter walked up to the window and drew the double lined curtains shut, darkening the room except for a single beam of gleaming sunlight coming though a small slit. He took her hand and held the diamond in the path of the light. Instantly, the ceiling and walls were awash in a thousand small, brightly gleaming rainbows.

"It's so beautiful," Annika said. She wiped her sleeve across her eyes to take away the tears.

Peter reopened the curtains and started walking to the dining table where two envelopes sat in the center, but was cut off halfway when the phone rang. He backed up to the coffee table in front of the sofa, saw the number, and hit the speaker button.

"Hi, Alex," Peter said. "You're on speaker."

"So how freely can I speak?" Alex said.

"I just asked."

"Way to go, kid! Did she accept?"

"Of course I did," Annika said loudly from the other side of the room.

"Good choice, kid. How do you like the three carats of Canadian diamond?"

Annika looked at Peter. He flushed slightly. "I was going to tell you the diamond was a gift from Alex. But I got the band," Peter said.

"Don't worry, kid. It's conflict free, straight from the Ekati mines in the Northwest Territories."

"Thank you, Alex. That's very generous of you."

"Well, I hate to interrupt your moment of rapture, but there's big news on TV you may be interested in."

Peter picked up the remote and switched it on to the financial news. "What's going on?"

"Avarus Pharmaceuticals just bought out Chromogen," Alex said. "But there's a twist."

"Wow! Look at that!" Peter said, looking at the streaming stock quotes. The ticker for Chromogen was flowing by showing a 23-percent increase on the day. Mitogenica was down by 9 percent. The presenter came on and commented on the buyout being a big surprise since Mitogenica was touted to have the better drug waiting for FDA approval. Sadly, the CEO of Avarus had died in a head-on collision with a truck just two days before the announcement, and the Avarus board unanimously voted in Arthur Cormack, CEO of Chromogen, to be the acting CEO of Avarus until further notice. Annika came crashing back down to earth and stood there, flabbergasted at the new power now held by Arthur Cormack, the man who also held her future in his evil, greedy, and murderous hands. Peter threw a look of understanding in her direction and muted the TV.

"Now, that kind of thing is just unheard of," Alex said.

"Ouch! What happened to your investments?" Peter asked, trying to steer the conversation in a different direction.

"I'm a trader, kid! I got rid of Mitogenica days ago, at a great profit."

Peter was dumbfounded. "Really? Just days ago?"

"Well, have fun on your trip and don't gamble too much."

Peter grimaced and looked at the phone as if it was Alex himself. "Uh, I didn't get to that part yet, Alex."

"Oops! Sorry, kid. I'll leave you to it. You better get packing." Alex hung up.

"What's he talking about?" Annika asked.

Peter walked to the table and picked up the envelopes. He brought them over and let Annika open one. It was a plane ticket, first-class, for Vegas. Annika gasped.

"Vegas? This leaves at five tonight! That's just four hours from now!"

Peter held up his good arm. "You can always say no."

"You mean you want to get married this weekend?"

"It's no honeymoon, especially with this," Peter said, holding up his cast.

"I really wanted a proper church service with family and friends."

"Of course! But that takes a long time to put together." He put his arm around her. The bright blue sky stood behind him. "You'll be here in just two months." He have her a leading look.

Annika didn't understand. "And?"

"And we won't have to wait anymore."

At those words, Annika could feel her heart sink. It was another example of how nothing was going right for her. Was her life cursed? She looked down at the floor. "Yeah, we will."

"What do you mean?"

"It's that time of the month."

Frustration flashed across Peter's face just for a second. But he regained his smile quickly. Almost too fast, for a man who had been waiting for intimacy so many months—and would still have to. "It's OK. I love you. Let's get married."

Annika had never done anything crazy in her life. But being with Peter made her forget all about what lay waiting for her back in Cleveland. And for the last year it seemed that everything she messed up, Peter helped to fix again. He had been right about so many things. For a year in which everything had gone so wrong, maybe it would now start going right. Starting with this.

Annika nodded. "OK. Let's go. But on one condition."

"Sure. What?"

"You tell me what happened to you!"

Peter smiled. "That will be the most boring part of the trip, I assure you."

New York

"Mr. Hayes will be arriving shortly, sir."

"Thank you, that's fine. Go wait for him," Nolan replied to his security staffer. He looked back at the screen hanging in his office. It showed the image of a man's silhouette, obscured by smoke.

"When will your hardware be arriving?" Smoke asked in his hoarse, raspy voice.

"Next week. May I ask the urgency behind me building a replica of Lindell's Gen-Silico in my residence?" Ever since Sydney delivered the final hardware specs on Lindell's system four months ago, it had been Smoke's top priority to actually build the thing in Nolan's own office.

"You may not ask."

"How am I supposed to operate it?"

"I will send some people to do that for you."

"And then what?"

"They'll use it, you belligerent idiot!" Smoke's voice thundered from the loud-speakers.

Nolan didn't like being left out of The Trust's most important plans. This was not a good sign. He couldn't hold back. "For what?"

"Tell me about the support group for Lindell's trials."

"Still waiting for something. We're watching closely." For once, Nolan had been smart enough not to mention the possibility of a big break in the information flow. Fewer expectations meant fewer failures. Sydney's disappointment today would be dealt with internally.

"You do understand, Nolan, that The Trust cherishes transparency above all other qualities in its people."

Nolan studied the smoke-veiled image of a faceless shadow on his screen. "I see your point."

Smoke started to grumble, when the elevator door with direct access into the penthouse opened. But it wasn't Austin Hayes that stepped out. It was a man Nolan had never seen before. His thick white hair, bushy eyebrows, and severely weathered face placed him at about sixty. He was tall and gaunt, with slightly hollow cheeks, but his movements were quick and strong.

"Who are you? How did you get past security?" Nolan yelled.

"This is Roy Orvis Ingram. He is going to shadow you for a while."

Nolan's knees nearly buckled. The situation was clearly getting out of hand.

Roy walked over to Nolan and extended his hand, grasping Nolan's in a grip of cold stone. A scar ran down his left cheek starting at the top of the cheekbone and ending at mid-height of the face. It reminded Nolan of the elite old-money fraternities in Germany, where membership was impossible without expertise in fencing and courage that bordered on foolhardiness. The proof of both was to sport sunglasses and let your fencing partner swipe his foil downward across your face, aiming first at the sunglasses. It left exactly the kind of lifelong scar that Roy had.

"My friends call me Orvis. You can call me Roy," he said.

Nolan looked up at the screen in desperation. "But I've got everything under control."

"Good. Then Roy's job will be easy," Smoke replied.

"I don't need help."

Smoke ignored the plea. "Roy will manage the computer programmers when they arrive. Everything he asks, you do."

Nolan bowed his head in shame. "Understood."

The elevator opened. Roy moved to the darkened back corner of the office as Austin Hayes stepped out, accompanied by the driver and one of Nolan's security staff. Nolan regained his demeanor and walked over.

"Mr. Hayes, welcome. You're just in time for the briefing."

Austin looked around, impressed with the artwork and décor. "What is this place?"

"Think of it as the place of no return," Nolan said, as he took him to the screen in his office.

Austin stared in nervous fascination at the dark figure on the screen. Smoke's voice thundered, "Wrong again, Nolan. Mr. Hayes passed that point the moment he rode the elevator to the penthouse with you at the Regency-Excelsior five years ago. Didn't you, Mr. Hayes?"

SUMMER

———

CHAPTER FOURTEEN

———

Friday, June 10
Strathmore Mews
Downtown Vancouver, B.C.

Annika rested for a moment in front of the wall of glass that looked out on Vancouver's skyline under the pink and orange sky of an evening sun. She glanced down and moved her hand in the sunlight, watching her ring sparkle and trying to gain some assurance by it. The two months of living apart from Peter after their marriage in Vegas had been painful—especially because he never got a single chance to visit her. It was odd, for someone who had been so eager for intimacy before the marriage. And it wasn't like Peter to be so distant. She tried to understand that he was under severe pressure in his new job at Cypress Turbines. He was, after all, working for the CEO and traveling constantly. But what worried her was how different Peter had become. Was it the pressure of his job? Was it her own pressure? She had just defended her master's thesis two days ago in Cleveland. Peter had vowed up and down before to be there. But in the end he didn't have the time. The old Peter might have had disagreements with her, but he came through for her every time. It was such a disappointment to stay up all night alone, making the necessary revisions to her text. She handed in her final copy of the master's thesis yesterday. Then she took the plane out to Vancouver this morning. Her sparse possessions had been air freighted, and she had spent the day moving them into Peter's—no, their—home. The last of her boxes was already put away in the office. The dinner table stood polished clean and set for six. Annika was exhausted. The door buzzer sounded. Annika ran and opened the door. Peter came in loaded with several bags in each hand. The smell of hot Chinese food filled the apartment. He gave her a quick peck on the cheek and set the food on the table.

"Sorry I'm late!" Peter said. "It was a killer day at the office."

Annika started setting the food out. The smell grew stronger with each box she took out of the bags. Annika's mouth began to water. She realized she hadn't eaten lunch on the plane and it was past nine p.m. Cleveland time. Minutes later, the door buzzer rang again. Peter opened the door to his parents, Thomas, and Uncle Alex.

Alex beamed at Annika. "Hey, kid, you look great! Marriage definitely becomes you!"

Greetings were exchanged by all and they sat down to eat. Alex looked around the place and let his gaze settle on Peter's father, Joseph.

"How do you like the place, Annika?" Alex asked. There was clearly some bragging going on.

"The views are wonderful," she said. There was a hint of reservation in her voice.

"But?" Alex asked.

"Well, eventually we'll need something bigger."

"Then Pete had better keep working hard."

"So, Peter tells us you're starting your PhD with Dr. Lindell?" Peter's mother asked.

Annika nodded with a smile. "I start on Monday."

Peter's mother was shocked. "That's fast! If you need help with anything this week, just let me know."

"Thank you, but actually I'm not going to be here."

"Where are you going to be?" Peter's mother asked.

"Dr. Lindell is sending me to the International Conference on Alternative Medicine for Cancer in Switzerland. I leave on Monday."

"Talk about fast!" Alex said. "Are you presenting?"

Annika grimaced. "I'm not allowed to publish anything from my master's. I'm just going to listen."

Peter smiled. "Speaking of which, I have some news for everyone."

Peter's parents looked up.

Alex glared at Annika's belly. "What, already?"

"No!" Peter said. "I managed to get some time off at work. I'm flying with Annika to Switzerland."

"Like a honeymoon!" Alex said. "Nice work, kid!"

Peter turned to Annika. "I almost forgot! Thomas asked if we could pick up a book for him in Zurich."

Peter's brother spoke up. "It's a rare three-hundred-year-old account of the Anabaptist movement in Switzerland for my continuing studies. I'm really afraid it would be damaged in the mail."

Annika shrugged. "Of course."

"Someone from the Swiss Baptist Union will meet us there with the book," Peter said.

"And take a few pictures for my scrapbook, please!" Thomas added.

Peter pointed to his camera sitting on the kitchen counter. "It's all charged and ready to go."

The conversation continued until Annika was unable to keep her eyes open. Eventually, Peter's family left and he took Annika out onto the small balcony for some fresh air. Annika felt awake again and was mesmerized by the view of Vancouver's skyline at night. To the left, the reflected lights of Granville Island shimmered in the rippling waters of False Creek. The expanse of the city to the south glistened with thousands of lights as far as the eye could see. Annika breathed a sigh of relief and hugged Peter closely to her. She finally felt at ease. She was settled. And now she could begin the rest of her life. Even with today's news, Chromogen and Arthur Cormack seemed far away. And Dr. Lindell's research was looking more promising than ever.

Seven Mile Beach
Grand Cayman Island

"Are you sure you're doing the right thing?" Linda asked her husband.

Tyler Evans turned to look at her from their sixth-story balcony of the Royal Tortuga Grand Hotel. "Of course I am."

She walked over and put her arms around him. "You don't need to impress me, you know."

Linda was a breast cancer survivor that Tyler had treated at his clinic in Tijuana eight years ago. After repeated visits and treatments, they had fallen in love. She was ten years his junior and beautiful in every way.

"You of all people should want this," Tyler said.

"I do. Just not like this."

"Then how?"

"It's Dr. Lindell's formula. Let him go public with it."

Tyler shook his head. "That will never happen. He works for Mitogenica now."

Linda sighed. "You don't know that."

"Ian Ponce is there today. We'll give Lindell his chance."

Linda stood back and looked at her husband dubiously. She went back inside the air-conditioned room for some water. He knew that look. It said she knew something was wrong but didn't want to know what. There were other things about him she hadn't wanted to know. His past improprieties with female patients that had stripped him of his license to practice medicine in the U.S. The other patients of the Tijuana clinic he had been with before her. The incident with the armed men in the Vancouver Public Library back in April. And now, that his clinic was stockpiling all the key ingredients of Lindell's formula. Or at least Tyler's version of it. Tyler knew as soon as he went public there would be massive demand. Which was why he wasn't disclosing all the ingredients in his version of Lindell's formula to anyone. Linda never needed to know the details. But she would enjoy the benefits that came later. Starting with many more vacations just like this one.

Tyler turned to face the Caribbean Sea and drew the mist-laden sea air deeply into his lungs. The surf crashed on the beach just a stone's throw from the hotel. Each wave brought countless white flecks of sunlight, shimmering under the midday sun. The water at the beach was such a bright blue-green, it set aglow the deep emerald needles of the Australian pine trees which stood in a row along the shoreline.

Linda came out and handed Tyler a tall glass of chilled water. The glass instantly was coated in fine droplets of condensation from the humid sea air. "You just got an email from the clinic."

Tyler immediately went in and got on his laptop. "This is it! I can complete the paper now! Look!"

"What?" She came around to see a graph.

"Still a hundred percent cure rate with the rats!"

"Too bad I'm not a rat," Linda said with a grin.

Tyler wanted to answer that comment but held his tongue. After Ian Ponce received treatment, Tyler was emboldened and started treating several other patients at the clinic with the new formula. Free of charge. They would be the subjects of his next publication. He looked up at Linda. "If you were a rat I'd still love you."

"As long as you weren't a cat. So tell me, why are they going to let you present this little revolution instead of your original boring review paper?"

"They aren't. Everyone comes up at the last minute with the latest revision on a flash drive."

"And this is your latest revision?"

Tyler nodded. "Exactly."

"Well, if anyone is sleeping this will wake them up fast."

"I'm counting on it," Tyler said. He glanced at his watch. "Ian must be there by now."

"What's he going to do?"

"Tell Lindell everything."

"And if Dr. Lindell doesn't believe you?"

Tyler shrugged. "Ian is cured of his cancer. And I'll send out my paper to him tomorrow with the formula. That's proof enough. Then we'll see what he does."

"You're going to get yourself into trouble."

Tyler sat down at the desk and brought up a video screen on the laptop. A webcam sat next to the laptop on the desk. Tyler slid a recordable DVD into the laptop's player. Tyler plugged in the webcam and adjusted it until it showed the chair sitting just a few feet away from desk.

"Honey, can you please draw the sheers over the window? We need diffused light."

Linda walked over and obliged.

"Ah. Perfect," Tyler said. He walked to the chair and sat. He looked up at Linda. "How do I look?"

"Like you're on vacation."

"OK. Let's make some history. Roll it."

Linda scrolled with the mouse until it found the right place. She clicked, and the record button lit up. The DVD started spinning in its drive.

Tyler lost his smile and spoke slowly and clearly. "Hello, Dr. Lindell. My name is Tyler Evans. Six months ago you cured some friends of mine of terminal cancer in your trial with Mitogenica, using a formula that shouldn't exist. We analyzed and replicated that formula. And now we're going to tell the world."

The Center for Natural Medicine
Vancouver, B.C.

Carter Feldman smiled as he held the door open for Ian Ponce. As Ian entered Lindell's office, Carter managed to restrain himself from explaining that he was not the doorman. Ian looked around the lab and was impressed with all the high-tech equipment. Well, that's how it was supposed to be. Lindell liked to bring his patients into his lab at least once so they would gain some confidence from seeing the high level of sophistication. Too bad the other technicians weren't here today.

Lindell led Ian to the far end of the lab where his desk sat in the corner opposite the room which held the Gen-Silico supercomputer. In between the two was Carter's desk. Lindell had arranged his computer monitors so their backs were facing Carter.

"Mr. Ponce, please sit down," Lindell said.

Carter always resented how Lindell treated his patients—so much differently than how he treated his most important lab technician. Lindell respected his patients. He was nice to them.

Ian Ponce sat down in the chair across from Lindell's desk as Carter went to his own desk and started pulling up the latest MRI results from the day before. As Carter typed away, he noticed something odd about Ian. This was not the typical face of a man dying of cancer. This was a face of certainty and purpose. A face looking into the future. He had never seen that before with any patient in this trial. Or any other cancer trial.

Lindell spoke. "I'm sorry, Mr. Ponce, but I have not had a chance to look over your new baseline data yet. We were just given the file a few minutes ago from the University Hospital." Lindell looked over to Carter as the computer hard drive whirred away, dumping its data into the memory for processing. *Oh, great,* thought Carter, *now he's going to blame me for this?* After all, Ian Ponce did insist on an appointment the very next day after his baseline test. His second baseline test.

Ian smiled. "No problem. Actually, I must apologize for all the trouble I caused you when I dropped out of the trial last month, just after the first baseline tests."

"Trials never go as we think they will," Lindell said.

Ian smiled. "Tell me about it."

"So, after this we'll review your treatment schedule and the follow-up visits to check your progress." Lindell eyed Carter, impatiently waiting for the data.

Finally, colorized MRI scans of the prostate area popped up on the screen. Carter sent the images to Lindell's screens. It was not a good picture. The first baseline scans showed several cancerous nodules in both lobes of the prostate and extending beyond the prostate capsule at several sites. There were indications of a slight urethral obstruction and numerous but small nodules on the bladder and rectum. That gave the tumor a stage of T4. Several regional lymph nodes were positive, but they were all smaller than five centimeters across, yielding a stage of N2. At least the cancer was still contained within the pelvic region, leaving the metastatic staging at M0. Carter flipped through the records. A biopsy taken at baseline had also revealed a Gleason score of 4. He looked at the micro photographs. They showed sheets of cells with randomly scattered lumens. They were no longer able to organize into complete gland units. Damn. Not good. The blood work showed a Prostate Specific Antigen level of 14.8 nanograms per milliliter, well beyond the normal upper limit of 4.0 nanograms per milliliter. PSA velocity, the rate at which PSA levels were increasing, was a dangerously high 0.27 nanograms per milliliter per month. Every time Carter saw numbers like that it made him squirm because he knew how bad the prognosis was.

"Those are from last month," Carter said. He scrolled down his file list, brought up the scans from the day before, and sent them over as well. "Here are yesterday's." When the MRI images came up on the screen, both Carter and Lindell nearly fell off their seats. The regional lymph nodes all appeared perfectly normal in size. There were no visible nodules on the rectum or bladder. The prostate itself was nearly completely normal in appearance. Only a single small cancerous nodule was visible, completely contained in the left lobe of the prostate. A cancer that was at T4 N2 M0 one month ago was now at T1 N0 M0. It was impossible. Carter pulled up the blood work results. The PSA was down to 5.7 nanograms per milliliter. Carter's mouth dropped open. It was nearly normal. All of that, without any treatment at all. The odds of spontaneous remission were so small that he had never expected to see one in his entire career.

"Carter, can you please double-check the dates on these files?" Lindell asked, surprised as well.

Carter's fingers danced on the keyboard, and the files listed on the screen. He slid his finger down until he came to the right two.

"The dates check out," Carter said. He eyed the pictures again side by side. The major blood vessels and bones were definitely the same. There was no mistake. *Too bad this wasn't a result of taking Lindell's formula*, Carter thought. He could probably get twenty grand for news like that.

Lindell raised his eyebrows. "I have some good news for you, Mr. Ponce."

"You mean, like the cancer is all gone?" Ian asked rhetorically.

"How did you know that?" Lindell asked. He was starting to look puzzled. Carter rarely saw Lindell look puzzled at anything.

"Because last week I had CAT scans done down in Tijuana," Ian said.

"Tijuana?" Lindell asked, mystified. "Why?"

"To prove that we have replicated your magic formula." Ian had the smile of a poker player who had just delivered a royal flush on a table with a full pot.

Carter immediately perked up. Something was happening and he had no idea what. With a few rapid keystrokes, he started recording the conversation using the microphone on his webcam.

"What on earth are you talking about?" Lindell asked with a straight face. But he fumbled with his pen and pad of paper, and had to slap them clumsily against his thigh with his hand before they fell to the ground.

Ian sat back in his chair. "Dr. Lindell, do the names Jim Caldicott, Raj Prahalad, and Janet Riedman mean anything to you?"

Lindell's eyes shot down to his leg. "No. Should they?" His voice wavered and he gripped his pen and paper tightly in his hand. Had Carter just seen Dr. Lindell lying? Carter made a search through his records on all the names as fast as he could. He certainly didn't know them. And they weren't in the records.

"Yes, they should. You cured them all of their cancers," Ian said.

That stopped Carter in his tracks. He looked to Lindell, who was now sweating. He actually looked worried. Carter had never seen him like this. Lindell tried to regain his composure.

"I certainly can't discuss any other patients in the trial," Lindell said.

"That's the problem. Everyone in Mitogenica's trial gets Mitaxynil and one of your three natural supplement cocktails."

"Everyone knows that," Lindell said.

"But the three that were cured just got your cocktail. The fourth cocktail. So they're not really in the trial, are they?"

Carter nearly fell off his seat. He was only aware of three formulas that Lindell was using. He felt the blood draining from his face and the floor fall out from beneath him. Lindell had found his cure and was testing it already?

Lindell looked limp. He wiped the sweat from the top of his head with a trembling hand. "That's impossible for you to know."

Ian explained how they had tested the pills and IV solutions given to every patient. How Tyler had analyzed the cocktails at labs in Mexico and one by one replicated the formula. How they had tested it on dozens of rats with a 100 percent cure rate. How they were going to go public with it at two international cancer conferences, first on Grand Cayman Monday morning, then in Switzerland just days later. As Carter took all this in, his heart rate started going ballistic. Now others knew about it, too? And were about to go public? Carter looked frantically at the door. He had to get out and tell Sydney.

Lindell slowly shook his head. "I need more time. I have to prove this in a larger trial with human patients." His voice was rising.

"And when is that going to be?"

"I can start in about two years."

"That's too late. People will die!" Ian said loudly.

"But the formula's not ready yet!" Lindell said, almost yelling.

"It looks ready to me!" Ian yelled back, pointing at the monitors with his MRIs.

"Is it? Look! You still have your cancer." Lindell showed Ian the small remaining clusters of cancerous cells.

Ian stood there, dumbfounded. "But the CAT scans came back clean."

"They might if you used outdated machines."

Ian sat down heavily on the nearest chair. "I was so sure."

Lindell pointed at the monitor. "This is what happens when you don't get the science right. Let me get it right! Please!"

Ian looked down at the floor and shook his head. He spoke quietly. "I don't believe you. You work for Mitogenica now."

"Only to get their experimental data! It helped me complete my model!"

"You'll get proof that we replicated your formula first thing Monday morning via courier."

"And when does Tyler give his talk?"

"At eleven fifteen Cayman time. That's nine fifteen here."

"That's very little time," Lindell said.

"Trust me, you can get used to that concept," Ian said. Ian handed Lindell a card.

"What's this?"

"My number here, and Tyler's at the Royal Tortuga Hotel. If you change your mind, call us." Ian started for the door. He put his hand on the doorknob.

Lindell called out, "If you wait, I'll give you the real formula. Today."

Ian froze on the spot. Carter couldn't believe that Lindell was using Ian's life as a bargaining chip. But then again, it was Ian who pulled the first hand. Carter could not imagine what was going through Ian's mind, but he knew in Ian's place, he would have taken the offer instantly.

Ian didn't turn back. He kept looking straight out to the hallway. "There's far more than my life at stake here."

"That's why I'm begging you to wait!" Lindell pleaded.

Unbelievably, Ian Ponce walked out the door without another word. Lindell looked again at the MRIs on the screen and wiped the hairless crown of his head several times with his hand.

Carter stared blankly at Lindell. "I thought I knew all the trial participants."

"Those were never going to be included in the trial," Lindell said.

"So when did they come in?"

"Saturdays. When you weren't here."

"But why?" Carter typed as quietly as he could and immediately started searching through all other subdirectories besides the usual data files. There! Hidden among Lindell's plant extract database were suspiciously large subdirectories. Three of them. One for each of the patients. Carter pulled them up.

"In less than two years I will begin enrollment in the most important alternative cancer treatment study ever. I wanted to be ready with the right formulation."

"By slipping a few guinea pigs into Mitogenica's trial?" Carter silently slid his thirty-two-gigabyte flash drive in the USB port of his server and started copying the files.

"I was going to put them back on the proper drugs if they didn't respond favorably," Lindell said. He started typing on his own workstation. To Carter's horror, the very files he was copying were being deleted as he watched. But he was sure Lindell had no idea what he was up to. When the directories were emptied, Carter saw that he had managed to get about half the data. That was enough. He had their names, too. He copied the recording he had made on the memory stick and slowly withdrew it. Lindell stood up and started for the door.

"Where are you going?" Carter asked.

"I have to get more analysis done on Mr. Ponce's blood samples." Lindell disappeared.

Carter nodded as he pocketed the memory stick. His mind was spinning at high speed. He was going to have some serious damage control to do. Not only that, but his many months of projected cash flow had just come to a screeching halt. The end game was already in play. Carter exited the Center for Natural Medicine and started heading for the Student Union Building. He felt like a little boy who had not only dropped the ball but watched it go rolling down a hopelessly steep and large hill, only to be crushed into a hundred pieces by a large truck speeding by down below. He closed his eyes in deep thought. Wait. There was still a way he could turn this to his advantage.

* * *

Ian Ponce walked beside the grassy boulevard of Main Mall. Lindell's offer was still reverberating in his mind, and he couldn't help but wonder if that was the stupidest decision he ever made. He tried to calm himself. The campus was peaceful. It was relatively empty this time of year, except for a core population of grad students and the professors who were scrambling to fit most of their year's research into the summer months. Tyler found shade from the midday sun under a row of massive red oaks, with dense green branches that spanned the sidewalk and half the grassy lane. He dialed his phone, cursing when he got Tyler's voicemail. He tried again, with the same result.

"Damn it, Tyler!" he said under his breath. He dialed the hotel.

"Royal Tortuga Grand Hotel, how may I help you?"

"Put me through to Tyler Evans, please." Ian waited until the call rang through.

"Hello?" a familiar voice said.

"Damn it, Tyler, why is your cell phone off?"

There was fumbling on the other side. "Sorry! Batteries ran out."

"You have to be reachable twenty-four-seven now!"

"I'll fix it. Did you tell Lindell?"

"Yes," Ian said. He wondered if he should really tell Tyler everything.

"How did he take it?"

"He wants two more years."

"That's too long."

"Yeah. Are you ready?"

"I got the final data from the lab last night," Tyler said.

"I asked if you're ready!" Ian said angrily. Several students picnicking on the grass looked up and started to stare. He glanced away.

"Hey! What's with you?"

Ian stopped walking. "The cancer isn't all gone."

"My God, I'm so sorry," Tyler said.

"Maybe I just need more treatments," Ian said. He knew that was speculation.

"I fly direct to Zurich from here on Monday. But come to the clinic next week. We'll fix you up."

"When will you finish the paper?"

"Tonight."

"Good. Once you present at the conferences, I'll post the paper on the blog."

"You've got the clinic's phone number and email, right?"

"Yes. In bold print."

"We're making history, my friend. Hang in there," Tyler said.

That was far less comforting than a clean MRI. "I'm trying to."

"Listen, I may not be reachable Sunday morning."

"Just before the conference starts? Why not?" Ian asked.

Tyler hesitated. "We're heading up to Rum Point for some sun."

"Fine. Call me when you get back." Ian hung up and shook his head in disgust. He still had his cancer but Tyler was off to smell the roses. Ian put the thought out of his mind and walked on to his car. He knew he was doing the right thing. It was strange, though, that it felt like such a mistake.

UBC Campus
Vancouver, B.C.

Carter walked through the south entrance of the Student Union Building and hauled his flabby body up the stairs in four massive strides. He walked to his normal corner where all the student body government offices were. The halls were deserted. He had no doubts that this morning's development qualified as an emergency. The palms of his hands were sweating profusely. He wiped them on his jeans and dialed Sydney's number.

"Carter? This is a surprise. What's happening?"

Carter went through the entire scene he had just witnessed between Lindell and Ian Ponce. The cures. The Tijuana lab. The mice. The plans to go public. Everything minus the names. Sydney said nothing during the entire story.

Finally, she spoke. "You did the right thing calling me, Carter. That's wonderful news."

"It is? Yes, I guess it is."

"Did you get any names?"

Of course she was going to ask that. "Yes, and most of their medical files."

"How?" Sydney asked, starting to use that helpless tone again.

"I found them hidden away in Dr. Lindell's files."

"That's perfect. When can I get the information?"

"Well, that's a problem," Carter said. The phone almost slipped out of his sweaty hand. He tried to dry it on his shirt.

"Why?" Sydney sounded almost hurt.

Here it comes. Carter knew he had to bargain over the phone. He would never be able to pull it off in person. "This is special information." He started to waver. He had to get a grip. He had rehearsed this in his head already. "I need fifty thousand for the names and files. And another fifty thousand for the data arriving from Cayman Island." Carter stammered the last words before his pounding heart made him stop for a deep breath. He could feel each heartbeat in his ears. He had no idea how Sydney would handle this.

"I'll need a few days to come up with that kind of money. But I'll tell you what. You give me the names of the people right now, and I'll agree to your terms." She took that surprisingly well.

"So when can we meet?" Carter asked, pressing the point.

"Monday. I'll let you know the place later."

"OK." Carter gave her the three names of the patients cured of their cancer in Lindell's trials. For a brief flash, Carter realized that there were real people attached to each of these names. But Sydney was harmless. She just wanted information.

"Thank you for the names. And Carter?"

"Yes?"

"Thank you again for trusting me. I knew I could count on you." Her tone was unmistakably romantic.

Now that the deal was made, Carter allowed himself the luxury of fantasizing about Sydney as she spoke. He adored her high cheekbones and eyebrows which looked like they were always half raised in a look of questioning. He loved the smell of her perfume and the touch of her long legs as they rubbed against his under the table. Just once it would be nice to have her run her fingers through his hair. He started to feel those warm tingles running through his body again. "You can always count on me," he said. He was jelly.

Sydney spoke again. This time seriously. "Just one more thing."

"Yes?"

"Tell nobody about this. I really mean nobody."

"Of course not."

"Good. Because if you do, I can't guarantee your safety."

Sydney's words hit him like a plank of wood across the face, and Carter's fantasy vaporized in an instant. Was that a threat? Did she know about Sam? He stammered back, "OK."

"Good. I'm glad we understand each other," she said, and hung up.

Carter struggled to calm himself as he walked back down the stairs into the main area of the Student Union Building. He pointed himself toward the snack shop. He desperately needed sugar. Of course she didn't know about Sam. That was an idle threat. She was only taking care of her own interests. He would wait a few minutes, then he was going to call Sam and get the same price. Or better. She would never know. Even if she found out, it would be too late. Because by this time next week he would be in Toronto with his mother. She had gone by her maiden name ever since the divorce twelve years ago. He would lie low for a year or so with no official address or phone number attached to his name. With his quarter of a million dollars, cash. It would be perfect.

CHAPTER FIFTEEN

—

Saturday, June 11
Vancouver, B.C.

Sydney Vale couldn't help thinking about yesterday's conversation with Nolan as she drove her car along Inglis Drive toward the small parking lot at Vancouver International Airport's South Terminal. He had been infuriated about the sudden and unforeseen turn of events, but had agreed to come up with the money with only the slightest hesitation. She was almost surprised when he called less than two hours later, telling her that he had a private jet reserved for her to go to the Caymans Saturday night. Damn, they were fast. But Sydney no longer marveled at anything The Trust could pull off. They had, after all, recruited her and Andrei six years ago directly out of *Glavnoye Razvedyvatel'noye Upraveleniye*, the Russian foreign military intelligence directorate. They had even supplied the bodies as a perfect cover to an explosives exercise gone horribly wrong. It was an easy choice. Her next assignment would have had her living out of a shack in Chechnya. It took a few months to perfect their English and falsify rock-solid backgrounds. Stalina Rzymski and Andrei Petrov were then truly dead. Sydney Patricia Vale and Owen Blake Sarton were very much alive. She resented like hell that the fat little jerk Carter was going to walk away with a hundred thousand for doing nothing more than being in the right place. The Trust paid her less than that to kill their mid-level targets. She and Owen had been saving every penny in a secret account, but it would take many more years before they could comfortably retire. Especially after the mishap last year. She shook her head and tried not to bite her lip as she parked her car and got out. The Trust had gotten into a turf war with the Italian mob over some businesses in the south of Italy. She and Owen were sent in to take out several members of the very powerful and troublesome Dostinelli family. Sydney still vividly remembered breaking into the empty Dostinelli stronghold just north of the Vatican in Rome. Intelligence told them the entire family was out that afternoon, attending the funeral of former family leader, Umberto Dostinelli. The timing was perfect—when the family was in a temporary leadership vacuum. Simple explosives would look and smell like a competing mob hit. But as Sydney and Owen planted the bombs, the trap was sprung and twenty armed men stormed the house, surrounding them in the main gallery. Sydney threw her bomb directly at them, knowing they would never shoot for fear of detonating it. As it flew through the air, she was the one who shot. The blast killed four Dostinellis but also blew Owen and her straight out the second-story windows and onto the Via Cola di Rienzo. She couldn't even remember how she made it to her car with two burst eardrums, a concussion, a dislocated left shoulder, and a broken leg. She did remember the searing pain of cuts all over her body. Somewhere along the drive, she had become aware that Owen was in the car with her and near death himself. By the time she got to the safe house, she had lost two liters of blood and was going into deep shock. Nolan sent them both to fully recover in Vancouver while playing the corporate espionage game. For far less money. That had started to change with the hits on Mitch Purcell and the other Chromogen patients. But Sydney was livid that Nolan refused to let her handle the more high-profile Gian Muratte assassination. He may have been CEO of Avarus Pharmaceuticals, but he was also married to Maria Dostinelli, heiress to the Dostinelli family's mob operations in Italy. That would have been a fitting payback for what happened in Rome two years earlier. But Nolan wanted to avoid sending in a known face, whether she was skilled at concealing herself or not. That was fine. She would still have her day, Sydney kept telling herself.

Sydney left her car and walked to the terminal building. The South Terminal was small, fast, and private. It was only used for corporate charters, float planes, and a couple of regional airlines. *This will be fast*, she thought, as she patted her purse by her side. Her baggage was waiting for her on the plane. Minutes later, she had her clearance and walked out onto the tarmac, escorted by the co-pilot. She couldn't help but cast a broad smile when she saw it. A Bombardier Challenger 605 equipped with two GE CF34 turbofan engines. She had always envied the pilots in *Voyenno-vozdushnye sily Rossii*, the Russian Air Force. She had dated a training pilot once just to get a ride in a Sukhoi-27 trainer. She never did get to fly in a MiG-29. The corporate jet she was now in was as close as she would get to her dreams. But as dreams go, this wasn't bad either. The nine boardroom-style seats were covered in racing green leather with hardwood trim that set off the polished wood veneer paneling throughout the cabin. Then there was the wet bar. Luxury bathroom. And gold trim finished it all off with the unmistakable message: the rich fly here.

"You have a package waiting for you," the co-pilot said. He joined the captain in the cockpit.

The engines were already starting as Sydney walked past the three-seat divan toward the club seating at the back. Between the two facing seats on the right sat a large black hardshell suitcase. She grabbed on to it to steady herself as the plane pulled out toward the runway at a fast clip. Sydney opened the case to find multiple compartments inside. The most important was on top. It contained a cold bag with a thick, insulated casing. She opened it. There were three glass vials with shiny steel fittings at each end. Each vial bore a bright yellow triangle with the international biohazard symbol. She marveled at where Nolan had sourced this so quickly. Sydney closed the insulated casing and removed another beside it. It contained three large spines, each as long as her hand, mounted on a grip and plunger device designed to mate with the metal fittings on the glass vials. She took one out and lightly touched the tip of her finger to it. A tiny red droplet of blood formed where the spine had made contact. Impressive.

The engines picked up speed and the plane rolled out onto the runway. The captain's voice came on the intercom, warning that takeoff was in a minute. The seat-belt light flashed on. A small pink leather Prada purse was next. Sydney looked inside. Oakley sunglasses. Makeup. Magnetic card key apparently pre-configured for the Royal Tortuga Hotel. Fake passport of impeccable quality. The picture was perfect. She flipped through it. Several stamps already. Also in the purse was a car rental slip for a yellow jeep. Pickup at the airport tonight. Lower in the suitcase was the typical high-class tourist garb. Then scuba gear. Sandals, of the right size. Sunscreen. *Only a woman had the brains to pack a case this well*, thought Sydney.

Sydney looked at her watch. Eight thirty p.m. Cruising speed of about 530 miles per hour. Georgetown was 3,100 miles away. She did a quick calculation in her head. Just under six hours. Maybe better with today's tailwind. That would put her on the ground at five o'clock in the morning Cayman time. That meant she had to go to sleep soon. Sydney felt herself pushed back into her seat as the engines roared to full throttle. She watched the hangars of the South Terminal fall quickly behind as the jet rapidly accelerated down the runway. The nose gear lifted off the ground and the whole cabin seemed to tilt upward until it was near vertical. The runway and the Pacific Ocean below fell back quickly as the Challenger raced to find its cruising altitude. She looked around to remind herself that this plane ride was just for her. If she did well, perhaps she would finally move back into the work The Trust had originally recruited her for. The work that paid so much better. She breathed a sigh of relief knowing that the boring assignment in Vancouver was finally coming to an end.

Sunday, June 12
Grand Cayman Island

The single main road that encircled Grand Cayman along its perimeter was anything but peaceful during rush hour—on any given weekday it was packed with bumper-to-bumper traffic. Especially where it turned northward along Seven Mile Beach to become West Bay Road. But on the weekends, peace descended again on Grand Cayman and the traffic grew sparse. Tyler Evans and his wife Linda pulled out of the parking lot of the Royal Tortuga Hotel onto West Bay Road and headed south into the hot, sunny morning. Snorkel gear rented from the hotel filled the trunk, along with beach towels, bottled water, and plenty of sunscreen. Tyler glanced in the rearview mirror and paid no attention at all to the bright yellow jeep pulling out onto the road behind them from the parking lot across the road. Tyler read to his wife from the tourist guide as she drove.

"Look at this! Life can be so easy. Especially if you're willing to put up with a few mosquitoes."

"What does that mean?"

Tyler went on. Grand Cayman was once the very definition of a tropical paradise. Life had changed little on the island from the time of the original settlers in the early 1700s until the end of the nineteenth century. For generations, nature provided everything they needed, including all the building materials for their thatch houses, hats, shoes, and baskets. And unique to the Caymans was the special silver thatch palm. Its leaves were so resistant to the ravages of salt water that it became the main material used to make maritime rope—and was heavily sought after by fisherman and turtlers from Cuba and Jamaica. New leaves of the silver thatch palm were hung, dried, split, and then spun into three-stranded ropes 150 feet long. One coil of such rope could be taken to any grocery store on the island and exchanged for a pound of flour, a pound of sugar, a tin of syrup, a pint of kerosene, and a bar of soap. It was not much, but you could live on that in a peaceful, tropical paradise. And for generations, many did.

"Tell me if you see some," Linda said.

"See some what?" Tyler asked.

"Silver thatch palm! I want to see what they look like."

"Sure. Let's cut through the island at Frank Sound, after the lighthouse."

Forty minutes later, Linda turned north onto Frank Sound Drive, toward Old Man Bay and the Northside. Tyler buried himself further in his guidebook. As they drove past the Queen Elizabeth Botanic Park, he thrust his finger toward a group of trees to the left. "Hey! There they are! Silver thatch palm trees!" Tyler said excitedly, eyeing the tall, thin green trunks supporting large fans of palm leaves that were silvery white on their undersides.

Ahead, Tyler saw the sign on the right side of the road, "Welcome to Rum Point," painted on large wooden barrels that were stacked in front of a long column of palm trees. He motioned for Linda to turn off the road. As they unloaded their gear, Tyler was surprised to see the same the same yellow Jeep he had noticed earlier. It pulled in to the same parking lot, just half a minute after they did. Tyler closed the trunk of the rental car. He noticed an exquisitely shaped blonde woman exit the yellow jeep. She wore large sunglasses and a baseball cap pulled low. She smiled at him. Something seemed vaguely familiar about her. Did he know her? He quickly brushed the thought away as the full force of the day's heat hit him. It was ten o'clock in the morning and already the ninety-degree heat was becoming unbearable with the high humidity.

"Let's get to the water," Tyler said to his wife.

"I need something cold to drink," Linda said, pointing to the wooden restaurant shack up ahead. On the way, they passed a post with several rough-hewn planks nailed to it. One of the planks was painted purple, with bright green and blue lettering which read "Relax: You are on Cayman Time." Linda went for drinks while Tyler ducked into the changing room. He walked out toward the sparkling blue-green water of North Sound and the Caribbean Sea beyond it. Linda joined him and they passed another plank sign, with colorful planks pointing to multiple different countries. One of the north-pointing planks read "Canada eh?" Tyler wondered how Ian was doing. He felt terrible that the cancer wasn't gone after all. But he was sure they would get it right in the end. He and Linda set their towels and gear down in the shade of the towering Australian pines lining the beach. She put her things on the lounge chair and started to get settled.

"Maybe you'll see some stingrays today," Linda said.

"That's what I brought this for," Tyler said, holding up a small disposable underwater camera. With a kiss, he took his snorkel gear to the beach. The water felt warm as he waded in. A small group of children played near the long cement jetty to the right. Boats and snorkelers were scattered throughout the water close to the beach. Some snorkelers nearby shouted that a small school of stingrays was approaching. The kids on the jetty ran down to the end to get a closer look. Tyler swam in that direction.

He looked underwater through his mask and could see several faint dark shapes up ahead moving gracefully through the water. He popped his head above water to see Linda on the beach, perfecting her tan. But as he waved, he noticed the blonde woman in the water just a few meters behind him. Wasn't that the same one from the parking lot? He shrugged it off and headed for the school of stingrays. There was no law against beautiful women swimming near him.

Seconds later, he felt something tugging on his flap. He looked back to see the blonde woman smiling at him and waving in the water. Tyler's heartbeat picked up a bit when he saw she was wearing a very small bikini. He hoped Linda wasn't watching him now. He smiled back and slowed down. The blonde woman swam up next to him and pointed up ahead. He could see the stingrays getting closer, and nodded. He felt a quiver of adrenaline when the woman put her hand on his left shoulder and drew him gently closer. What was she doing? Her leg brushed against his. It was supremely smooth. Bubbles erupted from her mouthpiece as she spoke to him underwater. Tyler couldn't understand what she was trying to say. He let her pull him closer. Almost imperceptibly, she strengthened her grip on his left shoulder until it was quite firm and spoke again in a flurry of bubbles. Tyler still struggled to understand her. He then realized that her thumb had been wandering downward on his chest in three distinct movements, each time stopping between two ribs. As if she'd been counting them. Her smile suddenly disappeared, and was replaced by a grimace of extreme exertion. The grip on his shoulder was tighter than a steel vise, and her other arm thrust toward him at unbelievable speed. Before Tyler could react, a searing pain exploded deep in his chest. He screamed in a burst of muffled bubbles. Tyler pushed her away, expecting a fight to ensue. But she swam off at high speed. He started to calm from his initial shock, only to feel the pain in his chest come racing back with agonizing ferocity. He gripped his chest where the pain was, and to his horror realized that something was sticking out of it. He looked down and felt a thick, black barb with a rough surface. Tyler screamed as a new wave of incredible pain erupted in his chest, exactly where the barb was. His eyes went wide and his entire chest expanded in an attempt to get air. He wanted to get his head above water to yell to Linda, but in his panic he could not find the bottom with his feet. Suddenly, he felt himself calm down as he was drawn into an irresistible sleepiness. He felt relaxed and sedate. Everything was going to be OK. His eyes closed of their own accord, and he had just enough time to curve his mouth into a peaceful smile before everything went black forever.

* * *

One hour later, a smartly dressed Sydney Vale rode the elevator up to the sixth floor of the Royal Tortuga Grand Hotel. Her performance at Rum Point would certainly score points with Nolan. He would doubtless see the logic in bringing her back as a full-time assassin for The Trust. The elevator doors opened, and she walked calmly down the hallway with her Prada handbag in one hand and a rolling Gucci suitcase in the other. Nobody would question her with that kind of gear. She smiled at the young couple walking past her and slowed her pace as she neared room 657. She turned around to watch them disappear into the elevator, then put on thin leather gloves and inserted her electronic card key in the lock of the door. She withdrew it with a flick of her wrist. The little green light came on and the lock opened. She quickly entered and locked the door behind her.

Papers filled with scribbled notes were neatly stacked in a pile next to a laptop computer on the desk. A stack of recordable DVDs and a webcam sat on the other side. A stack of printouts of the article Tyler had written sat neatly at the back of the desk. Sydney took her suitcase, which was empty, and loaded it with everything on and around the desk. Everything in sight that might contain the information went in. She started a quick run-through of the room before leaving. Under the bed. In the drawers. The closet. Through the suitcases. Every trace of the publication had to disappear. As she looked through Tyler's own suitcase, the phone suddenly rang. She jumped. It took several seconds for her heart rate to get back to normal, just until the ringing stopped and the message light went on. She finished her run-through and walked over to the phone. With gloved hands, she picked up and pushed the messages button. A pleasant but mechanical-sounding female voice started talking.

"You have two new messages. Message one, from eight twenty-seven this morning."

"Mr. Evans, this is Tony at the front desk. I just wanted you to know that the courier finally showed up and your two packages should make it to Vancouver in time, first thing Monday morning. Have a great day."

The female voice returned. *"Message two, from eleven fourteen this morning."*

"Tyler, it's Ian. Did you get the paper finished up and sent out? Let me know. And give me a call when you get back from the beach. I think someone's been following me. Just let me know you're OK."

Damn. The package already made it out. That was a complication. Sydney glanced down at her watch. She had to rush. A few moments later she was loading everything into the back of the yellow jeep. The Challenger had a time slot for takeoff in just under an hour. She couldn't miss that flight. Just before leaving the plane that morning she was informed of an urgent new mission. As she drove, she picked up her phone and dialed the current number of the month.

"This is Central. Voice check."

"Sydney Vale."

A few seconds later the channel was opened.

"Sydney. I trust you have good news for me."

"Mission accomplished. But Tyler sent out two disks via courier to Vancouver. One of them to Ian."

"We can handle that. Any interference from our friends?"

"Nothing at all. I was actually surprised," Sydney said.

"I'm not. You're going to make your flight, then?"

Sydney glanced at her watch. "No problem. What's the urgent new mission?"

"We have a small tactical force assembling in Vancouver today. You will be briefed when you arrive."

"Briefed on what?" Sydney asked. She was getting concerned. This was out of the ordinary. If there was anything that needed doing, it could be done by her and Owen.

"I suggest you use the plane ride to catch up on your sleep. You're going to need it," Nolan said. He hung up.

Vancouver, B.C.

"Damn it, why don't you pick up?" Ian Ponce mumbled angrily. Ian had installed himself at one of the outside tables of the Café Torrefaction on Robson and Thurlow Streets early in the afternoon. He did his best thinking there, and was reviewing the latest data from Tyler's clinic in Tijuana. He had questions for Tyler and tried several times to reach him and got nothing but his voice mail. The hours had ticked by and it was already eight o'clock at night. He called Tyler's room at the Tortuga Grand Hotel and waited for the message tone to sound. "Tyler, damn it, where are you? Will you please call me?" He hung up. Something didn't feel right.

Ian sipped his coffee and finished off his low-fat blueberry muffin. Five more minutes, then he was going home. The evening air was starting to chill. He watched the continuous stream of people walking down Robson Street as the summer sun gave the last of its evening light. He turned his laptop back on to double-check the timing of Tyler's paper. He scrolled down the list of talks to be given Monday late in the morning. Tyler Evans's name appeared in the plenary session at eleven fifteen, A Review of Alternative Therapies in Late-stage Cancer Treatment. Tomorrow would be history in the making. He flipped back to the file he was finalizing for upload to his Web site. He saved the latest version to the hard drive, then his USB memory stick. He shut the laptop off and downed the rest of his coffee. He picked up his phone to try Tyler one more time and noticed that the bum across the street was staring at him. The bum had been sitting there all afternoon, dressed in filthy, tattered clothing with an upside-down hat in front of him to collect change. But he didn't have the vacant stare of a normal bum. He was carefully reading Ian's face. And his eyes were intelligent. The bum looked back to his hat. Ian quickly grabbed his laptop and stood up, still watching the bum. Ian walked around the corner of the café and started moving northwest along Robson Street, away from the bum. Just as he threw a quick glance backward, the bum stood up. Not with the feeble motion of a body worn by years of malnutrition, alcohol, and the elements. His movements were quick and strong. And he was moving toward Ian. Tires screeched and horns started blasting as the bum stepped out into the traffic moving along Thurlow Street. Ian broke into a full run, carrying his heavy paunch as fast as his legs could bear. A few buildings down and Ian found himself in front of a small restaurant. Without looking back, he ran straight in past the tables and through to the kitchen. Ian ran headlong into one of the cooks, sending him sprawling on the floor with two plates of food. The cook yelled at him as he got up, but Ian didn't dare stop. He ran to the back doors and shoved them open. He picked up his pace in the dark alley, still heading northwest, until he spotted a narrow passage between two buildings on the other side of the alley. Ian was struggling to breathe as he emerged onto Haro Street. Sweat was dripping down his forehead into his eyes. He mopped his forehead with a handkerchief and kept up his pace until reaching Bute Street, where he swung left and followed the alley between Haro and Barclay. He slowed to a quick jog and crossed over Jervis, finally slowing to a walk. His heart was heaving dangerously fast. He looked all around and saw no sign of the bum. Up ahead he saw the bright red neon sign of an Internet café. Ian walked in and followed the arrows pointing to the computers downstairs. Perfect. Out of sight. The small chair beneath him creaked loudly as he let his full weight fall on it. Ian could feel his heart rate starting to slow. Ian sat down, inserted his credit card into the reader, and logged on. He took out a flash drive and thrust it into the computer's USB port. Ian logged on to his cancer blog and started downloading the full contents of his drive, all the time watching the stairs for anyone suspicious. The next person to open his page would see history unfold in front of him or her. Ian yanked out his flash drive. He allowed himself just another minute to fully catch his breath. Then, he hurried up the stairs and onto the street. Two streets removed from Robson, there was considerably less traffic and fewer people around. For a second, Ian started to backtrack to his car. But he realized if they knew enough to follow him, they would know where his car was parked. They could already be waiting there for him. Ian spun around to the northeast. Two blocks up on Robson Street, Ian saw several taxis drive by. That would be the safest way out of here.

Ian looked around. The usual crowd of people lined the streets, on their way to shopping, dinner, or a movie. Nobody even glanced at him. The bum from the café was gone. Ian started calmly walking north to Robson. It was just a block and a half away. More taxis drove by up ahead. Two were empty and available. Ian's adrenaline started to flow. He wanted so badly to run, but that would draw attention. Just as he got to Haro Street, the traffic shifted and he had to stop for the walk signal. Standing on the corner, Ian felt totally exposed. He looked down at the pavement as the cars went by. Finally the walk light came on, and he strode out quickly to cross the street. Coming toward him from the other side was a family of four, a couple of teenagers, and two men in suits. Nobody suspicious. The men in suits were intently discussing something and appeared oblivious to Ian's presence as they walked straight for him. Ian shifted course. Oddly, they shifted too. But just before colliding they separated and walked on either side of Ian. The man on the left bumped into Ian hard.

"I'm terribly sorry!" he said with a thick British accent.

Ian burst into a short sprint to put distance between himself and the man. But the man didn't pursue. He looked at Ian oddly and kept walking with his associate. Ian breathed a sigh of relief and felt stupid at his paranoia. He turned back toward Robson and kept walking. Until he became aware of a sharp stinging sensation on his left forearm. He lifted it up to take a look. There was a single droplet of blood exactly where it stung. He wiped it away with his right hand. A small, perfectly round puncture hole remained, and immediately started filling with blood again. *That's odd*, Ian thought. A bee sting? It didn't feel like it. He looked behind him to where the two men in suits should be by now. They were gone. He shivered as a cold breeze wafted over him. His left arm in particular felt cold. Icy cold. He felt it with his right hand, expecting to feel coldness but instead felt nothing at all. He realized then that his entire left forearm was completely numb. Ian's heart started racing as he tried to understand what was happening to him. He was halfway to Robson Street. He increased his pace as fast as he could. He watched a taxi pulled over to the side and let the passenger out. It flicked its turn signal on and waited for the traffic to clear so it could pull out into the street. Ian started sprinting.

"Wait! Taxi! Taxi!" Ian shouted. But it was too far away. The taxi left.

Ian felt his gait become lopsided and realized his left arm was dangling like a piece of meat at his side. The numbness in his arm was spreading now, through his shoulder and up into his chest and throat. His cheeks and tongue felt fat. Ian brought his right hand up to feel his mouth. But his mouth didn't feel his hand. And the hand came back covered in drool. Ian realized he could no longer talk. Or scream. He suddenly felt a heavy weight on his chest and slowed his pace as he tried to catch his breath. But it was OK now. He was there, at Robson Street. It was busy with cars and people. He leaned against the side of the building at the street corner and looked against the direction of traffic. A taxi was headed toward him, with its light on. Ian felt so relieved he barely noticed how difficult it had become to breathe. He tried to step out and raise his right arm but that was completely numb now, too. Ian's legs buckled and both knees hit the pavement with a loud thud. But he felt nothing. Everything around him seemed to go cloudy. He was barely aware of the people that were stopping around him. From his position lying flat on the sidewalk he could still see the traffic flowing across the intersection. His eyes followed the taxi he had spotted seconds earlier as it drove past him and up the street. Not a single muscle in his body responded to Ian's frantic attempt at movement. The scenery around him blurred into a mélange of random colors. Only a fuzzy realization in the back of Ian's mind told him that he was no longer breathing. But all he could do in response was allow his heavy, sleepy eyes to close for the last time.

CHAPTER SIXTEEN

Sunday, June 12
Shaugnessy
Vancouver, B.C.

Several blocks south of Vancouver General Hospital, Carter Feldman paced around his tiny, filthy living room. The stench of overused cycling clothes, stale pizza, and beer hung in the air like a thick fog. He had little time to take care of that in the last two days. Both Sydney and Sam agreed to pay one hundred thousand each for the information on Dr. Lindell's patients. For Carter, that was a one-way ticket into a new life. The movers would arrive on Tuesday and he would fly out the next morning to Toronto. He looked around and sneered at his own apartment. He lived in one of the typical 1970s low-rise buildings that wrapped itself halfway along the block with just a thin slice of green on all sides. Parking was on the street, for those with cars. He had a ground-level one-bedroom apartment facing the back, with a glass door that opened to a bit of grass, some small trees, and a dark alley. Well, it was cheap. But he didn't need cheap anymore.

Carter walked over to last night's pizza box on his coffee table, flipped the lid open and took a piece. Pepperoni pizza seemed to keep its flavor best the second day, which is why he always ordered it. He sat down across from his widescreen TV and flipped from channel to channel. Sam would be here any minute. He had been somewhere on the East Coast when Carter called Friday and the first flight he could take into Vancouver had arrived at 10:57 p.m., just twenty-three minutes ago. Carter tried to calm himself but couldn't. Sydney's words kept reverberating in his head. *I can't guarantee your safety.* What did that mean, anyway? He realized that he had left two flash drives sitting on his coffee table. He grabbed one of them and pocketed it. Just as he leaned back into the sofa, the door buzzer went off. Carter felt his heart skip a beat. He jumped off the sofa and hit the intercom button. "Who is it?"

"I'm not a Victoria's Secret model." Sam's deep voice was unmistakable. As was his sense of humor. Carter buzzed him in. A few seconds later, there was a knock at the door. Carter opened the door and Sam walked in with a small briefcase. Sam was a large man who spoke slowly. He reminded Carter of most artists' conceptions of early man. He was just missing the bearskin toga and wooden club. Sam set the briefcase on the coffee table and eyed Carter.

"Before we get into this, I need an honest answer."

"Sure."

"Are you selling this information to anyone else?"

Carter's whole body seized up at the question. "Never!" he blurted out.

"That's good."

There was a worrying amount of relief in Sam's voice. "Why?" asked Carter.

"Tyler Evans won't be giving his paper tomorrow on Grand Cayman."

"Because...?"

"He died on the beach this morning."

Carter's heart went into overdrive. He struggled to breathe evenly. The last thing he wanted to show Sam was any sign of nervousness. "Wow. I don't know what to say."

"I'd say your information just got a lot more dangerous. Where is it?"

"Where's the money?" Carter asked.

Sam opened his briefcase and handed Carter five bundles of hundred-dollar bills wrapped in mustard-colored straps. Each bundle was marked as ten thousand dollars. Carter once read that it took twenty-two pounds of hundred-dollar bills to make a million dollars. He felt the weight of the bundles in his hands. This was a good start. Carter picked up the flash drive and handed it to Sam.

"I need to verify it," Sam said, as he took a small computer out of his briefcase and started it up.

Sam was just about to pick up the drive when the buzzer rang. Carter gasped and nearly jumped a foot in the air.

"Expecting someone?" Sam asked.

"No!"

Sam nodded toward the intercom. "Go see who it is."

Carter pushed the button. "Yes? Who is it?"

"It's Sydney. Can we talk?"

Carter went pale. He glanced at Sam.

Sam frowned. "Who the hell is that?"

"Nobody. I can get rid of her in a minute," Carter said.

"Do it," Sam said. He shut his laptop and took his case with him into the bathroom. He turned the light off, but left the door open a sliver so he could see into the living room. Carter buzzed the front door open for Sydney. His mind raced through every possible reason she would have for coming at this time. She wasn't supposed to come until tomorrow. And not here. She never came here. They always met somewhere else. The knock came far too soon, and Carter reluctantly opened the door. To his further dismay, Sydney was not alone.

"Who is that?" Carter asked, looking at the man behind her.

"A friend of mine. You can call him Owen," Sydney said. They both walked in. Owen closed the door behind him. Sydney wasn't playing the flirt anymore. Something was different about her tonight. The soothing voice was gone. There was no perfume. No makeup. She was dressed in jeans and a tight-fitting T-shirt covered by a light jacket that fell loosely to her knees. Carter didn't like this version of Sydney at all.

"I wasn't expecting you," Carter said to Sydney.

She looked at the mess and snickered. "I hope not. Do you have the data?"

"I thought you were coming for that tomorrow."

"Plans have changed. We need it now."

Carter could feel another surge of adrenaline kicking in. This was not good. "OK. The data is right there on the table," he stammered, pointing to the flash drive. Out of the corner of his eye, Carter could see the bathroom door slightly ajar. Sam must be fuming at him.

Sydney nodded to Owen, who pulled out a laptop and plugged in the hard drive. As the laptop started up, Sydney turned to Carter.

"By the way, you weren't planning any travel in the near future, were you?"

Carter broke out in a cold sweat and his heart rate skyrocketed. "Why do you ask that?" he said in a shaky voice. The airline ticket was on top of the TV in plain sight.

"We wouldn't want you to skip town to go be with your mother in Toronto." Sydney hadn't even bothered to look at the ticket. She didn't need to.

Oh God, thought Carter. "It was just for a visit."

"A one-way ticket? Did you really think you were dealing with such amateurs?"

Carter could feel the floor give out under him. He was on the verge of panic. This was much worse than he ever anticipated. What was next?

Owen plugged the stick into the computer and after several seconds nodded to Sydney.

"OK. It looks like it's there," Sydney said.

Carter looked past Sydney to the sanctuary of the back alley outside his sliding glass door. He looked back to her and sheepishly murmured, "What about my money?"

Carter barely finished his last word before Sydney pulled a silenced gun out from under her jacket and jammed its muzzle firmly in the center of Carter's forehead. "What about it?"

Carter fell back a step in sheer terror, but Sydney kept the weapon firmly against his head. "What about the information coming in from Tyler Evans?" Carter pleaded.

"I got that myself already."

Carter was dumbfounded. "How? It's not even here yet!"

"I was on Grand Cayman yesterday," Sydney said.

Carter instantly connected that to Tyler's Evans's demise. The thought terrified him. "Wait! There's other data from Dr. Lindell I can get you!"

Sydney frowned. "We're going there next." She started to pull back on the trigger.

Carter started to go into shock as he realized he was about to die a gruesome death. But in the next second, the bathroom door swung open and Sam's voice thundered into the room.

"Stop right there."

No sooner had Sam spoken than Sydney instantly reached under her jacket with her left hand and pulled out another pistol, aiming it directly at him. Her motion was so fluid, Carter didn't perceive the slightest movement of the gun touching the center of his forehead. Owen rapidly drew his own gun at the same time. After several seconds of silence, Carter managed to take his eyes off the gun that could end his life any moment and looked over to Sam. He was holding two guns with rock-steady hands, one pointed at Owen's head, the other at Sydney's. Carter was surprised to see Sydney actually start to look nervous. Something was running through her mind.

"Who the hell are you?" Sydney asked Sam.

"I'm someone who's brought a lot of money for the data on that flash drive. And I'm not leaving without it," Sam said.

"I can't let that happen," Sydney said. "And you're outgunned."

"Wait! Wait! I have a second one in my pocket!" Carter blubbered.

Sydney glanced at Owen for a few seconds in consideration of the news. But before they could react, a brief flurry of motion outside the back window caught Carter's attention. Break-ins were common in the area, and he was highly sensitive to any movement in the alley. Even now. He turned again and through the opening in the sheers could see some shrubs still wavering. Sydney caught the look on Carter's face. She pushed her gun against his forehead harder. Carter leaned his head back with a grimace of pain but he dared not take a step away.

"What is it?" she demanded.

"I think there's someone out there," Carter said.

"Friends of yours?" Sydney asked Sam.

Sam shook his head. "I work alone."

Carter breathed incredible relief when Sydney lowered her gun from his head. She kept one on Sam and stepped toward the sliding glass door. Carter strained to look through the glass door himself, but his view was blocked by Sydney as she stood right in front of it. She gently spread open the sheers open with her pistol. Without warning, the darkness outside was transformed into a light show with multiple brilliant flashes coming from several sources, over and over. The glass door shattered into small pieces. The room filled with flying fragments of glass, wall, ceiling, and furniture. Carter's mind raced through similar scenes from all the action flicks he had ever watched. He quickly realized there had to be a small army out there with automatic weapons. Sydney, Owen, and Sam opened fire in return with blast after earsplitting blast. When the first wave of firing was over, Carter watched Sam and Owen fall to the ground, motionless. Sydney turned to look back at Owen. Carter nearly convulsed when he saw her face full of cuts from the broken glass, and multiple wounds all over her upper body. Blood was oozing out of every wound, soaking Sydney's shirt. She looked down in horror at the sight of her own blood streaming from her chest and stomach. She fell to her knees and propped herself up against the wall next to the shattered glass door. Blood started gurgling in her throat and she coughed violently. She looked at Owen's motionless body.

"Andrei! Andrei!" she yelled. There was no answer, no movement.

Sydney reloaded her pistols as she coughed up more blood. She glared at Carter in half surprise, half contempt. Then Carter realized he had not been hit—not even once. In a swift reversal he didn't have time to understand, a quickly dying Sydney looked up at him and gasped, "Run, you idiot!"

Carter bolted down his short entranceway and lunged for the front door. As he reached for the doorknob, more automatic gunfire erupted from behind him. His hand recoiled and he threw himself against the side of the entranceway for shelter. Two men dressed in black fatigues jumped through the shattered back doorway with machine guns. They didn't see Sydney, who was still sitting on the floor behind them, around the corner from the doorway. Carter stood motionless up against the wall, paralyzed with terror. Both aimed their weapons straight at him. But before they could shoot, Sydney screamed and opened fire on them with both pistols. The men started shooting as they went down. Carter froze in place as one machine gun swung in an arc directly toward him, discharging a continuous stream of bullets that cut through the ceiling and then the wall just inches from where he stood. He felt a small, sharp impact on his cheek from scattered fragments of wall, and in the next instant heard a metallic clang as a bullet struck his titanium bike, which stood against the wall in the entranceway. The firing stopped and gave way to a sudden, eerie silence he knew would not last. Sydney lay on the floor, covered in blood, her empty eyes staring out into nothingness. Carter felt himself breathing rapid, shallow breaths. He grabbed the doorknob with his right hand and yanked the door open. His left hand shot out and gripped his bike, pulling it into the hallway with him. He jumped on the seat and started pumping the pedals with every ounce of strength he had.

The fire exit doors stood at the far end of the hallway, but halfway there the hallway was intersected by the front and rear exits. Carter raised his heavy torso in the air and heaved each breath in and out, gaining precious speed with each turn of the pedals. Just as he was about to reach the intersection, a man in fatigues jumped out with a machine gun. Carter smashed into him before he had time to fire. The man's head impacted the far corner of the wall and he fell limp. Carter went sprawling onto the ground, hitting the wall with his shoulder. He screamed in pain, not knowing if something was broken. He picked up his bike and spun around. The man had come from the back way. Carter aimed his bike for the front entrance, just feet away, and lunged for it. In seconds he was out in the cool night air, speeding away. At the first intersection, he turned down Laurel Street. The neighborhood was totally quiet this late on a Sunday night. Carter looked back. Nobody was pursuing him and his apartment building was out of sight. Douglas Park lay up ahead on his left. As he kept pedaling, he took out his cell phone to call 911, but a wave of guilt came over him. He had to warn Dr. Lindell first. Carter pushed the speed dial for Dr. Lindell's cell. It rang and rang. Damn! Nobody picked up. Lindell's voicemail came on. Carter held the phone in front of his face to speak into it. He gasped into the phone between labored breaths.

"Dr. Lindell, you have to get out of there! They're coming after you!"

Just then, Carter noticed a bright red flash of light coming from his cell phone. By reflex he held it out to get a better look. For just a split second, a small dot of bright red light fell in the center of the display. The next instant, the phone exploded painfully out of Carter's hand. His whole hand throbbed with pain and felt like it was on fire. He held it up and noticed in revulsion that half his middle finger was missing. Carter glanced behind him. He could barely make out a lone man in black fatigues, standing at least three blocks back in the middle of the street. He held a rifle with a large scope. An intensely bright beam of red light emanated from the tip of the gun and shone out in the night air. Carter had no time to react when he noticed that the beam disappeared into a single bright red point, and that he himself was glowing the same color of red between his eyes. The last thing Carter Feldman ever saw was the muzzle of the gun erupting with a brilliant flash of white light.

UBC Endowment Lands
Vancouver, B.C.

Somewhere along the row of houses between Western Parkway and Wesbrook Mall, Elliott Lindell walked through his front door short of breath and in a hurry, carrying the last of his data archives from the lab. He slammed the door behind him and paced down the stairs into his basement office. His favorite working music, Schubert's *Symphony No. 8* performed by the Vienna Philharmonic, played in the background, as it had all day. He unloaded his arms on the table next to his Gen-Silico workstation. Ever since Ian Ponce's confrontation on Friday, Lindell had been racing to secure his data, just as he had in September. He never expected the fourth cocktail to work as well as it had. And he certainly never dreamed anyone would take samples of it and try to copy it. Let alone go public. Lindell glanced at his watch. Almost midnight. There was little time left to convince Ian and Tyler to backtrack on their plans. Lindell imagined Gwen Riley's reaction if the news broke on his cure. Of course, Gwen would be the least of his worries if that happened. Which was why he had been so busy over the last two days.

Lindell made sure his watch and wallet lay safely on his desk. His Tag Heuer and credit cards would be wiped out by the high-intensity magnetic fields. He walked to the other corner of the basement and placed the last of his lab computer's hard drives on top of a metallic box the size of a briefcase. A large green light shone on its display panel, assuring that a full eight thousand Gauss magnetic field was at work to completely erase any magnetic media placed on top. It was the only way to truly erase the contents of a hard drive. Seventeen other hard drives that had already been degaussed since Friday lay scattered on the floor next to the table. Now he felt safe. He took out a handkerchief and mopped the sweat off his face and head with it.

Lindell turned back to his Gen-Silico workstation. It was a much smaller version of the supercomputer he had in the lab. He couldn't run his model on it, but he could view the results of a run. And now it contained the only copy of his computer model, together with his latest results in one twenty-gigabyte directory. Tomorrow, he would erase even that and bring everything to the cabin. He would complete his work on the model there. Lindell called up the results of today's run of the model, using the results of the blood tests he had done on Ian Ponce. It confirmed what he suspected all along. He didn't have to wait for Tyler Evans's data to arrive in the morning. He already could tell from the metabolites in Ian's blood that Tyler Evans and his Tijuana lab had cut corners on half the ingredients in his cocktail. And two key Chinese herbs were missing altogether. Despite that, Tyler's lab rats were all cured. But Lindell's model showed an initial regression in tumor size for only a quarter of the human genotypes in his library. And even for those, the cancer would come back. Lindell shook his head in disgust. Ian was one of the lucky ones to benefit from Tyler's version of the formula. But once large-scale trials started, Tyler's formula would be easily discredited by the same big pharma interests that had always kept natural treatments at bay. Only a total cure would be unstoppable. Lindell grabbed his mug of coffee leftover from lunchtime and downed the remains which were cold and bitter. He had to tell them to stop now.

As Lindell put his mug down, something caught his attention. Movement. Lindell turned to look at the four small screens next to the stairs. They showed live video from his security surveillance system. That's where the motion had been. He set up a copy of the video feed on the large monitor in front of him. There! Just as it came on his screen, he caught a glimpse of a dark figure running into the hedge at the side of his house. But the alarm was not triggered. Odd. Lindell kept an eye on the screen and reached for his cell phone in case he had to call the police. It was then that he noticed his phone was flashing a missed call on the screen. From Carter. Lindell played the message. Carter's frantic and labored voice came on.

"Dr. Lindell, you have to get out of there! They're coming after you!"

The sound of Carter breathing heavily lasted a second more, then the connection was abruptly severed. Lindell called up the message details. He had just missed it by ten minutes. He stared back at the surveillance feed and his pulse leapt. The scene from the front door showed two men dressed in dark fatigues. One worked on the door while the other held a silenced gun up to the camera. After a brief burst of light, the picture on the screen went black. Lindell heard successive bangs at the front door followed by the sound of the door frame cracking wide open. Loud voices shouting commands filled the ground floor. Lindell leapt up from his chair and ran to the security panel at the foot of the stairs. He pounded his fist on the large red button at the bottom of the panel. His basement office was also his panic room. A heavy steel door slid shut upstairs at the basement entrance, and a second closed shut in front of Lindell at the base of the stairs. Just as the second door was locked in place, the other end of the house shook with a small explosion. All the lights went out. In the split second of total darkness that followed, Lindell went into a full-blown panic. He wasn't ready for this. He spun around and saw his computer was still running on its uninterruptible power supply. Dim emergency lighting came on in the panic room. He raced back to his terminal. Just as he started typing, he heard the sound of loud machinery upstairs. With shaky hands and shallow, rapid breaths, Lindell called up the same program he had used in September to send the model to Annika. This time the model would be split into four encrypted portions, each traveling to a separate node in Rome, Paris, London, and Bermuda. Then it would be retransmitted to the cabin, with reassembly and decryption taking place on his Gen-Silico there. There was just one problem: time. The query screen came up.

"Start encryption?"

Lindell clenched his fists in frustration. He turned to his other screen with the surveillance cameras. On the lower left picture, he could see a man pressing a large power drill into the locking mechanism of the first door upstairs. Through both doors, he heard the high-pitched scream of metal cutting metal. There was no time. The encryption algorithm took too long. Lindell hit the "N" key. The screen replied with the message "Transferring unencrypted data." The status bar popped up and started to rapidly fill as the transfer progressed. Lindell grabbed his watch and wallet. He typed in the next command: "Internal degauss." As a precaution, Lindell had degaussers built around the hard drives in his home Gen-Silico and also at the cabin. After the files were transferred and safe, the degaussers would render the hard drives completely useless within two minutes. The whining of the drill upstairs came to a stop, and with a loud crash the first door was breached.

Lindell watched the file transfer status bar as it reached 100 percent. Loud footsteps pounded on the stairs to the basement. The drill went into action again, filling the room with a deafening high-pitched whine. Lindell was just about to start the degauss program when a large red box flashed on his screen. It was the last message he wanted to see: "Fatal Transfer Error 105." The Gen-Silico at the cabin wasn't responding. Instead of relaying on to the cabin, Lindell's only copy of his computer model was split in four pieces and parked in his grandfather's former residences in Rome, Paris, London, and Bermuda. The whine suddenly changed pitch as the drill bit broke through the lock mechanism. Lindell turned and watched as the thick drill bit poked through the door into his room. The door had three large bolts holding it in place. The drill was withdrawn, and the deafening screech started again on the next bolt. Lindell had no choice but to start the degauss process. He thrust his finger on the return key and then ran to the back corner of his basement, which was poorly lit. He pressed hard on one of the dark wood panels at the bottom corner. The wood paneling gave way at the seams, opening inward on hidden internal hinges to a small secret room which lay outside the house's foundation. He heard the drill bit break through for the second time. The drill stopped spinning just for a moment, then soon resumed on the third and last bolt. Lindell shut the panel behind him and locked it from inside. He slid a two-inch-thick alloy steel bolt into a receptacle in the concrete wall. The room was less than two meters across in each direction and lit by a single, dim light bulb hanging by a wire from the ceiling. The space was surrounded by reinforced concrete on all sides except the one furthest from Lindell's house. That wall was made of cinderblock and old red brick, with a makeshift steel door in the center. A safe was embedded in the concrete wall on Lindell's left. Lindell opened it with a digital code and scooped up the contents: passport and credit cards under a false name, cash in dollars and Euros, a flashlight, and a loaded handgun. Lindell opened the steel door in front of him. A wave of stale air swept over him. It reeked of damp and mildew. Lindell shone the flashlight ahead and stepped down into the long forgotten passageway lined with decaying bricks nearly a century old. The tunnel filled with the echoing sounds of Lindell's hurried footsteps toward the exit at the far end, over half a kilometer away. Lindell cursed himself silently for not having gone earlier to the cabin. He had planned to leave that very morning, but his logic was blinded by his curiosity about Tyler's version of the formula. Just one more run of the model, Lindell had thought, to see where Tyler had gone wrong. Now his life's work lay unencrypted on four computers around the world. And if the people upstairs were to get a hold of it, he would be as good as dead. Lindell looked on into the blackness of the tunnel ahead and continued walking as fast as he could. If it wasn't for his grandfather's friends in Bermuda, he would already be dead. It was they who had made this house on the UBC campus such a compelling buy.

Back in 1993 when he first got his position at the Center for Natural Medicine, Lindell quickly received word from his grandfather's estate managers of a special property that was soon to come on the market. The UBC campus had changed much during the years. It was often forgotten that during the 1930s, a large swath of land between McInnes Field, Wesbrook Mall, and Walter Gage Road was kept as a military reserve. During the years surrounding World War II, a wireless station was installed there while the military barracks of Fort Camp were constructed at the northwest corner of campus. When the threat of a Japanese invasion at the coast became real, large cement bunkers and gunneries were installed along the beach beneath campus, and a system of tunnels was built to join the wireless station with the barracks straight across campus. The tunnels made several strategic stops along the way, one being under the 1925 Mainstacks Library. There were also extensions and underground storage bunkers. Since then, some tunnels were closed. Others, forgotten. But not by the former owner of Lindell's house. His basement connected to the end of the longest tunnel, which still went straight out through the library and branched off to a secondary tunnel. That tunnel ended in the middle of the Marine Drive Forshore Park between Cecil Green Park Road and Northwest Marine Drive. It reminded Lindell of his grandfather's many apartments throughout Europe. There was always an air of secrecy about them.

As he ran, Lindell realized what the problem was with the Gen-Silico supercomputer at the cabin. He hadn't properly configured it yet. He could do that and complete the transfer from any place. It was simple. And it was safe, because the only thing connecting the cabin with the other computers was a connection to a satellite. He just had to get to the cabin. After nearly five hundred meters of half running, half stumbling on the unsure footing of an eighty-year-old brick tunnel floor, Lindell paused to catch his breath. His shirt was drenched with sweat and his feet were aching painfully from multiple blisters and bruises. The echoes of his own noise died down, and for the first time the tunnel filled with the peaceful sound of dripping water. Lindell rested in place and let himself breathe loudly. After a minute's rest, he put his foot out to continue his journey but stopped short at the sound of someone else in the tunnel. He couldn't tell from which direction the sound was coming. He took his gun out and aimed it forward together with the flashlight. He went forward cautiously. Soon, the sound of his own footsteps changed. The echoes became shallower and quieter. He realized he was getting close to the end. Quickening his pace, he pointed the flashlight downward to make sure of his footing. But he had gone no more than twenty paces when three blinding bright lights came on in the tunnel in front of him, aiming directly at his face. Squinting against the painfully bright light, Lindell brandished his gun with a shaking hand.

An unfamiliar voice shouted, "Drop the gun, Lindell!"

"Who are you?" Lindell demanded.

"Drop the gun now!"

Up above ground at the northwest tip of the UBC campus, the graduate students of the Green College residence slept soundly in anticipation of their next week's research. Some still worked feverishly on writing their thesis or research papers to make their deadlines. Nobody heard the multiple gunshots ringing out beneath their feet, muffled by brick and earth and eighty years of a forgotten history that apparently wasn't worth caring about.

New York

Most of New York lay at rest in the early hours of the morning as Nolan Vasquez paced back and forth in his gallery under the watchful eye of Roy Ingram. A large part of his precious gallery had been taken over by a makeshift computer room to house the new Gen-Silico supercomputer. Ever since it had become operational over a month ago, Roy's people had installed themselves there full time, and there was nothing Nolan could do about it. Roy smirked as he lifted Nolan's prized Fabergé teapot and poured himself a cup of tea, rather than the espresso that Nolan always had. The rest of Nolan's penthouse, including his prized Fabergé tea service, had been abruptly commandeered as of Friday night. Nolan glared back at Roy with hatred in his eyes. He still didn't understand how Roy found out so quickly about Lindell's fourth cocktail and the patients' plan to go public. Nolan got the news directly from Sydney early Friday afternoon. Three hours later, he was in the midst of planning to take care of that himself when Roy touched down on the building's helipad with a crew of people, equipment, and a list of orders that were not to be questioned. Several of Roy's men were still in the penthouse, and Nolan had no idea what they were doing. Worst of all was the deception. Owen and Sydney should have been part of the whole operation. Not cut down like the enemy halfway through.

"You shouldn't have killed them," Nolan said. Roy's tactical team had since sanitized Carter's apartment and moved on to Lindell's house to secure the model. But they were already seven minutes late in reporting.

"That's right. With their track record, you should have long ago." Roy gazed blankly at Nolan's artwork that hung on the wall as if it was a billboard. He clearly had no appreciation for art or antiquity.

"You know nothing of their track record!" Nolan shouted back. He immediately regretted his loss of control. Roy was a mystery to him. The Trust was organized into cells, each cell administering its own industry with no knowledge of the others. If needed, the cells were only coordinated remotely, at the level of the Overseers such as Smoke. Nolan had never heard of Roy or anyone like him in The Trust. Face-to-face contact was simply unheard of, let alone this ridiculous level of micromanagement. Something more was going on. Nolan's train of thought was interrupted by the loud ringing of the phone on his desk. Roy was closest and hit the speaker button. The usual computerized female voice came on.

"Central operations. Voice print authentication confirmed."

"What's your status?" Roy said loudly into the phone.

There was a moment of hesitation. "Everything is secure," a man responded. Background noise made it clear he was inside a moving car.

"I asked your status!" Roy demanded.

"We didn't get the model."

"What?" Roy yelled back.

"Lindell erased everything at his lab and his house."

"That means nothing. Bring it all in."

"Lindell used military spec degaussers, sir. It's all gone."

"Then bring Lindell in. He'll tell us where his backup is."

"Sir, Dr. Lindell is dead."

Roy's arrogant sneer vanished. Nolan watched gleefully as Roy lost his cool. "You were supposed to take him alive!"

"He escaped when we took the house."

"How?" Roy demanded.

"Through an old military tunnel that connected to his basement."

Roy spun around and glared at Nolan. "And you didn't know about that?"

Nolan shot back. "You killed the only two who could have known."

Roy turned back to the phone. "Then what?"

"We discovered the tunnel in time to intercept him at the other end. But he opened fire on us with a handgun. We had to shoot back."

Roy gritted his teeth. "No, you didn't have to." He let himself fall heavily into the chair next to Nolan's desk. Nolan watched the scar on Roy's cheek quiver. Roy spoke in a quieter tone. "Put his body with Carter's in the lab. Everything else stays the same."

"Yes, sir."

"Did your men at least succeed in Cleveland?"

"The target was eliminated this morning, sir."

Roy leaned forward and punched the disconnect button.

"What happened in Cleveland?" Nolan asked.

"We had to plug a leak at Glenville University Hospital."

"Who?" Nolan was getting very worried. Roy would claim this was yet another failure on his part.

"One of the research staff was selling data. Trevor Wilkins."

Damn. Nolan scolded himself. He should have checked Trevor more carefully. He forced a confident smile. "But he won't have Lindell's computer model."

Roy stood up and poured himself more tea from Nolan's set. "Lindell had a backup. I just need to find it."

Nolan felt his control over the situation quickly evaporating. "You? Don't you think I'm better suited for that?"

Roy leaned forward with his teacup to set it on the table next to the tea service, but in the process purposefully scored the sterling silver teapot with the unglazed under-side of the cup. Nolan watched in horror as a deep and wide scratch appeared on his prized possession. If it weren't for Roy's men that still walked the floors of his pent-house, he would have attacked Roy on the spot. There was only one other tea service like this on the planet. But this particular set was unique because it did not officially exist. During the 1890s, Czar Nicholas II was desperate for J. P. Morgan to help him open up the U.S. capital market to Russian bonds. The czar knew of Morgan's famous love for antiques. So the czar commissioned Fabergé to remake the original 1885 Imperial tea service—off the books. He shipped it to Morgan hoping the gift would stir up some sympathy during a time when political instability in Russia was growing dangerously high. How it fell into the hands of Morgan's enemies in The Trust was an untold story. But the hallmarks and design of the service made its authenticity undeni-able. If it was ever made public, it would rewrite history.

"That piece is priceless!" Nolan yelled.

"A little bit less priceless, now. Don't ever question me again." Roy slowly ran his finger down the deep scar on his left cheek as he proudly eyed the similar scar on Nolan's teapot.

Nolan leaned forward until his face nearly touched Roy's. "A thug like you can never replace me. I've made hundreds of millions for The Trust."

"If Lindell's model gets out, there'll be nothing left to replace," Roy retorted.

"Then I suggest you start looking at Gwen Riley and Lindell's student, Annika."

Roy pushed Nolan away. "We already are."

Nolan turned and stormed into his kitchen. His butler stood there aimlessly.

"Make me a damn espresso!" Nolan yelled at the top of his lungs.

The butler sprang into action. Nolan could hear Roy cackling with pleasure in the background at the scene he had just witnessed. That was good. Theatrics were important, especially for people such as Roy. Because Nolan still had an ace up his sleeve, and Roy needed to keep looking in the wrong places until it came time to put the card into play.

CHAPTER SEVENTEEN

Monday, June 13
The Center for Natural Medicine
Vancouver, B.C.

Annika eyed Peter half suspiciously as he held the door open for her.

"You're being awfully nice to me lately," she said with a smile.

Peter smiled back and briefly held his hand up for Annika to wait. He was in the middle of a phone call. He nodded several times into his cell phone. "Tell him I'll be right in. Thirty minutes. I'm taking my wife in for her first day as a doctoral student."

"More stress at the office?" Annika asked.

Peter nodded. "Sorry. There's a lot to wrap-up before we go."

Peter had been called into the office twice during the weekend, but had made it up to Annika by coming back with flowers each time and taking her out both nights for dinner to the place of her choosing. When he was called out on Sunday after lunch, he also booked Annika for all afternoon in the spa just a block away, to relax her before the long flight to Switzerland. She couldn't really say no to that.

"If you need to get going, I understand."

Peter shook his head. "I'll walk you there."

They walked up to the front desk where a young, attractive receptionist was busily talking on the phone while typing into her computer. The nameplate on her desk read Sharon Rispoli. She acknowledged their presence with a slight nod of her head. She looked twice at Annika and flicked back a lock of her shiny black hair. Eventually, she finished and put the phone down.

"You're Dr. Lindell's new student, Annika?"

Annika was surprised and impressed. She hadn't been there since November. "Yes!"

"It's hard to forget the grad student who gets to fly off to Europe on her very first day," Sharon said with a scowl.

Annika went slightly red. "Yes, um, of course."

Sharon handed Annika a paper form and a pen. "Please fill this in so I can give you the keys to the building."

As Annika was filling in the form, a short, balding man in a courier uniform rushed in the building. He was nervous and fidgety and looked at his watch several times. He looked as if he was always running late. Sharon looked at him with disapproval.

"Where's Jim?"

"Sick today."

Sharon looked at the large white clock on the wall. "It's eight o'clock. You're half an hour early. I get most of my mail-outs in the next half hour."

"Sorry, I got the route all screwed up."

Sharon frowned and held out a stack of packages for him. He exchanged them for two incoming parcels and held out a pocket computer for a digital signature. The courier smiled and rushed back out.

Sharon raised an eyebrow at the packages and glanced at Annika. She walked over with a set of keys in her hand. No sooner had Annika signed her name than Sharon pulled the form out of her hands and thrust the keys forward, together with a small but thick cardboard envelope.

"Annika, could you please take this package to Dr. Lindell?" she asked. The envelope had "URGENT" and "CONFIDENTIAL" written on it in large, red block letters.

"Of course," Annika replied as she took the package. "Is Dr. Lindell in yet?"

"He's always in at this time. His phone has been off the hook since I arrived," Sharon said.

As Annika started for Lindell's office, Peter gently grabbed her shoulder. "I need to go now. I'll see you this afternoon, OK?"

Annika smiled and put her arm around Peter. "OK. Thanks."

He gave her a long kiss and turned for the exit. Annika went the opposite direction down the hallway. Just before turning left at the end, she looked back to see Peter watching her, smiling. He waved and blew a kiss good-bye. She stood and did the same. He waved her on and started for his car. Annika resumed her walk to Lindell's office, thinking about her upcoming trip with Peter and their honeymoon in Europe. She looked down the hall and broke into a broad smile just as Dr. Lindell's office door flew off its hinges and across the hallway with the speed of a bullet. In the next instant, the entire hallway turned painfully bright white and a blast of intense heat washed over Annika's entire body. She had no time to react before the shock wave hit her. She could feel her hair blow straight back while her clothes were tugged so hard, it felt like they would be pulled right off her body. As the deafening blast hit her, Annika felt her entire body lift off the floor for a brief second, until she tumbled backward hard on the concrete floor. Annika looked down the hallway in horror as bright flames surged out of Dr. Lindell's office and came speeding directly toward her. She felt an intense flash of heat on her arms and face which quickly grew unbearable—until the window at the other end of the hall shattered and the flames were sucked out through the new opening. Thick, black smoke billowed out of Lindell's office and through the broken window.

"No!" Annika cried. She quickly realized where the blast had come from. She also became aware of a throbbing pain in her ears and head. As she scrambled to get her footing, she felt someone grip her arm from behind and with surprising force haul her straight up and onto her feet. She spun around.

"Peter!"

"Let's get out of here!" he yelled.

They both started running, and within another second the building's fire alarms all went off in deafening unison. Flashing strobe lights and exit signs lit up in front of them at the main entrance. Office doors all along the hallway were opening and people dressed in lab coats were rushing out. Annika struggled to walk straight. She felt Peter's arm firmly around her, helping her walk to the exit. Sharon was yelling into the phone and waving frantically at them.

"Get out of the building now!" she screamed.

Peter kicked the exit door open with his foot and took Annika out onto the strip of grass just outside the front.

"My God, are you OK?" Peter asked. He looked over her body for injuries.

Annika could feel a hot, burning sensation all over her face. "My face really hurts!" she screamed.

Peter touched it lightly. "You've got some heat rash."

"From the blast?"

Peter nodded. "The guys in the foundry at Alameda got it all the time. Give it ten minutes. It's not too bad."

Annika looked back at the center, the back end of which was now engulfed in flames.

"Dr. Lindell!" she cried. "Dr. Lindell was in his office!" Annika broke down in tears.

"We don't know that for sure."

"But Sharon said he was on the phone all morning!"

Peter put his arms around her. They could hear the sound of sirens in the distance. "Shhh. Let's wait for the firemen to do their job."

"But what am I going to do now?" Annika sobbed, tears streaming down her face. The lab's fire alarm was overshadowed by the loud sirens of multiple fire trucks approaching. They were so loud it was painful. Annika put her hands over her ears.

Peter helped Annika get to her feet. "Come on. Let's go back home."

Through tear-stained eyes Annika nodded. Firemen started jumping out of their trucks and directing everybody away from the building. Annika watched Sharon standing close to the main entrance in intense conversation with the fire chief. The chief relayed a flurry of orders to his men, who rushed back to their trucks and donned air tanks and face masks. Annika turned back to Peter and held on to him tightly. He helped her into the Lexus. She strapped herself in, and felt overwhelmed by exhaustion. She let her head lean against the window and closed her eyes. She was barely aware of Peter getting in on the driver's side, or the gentle purr of the engine starting. She felt herself drifting off, hoping that the morning's events were just a bad nightmare because they were far too terrible to be reality.

When Annika woke up, Peter was laying her down on the bed in their apartment in Strathmore Mews.

"What happened? How did I get here?" Annika asked.

"It's OK. I carried you."

Tears started to well up in her eyes as the memory of the explosion came flooding back. "Everything's ruined!"

Peter put a pillow under Annika's head. "You need to rest now."

"But our trip to Switzerland! Our honeymoon!"

"I still have my ticket. And you still have yours."

"You really think we should go?"

"It's your decision. But I think we should." Peter's words were comforting, but his face was strangely indifferent. Almost calculating.

"But what do I come back to?" Annika asked.

Peter leaned down and kissed her on the forehead. "You come back to me. To us."

Annika smiled weakly. She felt guilty for doubting his sincerity. "I love you so much."

"I really need to go. You can decide when I get back."

"Sure. OK."

As Peter walked out, Annika turned over and looked at the alarm clock. It showed ten after nine. She tried to block the morning's memories from her mind, and felt herself drifting off again as the door to the apartment shut around the corner from the bedroom door. Annika closed her eyes, only to see the explosion playing out over and over again. She tried to calm herself but could only worry and wonder what her future held now. She forced her eyes to remain closed and tried to give in to her exhaustion. But it seemed only moments after Peter left, the buzzer rang. Annika sat up in the bed. Had Peter forgotten something? She gasped as she read the clock. One thirty in the afternoon. The buzzer rang again. She forced herself out of bed and went to the door. She opened it to find a uniformed police officer standing in the hallway.

"Are you Annika Grafton?"

Annika felt cold with the door open. She wrapped her arms around herself and leaned against the door frame. She nodded. "Yes."

"I'm Officer Ginsburg with the RCMP. I understand you were at the Center for Natural Medicine this morning just before the explosion occurred."

"Yes, I was. Just down the hall from the lab when it went," Annika said weakly.

The officer nodded as he looked her over carefully. "You weren't burned at all? You didn't inhale any smoke?"

"No. I don't think so," Annika said.

"Before the explosion, did you smell anything in the air? Any kind of chemical or acrid smell?"

"I really can't remember. I don't think so."

"What about rotten eggs?" the officer asked.

"You mean from the hydrogen sulfide they put in the natural gas? Was there a gas leak in the lab?"

"Did you smell a gas leak?" the officer asked.

"I don't remember. Why are you asking?"

"They're just routine questions, ma'am. We're still trying to piece together exactly what happened this morning," Ginsburg said, without giving up any hint of information.

"Was Dr. Lindell in the lab when it exploded?" Annika asked.

"It was a very hot fire, ma'am. It took a long time to put it out."

"Was anybody inside the lab?"

Ginsburg nodded. "Two people. We've positively ID'd them as Elliott Lindell and Carter Feldman, the lab technician."

Annika looked down and watched the tears falling from her eyes hit the floor. "Are you sure?" she asked, still looking down.

"Yes, ma'am."

The last glimmer of hope that Dr. Lindell was alive had just been snuffed out. Mitch Purcell and the other patients Annika had helped in Chromogen's trial were gone. Everything she had planned and worked for since her father's death was all in vain. If it wasn't for Peter, she would be alone. Thank God for Peter. Annika looked up at the officer. "Then why are you here?"

"Some of Dr. Lindell's personal effects survived the fire. There was an inscription on his cufflinks that nobody understands." Ginsburg held out an enlarged photocopy of the back of the cufflinks. The words were inscribed around the Tiffany's insignia. "With all my love, Emily."

Annika looked at the words over and over. "I don't know."

"Dr. Lindell has no surviving family that we know of, and Emily was not his mother's name."

Annika shook her head. "I'm sorry. I have no idea who Emily is." Annika sniffled and wiped away her tears with her hands. "This was an accident, right?"

Officer Ginsburg hesitated for a second. "We're still trying to piece everything together, ma'am."

Annika caught the hesitation immediately. "So you don't know for sure that it was an accident?"

He handed her his card. "If you remember anything else, please give me a call."

"OK," Annika said. She watched Officer Ginsburg turn and walk to the elevator bank. Just before he hit the button, the doors sprang open and Peter walked out. Peter walked past the officer with a puzzled, questioning look on his face, toward Annika.

"Who was that?" Peter asked.

"Just some routine questions, I guess," Annika said. She rubbed the remaining tears out of her bloodshot eyes. Her face was pallid. She looked utterly exhausted.

"Questions about what?" Peter asked.

"About the lab. There might have been foul play," Annika said.

Peter seemed surprised. "What? Are they sure?"

Annika shook her head. "No." She walked back inside and sat down. Peter followed.

Peter sat next to her and put his arm around her. "How are you doing?"

His arm felt like that of a stranger. Annika fought the urge to move away from Peter. She told herself it was all in her head. "I just can't keep the scenes from this morning out of my head."

Peter got up and walked over to the living room table where his plane ticket lay. He held it up. "What about Switzerland? The plane leaves in two and a half hours."

Annika buried her head in her hands. "It doesn't feel right to go when everything is such a mess."

Peter walked over and sat down again next to Annika. "I understand. Let me have your ticket, and I'll cancel them both."

Annika breathed a sigh of relief. That was the old Peter talking again. She reached for her purse and opened it. Something immediately caught her eye. It was the urgent package she'd been given for Dr. Lindell that morning. She pulled it out.

Peter looked at it with intense interest. "What's that?"

"I totally forgot about this. It was for Dr. Lindell." It was partially torn open. A small note stuck halfway out through the rip in the package.

Peter was gazing at the package. "So what are you going to do with it?"

"Give it to the police, of course."

Peter raised his eyebrows. "Don't you want to see what was so urgent for Dr. Lindell to get on the day he died?"

Annika eyed the package. She did want to see it, more than anything. "Yes." Annika pulled the note out and started reading.

> *Dr. Lindell,*
>
> *The world needs to know about your cure for cancer far faster than in two years. We hope you will agree to go public yourself before we do on Monday. The proof that we have replicated your cure is here on this DVD. When you get this, there will be little time to make your decision. Call me, so we can do this together.*
>
> *Sincerely,*
Tyler Evans.

Annika looked up at Peter. The disbelief on his face almost matched the shock on hers.

Peter stared at her. "Did that say cure for cancer?"

Annika dug into the package and produced a DVD. "Let's find out."

She walked over to the far wall and slid the DVD into the player which sat underneath the large widescreen TV. A bright blue sky lit up the TV screen. Cars ran back and forth on a busy street. Freshly whitewashed buildings with red tile roofs across the way looked like they belonged to a rich neighborhood somewhere in the third world. Somewhere hot. The camera panned left and completed a half turn. Two men dressed in white lab coats and wearing sunglasses stood in front of a large white mansion with red tile roofing and finely crafted iron fences in front. A large sign in front of the building read "Excelsior Health Clinic." Just behind the clinic stood the tall stonework bell tower of a Catholic church. The men in front of the clinic both held bottles of Dos Equis in their hands and smiled broadly as they waved to the camera. One of them held up a small white rodent in his hand, and they toasted their beers to the small animal. One of the men tipped his beer bottle into the rodent's mouth. The men laughed. The scene moved inside the health clinic and down to the basement, which was lined with bare, gray cinderblock. Old fluorescent lights hung overhead. Cages upon cages of rats were stacked up on several tables.

The scene shifted to what looked like a hotel room. One of the men from the first scene was sitting on a chair next to a small desk. He spoke.

"Dr. Lindell, this is Tyler Evans. What you just saw is the medical clinic in Tijuana where I have successfully re-created your formula and tested it on three cancers that we artificially induced in Sprague-Dawley rats. In all cases, for breast, colon, and prostate cancer, we achieved a hundred percent rate of remission within the test period of eight weeks after administration." He held up several graphs to the camera, which slowly refocused on them.

Peter and Annika both sat back, stunned.

"Is this for real?" Peter gasped. "I thought he wasn't finished yet!"

Annika's mourning for Dr. Lindell suddenly gave way to a slight feeling of betrayal. "He told me nothing about this!"

Tyler Evans continued. "All the data is on separate files on this DVD, including our formulation of the cure you used on the three patients in Mitogenica's trial. I am going to present this data Monday morning here at the plenary review session in the Cancer Conference on Grand Cayman. Then I'll fly to the Complementary Medicine conference in Davos, Switzerland, and present the same data there on Wednesday."

Annika turned to Peter. "That's today! And he'll be in Switzerland, too!"

Peter nodded his head vigorously, but held up his hand for Annika to stop talking. "Shhh! I want to hear this!"

Tyler Evans kept talking. "Of course, this is just the beginning. Ian Ponce is the first human to go into total remission on this formula. But he won't be the last. By this time next year, I will be presenting data from human trials. We want to work with you, not against you. But the world has to know about this. Please call me." The screen went black.

Annika grabbed Peter's arm. "I have to meet this man! He may be the only one who can carry on Dr. Lindell's work!"

Peter was in deep thought. "Yeah." He looked worried.

"What's wrong?"

"Do you think there's any connection between Dr. Lindell dying today and this guy going public?"

"What do you mean?" Annika asked.

"Don't you think somebody would want to stop this?"

"This," Annika said, pointing to the TV screen, "cannot be stopped."

"You really want to make this trip?" Peter said.

Annika nodded. "More than ever," she said, with fire in her eyes.

"You don't think it's dangerous?"

"This is all I have left, Peter."

"You have me."

"That's not what I mean," Annika said.

Peter shook his head and looked at his watch. "We have to get going right now. Are you fully packed?"

Annika jumped up and took the DVD out of the player. She slid it back into its case and put it in her purse. "I am now."

Mitogenica Inc.
Vancouver, B.C.

Gwen Riley sat at her desk and stared in disbelief at the story on the Center for Natural Medicine in the online edition of *The Vancouver Tribune*. She gripped the armrests of her chair until the whites of her knuckles showed. Live streaming video on her screen showed thin wisps of smoke still rising from center. Fire trucks surrounded the building and firefighters were cleaning up the mess from the explosion. A shot from a helicopter then showed the entire back upper corner of the building gone. Gwen felt sickened as she could see inside Lindell's lab and recognize the blackened equipment and offices she had visited in the past. Then came the footage taken by a student on his cell phone. The *Tribune*'s Web site played that one every few minutes. It showed a far grimmer picture, just after the explosion. Thick black smoke rose in a column above the center. Yellow flames broke through the windows and people came streaming out of the front entrance with true panic on their faces. One student ran out, blackened with smoke, and collapsed on the ground right in front of the camera. The shakiness of the amateur video made it all the more grotesque. Gwen had actually seen the column of black smoke from her office in Mitogenica that morning, and had not known what it was. The story was now all over the news. It was rumored to be a natural gas leak, but the police were still investigating. Two bodies had been recovered: Dr. Lindell and his lab technician. Predictably, Austin had called her after the news broke. But the surprise was that he had called from Los Angeles International Airport, on his way up to Vancouver. Gwen looked at her watch. There was little time left. She was livid that John Rhoades had been incommunicado the entire weekend, and even this morning. In particular because over the weekend she received some new information on John that he himself should have shared with her. She now realized that she had seriously misjudged the situation. One thing was sure: it was no gas leak in the center. She had to find out the real story behind it. And only John Rhoades could tell her that. Gwen tried his number for the tenth time that morning. Finally, he picked up.

"Where the hell have you been?" Gwen demanded, nearly shouting.

"Busy."

"I need you here in twenty minutes. I mean it."

"What's so urgent?"

"Austin Hayes is on his way here now."

"OK. I'll be there."

Fifteen minutes later, John Rhoades knocked on Gwen's door. She was prepared to launch into a tirade about how miserably he had failed until she saw his appearance when he entered. He looked tired, ragged, and beaten. He was scraped and bruised all over, and had a long, thin bandage on the side of his head. But his movements betrayed not the slightest pain or discomfort.

"My God, what happened?" Gwen gasped.

John kept his emotionless face of stone. "I was shot."

Gwen gestured toward her screen with the news on. "Were you involved in that? He nodded. "We were tracking Sydney Vale Saturday night."

"She did all this?"

"No, she's dead. So is her partner."

Gwen grimaced in disgust. "You didn't!"

"Not us."

"Who, then?"

"That's what Austin's lead may tell us."

Gwen's assistant Nadine rang through. "Ma'am, Austin Hayes just checked in through security. He's coming up now."

John nodded and walked outside Gwen's office, hiding around the corner of the hallway. A moment later, Gwen watched through her open office door as the elevator opened and Austin Hayes walked out. Gwen hid her shock at the sight of a man that was clearly no longer the Austin she had seen only six months ago in New York. He had aged terribly, gained weight, and looked disheveled. And worried. Gwen smiled on the inside at her opportunity for control. She stood up and held her hand up for Austin to stop.

"First, deposit your cell phone and anything else electronic on Nadine's desk."

Austin protested. "What? Since when?"

"Since now, or I'll throw you out of here myself."

Austin bowed his head in resignation and left his phone and PDA in the center of Nadine's desk. He then continued on and closed Gwen's door behind him.

Gwen turned her mouth down into a twisted scowl. "You monster. You had something to do with Lindell's death, didn't you?"

Austin waved both hands in the air and shook his head. "No way."

"Then why are you here now?"

"To give you your final warning."

"Warning? Mitogenica stock is up thirty percent since we last spoke. And your precious Avarus Pharma is down ten."

Austin shrugged it off. "I know the rumors about your trials with Lindell."

"Well, the market likes something about us lately. Our stock is up."

"So what? That only works in our favor."

Gwen folded her arms tightly in front of her. "How's that?"

"When the FDA makes its decision, it gives that much more room for your stock to fall and Avarus to rise. The shorts will make a killing."

"And if you're wrong?"

"We won't be, Gwen. When are you going to start believing that these friends of mine are in control?" Austin's tone almost sounded like pleading.

Gwen got up from her chair and stared Austin down. "What's in this for you?"

Austin ignored the question. "The FDA's decision is imminent, Gwen."

"Or do you mean your friends' decision?"

"It's more or less the same. So I suggest you think hard about this one."

Gwen turned around and faced her window, looking at the place where she had seen the column of smoke earlier that day. "I'd tell your friends they can go straight to hell, but I'd prefer that they make a long stop in prison along the way."

Austin clasped his hands together in a fist and rested his head on them. He closed his eyes for a moment and breathed deeply. "If you turn over Lindell's model now, we can negotiate a good deal for you."

"I don't have it."

"Come on, Gwen. Then what's up with all the computer power you bought last year?"

The conversation was swinging in a direction Gwen didn't like. She glared at Austin. "If you had anything to do with Lindell's death, so help me I'll see you rot in prison alongside your friends. Now get out of here."

Austin stood up to leave. "I'm sorry, Gwen. I'm just the messenger."

Gwen turned her back to Austin and faced the window again. "I don't believe anything that comes out of your mouth anymore."

Austin walked out and collected his things from Nadine's desk. When the elevator doors closed, John Rhoades came out from around the corner opposite the elevators and walked back into her office, closing the door behind him.

"Did you plant your devices?" Gwen asked.

"Of course. Did you get the conversation?"

Gwen turned to check the small webcam that was hidden in a dark gap between two books on her bookshelf. She pulled up a small video screen on her computer. It showed Austin sitting down and starting the conversation.

"This won't be very useful without knowing who his friends are."

"We'll find out. We've got full GPS tracking and short-range voice broadcast from his cell phone."

"For how long?" Gwen asked.

"Unlimited. They feed off the phone's own batteries," John said.

"Voice broadcast? Why didn't you plant those on Sydney and Owen?"

"Too risky. It's a continuous signal and they would scan for that sort of thing."

Gwen leaned back in her chair. "So, do you have anything you want to tell me?"

"Such as?"

"Like what happened in April with Cypress Turbines." There. Gwen caught the first glimmer of emotion in John Rhoades's face. It was more surprise than anything else.

"There's not much to tell."

"That's not what the CEO Will Conleth told me. And Peter Grafton was involved."

"Peter Grafton? So what?"

Gwen looked at John incredulously. "So what? The strongest living link to Elliott Lindell happens to be married to him. Is he a threat here?"

"Not in my judgment." Back to the emotionless face.

"But you're still doing a background check on him!"

"That's routine for my line of work."

"But not for Peter's line of work, Mr. Rhoades!"

"I'm checking you, too, Ms. Riley. Or is it Emily Hargraves?"

Gwen stopped dead at those words and struggled to save face herself. She let out a snicker. "I'm surprised it took you so long."

"What's going to take longer is figuring out your real intent here."

"That's none of your business. I'm paying you to watch Austin and Annika."

"We've got that covered."

"I want to know everything that happened this weekend."

John leaned forward and put a compact eyeglass case on Gwen's desk. "Try them on."

Gwen removed a pair of glasses with thick but sleek tortoiseshell frames. "What are these?"

"Austin's friends will soon show their faces. There's a mini camera and microphone in the right frame. Pull on the left."

Gwen yanked on the left frame. With enough force, the left side came out completely, revealing a USB connector. "Impressive."

"It can store twenty gigabytes of video and sound. More than you'll need."

"I usually wear contact lenses," Gwen said.

"Three-point-five in each eye. Right?"

She nodded. "Very good. But you never answered my question about what happened this weekend."

John looked down at his watch. "I can't for another twelve hours."

Gwen was furious. "You're playing a dangerous game."

John got up to leave. He glanced at Gwen's screen, which still showed the news footage of the morning's explosion. "Apparently you are, too."

Gwen called out after John, "And I still forbid the use of guns." She got no answer, but knew that he heard when the elevator doors shut several seconds later. She called for Nadine, who hurried through the doorway.

"Yes, ma'am?"

"Get the CFO in here immediately."

Nadine nodded. "Right away, ma'am."

Chapter Eighteen

—

Monday, June 13
Vancouver International Airport

Mid-afternoon traffic through Vancouver had been much worse than normal owing to an accident on the Oak Street Bridge that had everything backed up along Granville and Oak to downtown. Annika and Peter rushed from their car to the international check-in at top speed. By the time they cleared security at Terminal D it was already four fifteen. Boarding was nearly complete for their flight to Frankfurt, but they still had to walk all the way to gate fifty-five at the end of the terminal. The loudspeaker in the terminal called repeatedly for the boarding of their flight, and with each reminder they picked up their pace a little more. Annika struggled to keep up with Peter and felt herself starting to sweat until, amazingly, he stopped halfway down the terminal at the Starbucks. She stared at Peter in bewilderment.

"What are you doing?" Annika asked. Another urgent announcement for their flight came over the loudspeakers.

Peter thrust his tickets into Annika's hands and quickly grabbed two large bottled Frappucinos. He aggressively barked out orders for several snacks. Annika had never seen Peter so forceful. She put a calming hand on his shoulder, only to have him spin around and whip his arm up as if to slap it away. She recoiled in shock. Peter quickly regained his calm and smiled.

"These will be nice on the other side of this flight."

"We might not get on the flight!"

Peter pointed down the terminal to their gate. The last two people were just going through the gate to board the flight. "Where's the problem? I do this all the time."

Not with me you never have, thought Annika. This was not like Peter at all. He usually abhorred being late for anything—flights in particular.

Peter paid and they dashed along the moving conveyor belt for the gate. Just as they arrived, Annika heard their names announced over the PA system. The flight attendant at the gate was glaring at them. Annika looked away with embarrassment, and noticed a large TV showing international news in the middle of the seating area. Annika presented the tickets to the attendant. She looked back at the large TV. She had almost forgotten the reason she was flying to Switzerland. "Tyler Evans gave his talk just hours ago. I wonder if it made news yet."

Peter turned to watch. A travel weather update was just ending. The scene then shifted to a residential building on fire as seen from a helicopter. The camera zoomed in on the fire. All the windows had been blown out and thick black smoke mixed with bright orange flames billowed out of every opening in the structure. As the camera zoomed back out, Annika couldn't help but take a step closer to the TV when she saw the building was whitewashed, with small portions of red-tiled roofing still intact.

Palm trees were everywhere. Just behind the burning building stood a familiar tall stonework bell tower and a Catholic church.

"Oh my God, Peter! Isn't that the clinic in Tijuana?"

The attendant interrupted. "Ma'am, we have to close the gate now." She held out their boarding passes.

Peter started walking to the Jetway. "Can't be. Come on, let's go."

Annika grabbed his arm and stopped him just as the news announcer started speaking.

"Ma'am!" the attendant repeated.

"Just a minute! This is important!" Annika said.

The news announcer continued. "Less than three hours ago, several city blocks in the middle of Tijuana were rocked by powerful explosions that completely destroyed the high-end medical clinic Excelsior, which catered to U.S. and Canadian citizens. Several witnesses reported hearing automatic weapons firing for several minutes just before the blasts. Firefighters and police have not been able to enter the building yet, and so far there are no survivors reported. Was this an act of terrorism against U.S. targets? Or the revenge of a patient for a botched—"

The attendant stood directly in front of Annika and Peter, blocking the TV. "Either you get on that plane right now or you're staying here."

Annika relented and followed Peter down the Jetway. Both pulled their carry-ons quickly behind them.

"You were right," Peter admitted. "That really was the clinic in the video."

"I just hope it didn't affect Tyler's talk today," Annika said. She stowed her luggage and then reached in her purse and pulled out the courier package from Tyler Evans.

"What are you looking at that for?" Peter asked.

"This!" Annika said, holding up the note written by Tyler. It was on hotel stationery and had the phone number in small print at the bottom. She took out her cell phone and dialed.

"You're calling him now? Why?"

"I want to ask him how his talk went today. And arrange a meeting in Switzerland."

"But—"

Annika shook her head to cut Peter off as someone answered in a friendly tone, "Royal Tortuga Grand Hotel on Cayman Island. How may I help you?"

"Please put me through to the room of Tyler Evans," Annika said.

"Please hold the line." After a moment, the voice came back. "I'm very sorry, Mr. Evans is no longer staying with us."

"That's impossible. He's at a conference there all day today. I need to speak with him urgently," Annika said.

"Just a moment, I need to put the hotel manager on with you."

"What? Why?"

Another female voice answered. "Hello, I'm Rita Unger, the hotel manager. May I ask your relationship to Mr. Evans?"

That's a strange question, Annika thought. "I'm his daughter."

Peter's eyebrows shot downward and he glared at Annika disapprovingly. She smiled and shrugged.

"I'm very sorry. Mr. Evans had an accident while swimming yesterday."

"Accident? What kind of accident?"

"I'm very sorry. Mr. Evans passed away."

"Oh, dear Lord." Annika's face lost all color and she froze in place. Peter reacted. He gestured for some answers. Annika kept listening to the phone.

"You should contact your mother at home."

"What kind of accident?" Annika insisted.

"Mr. Evans was stung directly in the heart by a stingray out at Rum Point. That's never happened before here, ever. I'm so sorry for your loss."

"Thank you," Annika said. She felt numb. She put down her cell phone.

"What is it? What's wrong?" Peter asked.

"Tyler Evans had an accident swimming. He's dead."

Peter leaned toward Annika and put his arm around her. "I'm so sorry, honey."

"What do I do now?" Annika asked.

"You need to get some rest," Peter said. "We'll figure it out."

Annika stared out the window as the plane detached from the gate and took its position in the line for takeoff. Everything she had worked for in her life since her father's death had now been taken away from her. The patients she had tried to help in Chromogen's trial were now mostly dead because of her. A prison sentence now hung over her head, dangling by the thread of Arthur Cormack's whim. Dr. Lindell and his work were lost forever. Annika looked down at the disk sticking halfway out of her purse. It was all that was left of Dr. Lindell's life's work, and even the men that made it were now dead. Annika was barely aware of the plane's engines as they throttled to full power and sped the plane along the runway and up into the air. She had to make full use of the ruin that was left of her life. The plane climbed higher in the sky, and at the first opportunity Annika reached next to Peter's feet and pulled out his laptop.

"Hey!" Peter protested. "I need to work!"

"So do I," Annika said. She inserted Tyler's disk and pored over the lab data and their version of Dr. Lindell's formula. She ignored dinner service when it came and only took water. If this version of the formula worked, maybe she could find someone else to use it in more trials. Or maybe she could just make it herself and start treating people like nurse Caisse did with the Native American formula that became known as Essiac tea. Annika eventually found herself feeling groggy. She looked up from the laptop and realized for the first time that the cabin lights were off and almost everyone else in the plane was asleep. She looked over at Peter. His seat was fully reclined, his blanket was pulled up to his chin, and he gently snored between slow, rhythmic breaths. Annika lay back in her own seat and closed her eyes—just for a moment, she thought. But the more she lay there, the more she felt the exhaustion of a day that had turned her life inside out. And she had no plan to go forward. No way of telling the world what Dr. Lindell had accomplished. Drowsiness soon enveloped her. As Annika drifted off to sleep, a single tear ran down her cheek and fell onto the package she had intended to give Dr. Lindell that morning.

Tuesday, June 14
Twenty Thousand Feet Over Germany

Eventually, Annika cracked her eyes open to bright sunlight pouring in through the airplane window. She let out a groan as every part of her body started to painfully complain about being stuck in the same cramped position for several hours. The bright light hurt her eyes and she squinted.

"Hi, there!" Peter said.

"What time is it?" Annika asked.

"Quarter to eleven. We'll be landing in Frankfurt soon."

Peter's tray was down. What was left of his breakfast sat shoved up against the laptop which was open and on. Peter quickly folded the screen down. Annika could have sworn she saw Tyler Evan's data on it.

"What are you working on?"

"Just some stuff for the boss. Hey, you need to eat now." Peter pointed to Annika's own tray. A stale croissant and industrial-grade yogurt graced a small cardboard breakfast box. Beside it was a small plastic cup of airplane coffee that smelled like Peter's sports socks after his workout. Annika was starving, but she couldn't bring herself to even touch the food.

"Yuck," she said, cringing.

Peter brought out a cinnamon apple muffin, a date square, and the bottled Frappucino he had bought at the airport. "Now try this."

This time, Peter had come through with her favorite treats. Annika grabbed the muffin and started devouring it. The Frappucino tasted fresh and was cool. "You were right. This is good."

"Just good?"

Annika took another gulp. She felt herself waking up. "OK, it's great."

"So, did you find anything interesting on the disk?" Peter asked.

Annika noticed the cabin crew was starting to collect breakfast garbage for landing. She gulped the rest of her drink and in three quick bites finished the muffin. She started unwrapping the date square.

"His formula has twenty-six ingredients. Most of them I already know."

"Really? Like what?"

"The basics like vitamin D, tocopherol succinates, tocotrienols, green tea polyphenols, and intravenous vitamin C are obvious. But he uses only conjugated linoleic acids with two carbon double bonds."

"What's that?"

"Conjugated linoleic acid? You've probably heard it called CLA. It's a natural trans fat found in beef and milk products, much more so when the animals are grass fed."

"Trans fats? I thought those were bad for you!"

"They're bad if they're man-made, from hydrogenating vegetable oils. But the natural ones found in milk are quite healthy. They've been shown to kill cancer cells."

"And it's part of the formula?"

"Yes, but it shouldn't be," Annika said.

"I don't follow."

"CLA also occurs naturally in plants—pomegranate seeds in particular. Dr. Lindell always wanted to use the CLA found in pomegranate seed oil because it has three carbon double bonds on the nine, eleven, and thirteen positions. That seemed to be key in altering mitochondrial fatty acid oxidation and killing the cancer cells."

Peter leaned back in his seat. "So that's a problem, then."

Annika nodded. She took another bite of her square. "And not the only one."

"Such as?"

"They were far too lax in what they required for the other plant extracts. Dr. Lindell always had very specific demands on the phyto chemical components in each extract he used. Every extract had to be standardized to deliver certain quantities of each component."

"So they didn't get it right?"

"Well, there's no Chinese herbs here at all. The last time I spoke with Dr. Lindell, several rare herbs from China were critically important."

"Why?"

"I think he finally figured out how to reactivate cancer cells' mitochondria using those herbs instead of Gwen Riley's artificial drugs."

"Speaking of Gwen Riley, she would probably still offer you a job, you know."

Annika winced and shook her head. "I may as well work for the devil herself."

Peter was surprised. "You really think the devil could be female?"

"I do after meeting Gwen Riley."

Three hours later, their connecting flight landed in Zurich. In between short conversations, Annika had kept poring over the experimental data on the DVD time and time again. She was still running through the data in her head as they deplaned in Terminal E and walked to the underground train. After a short wait, the doors closed and they started their three-minute ride to the main terminal. The sound of chirping mountain birds, the large traditional *alpenhorn,* and cowbells filled the underground train. Peter noticed brightly lit picture boards flashing by on the far wall of the train tunnel. They gave the appearance of a smooth, fluid motion picture of the Swiss Alps.

"Look!" Peter said.

Annika turned just in time to see a young, pigtailed Heidi standing in green fields with the Matterhorn and blue skies in the background. She smiled, winked, and blew a kiss. The scene went dark and the train stopped at the main terminal. Annika and Peter made their way to Passport Control, which they quickly cleared, and went on to get their luggage. Both had packed minimally and rolled only one suitcase behind them with the carry-ons.

"Don't forget that Zimmerli guy is here with Thomas's book," Peter said.

"And Thomas wants his pictures of the scene of the crime," said Annika.

They exited customs to a large crowd of people bustling in the arrivals hall, waiting for their friends and family. One man stood out, holding a page of paper with "Grafton" written on it. He was a tall, bald, and elderly man with deep wrinkles in his forehead. Annika approached with a smile and made introductions. He smiled kindly. Annika immediately took a liking to him. And she was glad to have a distraction from everything that had happened in the last two days and all the decisions she would soon have to make.

Zimmerli handed over a heavy package. He spoke with a thick Swiss German accent. "This is the book your brother Thomas ordered."

Peter gently unfolded the paper wrapping. The book's black leather binding and cover were terribly aged, scored, and creased. It seemed barely intact. The thick pages of the book were rough-hewn and all of slightly different dimensions. Peter opened the cover. The front page was written with a strange form of calligraphy, but neither Peter nor Annika could read it, except for the date, which was 1539.

"Wow! What language is this?" Peter asked.

"German, of course!" Zimmerli said. "It was written right here almost five hundred years ago."

"It looks quite valuable," Annika said.

"It is!" Zimmerli responded.

Peter turned to Annika with a smile and rolled his eyes. "Uncle Alex!"

"What's your brother going to use it for?" Zimmerli asked.

"Research material for his dissertation on the history of the Baptist church."

Zimmerli cracked a broad smile. "Well then, you've come to the right place! Do you have time for a quick tour in Zurich?" Zimmerli asked.

"Definitely. Let's go," Annika said. She knew Thomas's salary as an assistant pastor would never let him afford a trip here. And he felt it would be asking too much of his uncle Alex to fund such a trip. Being a Baptist, he was so eager to get firsthand photos of the place where the Swiss German reformation started, which led to the birth of the Baptist denomination. As Zimmerli led the way to the train station in the lower level of the airport, Annika looked at Peter. "I didn't know Thomas could read German."

"I guess I didn't either," Peter said.

Twenty minutes later, the three of them walked out of Zurich Hauptbahnhof, the main train station of Zurich. The afternoon sun shone brightly in a cloudless, sapphire blue sky. Annika felt just a bit more awake after such a short night's sleep. They crossed over the Limmat River on the Bahnhofbrücke and turned right onto the Limmat Quai, a street running along the Limmat all the way to Lake Zurich.

"Now we're heading to the Altstadt, where the buildings are quite old," Zimmerli explained.

As they walked, the houses lining the river grew larger and more colorful. Along the Limmat Quai, the ground floors of many buildings were graced with majestic stone arches below which sidewalk cafés were crowded with those enjoying an afternoon coffee. Further down toward the end of the street, two giant spires jutted majestically skyward above all the surrounding buildings. Zimmerli pointed to the spires.

"That is the Grossmünster, where Ulrich Zwingli became the People's Priest in 1518."

Peter took out his digital camera and started taking pictures.

"Who's he?"

"He led the protestant reformation in German Switzerland," Zimmerli said.

"So he's the good guy!" Peter said.

Zimmerli chuckled. "No! Quite the opposite, in fact."

"Didn't he start the Baptists?" Annika asked.

Zimmerli shook his head. "His students did. They were the Anabaptists."

"What's an Anabaptist?" Peter asked.

"The word literally means to be baptized again. They wanted to get baptized as adults to show their faith in Christ. And many were martyred for it."

"Why? What was the big deal?"

Zimmerli's eyebrows shot up, and the wrinkles in his forehead stood out. "It was against church doctrine! They only provided for infant baptism."

"But that's just the church!" Peter said.

"Church, government, power, wealth. It was all connected back then."

"So what?" Peter said.

"The Anabaptists were considered radicals who threatened the very structure of church and government. Zwingli's job was to manage the reformation in Switzerland to avoid exactly that."

They stopped in front of the Grossmünster. The massive stone structure was set back from the street. Each of the two spires was set on a tall square tower built of dressed stone. Two levels of enormous arched windows graced each face of the towers at the top.

"It's beautiful!" Annika said.

Peter looked at Zimmerli. "So what happened?"

"Zwingli and the Zurich city council passed a law in 1526 that made re-baptism illegal and punishable by drowning to death."

Annika was horrified. "They killed them?"

"Listen, one day these people are sitting next to you in church. Their kids play with your kids. You might have lunch with them. The next thing you know, they tie you up and burn you at the stake. Or drown you, or torture you to death. And they did it by the thousands."

Annika cringed at the imagery that went through her head. She couldn't help but think about the explosion that had taken Dr. Lindell's life. She had never considered before how he might have suffered.

"So much for fifteen hundred years of civilization," Peter said.

Zimmerli slightly bowed his head. "Every country has its dark past. Now you know ours."

"I think there's still something special I need to get with this," Peter said, holding his camera up.

"Oh, yes. It was Felix Manz who started the Anabaptist movement. On January 5, 1527, he was taken to the bridge of the Rathaus just behind us there," Zimmerli said, pointing to a four-story stone building that stood at the river. "He was taken by boat to a fisherman's hut anchored in the middle of the Limmat River. His arms and legs were bound behind him, and he was thrown into the water and drowned to death right there." Zimmerli indicated the middle point of the river, near its mouth.

Annika couldn't bear the level of description. As Peter took his pictures, she turned back to the large church in front of them.

"So how old is the Grossmünster?" Annika asked.

"Construction was started around the year 1100. They finished it about 1220," Zimmerli said.

Annika looked back across the river which was lined by tightly packed houses in a row. Beyond, other churches sported large clock towers. Annika realized it was four o'clock.

"We still have to get to Davos today. We should get going."

"Of course. Let's go this way back, over the Münsterbrücke," Zimmerli said, leading them onto the nearest bridge. It was lined with square-cut cobblestones and ornate wrought iron fences on each side. They stopped at the middle and looked down the river toward Lake Zurich. One more bridge stood in front of the lake, but beyond they could see the rolling green hills surrounding the lake and far beyond the snowcapped peaks of the Swiss Alps. Peter took more pictures.

A bright flash of light hit Annika in the eye from the other bridge, just in front of the lake. She squinted against the sunlight in her face, and could just make out a man standing at the center point of the bridge. He was pointing something at her. When he took it down to pack it away, it looked like a large telescopic camera lens. Annika strained to get a better look, shielding her face from the sun with her hand. The man quickly mounted a scooter and sped toward the heart of downtown Zurich.

"What are you looking at?" Peter asked.

"I don't know," Annika said.

Peter finished with his pictures. "OK. Let's get going."

Davos Dorf, Switzerland

The two-and-a-half-hour train ride from Zurich brought Annika and Peter to the Davos train station just before seven p.m. A brief stop in the mountain village of Landquart had been a welcome breath of fresh air and a chance to stretch again. As they went through the rolling green hills and ever-nearing Alps of the Graubünden, they made detailed plans for the honeymoon part of the trip. Peter's travel agent had booked it all for them. After Annika's conference ended Friday afternoon, they would take an evening flight to Rome. After two days in Rome and two in Venice, it was off to Paris for three days, and finally three days in London. As the train's squealing brakes brought them to a halt at Davos Dorf, Annika realized she hadn't thought about Dr. Lindell, Arthur Cormack, or her PhD since Landquart. She smiled to herself. Perhaps she was going to be able to enjoy this time with Peter.

They walked off the train and southward down Davos's main road, Promenadestrasse. The town lay stretched out along a narrow valley in the Alps, each side of the valley ahead eventually rising through thickly treed hills up to snowcapped mountains. Small shops offering everything from Swiss watches to hiking and mountain-climbing gear lined the street. Cafés and restaurants were everywhere, most of them built into old chalet-style wooden houses with flower boxes beneath the windows.

"We've got to come exploring here tomorrow before the conference!" Annika said.

"Sure. Do you think they have a Starbucks in town?" Peter asked.

"Hey, isn't that the way up to the hotel?" Annika asked. Over to the right, two steel railway tracks ran up the mountainside starting from a building just in front of them. It was the *funicular*—the private cable car of the Hotel Schatzberg. Halfway up the mountain, the tracks disappeared over a small plateau which blocked their view of the rest of the summit. Only at the very top could they see the uppermost floors of the Hotel Schatzberg. Annika and Peter entered the small building and took their tickets. They walked up a set of steep cement stairs alongside the small train car which sat perched on the tracks. The car was bright blue and yellow, with the hotel's name in large, bold lettering on the front panel. A shiny steel cable hooked onto the upper end of the car ran between guide wheels and the tracks all the way up the mountainside. Annika had read that the cable was attached at the other end to the train car which now stood at the top of the mountain at the hotel. The two cars balanced each other out. The weight of one car going down was used to help pull the other car up along the cable connecting them.

Annika and Peter struggled to stay awake as a handful of others came in over the next few minutes. They heard a bell ringing and the cable car controller signaled that they were about to leave. The cable car smoothly accelerated up the tracks. Within seconds, they had cleared the small sheltered area at the base and were soon bathed in the orange glow of the evening sun. The town of Davos fell beneath them, and the whitecapped mountains on the other side of the valley stood out brilliantly against the blue sky. They soon passed under an old wooden bridge, which connected a hiking trail on either side of the *funicular* tracks. Several hikers on the bridge waved at them. In a few minutes they reached the halfway point. The single track divided into two and the *funicular* jogged onto the right track. On the left, the other car passed them on its way down. Further up the mountain, Annika could feel her ears popping. She felt lightheaded and remembered reading that the hotel was at 5,700 feet above sea level. The *funicular* slowed and pulled into its station at the top of the mountain. The bell rang and the doors opened. Annika and Peter walked out onto the stairway next to the *funicular*.

The driver spoke in English with a Swiss accent. "Your suitcases will be taken directly to your rooms."

Outside, the cool mountain air was refreshing. Manicured lawns and gardens surrounded the main building of the hotel and merged seamlessly with the forest nearby. The hotel itself stood four stories tall and stretched long enough to accommodate the balconies of thirty rooms along its length. The beautiful detail of the structure's Art Nouveau design glowed in the light of the setting sun. The main entrance brought Annika and Peter into a long hallway with a high ceiling, the left wall of which was made of windows affording breathtaking views of Davos and the surrounding mountains. The reception area ahead was teeming with activity. Signs for the Fifth International Conference on Natural and Alternative Medicine were being put up everywhere. Across from reception, a registration booth was already set up but was unmanned. Two young women at the reception desk wore dark slacks and immaculate white shirts just like the rest of the staff. Annika walked up to them.

"Annika and Peter Grafton," she said to the two.

"Of course, just one moment," said one, with a Swiss German accent similar to Mr. Zimmerli's. She looked down at her computer and with only a few keystrokes found the booking. She made a quick comment in Swiss German to her colleague, who then produced two room keys with speed and efficiency. Both smiled continuously.

"Room 423. Please enjoy your stay."

Annika and Peter walked over to the grand staircase which rose in wide, square sections around a large, open central column where the elevator stood inside an ornate wrought iron cage enclosing the entire shaft. Moments later, they arrived in front of their room. Annika opened the door and both were awed by the beauty and detail of the room, still perfectly preserved after more than one hundred years. Painted wood paneling covered the walls and ceiling. Solid wood furniture stood throughout the room; most of it looked antique, perhaps original to the hotel. A chandelier hung in the middle of the ceiling and brass wall lamps decorated each wall. At the far end of the room, two wooden stairs led up to the large inner and outer glass doors, which opened to the spacious balcony. Two large windows were on either side, each with an inner and outer window, separated by a half foot of space.

Annika opened both doors and they walked onto the balcony. The view of Davos and the sun setting behind the mountains was magnificent. The hotel was surrounded by snowcapped mountains covered with lush green grasses and forest at the base. The setting sun caused the snowy mountain peaks to glow bright pink-orange against a deep blue sky. Further up in the nearby hills stood a small lake so blue it seemed almost radiant.

"Wow," Peter said. "This is amazing. But why here for the conference?"

"A hundred years ago, this hotel was a famous sanitarium. People came to get treated for psoriasis, rickets, allergies, and especially tuberculosis."

"What, from the clean mountain air?"

"No! Just by exposure to that!" Annika said, pointing to the sun. "Up here you can get a good dose of vitamin D almost all year round in just a few minutes every day."

"Wasn't that just a fad?"

"A hundred years ago heliotherapy and photobiology were huge things. Especially in Europe."

"Photo-what?" Peter asked.

"Photobiology. It's the science of how sunlight interacts with living things. It was so big that a Danish man by the name of Niels Ryberg Finsen won the Nobel Prize in 1903 for his work in the field."

"For doing what, exactly?"

"He treated lupus, one of the forms of tuberculosis, using exposure to sunlight. Then he teamed up with a Swiss doctor named August Rollier and they opened a whole chain of high-altitude sanitariums across Switzerland to treat people for tuberculosis and many other diseases."

Peter couldn't help but let out a long yawn. "Sorry, it really is interesting." He walked over to the bed, lay down, and flicked on the TV with the remote.

"Aren't you hungry?" Annika asked.

Peter started channel surfing. "Starved. Why don't we get some room service?"

"Sounds good to me," Annika said.

There was a knock at the door. Annika opened it to find the bellboy standing there with the suitcases. He brought them into the small entranceway of the room and left so quickly Annika didn't have time to think of tipping him. She closed the door and opened her suitcase to bring out her toiletries.

"So what kind of food did you want?" No answer came. "Peter?"

Annika looked around the corner. Peter was already in a deep sleep and gently snoring. Annika covered him with a blanket, turned down the lights and got under the covers next to him. Once her head hit the pillow, she felt herself quickly drifting off. She turned over on her side toward Peter. Sleeping peacefully like that, he looked exactly like the Peter she had met and fallen in love with. She hoped she could get used to the new sides of him that had been coming out lately. After all, besides Peter she had nothing to go back to after the trip. So much had changed in her life. She was happy to feel herself falling into a deep, forgetful sleep. Because right now, happiness required forgetting.

CHAPTER NINETEEN

___

Wednesday, June 15
Hotel Schatzberg
Davos Dorf, Switzerland

That morning, Annika had awoken from ten hours of sleep feeling totally rejuvenated. Being up in the mountains away from everything gave her a supreme sense of peace she hoped would last her entire two-week vacation with Peter. When she got back to Vancouver, she could start worrying about life again. She had gone with Peter downstairs to a late breakfast and taken the ten-thirty *funicular* down into Davos for a morning of browsing for souvenirs, touring the coffee shops, and window-shopping for ten-thousand-dollar Swiss-made watches that apparently got regularly snapped up by whimsical rich tourists during ski season. Then they made their way for a late lunch at a little bistro on Promenadestrasse that looked more like a Swiss chalet from the outside, with heavily varnished picnic tables set up under the shade of large evergreens.

Annika sat across from Peter and read through her wish list for the upcoming European tour: Venice, Rome, Paris. Annika had grown up with the dream of seeing Europe, but knowing it was far beyond the family budget.

Peter took a deep breath after hearing the lineup. "What about London?"

"Haven't gotten there yet," said Annika. She beamed at Peter. He seemed so relaxed now. He was back to his normal self.

Their server arrived with lunch. Annika and Peter had relied on her to give them the most typical Swiss dishes of the region. Peter had taken *Kalbsgeschnetzeltes nach Zürcher Art*, which was fried veal in a white wine and mushroom cream sauce. It came with the quintessential Swiss side dish *Rösti*, basically a large hash brown seasoned and prepared to the exacting standards of Swiss culinary practice. Annika had gone light with *Aelplermagronen*, or Alpine macaroni. It was a large bowl of noodles with chunks of potato, all drenched in a cream sauce with onion, bacon, and aged parmesan. After a morning of walking in the fresh mountain air, both were famished. They quickly dug in.

Annika looked at her watch. "It's already one. We should hurry."

The keynote speech of the conference was to be given at two. Then, a series of presentations lasting until five thirty would end the first day.

"Hurry up and try this," Peter said. He took a large piece of rösti on his fork, set it on some veal, and moved it around his plate until it was dripping with cream sauce. Then he held it out across the table for Annika.

"It's wonderful!" Annika said. She likewise gave Peter some of her macaroni. "So what are you up to this afternoon?"

"I'll connect up in the room and do some work."

"We're on vacation!"

Peter smiled back. "And I'll sort out the rest of London."

"While I'm trying not to doze off."

"There's nothing too exciting in today's lineup?"

Annika shook her head. "No, that starts tomorrow in the oncology tract."

But she already knew the most important presentation of the conference would not occur because Tyler Evans, who would have given it, was dead. Annika had dreamed that one day she would present her own PhD work with Dr. Lindell at such a conference. Work that would change the world forever. Now she knew that would never happen. The next two and a half days of the conference would be rough. There was no escaping being reminded of what lay waiting for her back in Vancouver. And she just didn't want to think about that right now.

Vancouver International Airport

Gwen Riley had very few bad days in her career. This was one of them. Ever since Austin had called her on Monday with the latest threats, short sellers had been coming in at the last hour of trading and pummeling Mitogenica stock into the ground. Down 4 percent Monday, down 5 percent yesterday. In her rush out of the office to catch the three-thirty flight to New York, Gwen hadn't had the chance to see today's results. And she still hadn't gotten John's big news because he had been called away on urgent business. Gwen finished stowing her luggage and flipped open her PDA. Her stomach sank as she saw Mitogenica's stock was down 8 percent today. Damn. She was about to fly to the annual biotech investors' conference in New York. A place where she would need ready answers for such price action of her company's stock. But she had none. At least, none that she was willing to accept.

"Orange juice, ma'am? Champagne? Water?" the flight attendant, asked as she came by with a tray full of drinks.

"Just water, thanks," Gwen said.

"I'll take the champagne please," a familiar voice said from up ahead, on the other side of the flight attendant.

Austin Hayes stepped aside for the attendant, put his briefcase in the overhead compartment, and sat down in the seat next to Gwen.

"Get out of here," Gwen said with a frown.

"Is there a problem, ma'am?" the flight attendant asked.

Austin held up his ticket with the number 5B on it. "Sorry, Gwen, this is actually my seat."

Gwen looked up at the attendant and shook her head. "No, no problem."

"Thank you, ma'am," the attendant said, and turned to serve other passengers.

Gwen closed her eyes and turned her head away in an attempt to control herself. "You've got to be kidding."

"The time for joking is long past," Austin said.

"Let me guess. Your friends knew I would be in this seat and put you there?"

"I keep trying to tell you they don't play games."

Gwen held up her PDA, which still showed Mitogenica's stock price action for the day. "And they're doing this, too?"

"Of course they are. Time is running out."

"Time for what?"

"What do you think? Why are we both flying to New York tonight?" Austin asked.

"I'm going to present at the biotech investors' conference," Gwen said. "What about you?"

"I'm going to hear the FDA decide between two competing cancer drug companies."

"So tomorrow's the day?" Gwen asked. "My answer is the same."

"Gwen, please listen to me. Certain actions are being carried out right now, that soon cannot be undone."

Gwen's phone rang. She quickly glanced down. It was an unknown number. She ignored it. "Like what?" she asked. The phone kept ringing. She hit the call reject button to stop it.

Austin lowered his voice. "Like this." He pulled open his laptop and brought it out of sleep mode. A small window popped up in the center, taking up half the screen. Gwen watched as a video recording started, showing Annika and Peter walking along a bridge across a river.

"This was taken yesterday in Zurich," Austin said.

"What does she have to do with this?" Gwen asked.

"She's the next closest person to Lindell, after you."

The picture then rapidly zoomed in on Annika until her face filled the screen. She seemed to be looking straight at the camera. Overlaid on the picture were the crosshairs of a targeting scope. The intersection of the crosshairs lay perfectly still at the center of Annika's forehead. Her hand moved above her forehead and cast a shadow over her face. The picture froze there, with the crosshairs still trained on Annika.

Gwen was livid. "So now you have to threaten young girls?"

"Not me. Them. They're everywhere. And they think she has something."

Gwen gestured to Austin's screen. "Why are you showing me yesterday's news today?"

Austin pointed to his laptop and quietly said, "Here's today's news. Right now."

Austin's screen went dark for a second and then came alive with an eerie green glow. Large windows and a glass door took shape in a jittery, grainy image. The focus of the picture shifted through the large window and the green hue suddenly brightened. Gwen immediately recognized the face of Annika. She was sleeping peacefully in a bed. Peter was sleeping on her far side, face up. Once again the scope's crosshairs settled at the dead center of her forehead.

Gwen's phone let out a shrill tone, telling her that a short text message had arrived. It started ringing again. She brought the message up on her phone's screen. "Urgent. John Rhoades calling." Gwen picked up instantly. "What is it?"

John Rhoades's voice answered, his tone laced with worry. "We have a situation. We may need to use deadly force."

"What situation?"

"Look for yourself. This is live."

Gwen looked at the phone's small screen. It showed a video of a dark figure perched on the railing of a large balcony four stories up. The camera zoomed in on the figure to show he was holding a gun with a very large scope on it. The gun was aimed into the room which adjoined the balcony. Gwen looked over to Austin's laptop, then back to her cell phone. Gwen realized that, incredibly, she was looking at exactly the same scene from two different perspectives. Each of them equally deadly. Gwen could hear John shouting her name through the cell phone. She put the phone back to her ear.

"Gwen!" John shouted. "Annika's in danger. The time is now!"

Austin said, "I'm sorry they chose to do it this way. It would be great if you could rethink your answer. Right now." He looked at her cell phone, puzzled about who she was talking to.

Gwen turned aside and spoke into her phone. "Use whatever force you have to."

She looked back at her own screen. The whole scene shook slightly, and a puff of smoke obscured the center of the picture for just a split second. The dark figure perched on the balcony railing jolted backward violently and with arms flailing fell four stories to the ground. Gwen looked over to Austin's laptop. The scene showing Annika sleeping in her bed swung violently upward to show the ceiling and sky, and then a dizzying flurry of blurred images until it finally settled on the side of the building and row after row of balconies as seen from the ground. The glowing green image of a man holding a large, silenced gun appeared. He raised the gun to a point somewhere above the camera and fired two quick shots, each causing the picture to jerk to the side. The man's foot rose up above the camera, and everything went black.

"Well done," said Gwen. She hung up.

Austin was aghast at what he saw. "Who were you talking to?"

"My own people. They're everywhere, too."

Austin recoiled from Gwen with fear in his eyes. "That was a mistake. You obviously don't know who you're dealing with."

"And obviously neither do they," Gwen said. She leaned back and cut the connection. The flight attendant came by asking everyone to turn off all electronic devices. Gwen smiled politely as she hid her phone underneath her purse. She dialed with one hand. When the attendant had passed out of view, Gwen brought her phone up to make one last call.

Thursday, June 16
Davos Dorf, Switzerland

Annika awoke with a start to the sound of a ringing phone. She was so disoriented that it took three rings before she realized what the sound was. She climbed over Peter and grabbed the handset of the room phone. With a gasp, Peter sat straight up in bed, with messy hair pointing in all directions.

"What's going on?"

Annika pointed to the phone in her hand. "Hello?"

The voice was hurried and upset. "Annika! Why is your cell phone switched off? I've been trying to call you!"

"Who is this?"

"I'm Dr. Li Wong from Mitogenica."

Annika looked at the clock radio next to the phone. It was three thirty in the morning. Or six thirty yesterday evening by Vancouver time. Peter looked at her questioningly. Annika shrugged. She spoke into the phone. "Yes?"

"Gwen Riley and the Center for Natural Medicine agreed that I would take over for Dr. Lindell in running the trials."

"Take over?"

"Yes, and I wanted to inform you in person. Until I learned that you had jumped on a plane to Europe using the center's money."

"But it was Dr. Lindell that sent me!" Annika protested.

"Exactly! And not me! You have to get back here."

"That's fine. I'm back in two weeks."

"No! We've cancelled that ticket."

"What?" Annika suddenly felt very awake.

"Your new flight leaves the Zurich airport at ten a.m. today. That's the plane you will be taking."

Annika's jaw dropped. "But my husband is with me here!"

"This is by direct order of Gwen Riley."

"Gwen Riley?" Annika repeated. Peter immediately perked up at the mention of the name. The name that Annika was learning to despise.

"Be here at the center tomorrow morning."

"When?"

"Check your email when you get back. And don't be late!" The connection was severed. Annika fell back onto her pillow, shaking her head. She felt numb. All she could do was stare blankly at Peter, her long red hair falling in a tangled mess around her head.

"What? Who was that?" Peter asked.

"Dr. Lindell's replacement. I have to go back today."

Peter shot up out of bed. "Are you serious?"

"By orders of your hero, Gwen Riley."

"Oh, honey, I'm so sorry. When do we go?"

Annika quickly did the math. The Zurich airport was about a three-hour train ride from Davos. Then there was the *funicular*. "We have about two hours to get out of here. And before that you need to rebook your flight."

Annika climbed off the bed and walked to the bathroom. She drank a glass of water and started the shower. She heard Peter frantically negotiating with his travel agent to cancel the trip of her dreams and to rebook his flight. When she was done, she let Peter in for his shower and walked to the balcony. The clear sky was still full of stars. The very first hints of the morning's twilight edged over the horizon. Down below in the valley, shining streetlights dotted the streets of Davos and the larger hotels lit up their entire grounds. The rest of Davos lay peacefully sleeping. Annika took in her last picturesque view of Europe. Minutes later, she and Peter rushed with their suitcases to reception to check out. The first *funicular* of the day started down to Davos in five minutes and they had to be on it to make the 4:54 train to Landquart. Peter handed over the keys at reception and paid. The two sped off down the long panoramic hallway made entirely of tall windows on the side facing Davos. The sky was slowly brightening to a light blue on the east side. Peter shouldered the exit door open but stopped midway, looking back. Annika turned back to see the desk clerk from reception running toward them.

"Excuse me! Mrs. Grafton!"

"Yes?"

"There was a delivery for you late last night." He came over with a small package the size of a wallet. Annika's arms were loaded. She glanced down at the outer pocket of her large suitcase.

"Can you please put that in there?"

The clerk opened the zippered pocket and slipped the package in. "I hope you enjoyed your stay," he said as he left.

"Yeah, what little of it we had," Peter said under his breath.

Annika hung her head at the reminder. Peter pushed open the glass doors of the exit, and they ran out into the cold morning air to the *funicular*. A blast of wind rushed over Annika and chilled her still wet hair. She sat beside Peter on the cold, hard, wooden bench inside the *funicular* and started shivering as the bell sounded, its brakes released, and it started downward. She was cold, hungry, and with barely four hours of sleep behind her, exhausted. Once again their plans had been ruined, and she would likely have to wait for years before coming back to Europe. And it was her fault, again. But somehow, the thoughts that would have normally brought her to tears had little effect. Annika realized she was starting to no longer care. The rest of the way to the Zurich airport, she drifted in and out of a restless sleep void of expectations for the future.

When they arrived at the Zurich airport shortly after eight, Annika could feel the emptiness of her stomach and was desperate to find something for breakfast. But the lines for check-in were long and slow-moving. After waiting half an hour, she and Peter finally got to the check-in desk. Peter handed over the tickets and dropped Annika's suitcase on the scales. Annika's stomach grumbled and she hoped there would still be time for a breakfast of any sort. Scanning the check-in area for food shops or cafés, she heard the shrill and annoying ring tone of a cell phone. The ringing didn't stop. Annika looked at the people behind them. It didn't seem to come from here.

"Ma'am?"

Annika turned to the attendant behind the check in-desk. He was bent over, reading the name tag on her suitcase. "Is this yours?"

"Yes. Why?"

He pointed to a small bulge in the outer pocket. "It's ringing."

Annika had forgotten about the package she got that morning. She zipped open the outer pocket and retrieved it, ripping off the paper packaging. Inside was a cell phone, still ringing. Peter watched as she answered it, intrigued.

"Hello?"

"Annika, this is Elliott Lindell."

Annika nearly dropped the phone. She moved a few steps away from Peter and the check-in desk, turning her body so she faced away from the people close by. She half whispered into the phone. "Is this some kind of sick joke?"

"It's really me, Annika." The voice was unmistakably Lindell's.

Annika was barely able to keep her voice low. "But the explosion! The body! The police told me you were dead!"

"I had no choice but to let them stage my death."

"Let who? Who staged your death?"

"They work for Gwen Riley."

A dozen possible scenarios ran through Annika's mind as to why Gwen would orchestrate such a deception. Annika was infuriated. "What has she done to you now?"

"It's not what you think."

"Gwen Riley is always worse than what I think."

"No. These men work for Cypress Turbines, too. Peter can tell you more."

"Peter? Are you sure?" Annika snapped her head around for a fleeting glance at Peter. He was still busy with the check-in attendant. *Is Peter involved in this somehow?* Annika thought.

"Ask him yourself. And don't trust these men, Annika."

Annika realized she had forgotten the real reason behind Lindell's apparent death. "Did you really find your cure?"

"It's very close. At least for colon, breast, and prostate cancer. The others will take longer."

Annika was almost disappointed. She had dreamt of finalizing the model together with Lindell during her PhD. "So your computer model is finished already?"

"That's the problem. The model is in grave danger."

"Why?"

"My house was attacked. I didn't have time to upload my model to a safe place."

"So where is it?"

"That's not important right now."

"Can I help you somehow?" Annika asked.

"Yes. When you get back to Vancouver."

"I'm going there now!"

"What? What about the conference?"

"Dr. Li Wong from Mitogenica called and said that Gwen Riley had ordered me to return immediately. We depart in an hour."

There was a pause on Lindell's end. "This could work out better. I'll call after you arrive."

"Whoever these people are, Dr. Lindell, I won't let them win."

"Their eyes and ears are everywhere, Annika. Your home will be bugged. Trust nobody."

"But what about—"

"I have to go now." Lindell hung up.

Annika put the phone in her purse as Peter walked over. He looked frustrated.

"What took so long?" Annika asked.

"Finding two seats together," Peter said.

"Did you?"

"Yeah. Right next to the toilets. What was that all about?" Peter asked, gesturing toward Annika's purse.

Annika told Peter the entire conversation. At first he was as shocked as Annika, and then became even more curious about what Lindell needed from her. Annika brushed off the questions and theories.

"So, who are these men you know?" she asked.

Peter's defensiveness was immediate. "I don't know them. They're just corporate security contractors working for Cypress on a job."

"But they're working for Gwen Riley, too."

"Why not? They'll work for anybody who pays them."

Annika raised her eyebrows. "Really? Anybody?"

"Annika, you can trust them. They helped Cypress Turbines. They helped me."

"Like they were paid to do."

Peter frowned and shook his head impatiently. His face half twisted as if he was about to shout an obscenity at her, but he managed control himself. Barely. "Come on, we have a long haul to get to our gate."

Annika let Peter lead the way to the passport control area. She didn't want to see the flash of anger on his face anymore. The new Peter was back. Granted, he must be disappointed at the trip cancellation as well. But the old Peter had disappointments, too, and he never reacted like this. What had happened at Cypress Turbines to make Peter act this way? Annika remembered the faculty reception at UBC back in November—and seeing Gwen Riley together with the CEO of Cypress Turbines. Gwen was somehow involved in this. But Annika wouldn't find out how from Peter. Ever since moving out to Vancouver, she had felt there were things Peter wasn't telling her. And probably never would.

Dresdener Grand Hotel
Zurich , Switzerland

Elliott Lindell set down his cell phone and paced around the room. He rubbed his hand over the five days' growth of beard on his face, and winced at the pain. His right hand still throbbed every now and then after having his gun shot out of it. The men who did it claimed they were saving his life, under Gwen Riley's orders, but later it seemed obvious they were far more interested in saving his model. That was also the case when they saved his life in the hill country of Thailand. After the heroics, they had taken the computer files that belonged to him. It was just another reminder that he could trust no one. Except Annika, of course. Lindell walked to the window and surveyed the lush green forests around the hotel and in the distance Lake Zurich, which glowed in the morning sun. Annika being called back from the conference early was a new complication he had not anticipated. But also an opportunity.

Lindell's failed attempt at sending the model to the cabin had left four unencrypted portions of his life's work sitting on servers in London, Paris, Rome, and Bermuda: the last of his grandfather's secret apartments. Only his Gen-Silico at the cabin had the programming to recombine the four portions of his model, and it would do so only if they originated from the IP addresses where they currently sat. And only if the files were properly encrypted. Annika's original travel schedule would have given Lindell two weeks to reprogram the Gen-Silico to accept unencrypted files and then complete the transfer. Now he had just twenty-four hours. But the model would be in danger for a much shorter time as well. Once he triggered the transfer, he had to erase each of the four fragments of the model, lest these fall into the wrong hands. Encrypted, they would have been useless apart. But unencrypted, conceivably they could be reassembled, given enough time and computer power.

Lindell sat down at the desk and got online to start planning the travel which would take him to each of the four servers to erase the fragments, starting with Paris. There was a TGV high-speed train from Zurich to Paris direct, leaving at two p.m. Then would come Rome, London, and finally Bermuda. Bermuda, however, was safe. He would stay there to continue his work in hiding until it was safe to reemerge. The door buzzer rang; Lindell immediately stopped typing and lifted his hands from the keyboard.

"Yes?"

"Room service. Your breakfast, Mr. Rosen."

That was the false name Lindell was using on his latest passport and credit cards, thanks to his friends in Bermuda.

"Leave it there, please. I'll take it in myself," Lindell said loudly. His friends had advised him to show his face as little as possible now.

"Yes, sir."

Lindell waited in silence for a moment and then looked through the peephole. The hallway was empty. He opened the door and wheeled in the breakfast cart. The smell of freshly brewed espresso, pastries, and bacon and eggs filled the room. Lindell made a space for his laptop on the coffee table, opened his reconfiguration subroutines for the Gen-Silico, and started eating. He always programmed best after a good meal. And if he was going to secure his model, he had a lot of programming to do in the next four hours before leaving for Paris.

New York

Gwen Riley's bad day on Wednesday had only gotten worse over the last twenty-four hours. Upon landing in New York late last night, she was promptly informed by John Rhoades that Elliott Lindell was indeed alive and well somewhere in Europe. John's men had overcome those who attacked Lindell's residence and forced the assault group's leader at gunpoint to report Lindell as dead. The leader's own body was then placed next to Carter's in the lab to complete the deception. Gwen still cringed at the thought. Yet more murders that might be traced to her. More troublesome was that John had withheld such critical information from her for so long, apparently a condition demanded by Lindell before he fled the country to Europe. He had been rather mistrusting of John's men after they intercepted him in his escape tunnel and shot his gun out of his hand. A necessary act, considering that Lindell shot first and the bullet grazed John's skull. Lindell had revealed nothing about the model. But he had agreed to stay in hiding overseas until the situation was resolved. That was just the start. Since Gwen arrived at the biotech investors' conference, the whispers all said that the FDA decision on Mitasmolin and Chrotophorib would be made before the weekend. The prevailing opinion was that Mitasmolin would come out on top, but everyone was intensely worried about the losses that Mitogenica stock had made during the week. Somebody out there knew something.

Gwen looked three tables across from her in the dimly lit ballroom of the Regency-Excelsior Hotel. Austin Hayes sat there with Arthur Cormack and two men she had never seen before. One was an attractive, middle-aged man of Mexican or Spanish descent. The other was quite a bit older, with a scar on his left cheek. *What do you know?* Gwen thought. All other eyes in the ballroom were fixed on the large video screen at the front, and the current presenter who was plugging the wonder sleep drug recently put out by his company, Morpheonic Pharmaceuticals. Oncology was next, and Gwen was given the honor of opening the session with the usual CEO's pitch of Mitogenica's future prospects. Once again, she started running through the high points of the presentation in her head. Halfway through, her PDA rang out a news alert. She thumbed it open. What she read was simply unfathomable. The FDA had granted approval to Avarus for its new drug Chrotophorib without any black box warning for liver toxicity. And for Mitogenica, the FDA had given an "approvable" letter, stating that Mitasmolin could later be approved once some questionable test center practices were clarified. In theory, "approvable" letters allowed the FDA to tie up all possible loose ends in the drug trial before final approval. In practice, they were the death knell to the receiving firm. They made for critical delays in market launch, costing tens or hundreds of millions and giving the competition room to gain the upper hand—usually for good. This was obviously great news for Chromogen's owner Avarus. And apocalyptic news for Mitogenica. Gwen flipped to a real-time quote on her screen. Mitogenica stock was down 37 percent already within minutes of the news breaking. Twice the normal day's volume had already changed hands. This was every CEO's worst nightmare.

Gwen knew very well that most of the three hundred others sitting in the ballroom were seeing exactly the same news she was. At least two dozen cell phones had just gone off within the same thirty-second interval, and half the audience's faces were lit up by the display of their PDAs or laptops as they read the news. A small but steady stream of attendees was leaving the room, each one quietly but frantically talking on a cell phone. Others still at the tables talked amongst themselves. The current speaker seemed more and more distracted, not by the commotion itself but by the obvious fact that there was a much bigger piece of news out there than what he was presenting. Austin's words about perfect timing rang through Gwen's head, and she looked over to the third table on her right. Austin sat there, not returning her look. He almost looked ashamed. But Arthur Cormack was grinning like the Cheshire cat at Gwen. The older gentleman with the scar sitting next to Austin was staring at her with an expressionless face.

Gwen sat back in her chair, closed her eyes and bit her lip. Because the worst was yet to come. The last of the questions for the current speaker ended. As the conference moderator stood up and introduced Gwen Riley from Mitogenica, a pregnant hush fell over the audience.

Without missing a beat, Gwen paced steadfastly up to the podium as Mitogenica's logo appeared on the opening slide for her talk. The elderly man with the scarred face next to Austin Hayes stood up. He had somehow gotten one of the microphones from the floor staff that gave them to the attendees during the question and answer period. He spoke loudly.

"I'm very sorry to interrupt, but investors in Mitogenica must be terribly shaken today by the news of the FDA rejecting your newest drug, Mitasmolin. Could you possibly say a few words to calm your investors' fears?"

Gwen replied without emotion. "First of all, the FDA did not reject our drug. They issued an 'approvable' letter, which I have not yet seen. I have every confidence that Mitogenica will answer any remaining items the FDA has opened and will obtain granted status in the very near future."

"Fast enough to regain your investors' trust? After all, without trust you're lost, aren't you?"

Gwen picked up on the double meaning. "I promise you, I'm going to deliver more results than you can handle."

"Really? Haven't you already lost this round?"

Gwen stood firm and smiled. "I always play to win. So if anyone thinks they're winning against me, they're likely playing the wrong game."

Amidst growing murmuring throughout the ballroom, the moderator stepped up to the podium and held up both hands. "Please, everyone, let Dr. Riley give her talk. Then we will have time for questions after."

The older man next to Austin sat down. Gwen nodded in appreciation to the moderator and began the most difficult talk of her career.

CHAPTER TWENTY

Friday, June 17
Strathmore Mews
Downtown Vancouver, B.C.

Twenty-nine stories above the waters of False Creek, Annika and Peter dragged themselves through the front door of their apartment in Granville Tower I and let their belongings fall to the floor just inside the entranceway. It was only 6:40 p.m., but Annika's body was telling her it was time to sleep starting right now, and desperately so. After the news that Dr. Lindell was still alive, Annika hadn't been able to get any of the sleep she so desperately needed on the plane ride from Zurich. Her adrenaline was now rapidly wearing thin. But she had to stay alert, knowing that the apartment was likely bugged, and she had to watch every word she spoke. Annika unpacked the cell phone from Dr. Lindell and put it on the dining room table so she could hear it from anywhere in the apartment. She wondered what he needed her to do, and hoped it wouldn't interfere with her reporting in to the Center for Natural Medicine tomorrow morning. That might tip somebody off.

Peter called out from the fridge. "Hey, do you want some pop or something? Oh, wait, I know." Peter emerged with can of soda for himself and gave Annika a bottle of chilled Japanese green tea laced with pomegranate juice. He had bought that himself at the local food mart the previous week.

"Thanks, honey," Annika said. This was the old, more thoughtful side of Peter she loved so much to see. He sat down beside her on the sofa and put his arm around her. There it was. The way he touched her. The feel of his hand on her shoulder. It was different, like a stranger. Annika recoiled. She stood up with her tea. She knew she was being crazy. It was all the stress.

"Hey, what's wrong?" Peter asked.

"Nothing. I'm sorry, it's me." Annika tried to find something to do. Then she remembered. "Oh, I have to check my email, remember?"

"Why?"

"To see when I have to meet Dr. Wong tomorrow morning."

Annika caught a glimmer of suspicion in Peter's eyes. He shrugged. "Sure, OK." Annika headed for the office. She closed her eyes in frustration at her own uncontrollable, very mixed emotions. She sat down in front of her computer, powered it up and waited for the email to come in. She could hear Peter switch on the TV in the living room and turn to business news. Annika had not accessed her email since Monday morning. When her in-box popped up, there was a whole screen of unread mails. Near the top she saw the mail from Dr. Wong. The meeting time was shown in the subject header: seven thirty in the morning. Annika sank in her chair. That would make for a long day. She let her eyes run down the screen. They settled on a name that she hadn't seen or thought about for months: Trevor Wilkins, from Glenville University Hospital. The subject header was blank. She clicked on his mail and read the contents.

> *Annika,*
> *If you're reading this, they have already killed me. Just like they killed the others. I know what they are holding over you. I can free you from that. Run the executable file attached to this mail and all 29 GB of Chromogen's original data set for Chrotophorib will be downloaded to your computer.*

Annika's adrenaline came surging back. She read the words again, her mind racing back to that day in Trevor's office when he flashed the cards in front of her, saying his life was being threatened. And claiming to have Chromogen's original data. It would prove Chromogen had falsified trial data, and erased several patients. It would be enough to bury Arthur Cormack forever, and any threat he held over her. Annika double-clicked the attachment to the mail. A new window popped open on her screen. The word "connecting" flashed over and over in the window, until after several seconds it changed to: "Connection established. Select target directory for download." Annika quickly picked one in her data folder and hit the return key. The box changed color and showed "Downloading 12.7 GB compressed." At the same instant, Annika jumped at the sound of Dr. Lindell's cell phone ringing on the table. She came out of the office and nearly bumped into Peter, who had the phone in one hand and the TV remote in the other. Annika took the phone while Peter ramped up the TV volume. She held the phone closely between her ear and Peter's and pressed the connect button.

Annika spoke in a whisper. "Hello?"

"Annika, are you home safely?"

"Yes. Where are you?"

"I'm on a train."

"Where to?"

"That doesn't matter. Now listen carefully. You are the only one who can help me now."

Annika glanced at Peter, who listened intently. "I understand."

"Once you get the model, you have to send it by overnight courier to the address I am texting you right now."

"OK," Annika replied softly. The phone flashed the message on the screen:

> *The Sea Venture Trading Company*
> *21 Jennings Bay Road*
> *Southampton Parish*
> *Bermuda*

"Can't I just bring it myself?" Annika asked. Peter flashed an angry look at her.

"No. That would be far too dangerous."

"OK. Where do I get the model?" Annika asked.

"I have a cabin north of Vancouver. Do you know where Belcarra is?"

Annika stared blankly at Peter. He nodded. "One-hour drive," he said.

"Yes. We do," Annika responded.

"Good. You need to get there at ten o'clock tonight."

"Why at ten?"

"That's when it gets dark."

"Dark enough for what?"

"To not be seen. Go to the end of Senkler Road and follow the dirt road into Belcarra Park. Mine is the last house on the waterfront. Everything is locked, secured, and safe there. I have a boathouse at the back."

"I don't know how to drive a boat!" Annika gasped.

"You don't have to."

Peter raised his eyebrows at Annika.

"And then what?" Annika asked.

"There's no phone reception at the cabin. I'll give you further instructions via Internet."

"Wait, how do we get in if everything is locked?" Annika asked in a whisper.

"Use the keys."

"What keys?"

"The ones I'm about to send you," Lindell said.

"What? How?" Annika asked, perplexed.

"Annika, there is something very important you must remember."

"What is that?"

"No matter what happens, do not try to access the model on any computer."

"Of course not—"

"And be as fast as you can. Remember, somebody might be watching you even now." The connection was severed.

Annika looked blankly at Peter. "But what about the keys?" The phone beeped to announce that a short text message had arrived. The screen filled with numbers. Then a second message arrived. More numbers. Then a third.

Peter leaned over Annika's shoulder and saw the messages. "Digital keys for an electronic lock?"

"I guess so. When do we need to go?"

Peter looked at his watch. "It's only seven. We should leave at nine. Lots of time."

"I'm not so sure."

"Why not?"

"Come here." Annika took Peter into the office and explained Trevor's email, still whispering. Peter's jaw dropped when he saw the download window. It still showed two more hours of download time.

"The time isn't an issue, is it?" Annika asked.

"Not quite. But when this thing decompresses it will get a lot bigger."

"How big?" Annika asked.

"Whatever it is, I don't have a card big enough."

"I'm not leaving here without that data. It's my life!" Annika whispered.

Peter came closer. "There's got to be someone out there watching us."

"Then what do we do?"

Peter took her out to the living room. He turned the TV volume down and spoke loudly. "I'm starving. How does Chinese take-out sound?" He started putting his running shoes on.

Annika stared back blankly. "Sure, sounds great."

"Agh!" Peter let out a groan. "I really banged my foot at the airport. Could you go pick it up?"

"Me?"

"Yeah! And you can pick up a chick flick at the video rental next door." Peter leaned over and whispered into Annika's ear. "Go slow. Let them follow you. Then I'll drive to the computer store and get the flash drive."

Annika nodded. They both left the apartment to the sound of financial news on the TV. Peter went to the stairwell while Annika went to the elevator. She looked back at Peter and shrugged, with a questioning look.

"No security cameras in the stairwell," Peter whispered.

Annika took the elevator to the ground floor and walked out the main entrance, turning left onto Beach Crescent where it began a large semicircular arch around the back end of Wainborn Park. Just up ahead on her left, Annika noticed a large black van with all the side windows heavily tinted. It took every bit of willpower she had not to look inside as she passed by. But maybe this was overkill. Would someone really be watching her? A few paces more, and she turned her head to glance back. Two men in sunglasses sat in the front, one of them talking into a cell phone. Annika turned back, her heart pounding. Part of her brain was yelling, "Run!" while the other part told her to stay calm. With shaky, nervous steps, she kept going and soon turned right onto Richards Street and walked across to the left side. Annika's heart leapt as she heard a car engine start up. Out of the corner of her eye, she saw the black van pull out of its spot and start following her. Annika tried to keep her pace even but found herself speeding up. *How are we going to get out of here?* Annika thought. She reached Pacific Street just as the walk signal went red for her. As she waited to cross, she realized the van had stopped at the red light just across from her. She couldn't help but glance over. The driver was looking straight forward. Annika looked behind her. Down from where she had come, she saw Peter in the Lexus RX cross Richards Street as he drove along Beach Crescent. He was still going to need plenty of time to get to the computer store. She turned back and looked straight ahead. The signal changed, and Annika walked across the street. Just halfway along the block was the Great Wall Restaurant. It was not formally a take-away place, but if one called ahead the staff was glad to make and package an order. It was far better than normal Chinese take-out. It just took time. Time which they now needed. Annika walked in and ordered the usual chop suey, noodles, rice, chow mein, sweet and sour chicken, and their favorite: slow roasted crispy duck. That took forty-five minutes to prepare. Annika walked back outside to go to the All Night Videos rental store next door. She looked straight ahead but concentrated all of her attention to the leftmost side of her field of vision. The black van was parked across the street, and the driver was facing her. Just then, a stranger bumped into Annika head-on.

"Ouch!" Annika yelped.

"Sorry!" he said, turning away and heading down the street.

Annika looked again at the stranger. He looked familiar. She entered the video store and found herself staring at the large wall of new releases for several minutes as she tried to place the stranger's face. Wasn't he one of the campus cops at UBC that had helped with her purse? What would he be doing here? Immediately, Annika wanted to find and talk to him. But as she turned around toward the door, the driver of the black van entered. Annika's heart started racing. She spun back around to the wall of videos and picked up the first cover in front of her face, trying desperately to calm her shaking hands.

Regency-Excelsior Hotel
New York

Gwen Riley sat back in the deep, cushiony chair in the Regency-Excelsior's panorama bar on the thirty-fifth floor. A breathtaking view of New York's nighttime skyline lay through the windows in front of her, but she was in no mood to enjoy it. After being humiliated on stage at the biotech investors' conference that afternoon, Gwen had been bombarded by question after theoretical question on how quickly Mitogenica could recover from the setback and what the revised future cash flows might be. The questioning continued the rest of the day and into the reception after the conference. It was not a good day to be CEO of Mitogenica. Gwen frowned and stirred the remainder of her gin and tonic with the small plastic rod that came with the drink. She looked around the bar. Thank God she didn't recognize anyone from the investors' conference, and nobody seemed to recognize her. She pondered ordering a plate of bar food for just a few seconds, and then decided on room service. She got up and walked toward the elevator to go to her room just three floors below. As the elevator doors closed, she noticed a young woman at the bar staring at her and picking up her cell to make a call.

Three floors down and in front of her room, Gwen swiped her magnetic key card in the reader and pushed the door open. She stopped. Everything was dark. That wasn't the way she had left it. She walked to the main switch where the entranceway merged into the sitting area and flipped on the light. Gwen gasped at the sight of a man sitting in the desk chair—the same man who had been sitting next to Austin at the conference.

"Who the hell do you think you are? Get out of here!" Gwen started toward the phone. She was stopped by two large men who came out of the bedroom with silenced guns.

"Is this some kind of joke?" she demanded.

"You never let me answer the first question. My name is Nolan."

"What do you want?"

"I just want to talk."

"Then why the guns?" Gwen asked, looking at the two men.

"I want to talk somewhere else. On my terms," Nolan said.

"What if I won't go?" Gwen said.

"We can do this the easy way, or the hard way," Nolan said.

This was it. Austin's friends were making their move. Gwen knew it was her chance to strike back. She remembered the glasses that John Rhoades had given her. "The easy way involves me going to the toilet first."

Nolan nodded. "Very well."

Two minutes later Gwen came out wearing glasses.

Nolan nodded to one of the men standing to the side of Gwen. He took Gwen's arm firmly, and they walked out toward the service elevators at the far end of the hall. Soon after they got in, one of the men took out a sack made of thick black cloth. He brought it up to Gwen's head.

"You've got to be kidding," Gwen said.

"We could always do it the hard way," Nolan said.

Gwen frowned and nodded. "Where are you taking me?"

"I'm taking you to meet The Trust," Nolan answered.

Paris

Distant echoes of car engines, honking horns, and the odd police siren made their way with little effect through Elliot Lindell's open window in the northern corner of the Sixteenth Arrondissement. At just past three thirty in the morning, Lindell stood wide-awake at his computer, attentively watching the text on the screen in front of him. He had just sent the last of his reconfiguration subroutines to the Gen-Silico supercomputer at the cabin and they were now installing themselves. The screen flashed green, signaling that it was ready. Lindell breathed a long sigh of relief and started the data transfer program for the model. He hit the return key, and after several seconds the screen told him the other nodes in London, Rome, and Bermuda had been successfully activated and were now transferring their portions of his computer model to the cabin. Lindell got up and went to the kitchen for a *pain aux raisins* he had picked up last night at the airport. He took a bite and poured some freshly brewed coffee. That, and the fresh morning air pouring in through the open window would keep him awake. Lindell once again became aware of the faint sounds outside of a city that never slept.

His grandfather's apartment was nestled in a relatively quiet, upper-class neighborhood situated along Rue Léonard de Vinci, between Avenue Foch and Place Victor Hugo. From his living room window on the top floor of the building, Lindell could just make out the upper third of the Arc de Triomphe. Lindell had been fascinated by that view as a youngster those thirty-five years ago. He remembered eating breakfast on the Louis XV table that still stood in the middle of the room. Grandfather took him first thing in the morning to the *boulangerie* for the breakfast bread and pastries—the steaming hot fresh *baguettes, pain aux raisins, croissant aux amandes*, and *pain au chocolat*. Grandmother set it all out on the table with fresh butter, jams, and a large pitcher of hot chocolate. After saying grace, the young Elliott quickly broke open one of the hot baguettes and watched the steam rise from it as he smeared on butter and jam. The food there was magnificent. Which was why he sorely regretted having to rush off to the next destination after only two days in the city. Grandfather never explained the sudden change in plans. The day after they arrived in Paris, he simply came in the apartment out of breath and looking quite nervous, and announced they had to leave for Rome first thing in the morning. Which was exactly where Lindell would be going next.

The computer in the next room made a soft tone which Lindell knew meant the transfer was complete. He brought his coffee with him into the office and checked the transfer protocol. The transfer had been successful. Lindell then once again remotely logged in to the security system of the cabin, as he had just before reconfiguring the Gen-Silico. Upon the suggestion of his friends in Bermuda, Lindell had made the security system of his cabin remotely accessible so he would know from a safe distance if the cabin had been compromised or not, long before ever arriving. Lindell checked each alarm system and motion detector one at a time. Every door, every window, every corner of his property. Still safe. He powered down the computer, slid the casing off and removed the hard drive. He walked over to the other corner of the room where the degausser stood and placed the hard drive on the metal panel at the top of the device. Lindell flipped the degausser on and prepared to leave for the airport. Now, finally, with one portion of his model destroyed, he felt a sense of confidence that the model would be safely out of reach from those who attacked him days ago, trying to take it by force. And out of the reach of Gwen Riley and the men working for her. Lindell glanced at his watch. He had five minutes to get out and hail a taxi to Charles de Gaulle Airport for the first flight out to Rome. Only when the remaining fragments of the model on the other three nodes were destroyed would it be completely safe. Getting the model back in one piece, however, now depended entirely on Annika.

New York

Gwen could only tell that she had been taken down the elevator to the parking level, where a large vehicle had been waiting. A twenty-minute ride full of turns and loops had made it impossible to figure how far she had gone from the Regency Excelsior. Loud music had been played in the vehicle the entire time. The vehicle came to a halt and someone pushed her through a door on her left. Gwen tripped and would have fallen if not for a strong pair of arms that caught and steadied her. Once she had regained her senses, she realized she could hear machinery in the distance. She smelled damp in the air. She was pushed into a small confined space. Doors closed. She was in an elevator. From the time it took, she was going up very high. When the elevator doors opened, a heavy hand grabbed the cloth bag off her face from behind. Gwen stood next to Nolan in a large room covered with wood paneling and oil paintings. A grand chandelier hung from the lofty ceiling over a huge antique table. Ornate patterns of rosewood, teak, and walnut were inlaid into the massive, solid mahogany table. Several men stood on one side of the table, including Austin Hayes, Arthur Cormack, and the older man with the scar on his cheek. Gwen was careful to look around the room slowly, to let the camera in her glasses get a good shot of every face and detail in the room. Nolan took his place at the head of the table and motioned for Gwen to take a seat beside him. On the far wall stood a large video screen that was emanating light but no picture. As Gwen walked to the end of the table, she stopped in front of Austin. He hung his head in shame.

"Coward. Can't you even look me in the face?"

Austin glanced up. Gwen immediately swung her right hand with all her force and slapped Austin across the face. Gwen walked on, looking back as she spoke. "That's for bringing Annika into this."

Nolan let out a slight chuckle as the screen on the wall came alive. Gwen stared in disgusted fascination at the silhouetted figure on the screen. A raspy voice emanated from the speakers under the screen. "Annika brought herself into this long ago, thanks to your Dr. Lindell."

Gwen glared back at the screen, and decided to test the waters. "So you're the one who killed Elliott Lindell?"

Nolan spoke up first. "That wasn't part of the plan. At least, not part of his plan." Nolan gestured toward Roy, who sat silently.

Gwen sensed the tension between the two. She stared down at Roy. "Really? So how much planning does it take not to blow up an old man in his lab?"

"Silence!" yelled Smoke from the screen. He broke into a short fit of uncontrolled coughing and wheezing. Everyone in the room fell silent until Smoke regained his composure. He cleared his throat of phlegm, and his raspy voice boomed out, "You can end this today!"

Gwen snickered. "By giving you the Eden Project?"

"And Lindell's model."

"Wrong. I don't have it."

"Give us everything you do have, or we'll ruin what's left of your pathetic company!" bellowed Smoke.

Gwen smiled back. "I must be quite a threat to you."

Nolan picked up a small stack of papers and plopped them on the table in front of Gwen.

"What's this?" Gwen asked.

"Your last ten-K statement. Without FDA approval of Mitasmolin, you've got less than a year of cash left."

Gwen looked up at the screen and smiled defiantly. "Wrong again."

Nolan looked nervously at Smoke. "She's bluffing. The numbers don't lie."

Gwen smirked. "No, they're just outdated."

"What are you talking about?" Nolan asked.

Gwen looked at Austin. "After Austin's last visit on Monday, I instructed my CFO to sell all our remaining treasury stock to raise more cash."

Everyone around the table fell silent. Nolan and Roy were aghast. Austin failed to suppress a slight smile.

Gwen continued. "We sold thirteen million shares by end of day Wednesday at an average price of fifteen dollars, and then bought every one of them back again this afternoon at a seventy-five percent discount. We still have all our treasury stock in place, plus an extra hundred and fifty million cash."

"That's still not enough for your next drug!" Smoke said.

"It doesn't need to be. On Monday I'm going to file suit against the FDA for corruption. That approvable letter is a sham and everyone knows it."

Smoke burst out laughing. "Fine. Let them all go to jail. When the dust settles, you'll still be bankrupt."

"And you'll still be short one computer model of cancer cells." Gwen turned to look at Roy. "Or did you destroy that too, accidentally?"

Smoke answered. "Give us the model now, and the FDA will backtrack on its approvable letter in a week."

"I don't have it," Gwen said. "And obviously, you don't either."

Nolan stepped up. "Sir, Roy's attack on Dr. Lindell has proven to be a colossal failure. May I make a suggestion?"

"Sit down and shut up!" Smoke bellowed.

"I'm afraid I must insist. I think I know where Lindell kept a backup of his model."

That caught everyone in the room by surprise, Gwen most of all. Roy looked on guardedly.

"Continue," Smoke said.

"Shortly before Roy here had Sydney killed, she uncovered a purchase two months ago of a Gen-Silico 5300 GX2 supercomputer, complete with 18 terabytes of memory."

"By whom?" Smoke asked.

"The Vancouver-based Cascade Pacific Real Estate Company."

"And how is that linked to Lindell?"

"The same company constructed a high-tech log cabin far up in the northern corner of Indian Arm three years ago. Sydney also reported that Lindell took long boat rides from his place in Belcarra. We can only assume that Lindell was moving his operations up to his cabin."

"Good work," Smoke said. The rare compliment stunned even Roy.

"This is pure speculation," Roy protested. "It could be a complete waste of time."

Nolan nodded. "Precisely, which is why I have authorized a small tactical force to infiltrate the cabin and take whatever they can find."

"You did this offline?" Smoke asked.

"If I had gone through Central Operations, Roy would have interfered," Nolan said.

"When will they get there?" Smoke asked.

"Tonight. They will deploy shortly after nightfall and travel over the old logging roads to the north."

"I asked when!"

"The terrain is difficult. It's impossible to tell exactly when they will arrive."

The faintest of nods was detectable on the silhouetted image of Smoke. "Consider yourself back in charge, Nolan. Dr. Riley, we will release you to your hotel, but if you leave before this is resolved, you'll be dead long before reaching the airport."

"Understood," Gwen said.

She was led to the door, with Nolan close behind. She felt the thick black cloth bag being pulled down over her head again. From the room behind her she heard the silhouetted figure on the screen shout, "Everyone leave! Except Roy."

Gwen heard Nolan bark instructions to those around them. They got back into the elevator and started heading down at high speed. From within the dark cloth bag, Gwen found the falling sensation intensely disorienting. She addressed Nolan.

"If I were a betting woman, I'd bet only you or Roy will make it out of this situation alive."

Nolan answered. "In that case, I suggest you put your money on me."

"Why is that?"

"If Roy had his way, you'd already be dead."

Strathmore Mews
Downtown Vancouver, B.C.

As the elevator doors opened in front of her on the twenty-ninth floor, Annika said a quick prayer that she was not too early. The black van had followed her all the way back to the apartment building and parked across the street. Her arms were loaded with bags of food and several DVDs. It didn't seem right to only get a single movie after browsing for an hour. She put her key in the door and opened. Financial news was blaring at full volume to cover up Peter's gasping as he sat on the sofa trying desperately to catch his breath. His face was flushed and covered with sweat. His hair was dripping wet. Annika versed her words carefully, still assuming someone was listening.

"I got the Chinese food! Sorry it took so long!" Annika said loudly. She came close to Peter and whispered. "What happened to you?"

Peter held up a memory card. "I just ran up the stairs. We don't have much time."

"Why did that take so long?" Annika asked, surprised.

"I parked way over on Howe and Drake so they wouldn't see the car."

"You ran all the way from there?"

Peter nodded between breaths. Large droplets of sweat were pouring down his face and most of his T-shirt was soaked with sweat on both sides.

He held up the flash drive again. "It's eighty forty already. We have to do this now."

Annika grabbed the memory card, ran to the office, and pushed it into the USB slot of her computer. The transfer of Trevor's data had already completed and self-decompressed. The full file size was sixty-three gigabytes. Annika found the folder with the information in it and started copying to the card. Peter walked in with a towel. He pulled off his T-shirt and toweled the sweat from his hair and skin.

Annika whispered. "It would have been nice to have more than one memory card!"

"Sorry! I tried three stores, and that was the only one they had!"

Annika walked to the kitchen, snatched a pomegranate juice out of the fridge and took a few rapid gulps. Peter came out of the office holding a large, brightly colored envelope from International Federated Couriers. He had already written Lindell's Bermuda address on the front.

"What's that?" Annika asked.

"It's from Cypress Turbines. We just drop it in any of the Federated boxes and it gets charged to the Cypress account." Peter folded the envelope and slipped it into Annika's purse. He then spoke loudly. "So, what movie did you get?"

"Ah!" Annika walked over and proudly held up her find. "*Gone with the Wind*, the extended version."

"Great!" Peter slipped on a fresh T-shirt while Annika retrieved the memory card from the computer in the office. She came out holding up the card.

"All finished" she whispered.

Peter had already put the DVD in the player and started the movie. He motioned Annika to the door. She protested. The air was filled with the smell of sweet and sour chicken and crispy roasted duck. She gestured to her stomach. "I'm starving!"

Peter pointed to his watch and shook his head. "We have to go now!"

Annika hung her shoulders in despair. She grabbed her backpack and left with Peter through the doorway, catching one last glimpse of the food on the table as Peter silently closed the door behind them. To avoid the security cameras in the elevator, they went down the twenty-nine flights of stairs. By the time they reached the bottom of the tower, Annika was dizzy from the constant turning from one staircase to the next. Her feet ached and her knees felt ready to buckle. Her hand was sore from grabbing the railing so many times.

Peter pointed to the rear exit. "They won't see us this way."

They emerged between two of the neighboring towers and headed straight for Homer Street. The light outside was rapidly dimming. The sun was getting ever closer to the horizon behind the tall buildings next to them. Peter led the way up to Drake Street, and they crossed over four blocks to Homer, as fast as they could. Annika sped to a slow run when she saw the Lexus parked up the street just half a block from them. Inside, they would be well concealed. They jumped in and Peter started the engine. The time appeared on the dashboard clock. It was nine o'clock exactly.

"We'll just make it," Peter said. He pulled out into the street and headed up to Hastings Street, which would turn into Route 7a and take them nearly all the way to Belcarra.

Annika looked behind them. There was no black van following them. But she had the feeling she was forgetting something. Something she had to tell Peter. She let it slide for the moment as she caught her breath and tried to calm down.

New York

The twenty-minute ride back to the Regency-Excelsior Hotel had been just as convoluted as the ride out. When the door to the limousine opened, Gwen knew she was back in the underground parking of the hotel. Before she got out, the bag was lifted from her head. Nolan sat beside her and smiled, politely gesturing to the elevator just a few steps away from them.

"Remember, stay here or you die."

"The police might have something to say about that."

"The police will find you dead upon their arrival," Nolan said, without a glimmer of doubt in his eye.

Without another word, Gwen hopped out and walked to the elevator, punching the call button with her thumb. The doors opened and she got in. The limousine waited until the elevator doors were closing in front of Gwen. Gwen suddenly realized why. Just before the two elevator doors met at the middle, she hit the door open button. The limo was driving away, and she caught a glimpse of the license plate. Gwen then rushed up to her room and dug into her suitcase for the encrypted cell phone John Rhoades had given her. She dug out another device John had given her, one which looked like an MP3 player but only had one simple switch. She flipped it on, and a bright red light started shining, telling her that she was jamming any bugs that might be in her room. She dialed John and at the same time she turned on her computer.

"Hello, Gwen. Is everything OK?"

"No. Everything is far from OK. I was just kidnapped by someone calling himself Nolan."

"Where are you?"

"Back at the Excelsior in my room."

"Are you hurt?"

"No. But they'll kill me if I leave the hotel or call the police."

"We can handle that. We'll be there—"

"No. Don't. There's something far more important."

"What?"

"Lindell had a place we didn't know about. A secret cabin on Indian Arm." Gwen talked as she typed into her laptop and opened an encrypted virtual private network connection.

"How do you know that?" John asked.

"They had me meet one of their leaders, to threaten me. Lindell has a Gen-Silico supercomputer there. They figure he also has a backup copy of the model there."

"And what do you think?"

"Knowing Lindell, yes. I recorded the entire thing on the glasses you gave me. Just a minute." Gwen took off her thick-framed glasses and yanked the flash memory drive out of the right side. She plugged the socket into her laptop and started uploading.

"The video has all the faces and most of the voices of the people in that room. The one sitting next to me at the head of the table is Nolan. The one on the video screen is some higher-level leader. He has no face and no name. I heard them calling him 'Smoke.' You'll see why. This is about half a gigabyte, so it's going to take a few minutes."

"That's fine."

"No, it's not fine. They're sending a small group of people to the cabin tonight to get the model. Sometime around midnight, your time."

There was a brief pause. "We can make it."

"You have to. The model is all that matters. Stop at nothing," Gwen said with finality.

"Understood."

"I also got a license plate number of what I believe to be Nolan's limousine. It's at the end of the recording."

"Good. That could help a lot."

"I'm counting on you. Don't fail me."

"Don't worry. We'll get the model. And then we'll get you."

"I know you will," Gwen said. She hung up. Something didn't feel right. That was far too easy.

CHAPTER TWENTY-ONE

Belcarra, B.C.

Annika struggled to keep her heavy eyes from closing as Peter drove past ever sparser houses in the far corner of Port Moody. The last hints of twilight had disappeared a quarter hour ago, and the quiet neighborhood they drove through offered little inspiration for staying awake. Annika rolled down the window to blow cool, fresh air on her face as Peter had done for himself ten minutes ago. She regretted not taking one of her green teas with her, or some of the Chinese take-out. She was famished, thirsty, and could almost no longer resist the urge to sleep. The scenery up ahead wouldn't help at all. Ioco Road was bringing them out of the suburbs and into the dark forest with no streetlights. Annika slipped down in her seat and had just started to nod off when the car's satellite navigation system blurted out the next turn up ahead, right onto First Avenue. Annika was jolted awake by the loud voice. The last of the streetlights soon fell behind them and Peter switched on the high beams to illuminate the trees on both sides. A cluster of houses in a small clearing to the right was the only sign of civilization. The navigation system blurted out again to go left onto Bedwell Bay Road. A small clearing in the trees opened up on the right, and Annika could just make out the pitch-black form of Sasamat Lake. A waft of chilling air blew in through Annika's window as they drove past. Annika welcomed it. She felt herself come back to life a little more. She sat up. Bedwell Bay Road snaked along the lake for another five minutes and then veered left. The voice from the navigation system announced Senkler Road on the right.

"We're almost at Lindell's house," Peter said, pointing to the screen.

Peter followed Senkler Road until it ended, then turned right onto the dirt road that took them into the complete blackness of thick forest. Just as Lindell had described, about fifty meters in stood a small, discrete iron gate set into the dense forest, with nothing visible but a winding paved road behind it. Peter stopped at the gate and rolled down his window. Outside it was dead quiet and still.

"It's closed. Now what?"

Annika pointed to the security console next to Peter's window.

"Try this," she said, as she held up her cell phone. It showed the first digital sequence that Lindell had sent. Peter reached over and keyed it in. The gate slowly rolled open and he drove down to the house. As they neared, outside lights lit up the perimeter of the house and along the path going to the water's edge.

"Look!" Annika remarked. "The boathouse must be through there."

They got out of the car and started down the path. Then Peter motioned for her to wait.

"Shhh! Just a second." Peter said softly. "I thought I heard something."

They both listened. The night was quiet except for the calming chatter of crickets. Annika stood there for half a minute, expecting to hear the black van any second. But the only thing she heard was the buzzing of a mosquito near her left ear. She waved it away.

Peter nodded. "Let's go."

They walked around the back of Lindell's house and down a thin path which wound through the thick forest. The path ended at the foot of a small wooden dock, clear of the shelter of trees overhead. Annika looked up above the dark waters of Indian Arm. The night sky was perfectly clear and filled with more stars than she had ever seen before. A cool, mild breeze carried the water's smell with it. The surface of Indian Arm was nearly mirror smooth. Small wavelets lapped at the shore rhythmically. Dim lights along the walkway made the wooden dock barely visible. Their reflections quivered back and forth in the gently rippling water. Peter used his flashlight as they walked to the small boathouse about fifteen meters out along the dock. There was no doorknob and no lock. Just a number pad. Annika got her cell phone out of her backpack and called up the second key. She punched it in. A little green light went on and the door opened with a soft whirring noise. Inside, fluorescent lighting glimmered to life. Floating on the water was a small but sporty-looking dinghy with seating for six people. The outer finish looked metallic, but on the inside it was all fiberglass. The boat was pointed toward a large, segmented steel door that would have looked at home in any garage except that its bottom was beneath the water level. The steering wheel at the front was sheltered by a small windshield and surrounded by small, dark, flat-panel screens embedded into dashboard.

"So now what?" Peter asked.

"We get in," Annika said. She climbed down the small wooden ladder. As soon as her foot touched the boat, the small screen next to the steering wheel lit up. A large glowing green bar on the screen showed "Batteries 100%." The large segmented door in front of the boat started slowly lifting up.

Annika waved at Peter. "Quick! Get in!"

Peter rushed down the ladder and hopped into the center of boat. The boat thrust down half a foot into the water and pitched to the side, throwing Peter off balance. Just as Peter regained his footing, a red window started flashing next to the green bar on the dashboard. "Warning: Disengage Power Supply."

"I think we have to unplug it!" Annika said, pointing to the power cord. Peter did so. The electric motor silently kicked in. The boat lurched forward. Peter lost his balance and fell back onto the bench of seats, nearly tumbling overboard.

"Careful!" Annika gasped.

Peter steadied himself and leaned over the seats at the back, looking at the propeller. "Wow. I can barely hear it!" he said. They looked back as they left the boathouse behind and the doorway started to close. The row of dim lights along Belcarra's Marine Avenue shrank as they moved further into the waters of Indian Arm. The boat sliced noiselessly through the calm water.

"Where are we going?" Annika asked.

Peter looked at the dashboard and noticed an electronic compass. They were headed northwest. "It could be anywhere. The inlet is over fifteen kilometers long and most of it accessible only by water," Peter answered.

"How long will this take?" Annika asked. She hadn't expected it to be so cold on the water. She wrapped her arms around herself to keep warm. At the center of the dashboard, the glowing green numbers of the speedometer shone brightly. It read fourteen kilometers per hour.

"At this rate, anywhere up to an hour," Peter said.

In the distance, streetlights and house lights became visible from behind a large swath of land in the middle of the inlet. The lights of several moving cars were visible, but seemed to barely move from across such a distance of water.

"What's that?" Annika asked.

"It must be Deep Cove," Peter said. More and more of the suburb became visible. The boat then turned to the north. The lights of Deep Cove grew fainter and smaller as the boat headed straight up the inlet. After several minutes, the boat was surrounded by total darkness. Annika looked up. The stars in the sky above seemed to have multiplied from thousands into millions. If she looked carefully, she could see starlight reflected on the surface of the water ahead of them. It was the only way to tell the difference between land and water, but for now there was only dimly shimmering water as far as she could see. The cool night air over the water soon went from refreshing to chilling. A shiver rippled through Annika's exhausted body, and she huddled close to Peter to keep warm. All she could do now was wait, with no idea of where they were going or when they would get there. And the only thing that lay in front of them was the pitch-black of wild forest on both sides of the water.

Fiumicino International Airport, Rome

Elliott Lindell was jolted awake from his light sleep as the Airbus A321 hit the ground, the thrust reversers deployed, and the engines roared into action to brake the plane. It was a few minutes behind schedule, on the tarmac at just past eight in the morning. Lindell turned on his phone and PDA and got online. He was relieved to see that his gate at the Belcarra house had been opened just short of an hour ago with the digital key he had sent Annika. A few minutes later, the boathouse was also accessed and the boat successfully launched. Lindell kept reading his small screen all the way through immigration and to the taxi stand outside. It was just past eleven at night in Vancouver, and Annika should be arriving at the cabin in a few minutes. Lindell got into the next taxi in line and gave directions to via Fiduciario, close to the Vatican. Inside the taxi, Lindell accessed the cabin's security system. Everything was still safe. There was no sign of anyone within a hundred meters of the cabin. This was going to work.

Indian Arm, British Columbia

Annika's whole body shivered intensely next to Peter in the boat, and she could only wonder when they would arrive after what seemed like hours of riding in nearly complete darkness. She looked at Peter. His face was lit up by the green glow of the dashboard display.

"I'm freezing, too," he said weakly, still looking straight ahead. His eyes then focused on something. He pointed. "Hey, wait, what's that?"

Up ahead, in the middle of the dark forest, she could see the faint glimmer of arti-ficial light. Annika's heart leapt as the light grew brighter and closer. The boat started slowing. Without warning, the lights of a boathouse flashed on just a dozen meters ahead. Annika gasped in surprise at how close they were. A door to the boathouse started opening. Just as the nose of the boat entered, the motor went into reverse, allowing the boat to drift with amazing precision into the small dock. The inside of the boathouse was painfully bright to Annika and Peter after being so long in darkness. Peter jumped onto the walkway with a rope in hand and tied the boat up. He looked at the dashboard.

"Looks like we have enough juice to get back!"

Annika looked. The soft green glow of the battery indicator now read 65 percent charge. Annika swung her backpack over her shoulder, climbed out with Peter and walked to the door. It was made of polished steel. She noticed that the entire inside of the boathouse was lined with the same steel sheeting. As they approached, Peter reached out to turn the knob, but before he reached it, the door opened automatically. They walked onto a narrow pier that jutted out from the shore about twenty meters. Looking back, Annika noticed that the boathouse exterior appeared to be made from old, weathered timber. There was not even a hint of the polished steel lining on the inside. Ahead, the lights of the cabin and several other small structures shone through evergreen trees that grew everywhere, giving the entire scene an eerie shade of dark green. The lights were reflected on the surface of the calm water and undulated slowly with every small wave that washed in.

Annika joined Peter as he walked on ahead along the dock. They reached the land just as the noise of the closing boathouse door ended. With the new quietness that enveloped them, they could hear a constant, gentle humming sound coming from somewhere up in the trees. Annika stopped in her tracks.

"Shhh!" she said, straining to hear. "What's that sound?"

"I would guess a diesel generator," Peter said.

"What makes you so sure?"

"These." Peter pointed to four large steel drums next to them on the end of the pier. They were all marked "Diesel Fuel."

The shore around the inlet sloped gently up to the surrounding mountains. Up ahead and beyond the shoreline, they could see a set of steps disappearing into the forest. Once they cleared the dock and walked up on the rocky shore, they could see that the steps led up and into a narrow clearing in the trees. A large, two-story log cabin was set about fifty meters back from the waterfront in the clearing. The steps led up to a veranda which ran around the cabin on the ground floor. A covered balcony wrapped itself around the entire upper level. Lights seemed to run continuously along the covers of each and highlighted the bright, varnished look of the thick logs. The roof, however, appeared jet-black. And shiny. A large satellite dish looked skyward from the pinnacle of the roof.

"It looks pretty high-tech for a log cabin," Peter said.

As they kept walking, Annika saw the roof in more detail. Small discrete square panels coated the entire sloped surface of the roof. At the right angle, they took on metallic sheen. "Look at those!"

"Solar panels!" Peter said.

"Why would you need solar panels if you already have a diesel generator?" Annika asked.

"We'll find out inside, I guess," Peter said.

Annika looked around the cabin. The lights which illuminated their immediate surroundings only penetrated the first few trees of the dense forest around them. Behind that, everything was black. It gave her a very unsettled feeling that was hard to shake off. She kept telling herself that nobody knew they were here as she followed Peter up the steps to the front door. The door stood out because it was made of polished steel and was set in a thick steel frame embedded in the surrounding logs. The rest of the house was pure, classic log cabin. At least, on the outside. The only detail on the door was a small, circular dark window at face level. There was no knob. As with the boathouse, there was only a small number pad where the doorbell should be.

"Time for key number three, I guess," Peter said.

Annika took out the cell phone and recalled the last text message. She keyed in the ten-digit code. As the last keystroke was made, the door opened outward with a loud click. The inside was pitch-black until Annika took the first step. Then the entire ground floor lit up with the soft glow of scores of small lights running along the ceiling.

"Wow!" Peter exclaimed. "LED lighting. This guy doesn't miss a trick."

Annika closed the door behind them and realized that she had been shivering the whole time. But the inside of the cabin was warm and well lit. Annika felt safe. They were standing in a large open-plan room which covered the entire ground floor. In the far left corner there was a small open kitchen and dining area. Next to it, a large stone fireplace stood along the wall to the left. The middle of the room was arranged as a living area, with leather sofas and chairs centered around a large flat screen TV. In the far corner opposite the kitchen stood a back door which looked like the thick steel door in the front. Staircases going both up and down were on the right. Two large windows were set into every wall. Peter walked up to the back door and looked out, cupping his hands around his face and the small round window to see better.

"What's out there?" Annika asked.

"Just a path leading up into the mountains," Peter said.

Annika walked to the window between the back door and the kitchen, looking out. She pulled back and looked at the window itself. It must have been more than three centimeters thick.

"There's something strange with the window." She knocked on the pane several times with her knuckle. "It doesn't even feel like normal glass! What is it?"

Peter walked over and pointed to the bottom of the pane. There were three very obvious layers to the window. The middle was the thickest. "See those three layers?"

"Yes. What are they?"

"The thick one in the middle one is polycarbonate. This is bulletproof glass."

Annika swept her hand over it, and then turned to Peter. "How do you know what bulletproof glass looks like?"

"Shh! Do you hear that?" Peter pointed upstairs. She heard it, too. The humming noise.

"That sounds familiar."

"Dr. Lindell's computer. Let's go!" Annika said.

Lights came on in front of them as they ascended the steps into a central hallway upstairs connecting to six rooms. At the top of the staircase was a thick wooden hatch which sat upright against the railings bordering the staircase. It was large enough to close down and completely cover the staircase. A mating latch at the top of the stairs made it possible to lock the hatch.

The humming noise came from down the hall, the last room. As they walked down the hallway, it lit up automatically, as did the rooms on either side. The door on the last room was not like the other inside doors. It was the same thick polished steel as the front door. A sturdy bolt lock could be slid shut from the inside.

Peter looked impressed. "Was he expecting World War Three to break out here?"

Annika said nothing. She entered the office and stopped in her tracks at the sight of Lindell's massive Gen-Silico supercomputer, sitting in a log cabin at least an hour's boat ride away from civilization. She gingerly set her backpack down on the desk, next to the keyboard.

Peter came in behind her. "Well, that's what the diesel generator is for. These things use huge amounts of power."

"Look!" Annika said. Next to the large flat screen of the Gen-Silico, a normal computer display was set up. Large text on it read: *MESSAGE FOR ANNIKA*. She walked up and hit a key on the keyboard. A short message filled the screen. It was set up like a chat window.

> *Annika, this is Elliot Lindell. I'm using an encrypted Internet connection via satellite so we should be safe. You'll find the empty flash drives in a box in the left desk drawer. Simply insert a flash drive into the port next to this monitor and enter "Protocol 2." Let me know when you have started that. It will take about four minutes. Remember—do not try to run this model.*

Annika turned to Peter, who was already in the desk. He pulled out the box of flash drives and put one into the port.

Annika typed: *OK. What next?*

About fifteen seconds went by before the answer came.

> *Now you must go down to the cellar. In the back corner on the top shelf, there is a small sealed parcel about thirty centimeters along each side. It should weigh about five kilograms. It's marked "EDEN I." Please take that with you. I'll let you know what to do with it later.*

Annika looked at Peter, wide-eyed. She typed back: *What exactly is in the parcel?* Again, there was a delay.

> *It's the Eden Prescription, Annika. Enough pills and IV solution for three full courses of treatment. You must be careful with it. It's worth as much to some people as the model itself.*

"I don't believe it!" Peter said. "The cure for cancer is sitting in the basement? Here? Now?"

Annika typed: *Then what?*

Another delay.

When you are all done, hit the large red button on the Gen-Silico
marked "Degauss." It will wipe out all the hard drives in less than
a minute.

A horizontal bar which tracked the progress of the encryption and writing onto the flash drive showed it was only 9 percent complete.

Annika typed: *OK. We're going downstairs now. Can we make a coffee or some-thing in the kitchen?*

Peter was aghast. "Hey, are you nuts?"

Annika pointed at the slowly filling bar on the screen. It only showed 16 percent complete. "We've got the time! I can't survive the trip back without something to wake me up!"

Lindell wrote back.

Use whatever you can find in the kitchen. But when the copy is ready,
get back in the boat and go home quickly.

They rushed downstairs to the cellar. The lights came on automatically as they went. The cellar was particularly chilly and damp. The floor was bare concrete and the walls cinderblock. On one side of the basement were rows upon rows of large batteries, each with glowing LEDs indicating their charge. Over in the opposite corner stood a shelf filled with various tools, files, and other small objects. On the top shelf was the parcel. Peter grabbed it carefully and they went back up the stairs. The coolness of the basement had brought Annika to shivering again. Peter didn't notice. He set the EDEN I package on the kitchen table. They went up to the office to find the encryption and copying completed. Annika took out the flash drive and put it in her pocket.

"Well, so much for the coffee," said Peter. "Let's get out of here."

Without saying a word, Annika snatched another flash drive out of the box and stuck it in the port.

"What are you doing?" Peter cried.

Annika launched the Protocol 2 command again. "This is the most important piece of software on the planet," she said. "There's no way I'm going to make only one copy." She started back downstairs.

"Where are you going?" Peter called out after her.

"To get something warm to drink," she called back.

Peter reluctantly followed her down the stairs but paused at the back door. He cupped his hands around his eyes and looked out the window. He turned his body to get different angles of view. Annika had several cupboards open and looked back to see where Peter was. He left the window and started for the kitchen, looking very unsettled.

"Is something wrong?" she asked.

Peter shook his head as he approached. "We should hurry. Did you find anything?"

"Bingo!" she said, holding up a glass jar of freeze-dried coffee.

Peter looked in the cupboard closest to him. "I found some creamer. And there's some bottled water down here, too."

Annika took two mugs, partially filled them with water and put both in the microwave.

Peter walked over to the back door again and looked out. "How long is that going to take?"

"Two minutes. Hey, are you sure there's nothing wrong?" Annika asked. "Do you see something out there?"

"No, nothing," Peter said. "I just don't like it here."

"I do. This is the safest I've felt all day," Annika said.

"Don't you want to mail Lindell's model to him?" Peter asked.

"Sure. And as soon as we've had a coffee, we'll do just that."

New York

In the hours following their kidnapping and release of Gwen Riley, Nolan had seen and heard surprisingly little from his shadow, Roy. Even after being put back in charge officially by Smoke himself, Nolan assumed Roy would be there at every corner, observing, interfering, and demanding explanations. Instead, Roy had been busy on the phone, out of earshot, or in the computer room on the Gen-Silico, doing something with the two programmers Smoke had installed there weeks ago. If Nolan had time, he would actually be worried about it. But he was busy coordinating his own team to make their descent on Lindell's cabin, take the model intact, and reaffirm Nolan as the next obvious Overseer of The Trust, once Smoke had finally passed away. But for the moment, nothing was certain. Especially now that Nolan's plan had just received two major complications. He picked up his satellite phone to deal with them. Right on cue, Roy came out of the computer room with a worrying look of confidence. And it was clear he knew of the problems, too.

"Is there something wrong?" Roy asked with a sneer.

"Just after we released her, Gwen Riley launched countermeasures against our bugs in her hotel room."

"Of course she did," Roy said, not giving Nolan the courtesy of eye contact.

"Central Operations finally informed me that she also made a phone call on an encrypted cell phone."

"Yes." Roy's pleasure was obviously building.

"You knew that, too?" Nolan asked.

"That's how she could inform her security people about Lindell's cabin."

Nolan was infuriated. "You want them up there?"

"Of course I do."

"My best men are going there to get Lindell's model now!" Nolan yelled.

"That's part of the plan."

"Not my plan! They should know what to expect."

"Then tell them!" Roy fired back.

Nolan shook his head in disgust as he picked up his phone to call. He glared at Roy. "Why didn't you tell me earlier?"

Roy looked at his watch. "Relax. You sent ten men, I sent fifty. Gwen's people won't get there for a while yet."

At those words, Nolan relaxed immensely. Roy had actually brought good news and solved Nolan's other complication. "That's good. I must inform my men right now."

"Of what?" Roy asked.

"That it's your people in the cabin."

Roy stopped dead at those words. "What?"

"My team is still five minutes out. But the forward scout could see the cabin lights are on, and there's an unknown number of people walking around inside."

For the first time ever, Nolan saw that Roy was completely stunned. His mouth dropped open wide. "Those aren't my men. Mine were airlifted to Fannin Lake. They're watching yours from further up the mountain and waiting for Gwen's people to—"

Nolan clenched his teeth in anger. "To what? Engage my men so I take the losses?"

"It was your call to send them there," Roy said.

"If you weren't playing games, someone wouldn't have beat us there."

Roy glared back at Nolan, the scar on his check quivering. "Find out who it is. Now." Roy's phone rang. He put it on speaker.

"Sir, we picked up satellite communications from the cabin, still in progress."

"Did you get the other end?" Nolan asked.

"A mobile device in the southern part of Europe."

Roy stepped in. "You can't do better than that?"

"It's taking time to fix a location. The signal is too sporadic."

Roy grew impatient. "Who is it? One of Gwen Riley's people?"

"We don't know, sir. As soon as we have a location we'll notify you."

Nolan spoke. "I'll ready all our teams in the area—"

Roy cut Nolan off. "I'll take care of that. You deal with the cabin." He walked back to the computer room.

Rome

The hot morning sun beat down on the streets around Vatican City and the quickly growing crowd of eager tourists lining up along the Viale Vaticano. A steady trickle of newcomers appeared from all directions as tourists rushed through the streets to find their places in the growing line. One taxi went against the crowds, heading away from the Vatican and up toward Via dei Gracchi. Then it turned onto Via Fiduciario. Inside, Elliot Lindell was still linked via his PDA to his cabin's surveillance system. He puzzled over why Annika and Peter had not yet taken the boat back to Belcarra. By his calculations, the copy should have completed several minutes ago. Why were they still there?

The taxi pulled over at number 37, Via Fiduciario. Lindell paid and got out in front of a large stone building sitting on the streetcorner. Two massive wooden doors stood at the center, topped by an archway encased by a wrought iron grate. The doors were set in a frame of large blocks of polished white marble. A small brass plaque stood at the right with 37 Via Fiduciario deeply stamped at the top. Below were two rows of buttons for the ten apartments inside the building. At the bottom of the plaque was a number pad. Lindell keyed in the code and the door opened to a foyer leading to a large spiral staircase and the central courtyard. Lindell started up the stairs. Halfway up, his PDA let out a loud shriek. He immediately looked at the screen to see what he didn't want. One of the motion detectors at the cabin's far perimeter had been set off.

It could have been a bear or a deer. Lindell quickened his pace up the stairs. By the top of the next flight, another alarm went off. Then another. And another. Lindell broke into an all-out sprint up the stairs. He had to warn Annika and Peter. There were clearly many people closing in on the outer perimeter, about a hundred meters from the cabin He came to his door on the fourth floor and keyed in his code. He pushed the door open and ran to the office to turn on his computer for a better link. He started frantically typing into his PDA. Annika might still have a chance if she ran now.

CHAPTER TWENTY-TWO

——

Indian Arm, B.C.

Annika held her warm coffee mug in both hands and sipped slowly. She leaned against the counter and sighed in satisfaction as she warmed up and came back to life. Peter was pacing back and forth nervously with his own coffee.

"Why are you so on edge?" Annika asked. "We weren't followed."

"Do you know that for sure?" Peter asked.

"Nobody knows we're here except Dr. Lindell."

Peter looked out the window again. "We should already be in the boat heading back with the model."

"To where? A bugged apartment with people watching our every move? I feel much safer here," Annika said.

"I was thinking we should go somewhere else."

That was a surprise. "Like where?"

Peter looked at his watch. "It should be finished now. Let's go." He gulped the last of his coffee and moved to put the mug on the kitchen counter. Peter led the way and again glanced out the back window as he walked past.

Annika followed and looked out the window with hands cupped around her eyes. "What is it that you keep looking at out there?"

Out of nowhere, a face suddenly appeared outside the window, staring directly at Annika. Two fierce eyes shone brightly against the black night paint which covered the rest of the face.

"Peter!" Annika screamed, as her coffee mug smashed onto the floor.

Peter spun around to see Annika staring at the window, terrified.

"What is it?" he asked.

"There's someone out there!" she shrieked.

Peter ran to the back door and looked out the window with her. The man Annika had seen was now busy hooking wires into the locking mechanism of the door. He briefly looked at Peter, as if to size him up, and then went back to work on the lock. Peter grabbed Annika and they both backed away from the door.

"What do we do?" Annika screamed.

Peter looked all around them. "Let me think!" But something outside locked his attention. He fixed his gaze out the large kitchen window next to the back door. Annika saw it, too—more movement further out, between the trees. She jumped when she saw a small bright flash outside. A split second later, the blast of a gunshot echoed all around the cabin and a bullet slammed into the window with a sharp cracking sound. It ricocheted off, leaving a small web of cracks centered around a large white blister.

"Peter!" Annika screamed.

Through the cracked window, Annika could see a man outside running toward them, holding a gun aimed right at Peter's head. Peter and Annika froze in terror as several more shots rang out. Eight more bullets hit the window directly in front of Peter at head level, each leaving its own web of cracks, each weakening the window further. The man stopped just feet away from the window and fired one last shot into the center of the cracks. The sound of this bullet hitting the window was different. A loud but dull cracking sound erupted from the window as the bullet just managed to break through the last layer of glass. The deformed tip of the bullet protruded halfway out of the windowpane, exactly at forehead height. A very pale Peter froze and could only stare at the bullet in the window and the man on the other side of it as he carefully aimed the gun again at Peter and pulled the trigger. Nothing. The man looked down and swore as he took a spare clip from his belt and started to reload.

"Peter!" Annika cried again, frantically.

Peter regained his senses and bolted away from the window just as the next shot was fired and made it through the glass. They looked toward the front door on the other side of the cabin. More men were there at the windows.

"Where do we go?" screamed Annika.

Peter grabbed her hand. "Upstairs! Now!" he shouted, as he yanked her with him at top speed back to the staircase. As they got to the back wall and the foot of the staircase, Annika realized she had left the EDEN I package and the flash drive behind in the kitchen.

"No!" she screamed. "The package! The model!" She broke away and went back to the kitchen. Peter lunged for her hand as it slipped away and nearly lost his balance. As he steadied himself and turned to follow her, he heard a loud banging at the back window. Chunks of glass flew into the room as a hand-sized hole was punched out of the pane by repeated strikes. Peter stared wide-eyed as a gun was thrust into the room, aiming for Annika.

"Annika!" Peter yelled. He ran and leapt at the hand. Peter grabbed the gun and the hand holding it, pulling both down onto the jagged broken window pane with every last ounce of his weight. A loud scream sounded just outside the window as the gun fired a shot harmlessly at the floor. The hand released the gun and disappeared outside. Blood ran down the window pane. Annika ran back with the package and flash drive in hand.

"Let's go!" Peter yelled.

They flew across the room and started up the staircase. Just at that moment, the back door flew open. They heard footsteps behind them on the staircase, but didn't dare turn back to look. Running turned to sprinting up the remaining stairs. At the top, Annika headed for the office door directly in front of them. Peter grabbed the railing and swung his body in a wide arc up in the air, coming down next to the hatch. Annika turned back in the doorway, staring at Peter with confusion on her face.

"What are you doing?" she asked Peter. Then she saw the large man standing on the fourth stair from the top. The gun in his hand was aimed at her. Annika could only stare in petrified horror.

With one fluid motion, Peter snapped open the lock on the hatch and shoved with everything he had. Just as the gunman lined up his sights on Annika's upper left chest where her heart was beating frantically, the massive wooden hatch slammed onto his head. Peter threw himself onto the hatch and slid the thick metal bolts on each side into their locking holes.

"The office!" he said to Annika, and pulled her in through the open doorway. They both slammed the heavy steel door shut and locked it.

"What's happening? Who are these people?" Annika cried in a shaky voice. She was pale with fear.

Peter tried to calm himself. "I don't know," he said breathlessly. "I don't know."

"We're trapped here now!" Annika said, tears rolling down her cheeks. She looked at the computer monitor. She saw the messages from Dr. Lindell that must have arrived when they were downstairs having coffee. Large capital letters were shouting: "*DANGER! LEAVE NOW!*" over and over again. The second copy of Lindell's model was now complete. A message on the computer read that the flash drive was ready to disconnect. Reluctantly, Annika pulled it out and held it tightly in her hand. She couldn't help but wonder how far across the lake they might be now if she had left after the first copy. She shoved the copy into her backpack. Then she remembered the last thing she had to do. She punched the large red button on the casing of the Gen-Silico. The room filled with the sound of an alarm going off as "Emergency Degauss" printed on the Gen-Silico's monitor. A loud humming sound erupted from the Gen-Silico hard drives.

Annika sat down at the desk and with trembling hands typed: *We are trapped here. They tried to kill us. What do we do now?*

Lindell's response came back shortly after: *The office is the safest—*

His message was cut short as a loud explosion outside rocked the entire cabin. The ceiling seemed to sway slightly under the blast, followed by a loud crash on the roof above them. A shrill scraping sound tracked down the roof to the side. When it stopped, Annika and Peter both watched a large white mass fall off the edge of the roof and crash to the ground next to the cabin with a loud metallic clang.

Peter looked back at Lindell's half message. "That was the satellite dish," he said. "We're on our own now."

Loud footsteps and voices sounded outside the steel door to the hallway. Annika grabbed her backpack and the EDEN I package and held them close. She recoiled as several shots were fired at the door. The bullets didn't even make a visible dent on the inside surface. Automatic gunfire went off for several seconds. Peter and Annika backed away at the deafening sound of the gunfire, but the door held.

Annika spun around and grabbed Peter's arm, pointing to the window. "Peter!"

A man standing on the balcony outside was looking into the room calmly as he spoke into a radio. He carefully noted where the Gen-Silico was positioned relative to the door and the window. He spoke into his radio, listened, and then nodded. From his gear pack, he picked out a coil of something that looked like dough. Working efficiently and methodically, he pressed the coil against the lower left corner of the window and started to unwind it, leaving behind a continuous thick strand all the way around.

"What's he doing?" Annika asked, terrified.

The man now pressed a small device into the thick strand of dough. Two coils of fine wire came out of the device, and were connected to a small black box held by the man. The man quickly started backing off to the side.

"Oh no!" Peter yelled. He frantically looked around the room for shelter. "Get in the closet! Now!" He jumped at Annika and she went sprawling into the open closet with the flash card and EDEN I package in hand. Annika's fall was broken by knee-high stacks of blue folders piled throughout the closet. Peter fell just in front of her and grabbed the knob of the closet door to pull it shut. But the door was only halfway closed when an explosion ripped through the room and smashed the door shut against its frame. The force of the blast threw both of them to the back of the closet. Large chunks of the window flew past and embedded themselves in the walls, floor, and ceiling. The whole room filled with acrid smoke.

Stunned and with ears ringing, Annika looked over at Peter. He lay unconscious on the floor next to her. The door of the closet hung on a single hinge. The second copy of the model lay on the floor between them. Annika grabbed it and started shaking Peter.

"Peter! Peter!" she yelled. Slowly, he started to come around.

Then Annika heard someone enter the room through the window. Steps came closer and closer. Without warning, the closet door was yanked away. The man from outside now stood in front of Annika with his pistol in hand. He glanced back at the damaged supercomputer and then focused on the backpack Annika was holding.

"Give me the model or you're dead!" he shouted. He trained his gun on the center of her forehead.

Annika thought quickly. "Shoot me, and you'll never know the decryption key."

The man paused and pressed his earpiece in his ear, listening to instructions. He pulled a small metallic canister out of his pocket and walked over to the barely conscious Peter. The man dragged Peter out of the closet, only to land a solid punch into Peter's stomach, knocking the wind out of him.

"Does this look familiar?" the man asked, holding out the canister. As Peter fought to inflate his lungs with air, the man held the canister in front of Peter's mouth and started spraying. Annika watched in horror as Peter could not help but inhale the mist. But halfway through the breath, a bright green spot of light came to rest on the man's temple. Immediately, a deafening shot rang out from just outside the window. Annika screamed in horror as the man's head jerked violently to the side. His hands instantly went limp, letting Peter and the canister fall to the floor. The man toppled backward, dead. Another man in fatigues and black face paint jumped through the blasted-open window.

"Are you two OK?" he asked.

Annika screamed and backed further into the closet.

The gunshot had shaken Peter back to full consciousness. He sat up on the floor. "It's OK, honey! He's the one working for Cypress Turbines! His name is John Rhoades."

"He just killed that man!" Annika said with a shaking voice, pointing to the corpse lying next to Peter.

"To save our lives!" Peter said.

John grabbed Peter's hand and helped him up. "How much did you inhale?" he asked, gesturing to the canister on the floor. While John was talking with Peter, Annika slipped the memory card into her backpack.

Peter glanced back at Annika before answering, "Half a breath, I guess. What is it?"

"You don't have long. We have to leave now," John said. He looked at the Gen-Silico computer in disappointment, then walked over to Annika and picked her up off the floor.

"Wait! I have to bring these!" Annika yelled. She grabbed her backpack and the small canister from the floor. "How do you know what this is?" Annika asked accusingly.

Suddenly, brief spurts of gunfire started blazing sporadically downstairs and from the outside.

"There's no time. Let's go," John said urgently.

A fresh wave of gunfire broke out downstairs, this time sustained. There was shouting and then more shots. John led them into the darkness outside on the balcony. Another man stood at the corner of the balcony with his rifle and a night scope, making rapid shots into the dark forest behind the cabin.

"What's the situation, Logan?" John asked.

"There's just three of them left!" He took another two shots. "Two outside and one downstairs."

Gunfire erupted downstairs once again, followed by two small explosions and then nothing at all. An eerie silence engulfed the entire cabin and surroundings.

John spoke into his radio. "Status?"

"We're clear!"

"Good work," John answered.

The response came back. "Are you done? Did you get Lindell's computer model?"

John slightly winced at those words.

Annika turned to Peter. "See! They didn't come to save us! They just came for the model!"

"Is that true?" Peter asked.

John's blackened face nodded. "Gwen Riley wants to recover Lindell's work before someone else does. And that someone else just tried to kill you."

"You do have the copy of the model, right?" Peter asked Annika.

Annika glared at Peter. "Yes."

John spoke into his radio. "We've got it. Let's get out of here."

Annika and Peter followed him and Logan down the stairs to the front of the cabin facing the water. They held up there, out of view from the forest behind, while two others emerged from inside the cabin.

"There's no sign of anyone else," one of them said.

Annika looked around. "How are we getting out of here?"

"Very quickly," John said, pointing to the waterfront. A large speedboat was tied to some trees at the end of the shoreline furthest from the boathouse. "Let's go," he said, and started a rapid jog to the boat. Everyone followed. But no sooner had Peter and Annika left the cover of the cabin than a bright object went screaming loudly through the air just above their heads. It hit the speedboat dead-on. Instantly, the boat exploded into a fireball that lifted it several meters off the water. Annika felt a flash of intense heat on her face as the fireball seemed to hover in midair for a second before the boat fell back into the water as a mass of burning splinters. The forest lit up with flashes of light, and the air filled again with the sound of blazing guns.

"Get back! Get back now!" John yelled. He and Logan spun around and released a long barrage of gunfire into the forest. Peter and Annika ran for their lives back around the corner to the front of the cabin. John and Logan held down their corner while Matt and Ken raced to the other and started firing their guns toward the forest. The noise was deafening and came from all directions. Annika reached back to grab Peter's hand for comfort, but couldn't find it. She turned and saw that he was grasping his chest, his eyes wide and questioning.

"What's happening?" Peter forced out hoarsely. He was barely able to talk.

John Rhoades said, "It's the neurotoxin." He turned to Annika. "How did you two get here?"

"There's a boat in the boathouse!" Annika yelled, pointing to the small boathouse at the end of the dock.

John shouted quick orders at Logan and the others. John and Ken both took out thick guns from their gear packs and nodded their readiness to Logan. Logan braced himself on the corner of the cabin and aimed at the large fuel tank next to the generator about fifty meters away. One shot later, the fuel tank exploded into flames, and the humming of the generator came to an abrupt halt. All the lighting in and around the cabin went completely black. Much dimmer backup lights came back on inside and around the boathouse. For a few seconds, the gunfire died down.

"Flares!" John shouted. John turned to Peter and Annika. "Close your eyes now!"

Peter and Annika both closed their eyes and covered them with their hands.

Several loud popping sounds erupted from close by, followed by multiple small explosions overhead. Even through closed eyes Peter and Annika saw powerfully bright flashes of white light. Seconds later, the flares went out and everything was black again.

John yelled at them. "Move now! To the boathouse!" As they bolted across the grounds, Annika noticed two men at the opposite tree line, writhing on the ground and screaming as they held their hands to their eyes. Peter was struggling to keep up. He was in obvious pain and kept one hand on his chest. John swung Peter's free arm over his shoulders and took most of Peter's weight on his legs. The heavy footsteps of six people running for their lives pounded the wooden dock all the way to the boathouse, only to find it locked. John held his gun to the number pad.

"No, wait!" Annika shouted. "I have the code."

John stood back as she read the number off the phone and keyed in the code, her fingers moving faster than the eye could follow. Peter started gasping for air and fell on his knees. The gunfire resumed from a couple of points in the forest. The number pad flashed green and the door opened. Everyone jumped inside just as war erupted once again outside. Bullets slammed into the boathouse by the dozen—but none made it through the steel shell that lined every wall. John picked up Peter and hauled him onto the boat. The rest followed. The boathouse door opened and the boat started its slow and silent exit. Everyone but Peter and Annika was shocked at how slowly the boat moved.

Logan got into the driver's seat and pushed down on the accelerator without effect. "What kind of a boat is this?" he yelled.

"It's electric!" Annika said.

"Damn!" Logan yelled in frustration. "Can't this tree-hugging piece of eco-electro crap go any faster?"

"I think it's on autopilot!" Annika said.

"Matt! Make this thing fly!" Logan yelled. He jumped out of the driver's seat. Matt moved to the controls as the boat exited the boathouse.

"Both of you! Lie low in the boat!" John yelled at Annika and Peter.

Peter started grasping at his throat. Annika shrieked at John. "Please! You have to help him!"

"Who's got the antidote? He's going into shock!" John yelled.

"I do!" Ken answered. He took out a small kit and opened it to reveal a large, long needle and a vial. He quickly extracted ten cc's of liquid into the needle and removed any air bubbles with a few flicks of the finger. He ripped Peter's shirt and counted down the ribs. Just as he plunged the needle into Peter's heart, the boat cleared the protective cover of the boathouse and came into full view of the cabin and forest. Everyone was shocked to see the cabin swarming with armed men. A group of them ran down the dock to get as close as possible, and all opened fire on the boat simultaneously. Logan and John ducked low in the boat and fired back with everything they had. The men on land dispersed and took cover.

"Matt!" John yelled. "They're not firing paint balls at us!"

Matt was frantically trying to master the boat's control system. "Just give me a second!" he said. His hands swept over the controls in a frenzy of motion.

"We don't have a second!" John yelled as he continued firing. A constant shower of bullets was impacting the hull of the boat and the water around them.

Annika watched as Ken withdrew the needle from Peter's chest and threw it overboard. Peter's eyes rolled back and he started writhing for air.

"It's not working!" Ken shouted.

"It takes a few seconds to kick in!" John yelled back. He noticed a man with a rocket launcher on his shoulder emerge from within the cabin and take aim at them.

"Logan! Rocket!" John yelled, pointing at the threat.

Logan steadied himself as best he could and fired his rifle. The man with the launcher instantly fell backward, releasing the rocket as he hit the ground. The rocket flew straight into the cabin's open doorway and detonated inside. The whole cabin shook as debris was blown out of all the ground floor windows, followed by flames and billowing smoke.

The explosion snapped Annika out of her focus on Peter. She remembered their way in. "On the dock! Those large barrels are filled with diesel fuel!" she yelled.

Logan took aim. Several explosions echoed across the waters and Logan's face lit up bright yellow as a massive fireball engulfed the dock and most of the shore in front of Lindell's cabin. For a moment, the gunfire stopped.

Annika turned back to Peter and watched in horror as he suddenly went limp. Ken grabbed Peter's arm and felt for a pulse. He shook his head in frustration and immediately pinched Peter's nostrils, exhaled a breath into Peter's lungs, and started pushing down on Peter's chest in rapid compressions.

Annika fell back in the boat, limp with panic and despair. She was powerless to help. The sound of the guns around her suddenly seemed distant as she watched the life slip out of Peter's body.

New York

The sound of bullets and small explosions came screaming through the loudspeaker of the phone on Nolan's desk.

"I said report! Where's my team?" Nolan yelled into the phone.

A frantic voice shouted back, "Sir, the first team is all down!"

"What! That's impossible!" Nolan yelled back.

"Gwen Riley's people are very well armed. They've taken Peter and Annika with them in a boat. We're firing on them now."

"Well, try hitting them!" Nolan shouted.

"We are! The boat seems bulletproof!"

"What about Lindell's computer model?" Roy yelled.

"Nothing. It's all been wiped clean. If there were any backups, they were taken."

Roy didn't flinch at those words. Nolan started pacing around the room.

"Keep looking," Nolan said.

"We can't right now!"

"Why not?" Nolan yelled back.

"The whole cabin is on fire," the frantic voice replied. Fresh gunfire erupted in the background.

Nolan cut the connection and dialed another number.

"Who are you calling now?" Roy asked.

"The team in Rome," Nolan replied.

"Why?"

"Whoever is at the address we located will have the answers."

Rome

Elliott Lindell stared at the computer screen in front of him, trying not to fall into a full-blown panic. Ten minutes ago his screen had flashed a warning that his IP address had been located by an outsider. His security specialist friends in Bermuda told him that once he was located in any of his apartments, he had to get out in no more than fifteen minutes. Nine minutes ago, he had placed the hard drive on the degausser and the erase procedure started. It was almost complete. Lindell couldn't help but wonder what had happened to Annika after the satellite link had been broken. Was she hurt? Was everything already lost? Lindell gathered the last of his things and prepared to leave quickly. But as he approached the door, his security alarm went off. Someone had just broken through the main entrance down below. Lindell looked at the video feed from the downstairs security camera to see two men coming rapidly up the stairs. Lindell double-bolted his door from the inside. He looked through the peephole, waiting and hoping they would pass by on their way upstairs. But to Lindell's horror, they stopped right at his door and knocked loudly. Lindell quietly backed away from the door and went into the bathroom, locking the door behind him. He could hear the knocks getting louder and knew it would be seconds before they started breaking in.

Lindell stood in front of the floor-to-ceiling mirror in the bathroom, and for the first time in his adult life, he was happy with the very quirky arrangements of his grandfather's apartments. He reached under the bidet and pulled hard on a hidden lever. The whole mirror in front of him shifted. He pushed firmly on the right edge, and the entire mirror opened to a space where there should have been a half-meter-thick stone wall. Instead, there was a passage to the neighboring building. Lindell stepped into the passage and pushed on the wall in front of him. It opened likewise into the bathroom of a small bachelor's apartment. He closed the wall-sized mirror tightly behind him until it clicked into place, and then closed himself into his second apartment. Lindell exited through the front door of the studio and hurried down the stairs leading to the main exit on Via dei Gracchi, conveniently hidden around the corner from the entrance to the other apartment. Lindell quickly put more distance between himself and the corner. He hailed one of the many taxis going by. The taxi pulled in and came to a stop. But just as Lindell opened the taxi door, he heard running footsteps behind him closing in at top speed. Before he could jump into the taxi, a hand clamped down on his arm from behind and yanked him backward. Lindell gasped in pain as he was hauled onto the sidewalk. Lindell spun around to see an ugly, immense man still holding his arm. For a moment, the grip on his arm loosened and the large man flinched in shock. He called out to a second man who was just behind him.

"I don't believe it. It's Lindell! He's alive!" With his free hand, the man brought up a small metallic canister and held it in front of Lindell's face.

The second man spoke with a thick Italian accent as he pointed to the canister with one of his stubby fingers. "If you're Lindell, then you know what this is. Don't you?" His sickly smile revealed teeth stained by coffee and cigarettes.

Lindell immediately recognized the canister from Annika's story about Mitch Purcell. The men working for Gwen Riley had also warned him about it. He nodded and said, "Yes."

The taxi driver leaned his head out the window and shouted something in Italian. The second man drew a gun and pointed it at the taxi driver, barking back harsh-sounding words and twice as loud. Without a sound, the driver's head vanished into the vehicle. The taxi pulled away and sped off. Lindell watched his last hope evaporate as the taxi disappeared into the traffic. Both men led Lindell back around the corner to Via Fiduciario. The one who had threatened the taxi driver took out a cell phone and dialed. He spoke with nervous delight, announcing the capture that would assure his career.

"Sir, Lindell's alive! We're bringing him in now."

Lindell strained to hear more of the conversation, but a heavy hand shoved him violently from behind, causing him to stumble forward and nearly trip over his own feet.

"Over there." The man behind him shoved Lindell forward again to a black car with darkened windows.

The first man with the phone opened the rear door for Lindell and nodded toward the open door. Lindell leaned down to get in, but then wrenched back at the sight of the driver's lifeless corpse leaning back on the front seat. His blood and brains were spattered throughout the rear of the car. The man gripping Lindell from behind saw it, too, and instantly let go. His face went pallid. He shouted to his partner, and nearly dropped the metallic cylinder as he fumbled to grasp his gun with the other hand. He spun around, looking wildly for an enemy he clearly hadn't expected or prepared for, then regained his iron grip on Lindell much harder than before. Lindell winced in pain as his arm felt like it was about to ripped off.

The other shouted into his phone. "Backup! We need backup!" He also reached for his holstered gun, but too late. Lindell watched two men emerge with impossible speed from behind a parked delivery truck and take aim at the man holding the phone. A short barrage of silenced blasts into his chest left him in shock and powerless. His legs buckled beneath him and he fell to his knees against the car. Lindell tried to turn away to avoid the gruesome sight. But the captor gripping him from behind held on tight, using Lindell as a human shield. Lindell was able to turn his head—only to see three other gunmen jump out of a van parked just paces behind them. They aimed for his captor's head. Lindell instinctively ducked, and almost instantly the grip loosened. His captor fell to the ground, blood pouring out of a large hole in his skull, spreading quickly over the sidewalk. His lifeless hand opened and the metal canister rolled out onto the sidewalk, stopping at Lindell's feet.

"I'm hit! I'm hit!" the man with the phone said in a gurgling, weak voice. He stared in horror at the sight of his dead partner. He was using all of his strength just to lean up against the car and speak. His chest was covered in blood oozing from his wounds.

One of the attackers walked up to him, placed the dying man's cell phone on his forehead, and held it there with the muzzle of his weapon. He spoke loudly and calmly at the phone.

"With the compliments of Maria Dostinelli. This is for killing her husband, Gian Muratte." Two rapid shots through the phone and into the man's head ended his life. His limp body slumped over into the gutter next to the car. The screech of tires sounded in the street next to them as two cars came to a rapid halt. Lindell stood there, still shaking in paralyzed fear as the killers disappeared into their getaway cars.

The final one to close his door looked at Lindell and yelled, "Get out of here now!"

Their cars zoomed away at top speed. When the roar of the motors had died down in the distance, Lindell could hear the sound of sirens converging on his location from all directions. With shaking hands, he grabbed the metal canister at his feet and ran back around the corner and down the street as far as he could. He waved his arm frantically for the next taxi. He realized that he had gravely miscalculated the entire situation, and hoped that Annika was not facing the same threat he just had.

Indian Arm, B.C.

Multiple bursts of automatic gunfire pierced the cool night air over the waters of Indian Arm as Logan Helliker and John Rhoades took aim at anything that moved near the burning cabin. Most of the return fire came from further back in the forest, which was obscured by the smoke. The bright orange flames of the diesel fuel burning on the dock and along the shoreline gave good cover. But the fire was dying down, and they were less than two hundred meters out from the shoreline.

"Matt! We need speed now!" John yelled.

"I'm just about there!" Matt yelled. The display on the dashboard had changed appearance. Now small text covered the screen and Matt was changing the programming.

Peter started coughing and sputtering. He pushed Ken away and turned on his side, looking at Annika.

"Peter! Are you OK?" Annika asked through tears of joy and relief.

"I'm not OK. But I am alive."

"I got it! I got it!" Matt yelled. The boat's electric motor kicked into overdrive. All braced themselves at the unexpected power of the boat's engine. The gentle breeze flowing past them turned into a rushing wind, and the burning cabin fell quickly behind into the darkness. The gunfire faded and soon stopped.

Annika crawled over to Peter and threw her arms around him, crying. "I thought I was going to lose you!"

"I thought you were, too," Peter said with a weak smile. He was still clearly struggling to breathe normally.

"What did they give him?" Annika asked John.

"It's a drug that paralyzes the heart and respiratory muscles. But we gave him an antidote. He's going to be fine."

Annika wasn't impressed. "How did you get an antidote?"

"Gwen Riley had some friends analyze it and prepare a countermeasure."

"So you work for Gwen Riley?"

John nodded. "That's right."

"Doing what, exactly?"

"Protecting Mitogenica and Dr. Lindell. And right now, securing the computer model."

At those words, Annika glanced by reflex at her backpack sitting next to John's feet. She wanted to kick herself for doing it. He immediately noticed and picked the bag up, looking inside. He pulled out the package addressed to Bermuda and then the parcel marked EDEN 1.

"What's this?" John asked.

"It's nothing!" Annika replied.

"It's three courses of Lindell's treatment," Peter said. "It's the cure for cancer. And his model is in the envelope."

Everyone on the boat suddenly focused on Peter and what he had just said.

"Peter!" Annika spun around, furious.

"It's OK, Annika. You can trust them. They just saved both our lives." Peter looked at John. "That disk has the only copy of the model left. But only Lindell himself can run it. He warned us." Peter glanced at Annika to let her know he was holding back on purpose.

Annika gently pressed her hand against her jacket pocket. To her relief, the flash drive was still there. Perhaps Gwen Riley would get a copy of the model. But at least

Dr. Lindell would get one, too. She gave a brief smile to Peter to confirm she had it. John put the first flash card and the parcel into his own gear bag. "These will be much safer with us, Annika. When the time is right, we'll give them back to Dr. Lindell." Then, he threw Annika's pack back to her.

"You know he's alive?" she asked.

"It was us who saved him Sunday night. If he would have simply trusted us and taken us up here," John said, shaking his head in frustration.

"So you could give the model to Gwen Riley?"

"So we could protect it."

"Where is he now?" Annika asked.

John shrugged. "We took him to Switzerland until this all blows over. By now he could be in Bermuda, at the address on your package."

Annika and Peter huddled together in the boat as it continued back toward Belcarra. The entire time, Logan steadied himself on the front passenger seat and scanned back and forth across the dark waters through the night vision scope on his rifle. The dim light of the scope made his eye seem to glow in the darkness. Annika soon realized that once they reached Belcarra, she had no idea where she would go next. Or be taken to. She didn't have a chance to speak.

"Hey, guys!" Matt said in a forceful whisper. He pointed forward. The shoreline and Lindell's house in Belcarra were approaching.

"We can't all fit in the Hummer with the gear," John said. He turned to Peter. "Where's your car?"

Peter pointed to the right. "At Dr. Lindell's house."

John looked at the others. "Matt, Ken, you go with these two. We rendezvous in ten minutes at the oil refinery two kilometers to the south."

Matt took out a small GPS unit and pulled up a map. "Yeah, got it. Ioco Road."

John nodded. "Drive to the southern access road there and wait for us. We'll leave together."

"Where are you going?" Peter asked.

"We launched our boat from the campgrounds. The Hummer is hidden on a small dirt road in the forest."

Matt slowed the boat as Lindell's boathouse drew closer. He pulled up to the dock and the four jumped off the boat. Matt and Ken both drew their weapons and put silencers on them. Matt took out a pair of night vision goggles and put them on. They paced up the dock as John and Logan took the boat northward toward the Hummer. As they walked up the path to Lindell's house, Matt signaled to stop several times until he scanned the area completely with his goggles. Each time they got the "all clear" after half a minute or so. Finally, they reached the car.

"I'll drive, OK?" Matt said.

Peter nodded and threw him the keys. They piled in the car and Matt started the engine. But the gear wouldn't shift to drive. He tried again. It wouldn't budge. Matt looked back to Peter. "Is there something wrong with your car?"

"No. It worked perfectly getting here," Peter said.

Matt's next words were abruptly drowned out by a loud hissing noise coming from under the dashboard.

Matt yelled at the top of his lungs, "Get out! Get out!" He tried in vain to open his door. It was jammed shut. He pulled out his radio to warn John and Logan, but the blast of gas went directly on his face. The radio fell to the floor and he slumped over the steering wheel, unconscious. Ken went quickly after that.

Annika pulled frantically at her door handle and tried to lift the lock button, but they were both jammed in position. She looked over to Peter helplessly. Peter was grabbing at his seat belt and shouting something, but the words were lost in the confusion. She tried to speak, but found her mouth heavy and unresponsive. A warm numbness spread over her tongue, mouth, throat, and then lungs. From her lungs, the warmth spread to her legs, arms, and head. She fought for movement, but her muscles refused to budge and relaxed into a limp paralysis. The only thing she could still feel was her heart racing in her chest. She wondered if she was about to die. Powerless, she slumped over onto Peter's lap. Through a thick veil of blurriness, she watched someone approach the car window and look at her, then her eyes rolled upward and she slipped into oblivion.

* * *

One kilometer to the north, John and Logan powered down Lindell's electric boat and let it drift noiselessly in the darkness to the shoreline. They hit land just two hundred meters north of the campgrounds. They both put on their night vision goggles to find their way through the dense forest to the Hummer. John glanced quickly at his small GPS screen. He pointed westward, just ahead of them. He tried to keep his voice to a whisper. "Two hundred meters over here."

"Got it," Logan said.

Shortly after, they broke out of the forest and onto a small dirt road. They started walking in the direction of the Hummer.

"Stop!" John whispered, holding his hand up. He was listening for something.

In the next instant, Logan heard it, too. A vehicle approaching from the south. They ducked back into the forest, waiting to see the car's headlights. But the only lights to appear were three thin red laser beams slicing through the misty night air from a roofless jeep that came from around the bend at slow speed. Its lights were off. Three men stood in the jeep, one facing forward and two backward. Each man held a night vision rifle scope mounted on a large, silenced weapon. They systematically scanned every inch of forest around them. As the jeep neared, Logan and John put their backs up tightly against a pair of large trees and stood motionless. Red laser beams swept through the forest on either side of them, finding nothing but trees and bushes. The jeep kept moving and the lasers veered off to the north. Logan peered around his tree just for a split second. He never had time to look at his enemy's weapons back at the cabin, but these he recognized immediately. The rifles were Heckler & Koch 416 carbines—light, compact machine guns capable of up to nine hundred rounds per minute. They were also used by the military special forces of eleven countries—including the U.S. Army's Delta Force. The implication was clear: the men wielding these weapons were among the best-trained in the world.

"Who the hell are these guys?" Logan whispered.

"Ping is still working on it," John said.

Logan then remembered what lay ahead of the jeep. "They're heading right for the Hummer!"

The jeep disappeared around the next bend. John took out his radio. He called Matt several times. Then he tried Ken. No answer.

"Damn!" John said. "We're on our own now."

Logan grimaced and nodded. He had found his way to John Rhoades after a military career he started as a Recon Marine. Primarily trained in counterintelligence and reconnaissance, Logan's expert-level marksmanship with handguns and assault rifles alike was a surprise to all. After minimal training he could maintain accurate long-range sniping under any conditions that combat or the weather could throw at him. That combination made him ideal for special ops, and he was quickly inducted into Special Forces and became a Scout Sniper Leader. After a decade of active duty around the globe, Logan grew tired of losing comrades and in some cases nearly his own life. Then, during a mission in Iraq, he took two rounds in the chest—one just an inch from his heart. He knew it was time to retire. Or at least, what he thought would be retirement.

He readied his rifle. They got back onto the dirt road and started jogging north. Within a couple of minutes, they stopped. Someone was using headlights up ahead. John and Logan went deep into the forest and slowly approached their car from the west. They recognized the jeep that had passed them earlier. It was stopped in front of John's black Hummer. Its headlights were on high beams to illuminate the Hummer and the surrounding area. Two men inspected the Hummer. The other two held their weapons at the ready, scanning the forest around them.

"It's bulletproof glass and paneling," one of them said to the others. He felt the hood. "It's still warm."

Another man who stood next to the Hummer spoke as if he was in charge. "This has got to be theirs. I need to report this."

At those words, Logan brought his silenced rifle swiftly but silently up to aiming height. John crept sideways several meters to get a better angle at the others. He picked up a large stone, and motioned his intent to Logan. John picked a spot to throw the stone in order to divert the group's attention away from himself and Logan. The group's leader took out a satellite phone and made his call. John let the stone fly, and then took aim with his own rifle.

"Yes. This is Taylor. We found—" He cut his own words off and turned with the others toward the loud sound of the stone crashing in the forest. He didn't notice the bright beam of green laser light which shone out from between the trees and raced in an instant to its target on his own head. But a glimmer of green light reflected off the Hummer's window and caught his attention. Taylor spun around to see the green laser light come to rest in the center of his forehead. He drew in a deep breath to shout, and reached for his weapon. But before he could do anything, Logan's bullet slammed into his head. As Taylor fell backward onto the road, John released his own silenced bullet into one of the armed men. The other two men whipped around to see two bodies hit the ground. The green laser beam had already disappeared. The man with the rifle looked frantically for a target. In a panic, he sprayed the forest randomly with silenced gunfire, his red sighting laser arcing back and forth wildly among the trees. The other took out his sidearm and swung it threateningly at the trees. He bent down and picked up Taylor's satellite phone with his left hand.

"Help! They're here! Agh!" He screamed in pain as the phone was shot out of his hand. The next bullet slammed into his right shoulder. His right arm fell limp at his side with the pistol still in hand, and now useless. Before he could dive for cover, a third bullet hit him dead between the eyes. The last man standing had seen the source of the bullets. He concentrated all his firepower in the forest where Logan now lay protected behind a thick cedar tree. His magazine emptied sooner than he expected. But he was fast. He took cover by diving behind the bulletproof Hummer before Logan could return fire. Through the Hummer's windows John could see the obvious motions of the gunman's shoulders as he yanked out his spent clip, inserted a new one, and readied his rifle for firing. John also noticed the gunman wasn't wearing night vision goggles. From his own hidden position, John took aim and shot out the two headlights of the jeep. The blackness of night descended on the forest again. John put his goggles on and paced through the trees and bushes to get his shot. His target was frantically looking in all directions with wide, darting eyes that found nothing to focus on but empty darkness. In desperation, the gunman blindly opened fire in all directions. John ducked behind a tree and spun his rifle to the vertical, holding it close to his body. He could feel bullets ricochet off the trees around him. When the shooting stopped, John knew another clip had been emptied. He stepped out and took aim, only to see the man's head light up in a brilliant flash of light and then explode sideways. John looked over to the left. Logan stood smiling at him.

"Good shooting!" John said. He motioned Logan closer. "Come on, we have work to do."

They dragged the bodies into the forest and concealed the jeep behind a thick patch of bushes. Minutes later, both men jumped in the Hummer. John turned off all the vehicle's lights and drove by using his night vision goggles, with windows down and rifles ready to fire. John knew if they were caught, it was over for everyone.

New York

"Taylor! Report! Report!" Nolan yelled into his phone.

Another voice came over the speaker: "Sir, there's no response from Taylor's team. Another unit is on the way now."

"How many did you capture at Lindell's house?" Nolan asked.

"Four. Annika, Peter, and two of Gwen Riley's people."

Roy stepped up to the phone. "Was the girl carrying anything?"

"Yes, sir. A high-storage-capacity flash memory card."

"Excellent! Anything else?"

"Yes, a cell phone with several messages in its memory."

"What messages?"

"All of them are codes except one, which is an address for a company in Bermuda."

"Which company?" Roy demanded.

"The Sea Venture Trading Company."

Nolan shrugged at the information. "Just bring them in. And keep that flash drive intact!"

"Yes, sir. We are proceeding to Pitt Meadows Airport as we speak."

"Good. And when you find the last of Gwen's people, kill them on sight. We don't need them."

"Yes, sir."

The connection was cut. Nolan looked over at Roy. He was pacing back and forth, muttering to himself and staring off into space with narrowed, concentrated eyes. An hour ago, the astonishing news from Rome of Lindell's continued existence had shocked them both and thrown the whole operation into question. But it also gave them new focus on retrieving the model from Lindell's cabin—especially after Annika and Peter showed up there and nearly botched the operation for them. Now, however, there was time to consider the implications of Lindell being alive. And there were many.

"That name. I know that name," Roy said to himself.

"What name?" Nolan asked.

"The Sea Venture Trading Company." Roy walked over to the desk and dialed through Central Operations.

"Who are you calling now?"

Roy held up his hand impatiently at Nolan's face. It was his usual way of saying "shut up" while economizing on words. He looked up at the chandelier while talking on the phone. "This is Roy. Bring me the first three volumes of the archives. Now." He disconnected.

"Archives of what?" Nolan asked.

"The archives of The Trust."

"Who were you talking to?"

"The Citadel."

Nolan had been to the Citadel of The Trust only four times. It was used by the inner circle as a command and control center, for special meetings, and for their leisure. Rarely, lower order members in good standing were allowed to visit. It was more a stone fortress than a mansion, located near the Hamptons on Long Island. It was well isolated and had its own long stretch of coastline. It had been built in the late nineteenth century by one of J. P. Morgan's closest friends—one who later betrayed him and masterminded The Trust after Morgan's death.

"What do you expected to find in the archives?" Nolan asked.

"The answer to why Lindell has evaded us so well."

Nolan shrugged. "Gwen Riley's people were helping him."

"That's just the beginning." Roy dialed the phone again.

"Such as?" Nolan asked.

"If Lindell is alive, whose body was in the lab?"

"What about the team from Vancouver?"

Roy briefly ignored Nolan to listen to the phone. He scowled and slammed his fist on the phone. "None of them can be located by Central Operations."

Nolan felt a small victory. "You accuse me of failure when you let Lindell escape and your hand-picked expert team was wiped out by Gwen Riley's men!"

"How dare you question me! I report to the inner circle of The Trust." Roy's scar vibrated in nervous fury.

Nolan frowned in disregard. "You underestimated Gwen Riley's men just as much as I did."

"And Lindell. But that's about to change."

"Why?"

"Lindell was expecting the model in Bermuda. He must be headed there soon." Roy spoke into the phone to Central Operations. "Do we have any assets on site in Bermuda?"

The answer came after several excruciatingly long seconds. "No."

"How quickly can we get someone there?" Roy yelled.

"I can have a private jet ready for takeoff in seven hours at JFK."

"What about boats?" Roy asked.

More seconds. "We've got a high-speed hundred-and-twenty-foot yacht currently moored in South Cove Marina. It's just at the southern end of Manhattan."

"And what exactly is high speed?" Nolan asked.

"It's a surface piercing hydrofoil. Cruising speed fifty-five knots."

"When can it be ready?" Roy asked.

"Fuel up and crew ready in two hours. At six hundred and fifty nautical miles to Bermuda, it's a toss-up who gets there first."

Roy's response was immediate. "Dispatch teams on both. Keep me informed."

"Affirmative."

CHAPTER TWENTY-THREE

Saturday, June 18
Heathrow Airport, London

The bloody scene from the streets of Rome played itself over and over in Elliott Lindell's mind during the entire plane ride to London. He knew he wouldn't get a lucky break like that again. Whoever wanted the model was now closer than ever, if they didn't already have it from the cabin. And they knew he was alive, which was a very dangerous thing. Lindell watched the time. He walked into the telecom shop and purchased a disposable cell phone. He then ran downstairs and got into the Heathrow Express, always watching to see if he was being followed. Waiting for the doors to close seemed to take an eternity. But he dared not start until the train was underway. In the meantime, Annika's life hung in the balance.

Finally, the doors closed and the train slowly rolled out of Heathrow Station toward London. Lindell removed the SIM card from the disposable cell and put it in his own PDA device. He logged on to the Net and checked for connection attempts on the two remaining nodes in London and Bermuda. Nothing. There was still a chance to save Annika. Lindell patiently waited for the signal during the entire train ride. When the Heathrow Express pulled into Victoria Station, he still had nothing. Lindell took a taxi to Belgrave Square and exited in front of the familiar old building bordering on Chesham Place. London had, of course, been a favored place of business for Lindell's friends in Bermuda. In turn for being able to periodically use the apartment, they had ensured that it was kitted out with the very latest in security features and accessibility to the Net. Thus, it was the safest place to be in order to do the most dangerous work. The only thing not modernized was the means of getting up to the third floor. Lindell walked up the stairs with an even pace until he came to the name plate which read The Sea Venture Trading Company. He swiped his index finger down the small reader and the door clicked open. Lindell walked in through a large main entrance. Computer consoles were on almost every wall for access to everything from the security system to temperature control and the home theatre. The first door straight ahead was the office and also the panic room. Conventional doors had been replaced by electrically actuated sliding doors hidden in the walls.

Lindell spoke clear and slowly to ensure his commands were followed. "Voice command: activate security." All the consoles lit up, and scenes of the security cameras out front and in the stairwell flashed on the screen. Lindell started up the computer. He checked his pockets. No memory card! Then he remembered his phone. Of course. He quickly plugged his cell phone into the computer. Thirty-two gigabytes should be enough. The computer came online. He rechecked all the nodes again. Still nothing. Clearly, nobody had run the model yet. But it was only a matter of time.

New York

Roy had been nervously pacing into and out of the computer room for nearly an hour when the sound of an approaching helicopter brought him instant relief. The whine of the turbine engines reached a crescendo overhead on the roof's landing pad and then sharply died down. Seconds later, the elevator doors opened and an ancient, scrawny lady walked in with three massive leather-bound books which looked even older than she. Each volume was half a meter long and at least ten centimeters thick. Nolan was staggered that her pencil-weight arms could manage such a load.

"Over there," Roy motioned to the woman.

She nodded and gently laid the books down on the desk in the middle of the gallery. "Will that be all?" she asked Roy.

"Yes, thank you. I'm sorry, but we have arrivals due any minute up on the helipad."

"Very well." The woman left again in the elevator without further exchange. Nolan was shocked at the air of authority the woman seemed to hold over Roy. Who was she?

Roy started looking through the books without inviting Nolan to join in. Nolan walked over and watched. The only titles to appear on the books were volume numbers and dates, embossed in thick gold typeface. The deep red leather of the books was visibly worn by time but remarkably intact. Roy quickly set aside volume 1, which started on March 31, 1913. Volume 2 was also soon dispatched. Volume 3 started on September 1, 1929. The inner cover was speckled with small spots of mildew. A heavy, musty smell filled the air as Roy turned the first few pages. They were filled with beautifully scripted handwritten notes as well as inlaid clippings of newspaper articles. Some pages were laid out like a ledger and filled with numbers. Roy eventually turned to a front-page story from the *New York Tribune* with a large picture at the center. He stopped there and stood back with a look of triumph.

"That's why Lindell's places weren't on our radar."

"I don't understand," Nolan said.

"You don't show up on the radar screen when you are standing in the middle of the control tower," said Roy. He pointed to the picture in the article.

Nolan couldn't believe his eyes. "He looks just like Lindell, but twenty years younger."

The photo showed Lindell's look-alike dressed in a suit, smiling and waving from the driver's seat of a Rolls-Royce Silver Ghost convertible. Sitting beside him was a young, slim woman in a glossy silk dress, a fur shawl draped over her shoulders with the fox head still attached. She wore a bright hat with a low brim that hugged her perfectly shaped face. Her skin was flawless. Her eyes sparkled. A string of large pearls graced her neck. She smiled defiantly while holding a smoldering cigarette in a theatre-length cigarette holder. The caption below the photo read: "Successful banker and industrialist James Windsor Cartwright II and his lovely companion Ms. Fiona Hallows shortly before both perished in the tragic fire which destroyed Mr. Cartwright's mansion. Sadly, Mr. Cartwright is survived by no known family or next of kin." The newspaper article was dated October 10, 1929.

Roy announced, as if to the whole room, "This is the grandfather of Elliott Lindell."

Nolan was stumped. "What? Beyond the similarities, how can you know that?"

"Read further in the article. Everything he owned was left in trust to the Sea Venture Trading Company in Hamilton, Bermuda."

"Still—"

"I checked through Central Operations while the archives were on their way. Lindell's father, Dr. Francis Harvey Lindell, was born in Bermuda on April 15, 1930."

Nolan looked again at the woman in the photo. "That would make her three months pregnant the day this picture was taken."

Roy nodded, with eyes that were seeing far beyond the picture. "They both had good reason to disappear."

"Why is that? And why is his picture in the Archives?"

"Because, my dear ignorant Nolan, Lindell's grandfather was one of the architects of The Trust."

Nolan fell back. "He was *what?*"

Roy skimmed some handwritten script along the margins of the page and further below the story. It seemed to unlock a larger story he knew all too well. "Now I remember. James started as a mail boy for J. P. Morgan at the age of ten. His father was one of the inner circle working with Morgan. When James graduated from Harvard Law School, he was inducted into the inner circle shortly before Morgan's death. He and his father set up all the holding companies, offshore bank accounts—the entire structure of The Trust."

Nolan was surprised. "Why do you know this in such detail?"

Roy bowed his head and closed his eyes. Nolan could see his jaw muscles clench tightly. "Morgan wanted The Trust to continue his work of nation building by financing the New Industrial World. He wanted them to keep markets stable, like he did during the panic of 1908, at great risk to his own wealth. But many of his inner circle saw this as useless charity that would gain nothing. They saw that once they gained enough power, guiding the world by force would follow naturally. To get that power, they wanted to manipulate markets on a massive scale. Morgan, of course, disallowed that while he was alive."

"So where's the problem? Just wait until Morgan was gone."

Roy smiled cynically. "That's what they thought, too. Morgan died in 1913 and The Trust was born. In their bloodlust for empire, they unleashed the stock market bubble that ended in the crash of 1929 and then the Great Depression."

"And got filthy rich in the process," Nolan added.

Roy shook his head. "Morgan had made provisions for that."

"Like what?"

"We found out later that Mr. Cartwright here had been instructed to expose any member of The Trust who went against Morgan's wishes. You see, the crash was meant as a warning shot to the meddling U.S. government trying to stop them. Instead, it evoked a witch hunt. They tried to track us down and make us pay for what we did. It drove The Trust deep underground," Roy said with a tinge of regret.

"But not deep enough?"

"No. The week after Cartwright apparently died, packages of evidence turned up via mail at the authorities all over the country. Everyone in The Trust ever connected with Cartwright was jailed within weeks. Including my own grandfather. Few escaped."

"And nobody went after Lindell? I mean Cartwright?"

Roy scowled and shook his head. "We thought he was dead. With the Depression to manage and the government chasing us, The Trust soon forgot about Cartwright. Until now."

Nolan looked at the car, Cartwright's attire, the woman. "So how much was he worth?"

"Maybe two hundred million dollars. Does it matter?"

"That was a lot in 1929. What happened to it all?" Nolan asked.

"A lot of it was in art and antiques which went missing after the fire—or were assumed destroyed. The fire consumed everything beyond recognition, including those two," Roy said, pointing at James and Fiona. "The safe was found filled with ashes. No diamonds were recovered. Neither was the car."

Roy walked over to the phone and dialed.

The usual response came back. "This is Central."

"Roy Ingram. What did you get on the Sea Venture?"

"A lot, when we looked in historical records. There are very old links to multiple bank accounts, including the Liechtensteiner Private Bank in Zurich. That account pays the rent on the apartments in Paris and Rome. And one other we didn't see yet in London, on Belgrave Square."

Roy barked back to the phone, "Dispatch a team there immediately!"

"Already done. They will be there within the hour."

"What's the status of the boat and the plane?" Roy asked.

"The last of the crew is boarding the boat now. Departure is imminent. Our plane is en route to New York and will land in three hours. It will be ready for takeoff at three thirty."

Roy and Nolan both looked up at the sound of another helicopter approaching. "They're here," Roy said. He cut the connection and walked out of the office. He glared at two armed men standing by the entrance. "You and you, come with me." They started up the stairs to the helicopter pad.

* * *

New York

With a sudden jolt, Annika awoke to a frail consciousness. She slowly opened her eyes against painfully bright light. She tried to move but couldn't. There seemed to be motion all around. As her eyes became accustomed to the light, she let them fully open and saw that her head was leaning against a window.

She looked up to see something cutting across the bright blue sky over and over again. She looked down, and through blurred eyes saw the tops of buildings all around, and directly below a large rectangular splash of green. She realized she was in a helicopter. One of the buildings had a large raised square section on top with a brightly painted circle in the middle. The circle slowly moved closer and closer, and with a gentle thud, the helicopter landed in the middle of it.

The window fell away from Annika's face, but she was too weak to keep herself from falling. Her fall was broken by a pair of strong arms that grabbed her and dragged her out. There were voices. The haziness started to slowly clear. She saw the helicopter as she was dragged to the edge of the landing pad. A steady cool wind in her face brought her further back to consciousness. Half a dozen men were around the helicopter, taking others out of it. She could make out the tops of surrounding buildings, and far beyond the green of a large rectangular park lined with tall buildings. The similarity to pictures she had seen was unmistakable. *Is that Central Park? Am I in New York?* The view changed abruptly as she was picked up with a painful yank and draped over someone's shoulders. She was carried down a set of stairs and into an elevator. The doors opened and she was dragged through a large room with very high ceilings. She was placed on a chair where she could feel a thin plastic restraining strip pulled painfully tight on her wrists behind her.

She looked around to find herself in a huge gallery. Ornate furniture and antiques stood all around. The walls were covered in dark wood paneling. A great chandelier hung from the painted ceiling high above, and gilt moldings adorned every corner. Every wall had its own collection of oil paintings with large gilt frames. Directly in front of her sat a massive solid wood antique desk with nothing more than a small green light on it and a computer screen. In the corner closest to her was an extra room which looked out of place, as if it had been recently constructed. A thick circular ventilation tube led from the room straight up to the ceiling. Just outside the room stood a small modern-looking desk with a large flat screen monitor and a keyboard.

The elevator doors opened again, and one by one Peter and the two men working for Gwen Riley were brought in and put into chairs beside Annika. They were also restrained. They regained consciousness quickly. As the men who brought them left and the room fell silent, Annika realized there was a constant background noise. It sounded familiar, but she couldn't place it. Then she heard footsteps. A tall man with long jet-black hair walked in from a neighboring room and stood in front of Annika. He was dressed in a silk suit and his dark-skinned, aristocratic face fit perfectly in the room. The only flaw on his entire person was the scar on his forehead.

"Hello, Annika. My name is Nolan," he said.

"What do you want?" Annika asked.

Nolan motioned for someone to come in from the side room. A slim man in jeans and a T-shirt walked in with flash memory card in his hand. Annika recognized it as the very memory stick she had loaded Lindell's model on in the cabin. The man walked over to the small makeshift room in the corner and opened the door. A constant, gentle humming came out of the room. Annika remembered that sound—it was the same sound coming from the computer room in Dr. Lindell's lab. The man entered with the card and seconds later came out.

"It's plugged in," he said to Nolan. He then went behind the small desk to the side of the room.

Nolan said, "Annika, you should know that I authorized the killing of your husband Peter at the cabin. I'm prepared to do it again right here and now."

Annika watched as the man typed rapidly on his keyboard. He read the screen, spoke to himself, nodded, and kept typing even more rapidly.

Matt and Ken struggled against their restraints. Nolan looked at them and said, "You're not going anywhere. There are armed guards at every door and every exit." Nolan looked over at Annika. "If there's an encryption key needed for this, now would be the time to give it to me."

"I don't know any encryption key. There isn't one!" Annika said.

"Really? We'll see about that," Nolan said. He looked over to the man at the desk with raised eyebrows. "Ed?"

Ed didn't turn around. "This is the real thing. I've just matched several portions to some encrypted fragments that Lindell's lab technician Carter Feldman had recovered for us."

"Can you run it?"

"No, it's encrypted. Wait. This is odd." He was looking at the screen with a furrowed brow, scratching the back of his neck.

"What is odd?" Roy asked, walking over to look.

Ed's eyes scanned the monitor as text flowed past at an impossible rate. "Part of the program is clearly encrypted. But part of it is unencrypted. It shouldn't look like this. Unless..."

"Unless what?" Roy asked.

"The encryption program was faulty. Wait a minute." There was more typing. A wide smile spread across Ed's face.

"Now what?" Nolan asked.

"I've got it! There's an executable file here with extraction and decryption sub-routines. I think we're in!"

Nolan smiled. "Well, it seems that the rumors of Dr. Lindell's proficiency at encryption were greatly exaggerated." He turned to Ed. "Execute."

Ed typed in a command and the screen went blank for a few seconds. Then, text appeared. "OK. I've got several choices of cancer here. Breast. Colon. Lung. Prostate."

"Try the last entry," Nolan said.

Ed kept looking at the screen and typing as he spoke. "OK. It's loading." The screen went black again. A small flashing message appeared in the upper left-hand corner of the screen. Ed turned around to Nolan and Roy. "It's looking for the three-D projector."

Matt, Ken, and Peter looked at Annika for an explanation. Annika's face was as blank with surprise as theirs. Nolan looked on in amusement as Ed went behind the desk and rolled out on a raised trolley an exact copy of the large mysterious black object that Annika and Peter had seen on Lindell's desk.

Nolan walked over to Annika. "You have no idea what your Dr. Lindell was capable of, do you?" Nolan turned to Ed. "Connect it."

Ed took an optical cable that was connected to the black device and plugged it into one of the ports of the Gen-Silico inside the computer room. Nolan walked over to his desk and grabbed what looked like a remote control. With the press of a few buttons, the lights dimmed and blinds came down over the windows. The room fell into darkness. Ed's face shone brightly from the light of the terminal in front of him. He typed another command, and immediately the room filled with light emanating from the air itself.

Everyone looked up. Floating in the middle of the room were hundreds of oddly shaped round red globules. They undulated slowly and seemed to almost glow. Some were small, compact, and nearly spherical. Others were more elongated. They all had transparent membranes through which multicolored shapes floating inside could be seen. The shapes were moving. They were alive. Many of the globules had strangely elongated tendrils reaching far outside their membranes. They all looked real enough to reach out and touch.

"What are those?" Peter asked.

"Those are cancer cells," Annika replied, still looking on in awe.

"To be precise," added Nolan, "they are the most accurately modeled cancer cells anywhere on the planet today. With this in our hands, we will make hundreds of billions in treating cancer over the next generation."

"But never curing it?" Annika asked.

"Why would we want to cure it when we can make a hundred times more simply treating it over and over again? And then make even more money selling other medications that treat the side effects of the chemo drugs?" Nolan said with a laugh. He turned to Ed. "Proceed. I want to see this to the end."

Ed typed further. A gentle female voice came from the computer. "Advanced metastatic prostate cancer model simulation 468. Treatment regime version OY-371."

Everyone in the room watched as a cloud of diffuse, glowing blue appeared in the spaces between and around the cancer cells. Then hundreds of gentle, mechanical-sounding female voices filled the air. Each voice came from an individual cancer cell, reporting its status.

"This sounds like what we heard back in Lindell's lab!" Peter said.

Annika was too busy taking it all in to respond. The chorus of voices quickly became overwhelming. Nolan gestured to Ed. Ed stood up from his chair and put on two metallic-looking gloves which were covered in a fine wire mesh at the fingertips. He held them up in the midst of the globules and they glimmered brightly. Annika immediately recognized the gloves. They were the same as what Dr. Lindell had worn back in his lab months ago. Ed reached into the mass of globules and pulled them toward him, then spread his hands wide. They expanded in size enormously.

"That one," Nolan said, pointing to one.

Ed grabbed at it with his hands on each side. Amazingly, it followed his hands' motion perfectly, as if he was grasping a real object. He pulled his hands apart to magnify the cell until it was larger than Ed himself. The chorus of voices continued but at a lower volume. One dominant voice came through. It emanated from the center of the single large cell Ed was manipulating. He then cut his hand through the middle, and rotated it so everyone could see the cross-section.

Everyone in the room gasped and stared breathlessly at the impossible level of detail in front of them. In the nucleus, chromosomes were clearly visible, showing in minute detail the twisted double helix of DNA coiled up and re-coiled again along their lengths. A vast array of sub-cellular organs was vibrantly alive within the cytosol.

Liquids were being pumped to and fro. Protein molecules were being manufactured and transported in and around the cytoplasm. A network of fine, transparent tubules gave the cell its shape, and transported large molecules back and forth between the many oddly shaped sub-cellular organs. From the surface of the cell protruded tiny antennae of different shapes, which grabbed on to particles floating past the cell and dragged them inward. This was life at its most basic level.

"Oh my God," Annika said. "It's incredible."

Even Roy was impressed at what he saw.

Annika looked over all the detailed structures of the cancer cell, and noticed several clusters of jelly-bean-shaped organs—the mitochondria. Inside, the mitochondria had many layers of folds and sub-folds which resembled ribbons. They transported chemicals back and forth. Tiny holes flickered open and closed all over the mitochondrial surface. The mitochondria were far smaller and fewer than in healthy cells. They were being suppressed by the cancer. The cloud of blue diffused into the cell and quickly coated all the mitochondria, turning them a bluish tinge. Small patches of blue appeared all over the surface of the mitochondria and some bits of blue leaked into the insides of the mitochondria. The mitochondria responded vigorously. They started growing in size and shifting in shape. The ribbon-like structures inside waved more quickly. The pores on the surface flickered opened wider and stayed open longer.

"What's happening?" Peter asked.

"It's the pretreatment to reactivate the mitochondria," Annika said. "Our herbal equivalent of dichloroacetate."

The female voice from the cell came back. "Homeostasis alteration complete: down regulation of mitochondrial pyruvate dehydrogenase kinase at ninety-nine percent. Reversal of aerobic glycolysis at ninety-eight percent. Normalization of potassium ion channels complete. Warning: mitochondrial peroxide levels twenty-three percent above baseline and rising. Cell death probability: twenty-seven percent."

Annika leaned over to Peter. "This is where the real action starts."

The female voice returned. "Mitochondrial challenge with therapeutic agent OY-IV." Soon after, a diffuse cloud of luminous green flowed between and around all the cells. The green substance attached itself to the outer cell membranes in concentrated patches of brightly glowing green. On the large cell in front, large patches of green were all over the outer edge. The green started to diffuse into the cell. Small globules of the green substance started moving all over within in the cell, and attaching to different sub-cellular organs.

The female voice came back. "Warning: commencement of endoplasmic reticula and lysosomal signaling. Concentration of caspase activators in cytosol at critical levels."

The green then visibly started attacking the jelly-bean-shaped organs—the mitochondria. As soon as they were close by, the green globules jumped onto the surface of the mitochondria and rapidly permeated their entire surface. The green patches gravitated to the small holes which flickered open and closed. Once there, the green held the holes open—for good. Then the green started flooding into the mitochondria, and the entire cancer cell seemed to reel in shock.

"Warning: disruption of mitochondrial membrane potential. Opening of permeability transition pores." The jelly-bean-shaped mitochondria started to violently swell.

Annika leaned over to Peter. "This is the beginning of the end. There are some very nasty chemicals inside those folds of the mitochondria which will start digesting the cancer cell from the inside out. Once they leak out, they trigger a cascade reaction and it's all over."

The many small folds inside the mitochondria started to break apart, and the chemicals inside them rapidly started leaking out of the holes in the surface of the mitochondria.

The female voice spoke again. "Warning: inner mitochondrial compartmentalization disrupted. Irreversible release of cytochrome-C initiated. Probability of cell death: eighty-six percent. Warning: Executioner caspases released. Intracellular protein cleavage at fifty percent and rising."

Quite visibly, the organs and the whole structure of the cell looked like they were under attack. They writhed in the bath of lethal chemicals which surrounded them and ate into their very structure. The cell started to disintegrate bit by bit.

"Warning: DNA fragmentation initiated. Probability of cell death: one hundred percent."

The nucleus of the cell undulated as if in agony. The chromosomes began to twist and bend, and then flew apart into small pieces. The entire cell then split apart into dozens of much smaller pieces. Small chemical antennae appeared on the surface of each new small mass.

"Expression of macrophage activators complete."

"What's that?" Peter asked.

Annika said, "They signal nearby white blood cells to digest them as food. There is no waste in nature. Programmed cell death is incredibly efficient."

All the small cells in the background had also broken apart into tiny fragments. Not a single whole cancer cell was left anywhere.

"End of simulation. One hundred percent cell death achieved."

The lights came back on and Nolan was beaming like a medieval warlord who had just conquered the known world. He turned to Ed. "Get the entire list of ingredients used for this run. I want complete compositions and concentrations."

"I'm on it," Ed said, and started a flurry of typing.

Nolan continued, "And by next week I want it reconfigured to run any man-made molecule we care to throw at it."

Ed's face looked doubtful. He kept typing, more rapidly than before. "That's strange."

"What's that?" Nolan asked, his confidence untouched.

"The input for this run wasn't drawing from any data set."

Nolan quickly came back down to earth. "What does that mean?" he asked.

Ed started to look truly nervous. He started typing faster and his face grew paler. "There's no data list at all. I'm not sure the model was actually even running just now."

"But the model is on that card, isn't it?"

"Yes!"

"Then what were you just running?" Nolan asked in a raised voice.

"I don't know! Maybe just a very elaborate three-D movie!" Ed said nervously.

"Why would Lindell bury that in his computer model?" Nolan shouted.

"He's buying himself time."

"To do what?" Nolan yelled.

"I'm trying to find out!" Ed snapped back. He type several commands and watched for the results. When he saw them, he yelped in fear.

"What's wrong?" Nolan asked.

"The contents of the flash drive have been erased. It's been rewriting itself the entire time. There's nothing left."

"What?" Nolan yelled. "That's the only copy of the model left! Why would Lindell destroy it so easily?"

Something dawned on Ed. He looked much more worried. He called up a new window on his monitor and his eyes went wide. "NO!" Ed yelled.

"What?" yelled Nolan.

"A communication channel has been opened right past our firewall!" Ed said in a shaky voice.

"That's impossible! Our firewall is foolproof!"

"It didn't go through. It went around it!"

"How is that possible?"

"I don't know! I've shut down the hard line and it's still going," Ed yelled. Then his eyes fell on the flash drive itself, which was still plugged into the USB port of the computer. He yanked it out and watched his screen. "Damn it! This was the transmitter!"

Roy came over with his face contorted in rage, the scar on his cheek quivering. "What did we lose?"

Ed scanned his screen. "It must be a 4G connection. Nearly everything in the records. Unencrypted."

"Where did it go?" Roy demanded.

"I can't trace it unless it's still transmitting."

Roy nodded. "Put it back in."

With trembling fingers Ed picked up the flash drive and inserted it back into the computer. "Running the trace program now. It's reacquiring," Ed said. Sweat was dripping from his face onto his keyboard as he typed. "This guy is good. He's got repeater nodes all over the place." He spoke to the screen. "But I'm coming to get you."

Roy looked at Nolan in disgust. "The last time there was a breach like this in The Trust, the FBI was at the door inside of fifteen minutes." Roy looked over at the captives. "Nothing can be left to chance." He looked around Nolan's magnificent apartment and then at Nolan. "This place burns."

Nolan came forward. "What security breach? I put nothing on that computer."

"You didn't have to," Roy said.

"What's going on here? We have to tell Central Operations."

"There's no time."

Nolan grabbed Roy by his lapel and nearly lifted him into the air. "It's protocol! We have to go through Central!" Nolan yelled.

"This is Central Operations!" Roy screamed back, pointing to the computer.

Nolan put Roy down in shock. "What?"

"We routed it through here ever since they arrived," Roy said, motioning toward the programmers. "We had to keep a close eye on you."

Finally, all the mysterious work going on around the clock in the computer room made sense to Nolan. He was furious at the deception. "This is your failure," he shouted at Roy.

"The Trust won't see it that way."

Nolan walked to the wall and pushed an alarm button. Within seconds, over a dozen armed security guards appeared at every door. He said loudly to all of them, "Our security has been breached at the highest levels. You have fifteen minutes. This is not a drill."

The guards started running in all directions. Roy got out his cell phone and started barking a rapid succession of orders. Nolan went over to the wall behind his desk and slammed his hand on one of the wooden panels. It slid open to reveal a large safe. He placed his eye up to a scanner, and in a flash of laser light the safe opened. He removed a large steel case and placed it on his desk. The turbine engines of the helicopter on the roof came back to life and were soon whining at a high pitch. Several guards arrived with large steel drums on trolleys and placed them around the room. One drum went into the computer room. Every drum had a timer built into the top.

"How much time?" one security guard asked Nolan.

"Ten minutes. Activate them later on my mark," Nolan replied.

The guard nodded and adjusted the timing devices to ten minutes each.

"Incendiaries," Matt said under his breath. Ken was carefully watching the activity around the computer console where Ed sat.

Ed yelled, "I've got the IP address! It's a landline in London!"

Roy rushed over to the computer. "Do you have a street address?"

Ed pointed to a map on the computer screen. "Here. On Belgrave Square."

Roy motioned for one of the guards to approach. "It's the address we already have. When does our team get there?" Roy asked Ed.

Ed pulled up another window. His finger floated above a small moving light on the map. It was closing in on the address. Another dot was about two kilometers further away. "We have one man about two minutes out. Another two are here, a couple minutes later."

"Good job," Roy said. While Ed studied the screen, Roy took the guard's silenced pistol and brought it up to the back of Ed's head. Annika barely had time to gasp before Roy pulled the trigger. The monitor was splattered with blood and Ed fell dead, face-first on the keyboard. Roy yanked out Lindell's flash drive and threw it on the floor. He walked to the small computer room where the other programmer sat, opened the door, and went inside. Two muffled popping sounds sealed the fate of the man inside. Roy came back out and snarled at Nolan. "Like I said, The Trust is not going to see this as my failure."

Nolan stood there, stunned, as Roy dialed his phone again.

Roy spoke without emotion. "Central Operations will now route through the Citadel. Are the operators ready?" Roy nodded in satisfaction at the answer. He spoke further. "If the good Dr. Lindell creates any problems for you, please kill him immediately."

Annika went pale at those words and looked at Peter, who was equally aghast. She hoped to see some measure of confidence or optimism in Matt and Ken, but they too appeared to have none. Annika started reasoning in her mind that perhaps it was OK if she died with the others, as long as Dr. Lindell could escape and continue his work. Then she started to pray.

London

For the second time that day, Elliot Lindell watched the warning flash across his computer screen that told him his IP address had been located. He frowned at himself for the failure. The data stream should not have been traceable. He wiped his bald head with his hand and collected his thoughts. The last thing he wanted was a repeat of Rome, mostly because he knew his good luck would not repeat. Lindell walked over to the window and looked down to the street below. Nothing yet. He shook his head in anger. The data had only just started downloading onto his computer but he couldn't wait. He sat down and started typing, redirecting the dataflow to his node in Bermuda. Bermuda was safe, after all. It would get his model, and all the other information that came with it. When the reroute was complete, Lindell shut off the computer and slid off the casing.

He never had time to tell Annika that, for safety's sake, he had added several programs to the model in case it was captured. The most important was the program that sent the model over the Internet to his nodes around the world and then erased the model on its own flash drive. Next was the spy program that mined data on the local system and sent that, too, so Lindell could better identify who it was that stole the model. When he saw some of the files coming in, he realized they could bring down the people that were after him. But it was all floating in buffers in the Internet, waiting to download to Bermuda now. Lindell slid the hard drive out of the computer and placed it on the degausser he had at the far corner of the room. Now that he had deprived these people of his model, the unencrypted fragment on this hard drive would be like gold to them. The green light on the machine came on, indicating that the demagnetizing cycle had started. Lindell popped his head out the window for a last check in the street. Still nothing. He bolted out the door and down the stairs, feeling relief that this time he got away cleanly. He pulled open the door to the street and stepped out, only to watch a black car come screeching to a halt just paces away from him. The lone man in the car jumped out of the driver's side. Every muscle in Lindell's body went into reverse and he recoiled behind the door. Lindell pushed with everything he had, and heard the door's lock click into place just as the man on the other side impacted against the door. Lindell had only taken two large strides up the stairs when a gunshot exploded into the stairwell and the door flew open. The man dashed up the stairs and lunged at Lindell, seizing his left leg with an ironclad grip. Lindell grabbed the steel banister and with all his force kicked his right leg back. The hard leather bottom of his shoe caught the man below him square on the jaw, sending him sprawling down the stairs. Lindell ran up to his apartment and slid his finger down the print reader. Lindell's hand was already pushing hard against the door when the electronic lock released. Lindell shoved his was through the door. He could hear heavy footsteps racing up the stairs. He slammed the door just in time. But before he could take his hands off, a powerful shot blasted into the lock. The whole door reverberated painfully against his hands.

"Voice command: activate security!" Lindell shouted between labored breaths. The computer consoles came to life and the security system went into active mode. Before Lindell could turn to watch the camera shot from the hallway, another shot hit the lock and went all the way through, grazing Lindell's arm. He winced in pain and leapt back into his office. One, two, three powerful kicks from outside and the door sprang open. The large, stocky man had fierce, dark eyes and was breathing hard. His face bore Lindell's shoe mark and a look of hatred so intense that Lindell knew he could kill without a second thought.

"Secure room!" Lindell shouted. The door to his office started to rapidly slide shut, but the man was unbelievably fast. He bolted for the door and grabbed it with both hands, trying to pull it open with brute force. There was just enough space left in the door to fit his quickly reddening face. The electric motors of the door started to whine and Lindell could smell smoke. He dug into his pocket and pulled out the canister from Rome. Lindell took a deep breath, held his eyes open at just a squint, brought the canister up to the man's face and released its entire contents in a long spray. The intruder refused to give up, and took a massive dose of the chemical in his eyes, nose, and mouth. With a final scream of pain, the intruder triumphed over the door's motors and forced it open. But he hadn't taken more than two steps toward Lindell when his legs buckled and he fell to the ground, writhing, holding his face with both hands. Lindell jumped to the window next to him and opened it. A strong breeze came in, flushing the air out of the room and through the open entrance door. Lindell allowed himself to breathe again, and stared in revulsion at the man's eyes, which had already swollen to twice their normal size. The man clawed at his face and mouth, to no avail. His arms soon fell limp, and his eyes stared upward, motionless.

Lindell stepped over the body and ran down the stairs. He jogged until he got to Upper Belgrave Street and then slowed to a normal walk. Once again the sound of tires squealing came from behind him. He knew where they were going and what they wanted. He managed to stop himself from looking back, and kept walking at a brisk pace southward, on to Victoria Station.

New York

"Report! Do you still have Lindell in your sights? Report!" Roy yelled at the phone.

Nothing. The voice came from Central, not the patch through to London. "I'm sorry, sir, there's no response. But the other two are arriving now. We are opening a channel." Two new voices came through the line.

"We're here! We're here! One man is down."

"Is it Lindell?" Roy asked.

"Negative! He's one of ours."

"Where is Lindell?" Nolan shouted.

There was a pause and the sound of rapid running through the apartment. Finally the answer came. "Not here, sir. And the computer is compromised."

Nolan slammed his hands down on the desk. "He can't be far! Get out there and find him!"

"Yes, sir! Right away!"

Nolan looked at Roy. "He must be going to Bermuda next."

"We'll be there waiting," said Roy.

Nolan walked over to the oil painting hanging on the nearest wall and gently stroked the frame as he frowned and shook his head. He went into the elevator and held the door open with the steel case he had taken from his safe.

"Make sure you get the tea service!" Nolan yelled at one of the guards passing by. The guard nodded and ran outside. The sound of the helicopter's engine grew louder. Two guards joined Nolan in the elevator. Each guard was loaded down with several large black duffel bags.

Roy spoke to one of the guards nearest the captives. "Stay here until five minutes are left. Two bullets in every head, one in every heart. Then get out of here."

The guard nodded.

"Are you ready?" Nolan asked. He held his finger on the side buttons of his wristwatch.

"Ready," the guard replied.

"Mark!" Nolan said. He depressed the button on his watch. The guard hit a button on his black device. The timers on all the bombs in the room started counting down from ten minutes. Nolan stepped into the elevator and the doors started to close. But at the last second his hand thrust out and pushed them back open. He was staring through the glass door onto the terrace.

Nolan's face went deep red. "Which of you idiots didn't get my tea service packed?" he bellowed. He spun around to the two guards behind him in the elevator. "Get it! Now!"

They both made a dash for the terrace.

Nolan shouted even louder. "Wrap it in towels! I don't want a single scratch!"

The two guards backtracked to the kitchen in a panic. Roy had an amused smile on his face. He took out his phone and dialed just as the elevator doors started to close again.

"Transport the good Dr. Riley to the Citadel, and do it quickly." The elevator doors shut and Nolan and Roy disappeared.

"Peter, I'm so sorry!" Annika said through her tears.

"It's not your fault," Peter said, with tremors in his voice.

"Yes, it is!" Annika cried. Tears were streaming down her face.

All four watched from their chairs as the remaining guards ran to and fro, loading various objects into small crates, and taking the freight elevator down over and over. The last large batch of goods left on their way down to the parking garage when the timers hit five minutes. Four guards remained. They piled the rest of their goods beside the freight elevator, waiting for it to come back up. One of the guards came forward and started twisting a silencer onto his pistol. He spoke to the other three, who came closer to watch the execution.

"Hold the elevator for me. I'll be done quickly." He walked up to Matt. "So we heard you were too fast for Sydney." The guard stretched out his hand and touched Matt's forehead with the muzzle. "Well, you're not too fast for this."

"Please, no!" Annika cried out.

Matt glared at the guard defiantly and prepared for the end. But the guard paused at the sound of the elevator bell ringing and the doors opening. "Get that!" the guard yelled to the others, his eyes still fixed coldly on Matt.

Matt refocused his eyes on the elevator, which was not empty. John and Logan stood inside, armed to the teeth. Logan's rifle was already at firing level, and with lethal efficiency he emptied two rounds into the head of the guard next to Matt. John sprayed the other three with machine gun fire before they could un-holster their side-arms. Four guards fell dead to the floor, and silence filled the room.

John and Logan ran to the four to cut loose their restraints.

Matt yelled, "We have about three minutes and then the whole place is going to blow!"

"We're going now!" John said. He freed Matt first and started on the others.

Matt shook his head. "No! I have to get to the computer!" He rushed to the console and picked up Lindell's flash drive from the floor. He plugged it back in. Annika grimaced as Matt cleaned the programmer's blood from the screen. He started typing and watching the screen.

"What are you doing?" John asked.

"Lindell rigged this flash drive with a high-speed emitter and a spy program to extract all the data.

"Smart!" John said.

"He dumped their data through the Net." Matt looked at John's phone. "Give me your cell! Quickly!"

John threw the phone to Matt. "How much data?" he asked.

Matt watched the screen. "Good, it's reacquiring the link and sending more data."

"To where?" John asked.

"They traced it to London and found Lindell, but he got away. They think he's going to Bermuda next."

"How do they know about Bermuda?" John asked.

"The address was on her phone," Matt said, glancing at Annika.

John gritted his teeth. "Damn it! Are you sure he's going there?"

"No. Let's see where the data is going now." He plugged John's cell into the computer and then dialed. "Is Ping in the house?"

"Yes. He can handle it."

Into the phone, Matt said, "Ping, we have a data stream here in New York. Can you trace it?" Matt looked over at John and nodded.

John turned to watch the timers on the bombs. They all read fifty-seven seconds and counting. "We have little time."

Matt nodded. "Just a minute. I have to help out on this side."

"Matt, we don't have a minute! Let's go!" John motioned for everyone to follow him to the elevator.

"Just a second! Oh, Lindell is good! He's set up a string of virtual nodes on the Net. We're almost there!" Matt said.

Everyone started for the open elevator.

"Matt! Twenty seconds!" John yelled.

Matt was too busy typing and watching his screen to notice. "Almost there!"

Just then, bullets went flying through the room from the terrace outside. Peter and Annika ducked behind the large desk while John and Logan took cover next to them and fired back. Matt kept his head as low as possible but never took his eyes off the screen. Bullets ricocheted everywhere in the large room, impacting walls and hitting mirrors and the chandelier above. Annika saw in horror that the timers now read twelve seconds. She tapped John on the shoulder and pointed to them. Ten seconds. John nodded. With a loud shout, he and Logan stood up and fired everything they had at the terrace. The remaining windows broke, the frames splintered, and the two men outside finally fell from their wounds. Everyone piled into the elevator. The counters were down to five seconds.

"Matt!" John yelled again.

"I've got it! I've got it! It's all going to Bermuda!" Matt shouted. He bolted upright from his sheltered position and jumped into the elevator. Logan pounded on the door close button over and over, almost as fast as Annika's heart was racing in her chest. The doors shut, and the elevator started its rapid descent.

John looked at his watch with a frown and shook his head. "Brace yourselves!"

A powerful shock wave hit them from above. Annika felt it travel through her entire body almost at once, and her eardrums both popped from the pressure. The entire building seemed to shake. The elevator lurched violently to the left, slamming everyone together into one painful lump of flesh. A screeching sound erupted from the right side as the elevator was pushed against the guide rails. The last thing Annika saw before the lights went out was the floor number 45 flashing on the control panel. Then, in total darkness, everyone suddenly felt weightless as the elevator went into freefall.

Victoria Station, London

Elliott Lindell was nearly out of breath by the time he made his way into London's busiest tube station and across the way to the Heathrow Express. He stood just a few meters away from it and had to slow his pace and catch his breath. But his rush hadn't been to outrun those looking for him. Shortly after leaving his flat on Belgrave Square he had realized the next departure of the Express was just minutes away, and it would get him to the airport just in time to make the last flight to Hamilton, Bermuda. Perhaps that was why his grandfather had chosen to live close to Victoria Station, Lindell thought to himself. To make a fast escape. But from whom? Lindell speedily navigated his last few steps through the crowds that were between him and the train. Just as he approached, the warning tone sounded that the train was about to depart. He ran the last three steps and made it inside just as the doors closed. He looked down at his cell phone. How odd. He could see that the data flow to Bermuda from the computer in New York had resumed, but then was cut off again just seconds ago. What could possibly cause that? Lindell tried to take some comfort that it meant he just received more information. He already knew that his model had successfully downloaded in its encrypted entirety in Bermuda and would be there waiting for him when he arrived. And not only did he have his model back, but now also enough information to permanently cripple whoever it was that was trying to stop him. His sense of relief quickly disappeared as Annika and Peter came back to mind. Were they even still alive? Had he brought about their deaths? The train started to pull out of the station on its way to Heathrow Airport. Finally, on to sanctuary and the closest thing to a home he had left.

He could check on Annika and Peter from there. And he could rebuild. Then, out of the corner of his eye, Lindell noticed two men running down the platform after his train, looking for someone. Looking for him. He snapped his head down so they wouldn't see his face, and spun his body to face away from them. Damn. They had been just seconds behind him. Then a terrible thought went through his mind. What if that second flow of data had been allowed in order to locate the end point? That had to be it. And he knew what to do about it.

New York

When the emergency lights came on in the elevator, Annika saw that everyone was floating in the air and by instinct trying to grab on to anything fixed. The floor indicator above the doors was counting down in the low twenties.

"Get on the floor!" John shouted.

Annika felt Peter's arm reach around her and pull her toward him. His other arm was firmly grasping the railing. As Annika got to Peter, she grabbed on to the railing with all her force and planted her feet on the floor just as an incredibly loud squeal erupted from the outside. Anyone who was floating in the air immediately fell to the floor with a loud and painful thud.

"Emergency brakes!" John yelled. "We're not out of this yet!"

The floor indicator was now in the low teens. The acrid smell of something burning filled the air. The floors kept whipping by at a decreasing rate. Five, four, three—.

All held their breath as the elevator hit the ground level and kept going. Finally, the squealing stopped and the elevator came to an abrupt halt at the second underground parking level. Everyone waited for a few seconds just to be sure it had really stopped. Logan pulled out a large knife and jabbed it between the inner doors, prying them all the way open. The steel and concrete floor of the underground parking lot stood about waist height above the floor of the elevator. Logan jammed open the outside doors and they all got out.

"Let's get out of here, before the police show up," John said.

"You have to help Dr. Lindell!" cried Annika. "If they find him they'll kill him!"

"Then we'll have to find him first," John said. He looked at Matt. "Did they already send someone to Bermuda?"

Matt nodded. "One unit by sea already. Another will be airborne from JFK in a few hours."

John looked at his watch. "We might make it." He turned to Annika. "You're coming, too."

"Why?" Annika asked.

"Because he trusts you," John said.

"And he doesn't trust you?" Annika asked.

John left the question unanswered. "Everything depends on us getting that data. That means leaving now." He led the way to a parked van with darkened windows and motioned for everyone to get in.

Annika nodded and followed. "How do we get there?"

"I called in a favor with the CEO of Cypress Turbines. There's a corporate jet at LaGuardia."

CHAPTER TWENTY-FOUR

Ten Thousand Feet Over the Atlantic Ocean

The last remnants of pink twilight disappeared on the Caribbean horizon of the Atlantic Ocean. Elliott Lindell watched through the window as innumerable stars filled the night sky above Bermuda. His ears gently popped as the Hamilton Airways flight started its descent toward the L.F. Wade International Airport. Lindell glanced at his watch. Touchdown would be a little late, at 9:20 p.m. The lights of Bermuda lay far ahead, flat against the water. The fondest memories of Lindell's youth took place on what was then the very mystical island home of his grandfather. The stories he heard were nothing short of fantastic. They always started with Bermuda's unwilling first settlers who came ashore in 1609 from the wreck of the Virginia-bound galleon the *Sea Venture*. One of William Shakespeare's friends was aboard that ship when the great storm brought it to Bermuda, and his writings of the storm later inspired Shakespeare's *The Tempest*. Before then, mariners had universally described Bermuda as The Isle of Devils—a dangerous place inhabited by monsters. But the first settlers found not only a lack of devils, but that nature had provided everything they could possibly need. Abundant edible plants, wild hogs, birds and fish that could be caught by hand. Cedar forests which would supply a shipbuilding industry for generations. Nature, it seemed, had been wildly misunderstood and falsely represented. So taken with the story of Bermuda's first inhabitants, Lindell's grandfather had named his most important company after the ship that brought them there—and was destroyed in the process.

The plane made its final descent before landing. Lindell felt more and more uneasy about what might be waiting for him. On the way to Heathrow, he had remotely logged in to his computer in Bermuda and moved his model and all the pirated data to his compact one terabyte external drive that was always attached for backup. It was small enough to fit into the palm of his hand. If he had to run with it, he could. He just didn't know where he would run to. His lawyer friends and security consultants on Bermuda were close by. But they had always made it clear to Lindell that he must never go to them during threatening situations. They could only help avoid such situations in the first place. Once a situation started, Lindell would be on his own.

* * *

Several kilometers behind the Hamilton Airways flight, a much smaller private jet also made its way toward Bermuda's airport. John Rhoades closed the cockpit door as he came back into the main cabin.

"The pilot told me we'll be down in fifteen minutes. There's only one plane in front, from London."

Matt nodded. "It's got to be Lindell in the plane up ahead! It's the last flight from London today and it left Heathrow an hour after he disappeared."

"Agreed. Did Ping get a phone number?"

"Lindell accessed his computer here online via his cell, when he was in London. Ping could trace it to a disposable."

"Good. As soon as we land, contact him."

"Will do," said Matt.

"Now let's see his location," John said.

"Sure thing." Matt brought up an aerial view of Bermuda on the laptop he had set up on the table. The southwestern portion of the island was shaped like a massive fishhook which enclosed the Great Sound—a large bay about five thousand meters across. The straight part of the fishhook stretched due northeast for about twenty kilometers and separated into several islands at the tip. Matt pointed to the large island just under the northern tip. "That's where we land. Lindell's house is down here. It's waterfront." He pointed to the bottom of the fishhook and expanded the view several times. It was a true villa by any standards, but a castle in Bermuda, and set on acres of beachfront land. "It should take about half an hour to get there."

John smiled. "The speed limit in Bermuda is thirty kilometers per hour. We need to keep a low profile."

Matt reluctantly agreed. "OK, an hour, then."

"Are the bikes there?"

Matt nodded. "Two rental bikes and an SUV are waiting at the airport."

Thirty minutes later, they were all through immigration and walking out the front door of the airport. The motorcycles and car stood lined up at the curbside. Logan and Ken took the bikes. The others got in the car. The night traffic was sparse but slow coming out of the airport, right up to the narrow concrete causeway which connected to the main island of Bermuda. Then the road freed up.

Matt tried repeatedly to call Lindell on his cell phone as John drove. "I just don't get it. Why won't he pick up?"

John pointed to Annika with his thumb. "Let her try."

* * *

Up ahead on Middle Road, Elliott Lindell rode in the back of a taxi. He watched the familiar lights go by as they drove through Smith's, Devonshire, Paget, and Warick Parishes. Memories of sailing in the bright blue waters of the Great Sound came flooding back. And of course, the visit with Emily to the villa, so long ago. Shortly after that he had proposed to her in Europe. And then it all came crashing down. Lindell still wondered how someone as wonderful as Emily could metamorphose into Gwen Riley. The taxi went over a bump and Lindell was thrust back into the present. He realized that he hadn't yet turned on his cell phone. He reached in his jacket pocket and brought it out, switching it on immediately. Suddenly, over a dozen messages popped up on the screen. From Annika! Lindell quickly dialed the number.

* * *

A few kilometers back on Middle Road, the cell in Annika's hand started ringing. Matt grabbed the phone and looked at the number.

"It's Lindell!" Matt yelled. He hit the call answer button and put it on speaker.

Annika looked dubiously at Matt and John. She spoke loudly. "Hello, Dr. Lindell!"

"Annika! Thank God you're safe! Where are you?"

Annika could hear the relief in Lindell's voice. She knew that wouldn't last. "We're on Bermuda. Just a little ways behind you."

"No! What on earth are you doing here?" Lindell replied.

"I'm with the men who saved your life. They saved our lives, too."

"You can't trust them, Annika. They work for Gwen!"

Annika shot a glance at John and Matt. "You may be in danger. Can you stop and wait for us?"

"No! I'm almost there. There's no time to wait!"

"Please, Dr. Lindell. Where are you now?"

"Just inside Southampton Parish, crossing Church Road."

"We're just behind you, in Warwick Parish now," Annika said.

John interrupted. "Don't go inside your house! Can you wait for us outside?"

Lindell's answer came after several seconds. "OK. But I won't wait for long."

John gunned the motor and went far beyond the island's speed limit. The streets were dark and mostly empty. The car soon crossed into Southampton Parish and hugged the coastline on the right-hand side. A scattering of lights were visible far across the dark waters of the Great Sound. Annika kept her eyes fixed on a cluster of large, bright lights due north of them. After minutes that passed by like hours, they turned down the quiet and isolated Jennings Bay Road. At the end, a lone man stood against the backdrop of a well-lit mansion. It was Lindell. John stopped the car and Annika jumped out ran up to Lindell. She threw her arms around him. "I'm so glad you're alive!"

"And I'm glad you're safe too, Annika," Lindell said. He then cast a disapproving glare at John and his men. "How dare you bring her and Peter here!"

John spoke. "There's no time for that. The people that want your model are coming here for you and the information you took from their computer."

Lindell bowed his head. "I didn't think they would ever find me here."

Annika stepped up. "It's true! I heard them talking about it!"

Lindell looked at John. "I suppose you want the files."

John nodded. "They will be much safer with us."

"You mean with Gwen Riley, don't you?" Lindell said.

"No. They have her. These files are the only leverage we have to get her back."

"And my model?" Lindell asked. "Will they demand that, too?"

"If we must. But there's something urgent you need to discuss with Gwen Riley first."

"The only thing that's urgent is for me to get my model back."

John held up a flash drive. "We already have that."

Lindell stared at the drive in John's hand. "How did you get a copy?"

"I'm sorry! I made two copies in the cabin," Annika said.

Lindell looked back at John and the others. "Let's go inside. And you keep these two safe!"

"You have my word," John said. He pocketed the flash drive.

Lindell led them through a large gate in the thick stone fence. A paved walkway stretched down to his house and continued along to the waterfront. At the near end of the water, a motorboat and two Jet Skis were moored to thick iron rings embedded into the stone wall that lined the expanse of his private beach. The Great Sound lay behind it all, and was perfectly silent and still except for a handful of distant moving lights skimming along the water. Beyond those boat lights, the lights of the island's extremities shimmered on both sides of the bay. The air was cool and fresh, and smelled like the sea. Lights mounted on the ground, the fence, palm trees, and the three-hundred-year-old house itself lit the immaculately landscaped grounds from all angles. As they approached the house, Annika felt relieved to see not a single light on inside. Lindell punched a code into the number panel next to the front door. The door clicked open.

John held Lindell back with a hand on his shoulder. "We go first!"

Lindell gave the OK. John and Logan went in with weapons drawn. Lindell followed behind and turned on the lights inside the house. He pointed to the security panel on the wall. It showed green lights for all monitored areas of the house and property.

"This system is state of the art. We're the only ones here."

"Just a minute," John said. He and Logan disappeared down the hall. When they came back, John nodded. "Get the data, and then we're leaving."

Lindell walked past him and down the hallway. He called back to John. "Once I get my model back, then I'll talk to Gwen."

John nodded. He pulled out his satellite phone and dialed. Matt walked up to the security panel and started playing with the buttons. He scrolled through each of the security cameras as Logan and others watched.

"Wow. This is a first-class system. Look, I can zoom in on any of the cameras." He flipped from one camera to the next, zooming in and out. First the front of the house and the road. Then the back of the house. Then he started on the beach.

John nodded with distraction. He was listening to his cell. "Gwen! We're here with Lindell. He's not cooperating. You have to tell him."

"Tell him what?" Matt asked with interest. He homed in on the power boat. He toggled the camera to run along the shoreline.

"Wait!" John said. "Go back to the boat!"

Matt toggled the camera control and brought it back to the boat.

"Zoom in!" John said.

The boat suddenly expanded and filled the little security screen. Half the boat was in the darkness of night, the other half lit up by a floodlight. The camera struggled to find the right brightness.

"Pan left to the backseats!" John said.

"What's wrong?" Matt asked. He moved the camera. A man's head popped up into plain view from behind the backseats of the boat. He was watching the house with a scope, and talking with someone over a radio.

John and the others took their weapons out and started running down the hall. "Dr. Lindell!" they shouted.

Matt turned back to Annika and Peter. "You stay there!"

Two loud gunshots boomed out from the last room at the end of the hall. The sound of a window breaking immediately followed. Annika and Peter watched the screen as the man on the boat leapt up with a huge knife in his hand. He sliced through the rope which secured the boat in place and started the motor.

Down the hall, John pounded on the locked door. "Dr. Lindell? Open the door!"

Annika and Peter watched helplessly as the man on the boat picked something up off the driver's seat. He held it up and pointed it back toward the house. It was a machine gun. They didn't have time to yell out a warning. John kicked the door open to see Lindell sitting on the floor, holding his stomach tightly. The window behind him was broken wide open. Gunfire thundered out of the boat. As the bullets came streaming through the open window, everyone scattered to the floor. Annika and Peter watched the scene on the security screen rapidly change. A second man ran away from the house at top speed, heading straight for the boat. He held a small object in his hand. He didn't slow in the slightest as he approached the stone wall at the water's edge. He launched himself into the air and landed in the backseat of the boat. The driver immediately pushed the motor to full power and the boat sped away, soon disappearing behind a small island just off the coast. Annika and Peter ran down the hall to see the others surrounding Lindell. As he brought his hand away from his chest, he did not seem surprised that it was soaked with blood. Annika shrieked at the sight.

"The hard drive! They've got my model! The files!" Lindell gasped.

John looked at Logan and Matt. "Get that drive back! Now!"

Matt and Logan bolted from the room and ran to the SUV out front. They opened the back and each got out his own large duffel bag. Matt took two Glock .45 autoloaders and several clips of ammunition. Logan holstered his own Glock and then removed a large black plastic case. With both hands, he flipped open the two fasteners on the front and opened the case. Inside lay a SWS Sniper Weapons Systems .338 Lapua Magnum rifle, sitting half embedded in dense polymer foam. Although trained on the M40 as a Marine Scout Sniper, Logan had tried the SWS after hearing it was quickly adopted by the Israeli Defense Forces in 2007. Then it became his weapon of choice for long-range sniping. Four clips of bullets were neatly dug into to foam along the top edge. Logan set his PDA beside the case and called up a map of Bermuda. He removed the large rifle and slung it on his back.

"They're heading for the yacht," Logan said. He took the extra clips and stored them in his motorbike.

Matt nodded. "They can only go north out of the sound, right here," he said, pointing to the northwesternmost edge where the fishhook terminated. They both took out radio headgear.

"That's our chance. Radio check," Logan said, shoving his earpiece in his left ear and strapping the small microphone so that it protruded just to the side of his mouth. Matt quickly followed suit.

"I'll take the bike and head him off at the Dockyards. You go by water!" Logan said, then got on one of the motorcycles and sped down Middle Road. Matt ran down to the water, untied the nearest Jet Ski and jumped on.

* * *

Back inside the house, Lindell gasped. "Annika! Come here!"

Annika came closer and kneeled down beside him. "Yes?"

"Don't...trust..." Lindell struggled to speak.

"Who? Gwen?" Annika asked.

"Or them!" Lindell said, eyeing John and Ken.

Annika nodded, with tears running down her face. "You're going to be OK! You have to be!"

Lindell leaned toward Annika and used every bit of his energy to whisper, "There's so much more I wanted to show you. The password for the model is..." His breathing became even shallower and the color was rapidly draining from his face. He gave one more long gasp, and then fell back with eyes closed.

"Dr. Lindell! No! Please!" Annika cried. She tugged at his lifeless hand, sobbing.

John bent over and put his fingers on Lindell's neck. He shook his head. "I'm sorry. He's gone."

"What's happening?" Gwen's voice came through John's phone.

"Dr. Lindell just passed away," John said grimly.

Gwen was silent just for a moment. "Damn it! Where is the model?"

"We're on it." He cut the call and got on his radio. "Guys, talk to me."

* * *

Halfway up the island, Logan was racing out of Sandy's Parish along the now deserted Mangrove Bay Road. He could see the road ahead joined several small islands and bridges along the way to the Dockyards. Watford Bridge was the first. He looked to the right as he drove across. There they were. The speedboat with Lindell's killer on board, and Matt speeding behind it on the Jet Ski.

"I can see our boat! Matt is gaining slowly!" Logan yelled into his radio mouthpiece. He saw flashes of light coming from the boat Matt was pursuing. Matt swerved violently to avoid the line of fire.

Matt's voice was barely audible over the loud scream of his engine. "They're shooting at me! I can't get close!"

"Hang on!" Logan yelled. "I'll be at the Dockyards in a couple of minutes!"

Logan pumped the bike to full throttle and sped straight along Malabar Road, which soon turned into Cockburn and then Pender Roads. Up ahead, the one-meter-thick stone walls of the Royal Dockyards soon rose high against the horizon as Logan approached. A well-illuminated gate made of thick beams of solid wood was in the center of the wall. Logan slowed only enough to take out his handgun and blast the lock off the small inner doorway. He burst through on his motorbike and into the large lower level of the fort known as The Keep. Logan was completely surrounded by stone walls that were one meter thick and at least two stories tall. In front of him was the steep hill which the tall walls of the fortress enclosed. The fortress was built in the early nineteenth century by the Royal Navy, exactly at the gateway from the Pacific Ocean to the Great Sound. A large earthen ramp built against the eastern wall ran gradually up to the hill and the top of the stone walls. Logan turned his bike toward it and sped to the top where five bastions looked out to the sea. The second bastion provided an ideal view. He parked his bike between two antiquated cannons that lay on the ground next to the stone wall and he ran to the edge of the bastion. To the right, about nine hundred meters out, Logan could see Matt and the speedboat. To the left, a large yacht was bearing straight toward the motorboat. The yacht's hull was suspended clear above the ocean's surface by hydrofoils which sliced through the water without regard for wave, current, or wind.

"We've got company! High-speed yacht coming in from the north! It's got to be doing fifty knots, at least!" Logan yelled. He turned toward Matt and the speedboat, steadying his rifle on the massive stone wall.

"I can see them now!" Matt yelled through the radio. "We don't have much time!"

Logan reached back and grabbed his SWS rifle. He flicked open the bipod and set it carefully on top of the wall. On the top of the rifle, Logan's high-powered optical scope was coupled to his latest toy, a night vision frontal attachment which used white phosphorus technology, or WPT. Logan made his adjustments to the scope and looked through. He could see them clearly. WPT gave a crisp black-and-white image far superior to the green glow of standard gallium arsenide-based night vision scopes. Logan put the crosshairs on the speedboat's driver. The water was calm and the boat was making a beeline for the yacht. Logan breathed deeply. As he exhaled, he counted his heartbeats until they slowed, all the time keeping his target in the crosshairs. As the last of his breath left his lungs, he pulled the trigger. Logan knew how long to wait for impact. He was using a Black Hills Sierra MatchKing 300-grain cartridge. It left the muzzle at 850 meters per second and would slow down over its trajectory to 530 meters per second, or mach 1.6, by the time it hit the target. Just under one and a half seconds later, the driver of the small speedboat slumped over the steering wheel. The boat started slowing down quickly. Matt was gaining. Through the scope, Logan could see the boat's passenger frantically move the driver aside to sit in his place. The boat had slowed greatly. Logan readjusted. He released his second bullet. The second target fell on top of the first, motionless.

"Nice shooting!" Matt yelled through the radio as his Jet Ski streaked across the water toward the speedboat, now dead in the water.

Logan panned back to the left. The yacht was still hurtling on its hydrofoils toward Matt and the speedboat.

"Hurry! They're right on top of you!" Logan shouted into his mouthpiece.

Matt hauled the bodies off to the side. The bottom one had Lindell's hard drive in his pocket. Matt grabbed it and shoved it in his own pocket. He looked up to see the yacht suddenly slow less than a hundred meters away. Its hull fell into the water, creating a large wave traveling outward in all directions. A spotlight mounted on the front of the yacht came on and shone directly on the speedboat. Matt threw up his arm to shield his eyes from the painfully bright light. Four men moved onto the forward deck with rifles at the ready.

"Watch out!" Logan yelled.

The guns of the two men on the yacht lit up with multiple flashes. Instantly, the water around the small speedboat came alive with the sound of bullets hitting the surface. Matt threw himself on the deck behind the bodies and took out his two Glocks. Bullets pierced the hull of the speedboat all over, and Matt could feel several impacts on the bodies now sheltering him. He brought up one arm on each side of the bodies and fired repeatedly at the yacht. He heard the loud pop of breaking glass, and the spotlight went dark.

"That wasn't you!" Logan said over the radio.

Matt peered around the bodies. One gunman lay still on the deck. The other three were reloading. The yacht had drifted close enough that they didn't need the spotlight anymore. The first to raise his weapon didn't get a shot off before his body jerked suddenly to the side. As he fell, the other two opened fire. Matt ducked again as more bullets sprayed the boat. Several bullets smashed into the engine. He could smell fuel. And smoke. Matt looked behind him. Flames had already engulfed the engine. He glanced up at the yacht, getting ever closer. The two gunmen were about to fire again. To move would be certain death.

"I need some help here!" Matt yelled into the radio.

"I'm working on it!" Logan replied.

Matt looked up to the Dockyards from where he crouched. High up on the stone wall on the closest bastion, three bright flashes came one after the other. Matt looked over to the yacht. One of the men screamed in pain, then fell over the side into the water. The other simply dropped motionless on the deck.

"Get out of there! Now! Now! Now!" Logan yelled.

Matt looked back to locate his Jet Ski. It had drifted several meters away behind the speedboat. The flames at the back were growing quickly. Matt grabbed the seats and pushed himself toward the back. He planted his foot firmly on the backseat and launched himself over the flames toward the Jet Ski. He landed hard. The seat hit him squarely in the midsection and knocked the wind out of him. Ignoring the pain, Matt grabbed the handlebars and pushed the throttle to maximum.

Logan's voice came back in his earpiece. "Get to the marina. We'll go back by road!"

Matt headed for the small marina just a few hundred meters ahead, to the left of Logan's position. He glanced behind him to see the yacht turning in his direction and picking up speed. The yacht struggled to steer clear of the burning speedboat and smashed right through it, causing a small explosion as the gas tank ruptured. The impact caused the dead men on the yacht's deck to fall overboard. Nobody cared. Another gunman came onto the forward deck with a rifle.

"I got you!" Logan said under his breath. This time it was easy. The yacht was heading almost directly toward him. He placed the crosshairs on the man's chest, released the bullet. But just as he chambered the next round, he noticed a flurry of bright flashes from the back deck of the boat. As quick as he could, he pulled his rifle behind the cover of the wall. A wave of bullets slammed into the solid rock wall on the other side.

"They've spotted me! I'll see you down there!" Logan shouted into the radio.

He folded the bipod and slung his rifle over his back. He stooped low behind the rock wall and ran to the bike. Leaning forward as low as possible on the bike, Logan rode it back down the earthen ramp until he was safe. Then he sat up and gunned the motor, speeding across the enclosed grassy field of The Keep and through the gate. The motor of the bike whined as Logan sped onto Pender Road. He hugged the pavement and went into a tight left turn and down the short street toward the water, flashing his headlight toward Matt. Matt was just meters away from the rocky beach at the shoreline, with the yacht not far behind. He brought the Jet Ski to a rapid stop, banging it against the rocks at the shore. Matt leapt off, scrambling up the large boulders that led to the road at the water's edge. He jumped on the bike behind Logan, and they zipped down the road, away from the water. The yacht pulled into a tight turn, coming incredibly close to the outlying stone dock. As the yacht came around, several men on the back deck released a barrage of gunfire at Logan and Matt. Bullets ricocheted off the road and stone fences around them.

"Hang on!" Logan said. He turned sharply back onto Pender Road and sped behind a line of large boats up on trailers near the shoreline. A few bullets made it through between the boats and ricocheted off the stone walls of the factory on their left.

John's voice finally came through the radio into both their earpieces. "Are you OK? What's happening?"

Matt answered as Logan drove onward. "We've got the hard drive!"

"Good work. What's your status?"

"We're being pursued!"

"By a boat?"

"Do you know how fast this thing goes?"

"How many men?" John asked.

"Logan took down five but there are plenty more!"

Logan pushed the bike to its limits as they came toward a long building with steel siding. The bullets stopped dead as soon as they passed behind the edge of the building.

"We're good! For now!" Logan said to John.

"I'm looking at a map of the island. You're just about to get to an elevated part of the road that's well protected. Keep to the right and you'll be fine until you get to the first bridge about one thousand meters ahead of you."

"OK!" Logan said. He slowed the bike as they came to the end of the long building, then stopped just before they left its cover. The road ahead stretched upward into a long steady hill lined with more protective buildings on the left—after a section that was completely exposed to the yacht.

"Hey! What are you doing?" Matt asked.

"They're pacing the yacht to match our speed."

"I figured that, too."

"They can't stop so fast. Give it a few seconds."

Logan counted down in his head, then sped out onto the naked road between buildings. Matt looked to the left and saw the yacht go cruising behind the next row of buildings in front. Logan leapt into high gear and took the next right, going uphill onto Cochrane Road. That kept them on the far side of the tiny island they were on. They picked up speed as the bike cleared the top of the hill and started downward. They merged back onto Malabar Road. The next bridge lay dead ahead. As they reached the stretch of road just in front of the bridge, they could see the yacht. It had slowed down and was waiting for them.

"Damn!" yelled Matt. They both ducked low on the bike as more bullets came flying. The bike lurched to the side as one slammed into the engine and another ricocheted off the exhaust pipe. Logan barely kept his balance and gunned the motor to recover his speed. He took the right fork in front, toward the cover of more buildings. They came to a row of large houses. Logan eyed the cars parked out in front carefully. He came to an abrupt stop in front of a dark blue BMW Z4 M Roadster and jumped off the bike.

"Come on!" He waved to Matt. "We need better cover than a motorbike."

Matt pulled a small tool from his pocket and popped the lock on the BMW. The alarm barely had begun to sound before he hopped in the front seat and yanked out the wire that powered its speaker.

"My turn to drive!" Matt said to Logan, as the motor roared to life. He jammed it into first gear and pulled out onto the road. Matt spoke into his radio mic. "Hey, boss, I think things are going to get pretty messy if we plan on sticking around here all night."

John's voice came back immediately. "Roger that. We're leaving for the airport now."

"We're ten minutes behind you. We'll be there!" Matt said. He approached the next bridge along Malabar Road with caution. But as they got to the bridge and within view of the yacht, nothing happened. The yacht didn't alter its course. Nobody fired at them.

"Keep it cool," Logan said. "They don't know it's us in the roadster."

Matt continued driving just a hair above the island's official speed limit of thirty-five kilometers per hour, all the time keeping his eye on the yacht. It felt like treading water in a pool of sharks. They drove over Boaz Island, which stretched barely a hundred meters and offered no cover at all. Then came Watford Island, even smaller. There was still no activity on the yacht. Watford Bridge was next. That took them onto Mangrove Bay Road, which veered right and behind the cover of Somerset Village. In seconds they were on the far side of Sandy's Parish and completely hidden from the yacht. Matt floored the accelerator, easily dodging the odd car still on the road so late at night. He sped all the way to Somerset Bridge, where he slowed down again. The bridge had a clear view of Great Sound. Matt looked for the yacht, but couldn't see it.

"Look, way over there," Logan said, pointing.

Matt saw the dim lights of the yacht. It was at least a thousand meters distant and heading away from them—to the southeast.

"They're headed for Lindell's house," Matt said.

"We have to beat them. There's too much exposed road there."

Matt gunned the engine and made a beeline down Middle Road. Their first visibility of the sound came as they drew near to Jennings Bay—and Lindell's house. A small clearing in the trees let them see out over the water through the small inlet of Jennings Bay. The yacht was close. Matt sped up. Middle Road found cover behind trees again, and Matt quickly traversed the thousand meters leading to the next clearing at Frank's Bay. He looked. The yacht was closer than before and no longer heading for Lindell's. It was going in their direction.

"Damn it! They're following us!"

"Relax," Logan said. "They could be making a loop back to Lindell's."

The car was sheltered behind trees again for the next few hundred meters, but then came up right against the water of Little Sound. The yacht was barely two hundred meters out and bearing directly toward them. Matt pounded on the brakes to slow the car down.

"Keep it easy," Logan said. He grabbed his rifle from the back, brought the barrel up in front of Matt's face, and peered through the scope at the yacht.

Matt was getting increasingly nervous. "Well?"

"They're using scopes too. Keep your speed level."

Matt turned again to look. "They see us."

"They will if you keep turning to look!"

"I can make it. There's cover up ahead." Matt sped up ever so slightly.

"Not for another thousand meters! Back off!"

Too late. Logan saw two men on the yacht looking directly at them through night vision binoculars. They quickly took aim with their rifles and the yacht sped up to come alongside the roadster.

"Go! Go! Go!" Logan yelled to Matt.

Matt pushed the pedal all the way down. The engine screamed and the roadster sliced through air. Logan saw several bright flashes from the yacht.

"Get down!" Logan shouted.

Both men crouched down in their seats. They could feel bullets impact the car in the front and back. The window next to Matt took a hit and the top half shattered.

"Are you OK?" Logan asked.

Matt flicked his head to the side to shake the small pieces of broken glass from his hair. "Ask me in a minute." His eyes were on the road.

Their radio sounded. "Where are you now?" John asked.

Logan kept crouching and looked at his GPS. "Middle Road, just leaving South-ampton Parish." Another volley of bullets slammed into the car.

"What was that?" John asked.

"We're taking fire from the yacht," Logan answered. "They're in pursuit."

"Then they know where you're headed."

"That would be my guess, too."

"Damn it! We're only ten minutes ahead of you."

"Then get the plane ready for us," Logan said.

"Roger that. We'll see you there," John said.

Finally, Middle Road offered shelter behind trees again after Jews Bay. Matt took a deep breath but kept the speed up. Logan started checking his ammunition for the rifle.

"We're clear now until the airport. You still have your sidearm?"

Matt could feel the weight of his pistol pulling down on the holster, but glanced down anyway to make sure it was there. "Yep. And three more clips."

"Good. We're going to need them."

Sunday, June 19
St. George's Parish, Bermuda

A single black SUV drove quickly along The Causeway—the bridge which connected Bermuda's airport with the rest of the island. The vehicle entered the traffic circle leading to L. F. Wade International Airport. But instead of turning right to the airport parking lot, John Rhoades drove the SUV left along Kindley Field Road. There, opposite the public terminal of the airport, were the hangars and a row of parked aircraft. Annika looked out the window and recognized the plane they arrived in. John parked the SUV in the darkest corner behind the hanger, right next to the chain-link fence. He looked at the time. It had been twenty minutes since his last communication with Logan and Matt. He motioned for everyone to get out.

"We've got ten minutes until they're here. Let's go!" he said.

They all scrambled out in the darkness, and four figures ran up to the chain-link fence separating the public road from the secured tarmac. John and Ken helped Peter and Annika over the fence, then jumped it themselves with their duffel bags full of gear. John led the way, keeping close to the outer wall of the hangar until they reached the corner of the building. Lighting was minimal. John held up his arm to stop everyone there. Both he and Ken put on their night vision goggles. John poked his head around the corner and after a few seconds gave the all clear. They ran across fifty meters of wide-open tarmac to the Global Express that sat waiting. John opened the door to the plane and everyone followed. It was dark inside. Annika and Peter felt around to find two seats and sat down. Ken flicked a switch and a few dim lights came on inside. Just enough to see by.

"Do you have enough time?" John asked Ken.

"Barely. I have to start now," Ken replied.

"Hey, where's the pilot?" Annika asked.

John jabbed his thumb toward Ken. "You're looking at him."

Ken Dochlin was the flier of the group. Early in his training in the Canadian Air Force, Ken was dubbed an air combat prodigy. He was twenty-two years old when he was deployed to the Gulf War to fly sweep and escort combat missions in Desert Storm. But on his fifth sortie out of Doha, enemy fire took out one engine and destroyed his flight computer. The high-speed ejection from his CF-118 Hornet left him an inch shorter and with a spine so damaged, the doctors took him out of air combat duty for good. Ken rotated onto every other aircraft in the Air Force and then transferred into Coast Guard Search and Rescue before meeting John Rhoades.

"Get to it," John said.

Ken sat in the cockpit and the instrument panel lit up with myriads of multicolored buttons, lights, and several display screens. Annika and Peter felt increasingly confident as they watched Ken throw multiple switches and run through his preflight check of the instruments and controls. Meanwhile, John unzipped his duffel bag and brought out two pistols and several magazines of ammunition. He then took out more night vision equipment and brought it to the cockpit. Slowly, the sound of the twin turbofan engines coming to life filled the aircraft. Annika and Peter squinted as the normal interior lights of the Global Express all came on at once. John retrieved a rifle with a large scope mounted on it from his bag. He slammed in a magazine of ammunition and stood at the door, peering through the scope. The whine of the turbine engines grew louder and the air-conditioning blasted on.

"Everything's a go," Ken said.

John leaned his head in and gave Ken a nod. John's radio came crackling to life. It was Logan's voice.

"We're almost there! But we've got company!"

John answered, "The yacht?"

"No, it's too big for the channel here. But their speedboat fits just fine!"

Annika heard gun blasts over the radio. She crouched down in her seat and looked out the window. She could see a lone car speeding along Kindley Field Road and from somewhere behind them, several bright flashes going off. Annika's heart leapt as she heard more gunshots—this time through the open door of the aircraft. John steadied his rifle and looked through his scope. He let off several earsplitting rounds toward the flashing lights.

"Nice shot, boss!" Logan's voice said, with a hint of surprise. "Bet you can't do that again!"

"Get your asses on this plane!" John yelled back into the radio.

A few seconds later, tires screeched in the distance behind the nearest hangar, and after a few seconds Annika could see two dark figures sprinting across the tarmac. John stepped inside to clear the doorway. Matt jumped in first, followed by Logan, with his rifle strapped to his back. They were both breathless from their run.

"We're good! Let's go!" John yelled to the cockpit.

The engines screamed much louder than before and the plane started rolling. John reached to close the door, only to have Logan grab his arm to stop him.

"Your shots only slowed them down. They're still out there," he said, pointing to the water. The entire route to the runway ran along the shoreline, just two hundred meters away from the water. They would be an easy target.

John nodded. "You've got until the runway." He then joined Ken in the cockpit.

Logan un-strapped his rifle and sat down in the open doorway as the Global Express sped up. "Lights out!" Logan called to the cockpit.

Once again, the cabin went dark. Matt took the seat just behind Annika and Peter. From the dark cabin, Annika could see clearly out into the night. Not far to the north lay a thin channel of water just two hundred meters across. On the other side was the westernmost portion of St. George's Island. Annika could see multiple houses, buildings, and streetlights dotting the island. Then something else. There it was. A small boat on the water speeding to catch up with the plane. Several flashes of light went off from the boat.

"They're shooting!" Matt said loudly from his seat.

"I got 'em!" Logan replied.

Without warning, he let off a round, then with quick and efficient movements ejected the spent cartridge and chambered the next shot. He quickly fired off another five shots. The cabin filled with the acrid scent of burned gunpowder. Annika watched the moving light on the water slow down and fall behind them. No more flashes. She leaned back in her seat feeling both relief and horror. Relief that she was now much safer. Horror at the lingering question of how many men Logan had just killed.

Logan brought his rifle in and yanked the door shut. The plane turned onto the runway and picked up speed quickly as the whine of the engines increased to full throttle. Annika watched out her window as the lights of the houses just north of the runway went whipping by faster and faster. The nose of the plane then lifted off the ground and pointed almost straight up. They were pressed back hard into their seats as the plane pulled steeply into the air. The cabin lights flickered back to life. Annika held Peter's hand tightly and closed her eyes. She fought back the tears for Dr. Lindell. Leaving the island meant leaving behind the last moments of him alive.

Logan looked out his window at the lights of Bermuda falling quickly below. The plane banked left to head northward, giving Logan a perfect view of the dark sea around the airport. Far below, he could just see the outline of the yacht speeding along The Narrows, a ten-meter-deep channel which ran next to the very coral reefs that had sunk the *Sea Venture* in 1609.

"Well, that was pretty easy!" Logan called to the cockpit. He chuckled to himself. The yacht was helplessly bound to the water below them. "Let's see what you can do from way down there!"

Suddenly, two bright flashes appeared on the upper deck of the yacht. Logan pressed his face hard against the window for a better look. The bright flashes immediately became elongated streaks through the air above the water. The streaks shortened, and the small bright spots of light started heading directly for the Global Express at impossibly high speed.

Logan jumped up and ran to the cockpit. "Missiles! They've got missiles!" he shouted.

John yelled back to him, "We've got it on radar! Take your seat, now!" Instantly, the 'fasten seat belts' sign flashed repeatedly.

Logan spun around and shouted to Annika, Peter, and Matt, "Buckle up!"

The plane immediately banked hard to the left. Logan lunged forward and grabbed the armrest closest to him, on the seat occupied by Matt. The plane then dove vertically and Logan hung on with all his strength to the armrest. The bags in the back tumbled onto the ceiling of the plane and Logan's body was stretched out, floating in the middle of the aisle. Logan groaned as he struggled to keep his grip. Matt reached out and grabbed Logan's jacket to try and stabilize him. Annika and Peter both felt their stomachs twist. Annika looked out the window to see two flashes of light go speeding by the plane so close she could hear the hiss of the rockets. She recoiled with a gasp. The plane stabilized, and Logan dropped back to the aisle floor, feet first. He jumped into the seat next to Matt and strapped in tightly.

In the cockpit, John watched the radar screen carefully. The two small dots were still moving away at high speed. "That was close! What were they?"

Ken studied the small screen as well. "I hope not heat seekers."

As John watched the screen, the two bright dots turned in a narrow arc and headed directly back toward them. "I think we have heat seekers. Now what?"

"Hold on tight," Ken said. He banked the plane down toward the water. John watched the altimeter go from two thousand feet to one thousand, then five hundred, all the time gaining speed. The collision alarm sounded.

"Hey! Where are you going?" John yelled.

At the last possible second, Ken pulled up hard. They were pinned to their seats as the plane returned to a horizontal flight path dangerously close to the surface of the water. Then John saw it. Directly in front of them lay the yacht that had fired the missiles. They were approaching from the side.

"Please tell me the engines exhaust at the side!" Ken yelled.

"Just a second!" John said. He looked through his infrared goggles. Bright streaking flashes of colored light flared out of an exhaust port at the back corner of the yacht. "We're in business! I see a vent at the back!" Then he paused as he watched three bright figures emerge onto the upper deck. He switched back to night vision and saw they were holding guns. "Guns on deck!"

"I see them!" Ken said. He flicked on the plane's forward lights. In a flash, the boat was suddenly lit up brighter than full daylight. All three men covered their eyes against the blinding light. They never had time to take aim. Ken aimed the plane for the back of the yacht until they were so close that John thrust his arms in the air to shield himself. At that instant, Ken steered hard to the side. The plane rolled until its wings were near perfectly vertical. It missed the yacht by just a few meters. As they flew past, the jet wash pulled all three gunmen up into the air and threw them in the water. Immediately, Ken rolled the plane back again and hugged the water as close as possible, waiting.

The Citadel of The Trust
Long Island, New York

"They're flying right at us! They're going to hit us!" came the shouts over the satellite phone. For a second, an incredibly loud whooshing sound drowned out every other noise and voice on the line.

"What was that?" Roy yelled into the phone.

Somebody hollered, but not at Roy. "The missiles! Hard to starboard! Hard to starboard! Full power!"

The sounds of mayhem and more shouts and screams could be heard for another second, followed by a loud blast, and then nothing but static. Roy stood there in shock. He knew it was futile to ask any more questions.

Nolan couldn't help but smile. Roy's failure was his victory. At the very least, it would gain him leniency from the inner circle.

Roy glowered at Nolan severely. "That was a twenty-million-dollar yacht!"

Nolan shrugged. "Then perhaps you shouldn't have dispatched it." Nolan's phone let out a shrill tone, signaling that it had received a text message. He took it out and read the message, first with surprise, then anger. Then he smiled.

"What is it?" Roy asked.

Nolan held the phone up for Roy to read. "That was for hitting our speedboat on Indian Arm. Now we're even."

Roy's face twisted in frustrated rage. He snapped at the guard closest to him to bring over Gwen Riley, who stood close by bound tightly in restraints. Roy took the guard's gun out and held it to Gwen's head.

"Kill me and you're a guaranteed dead man," Gwen snarled.

Roy burst out laughing. "It's not you I'm going to kill tonight. It's all of them." He held out Nolan's cell phone and took a picture of Gwen with the gun to her head. He keyed in some words and sent the message back as a reply.

Roy then pushed Gwen away in contempt and threw Nolan's phone back to him. Nolan read the message Roy had just sent.

"Is there a plan behind this?"

"Of course there is." Roy walked to the door and opened it.

"Where are you going?" Nolan asked.

Roy didn't answer or look back. Nolan watched as Roy took out his own phone and closed the door behind him.

Over the Waters of Murray's Anchorage, Bermuda

Annika was still shaking from the twin explosions that had detonated not far behind the plane when they were close to the water. The blasts had been so loud, she was certain they would all perish, until the plane started gaining altitude again and kept flying without incident. Peter had his arm around her to calm her down. They both looked out the window at the burning wreck of a yacht which floated in the south channel just off the coast of St. George's Island. Bright yellow flames shot into the sky as the fire engulfed the hull of the boat. Then a large fireball erupted from the ship's remains, lighting up the water beneath it as it rose in the air. The burning wreck disappeared into the waters of the Atlantic, and the entire scene went dark as if a switch had been thrown to turn off the light.

"Another sunken ship for the divers!" Logan said with a smile.

John came back from the cockpit. "Is everyone all right?"

"Nice flying, Ken!" Logan yelled to the cockpit.

Ken gave a silent thumbs-up in return. He still had a plane to fly.

Logan turned to Annika and Peter. "I meant to tell you, when he puts on the 'fasten seat belt' sign, he really means it."

John scowled. It was a rare show of emotion.

"What's wrong?" Logan asked.

John held out his cell phone. Logan grabbed it and looked at the screen. It showed a picture of Gwen with a gun to her head. The text that came with the picture read: *Be here in three hours with Annika, Peter, and the hard drive or Gwen Riley dies. Instructions will follow.*

Annika's heart sank when she saw hers and Peter's names on the message. She wondered when the nightmare would finally end.

Peter grabbed her hand. "Don't worry, these guys won't let anything happen to us." Peter looked up to John and Logan. "Will you?"

Logan grimaced in frustration. "We won't let them win that easily. There's got to be a way."

"There is. I just don't know it yet," John said.

Just then, John's satellite phone rang, still in Logan's hand. Logan answered and listened. He looked over to John in confusion and held out the phone.

"It's for you. Somebody who calls himself Smoke."

John took the phone and listened. He walked several paces toward the rear of the cabin and looked to the front. His normally expressionless face showed the briefest flash of emotion when his eyes came to rest on Annika and Peter.

"I understand," John said into the phone. He cut the connection and headed into the area at the back of the plane where the gear was stowed. He closed the door behind him.

"Hey, are we keeping secrets now?" Logan called out. He looked worried for a few seconds and then walked up to the cockpit. Annika and Peter both looked at Matt for answers. A troubled frown flashed across his face before he turned and faced the window.

A minute later, John returned with a black case in his hand.

"What's going on?" Annika asked. "Can you please take us home now?"

"I'm afraid not," John said. His stone face softened. He looked apologetic.

Annika started to get worried. "Then where are you taking us?"

"There's one way out of this. And that involves you going back to Nolan," John answered.

"What? They'll kill us!" Peter shouted. Annika was shocked by the rage in Peter's voice.

Peter jumped out of his seat and launched himself at John. But in one rapid motion, John reached into the black case, pulled out an air gun and shot a large dart into his thigh. Peter stopped in his tracks and screamed in pain.

"I suspected you'd react like that," John said.

Peter didn't talk. He grabbed the flesh of his thigh around the deeply embedded dart. Hesitantly, he placed one hand on it and yanked it out. His legs buckled and he fell to his knees. He grabbed at the chair closest to him to steady himself, but quickly lost his grip and fell over completely. His head hit the cabin floor with a loud thud.

"Peter! Peter!" Annika screamed. She leapt from her seat and went to Peter, but he was limp and unresponsive. Before Annika could look up to John for answers, she felt the sharp sting of a needle jabbing into her own leg.

"Ow!" she cried. "Why are you doing this to us?" she yelled at John. With another squeal of pain, she pulled out the dart. But as with Peter, it was too late; Annika could feel that the contents had been injected and were going to work. She felt lightheaded. The cabin started spinning around her, far too fast for her to stand up. She eased herself down next to Peter, her back propped up against a seat. John walked over to her and stood looking down at her. His face was blurry.

"Why?" Annika asked once more, before falling into a helpless sleep.

John never answered. When Annika was all the way out, he turned to Logan.

"Did you pack a chute?"

Logan smiled. "Of course. I knew Ken might be flying."

"Good. You have a special delivery to make."

CHAPTER TWENTY-FIVE

Somewhere Over Long Island, New York

Annika woke to the pain of her ears violently popping and a rush of cold air blasting at her face. The wind was so powerful it whipped her hair back and forth across her face. She tried to stand up, but was bound tightly to her seat and handcuffed. The lights in the cabin were all off except for the dim emergency lighting. Through blurry eyes, she saw that the door of the plane was open. Incredibly, someone stood right at the doorway. He wore black fatigues and protective gear over his face and head. He had a large, bulky pack on his back and a smaller one in front. He looked at John Rhoades, who stood behind him, gave a thumbs-up, and leapt out the door. John carefully walked to the door and shut it. The pressure slowly normalized and the lights came back on in the cabin. John saw that she was awake.

"We're landing in twenty minutes." He went into the cockpit and shut the door.

In the next few minutes, Peter came to. Both wondered what was to become of them. The very men who had saved their lives just hours before were now their captors. And they were about to be taken back to the man whose last order was to put a bullet in their heads and hearts. All too soon, they could feel the plane begin its descent. Annika felt herself trembling with fear when the wheels hit the ground. The plane came to a slow crawl. Peter looked out the window.

"What do you see?" Annika asked.

"Nothing at all. We must be in the middle of nowhere," Peter said.

"Not quite nowhere," John said, coming out of the cockpit. "It's an old private airstrip on Long Island."

"Wait a minute! Someone's out there!" Peter said. He watched as four large SUVs pulled up beside the airplane. Armed men poured out of the vehicles and stood, taking aim at the aircraft. Matt and Ken opened the airplane door and got out with hands in the air.

"You've sold us out?" Peter yelled angrily. "To them?"

John nodded somberly. "Gwen Riley is our first priority. This is where we get off." He took both of them to the door and let them walk off the plane themselves. Multiple guns were aimed at them. John followed, holding out Lindell's hard drive for everyone to see. An older man came forward, nearly bald and with a deep scar running down his left cheek. He was the only one not holding a gun. He took Lindell's hard drive from John and returned to one of the vehicles, which promptly left. Annika and Peter were led to a separate SUV than John and his men, and a black cloth hood was placed over their heads before they got into the vehicles. Within a few minutes the airstrip was deserted and dark, except for the Global Express that sat dark and empty.

Ten minutes later, the vehicle came to a halt. The doors opened, and Annika felt a hand grip her arm and pull her outside. Her feet hit a layer of fine gravel covering the ground. The cloth bag over her head was removed. Annika looked up at a massive stone structure surrounding them on three sides. It was nothing short of a modern-day castle. The stone walls were at least four stories high, with dozens of tall, arched windows on every level, many of them stained glass. The driveway pointed straight out from the three walls surrounding them, and ended in a tall wrought iron gate with spikes along the top rail. Annika was certain she could hear the crashing of waves in the distance. That sound usually calmed her, but now it did little to relieve her sense of impending doom. The circular parkway where they stood surrounded a fountain which was lit from all sides. Water spewed from the mouths of cherubim and serpents alike onto a clam-shaped dish raised high above the center. The dish was held in the left arm of the centerpiece, an overly muscular male figure with a flaming torch in his right hand. His proud face was raised to the heavens and his eyes gazed straight up.

A man walked out of the entrance with two armed guards on either side of him. Annika recognized Nolan from the penthouse in New York.

"Welcome to the Citadel of The Trust," Nolan said as he approached. He motioned for them to move.

The armed men pushed Annika, Peter, John Rhoades, and his men through the entrance and down a tightly curved stone staircase into the basement. Annika expected a cold, damp cellar, but was shocked when she entered a room which was nearly a carbon copy of Nolan's penthouse in New York, minus the windows. The door slammed shut behind them. Annika noticed it was the room's only door.

Nolan laughed. "As you've seen, there's only one way into this place—and no way out."

Nolan walked to the front of the room to join over a dozen men that Annika had never seen before. But the woman that stood there, Annika knew. It was Gwen Riley, held under tight guard. The guards that had been at the airstrip surrounded the prisoners. Annika, Peter, and the others were placed next to Gwen. One armed guard each was placed beside Annika, Peter, and Gwen. John and each of his men were guarded by two. In the well-lit room, Annika noticed that the guards that had taken them inside looked different from those with Nolan. They were covered in thick black body armor and wore large plastic face shields that covered their faces entirely, even around the sides. Each carried a small machine gun, but also had two holstered pistols and plenty of ammunition on them. They reminded her of the men at the cabin. Annika shuddered. Nolan's guards were fewer and had been less armed. No armor. No masks. Annika watched Nolan talking with the others. They all looked at her, Peter, and the others like animals about to be slaughtered. Only one man didn't. His expression was apologetic and he kept looking at Gwen.

"Who is that?" Annika asked Gwen.

Gwen spoke softly. "His name is Austin Hayes. He is someone I once had respect for. Annika, don't worry. This is going to work out."

"It hasn't worked very well so far," Annika said. She was stunned at the sincerity in Gwen's voice.

Gwen nodded to the silent man sitting before a large video screen at the front. He had a large scar running down his cheek. "That's the dangerous one. His name is Roy."

The screen at the front of the room came to life. The lights dimmed slightly. Everyone turned to it and immediately all sound died to less than a whisper. Annika could barely make out an image in the darkness of the screen through thick wisps of smoke. Then a tired, hoarse voice began speaking, greatly amplified by the speakers.

"Nolan, I am tired of your failures!"

Nolan spoke back in protest. "We've cleaned up the mess left behind by Lindell's spy program. We have it contained."

"You've contained nothing!" the voice from the screen thundered. "These people have enough information to bury The Trust because of you!"

"No! It was Roy who turned my office into Central Operations!"

Smoke lunged forward into the light. A bitter face, wrinkled and withered by time, showed itself in plain light. But it was not just an old, timeworn face. The skin hung loosely over the facial bones. The cheeks were hollow. The cartilage of the nose and ears showed every detail through thin, fleshless skin. It was the face of a dying man. Everyone in the room fell back in sheer terror at seeing the face of the un-seeable. "You fool! Your incompetence forced our hand! Now we have nothing!"

Nolan was stunned. He spun around to Roy, who showed no surprise at all by what he had just seen and heard. Nolan looked back at the screen frantically. "We have Lindell's model!"

"And it's encrypted. It will take years to crack."

"If I rebuild my Gen-Silico I can do it in five years."

"I don't have five years."

"Then what are we waiting for?"

"For this!" Smoke said. He nodded to someone just off camera. A light came on in the room, and the camera backed away to reveal his old, decrepit body sitting in a wheelchair. An IV tube was stuck in his arm, leading up to a bag hanging on a rack. A second figure walked from the camera toward Smoke and turned around. Nolan, Annika, and Peter all gasped when they recognized Logan's face. Annika noticed Logan was holding up the package she had recovered from Lindell's cabin, marked EDEN 1. But there was something different about it. It looked slightly larger. Something was wrapped around it. There were wires and small canisters.

Smoke spoke again. "Even five months would be too long."

Nolan looked on, aghast. "What's going on here?"

"Not only did you let Mr. Rhoades and his people take Lindell's model from the cabin, but also the last batch of Lindell's cure in existence." Smoke pointed to the box Logan held. "Apparently it works on lung cancer, too."

John Rhoades interrupted, "The cure isn't yours yet."

Nolan could barely enunciate his words. "What's he talking about?"

John spoke again. "That box is rigged with enough thermite to destroy the contents."

Nolan spun around to the screen. "You made a deal? For what?" he shrieked.

Smoke leaned forward again into the light. "For you, you idiot!"

Roy nodded to the armed guards standing with the prisoners. They immediately inserted tubes into the side of their face shields. Annika suddenly realized that the men were not wearing face shields, but gas masks. They took out more masks from among their gear and fitted one on each prisoner. Roy was given one, too. The guard nearest Annika placed one over her face with such force she almost fell over. A loud hissing sound erupted from under the table. Annika could see a thick mist fill the room. The guards aimed their weapons not at the prisoners, but at every man in the room without a mask.

Nolan screamed in protest, "I did everything for The Trust! You still need me!"

"I have everything I need right here!" Smoke bellowed back.

As he coughed, sputtered, and struggled to breathe, Nolan spun around to Roy and reached for his gun. He barely had enough time to remove his weapon from his holster when the two guards next to Roy both opened fire, spraying his upper body with bullets. The remainder of Roy's guards raised their weapons toward the rest of those without masks.

Annika screamed as Nolan fell on the ground, writhing in pain. Austin Hayes, Arthur Cormack, and the rest of Nolan's men watched in terror as Nolan died in front of their eyes. Within seconds, they were falling one by one, grasping their throats for air that wouldn't come.

"Keep your masks on!" John yelled.

Annika saw Gwen Riley turn to watch Austin Hayes and Arthur Cormack lie on the ground, writhing for their last breaths. The dying Austin reached out his hand to Gwen, who walked over with her purse, opened it, and took out a syringe.

"This is the antidote," Gwen said to Austin.

He shook his head and waved his hand "No! It's too late for me."

"You're not like them!" Gwen said.

"Yes, I am. I'm sorry." He grasped Gwen's hand with the syringe and pushed it away. At those words, Austin's eyes rolled back in their sockets and he fell to the floor dead.

Annika watched Gwen return with a face as cold as stone. But as Gwen got closer, Annika could see a single tear running down Gwen's cheek. Gwen turned away from Annika and didn't say a word. After the last of Nolan's men stopped moving, Roy signaled for yet another minute of waiting to be sure. The time ticked by like a small eternity for Annika. She desperately wanted to rip off her mask and run, but knew she couldn't.

Finally, Roy motioned for one of the guards to open the door. Several men walked in with painfully bright UV lamps, shining them in all directions in the room.

"Close your eyes!" Roy shouted. "The UV light decomposes the chemical in seconds." Half a minute later, the UV lamps were gone and everyone's masks were off. John and his men quickly picked up the weapons which had been held by Nolan and his people. John checked Nolan's pulse. He looked up to the screen and nodded. Logan took the contents out of the box marked EDEN I, handed them to a doctor standing next to Smoke, and left the room. The doctor took one of the bags and hooked it up to the IV drip line already in place in Smoke's arm. He also opened one of the bottles of pills and gave some to Smoke with a glass of water. Smoke gulped the pills down, emptying the entire glass.

John turned to Annika and Peter. "Sorry about what I did on the plane. You had to be convinced you were prisoners."

Annika could still feel the pain where the dart went into her leg. "Please, let's just go."

"I think we're done here," John said, motioning for Annika, Peter, Gwen, and his men to leave.

A slow, gurgling laughter erupted from the screen. "Did you honestly think it would be that easy?"

Roy's men immediately turned their guns on John and his men, who returned the threat with their own guns aimed back. Two of Nolan's men had guns trained on Gwen Riley.

John looked up at the screen as he held his weapons steady on the heads of Roy and the guard next to him. "I'm surprised you sacrifice your people so easily."

Smoked laughed again. "Trevor Wilkins didn't just send Chromogen's original data to Annika. He also sent it to the FBI, the CIA, and three major newspapers. I'm surprised the story hasn't broken already."

John was stunned. He looked at Annika for an answer. Annika only shook her head. "I had no idea," she said.

Smoke continued. "What we did here was necessary internal housekeeping. You gave me Lindell's cure for nothing! And now you're going to give me your second copy of his model."

John was stone-faced. "You already took the copy that Annika made."

Smoke raised his hand in anger. The guard next to John smashed the butt of his rifle into the back of John's neck, sending him down on all fours. "The computer at Lindell's cabin logged two copies last night."

John visibly winced at that. He looked over at Gwen. She frowned and shook her head. "Mitogenica is back in the clear, now. Keep that model!"

John looked back to Smoke. "No deal."

"You and your men might survive this with your bulletproof vests. But Gwen Riley certainly won't," said Smoke.

"I don't care," Gwen said defiantly to Smoke. She glared at John Rhoades. "Get that model to Mitogenica."

"I can just kill you all," Smoke said.

Gwen raised her voice at John. "Shoot them! Save the model!"

"I can't! You'll die!" John shouted back.

"Yes, she'll die, John," Smoke said.

"I'll take my chances!" Gwen snapped back.

"You've got no chance!" John said. He started to approach Roy with the flash drive which held the model.

"You will stand down!" Gwen shouted at John.

"I can't let you die." John held up his hand with the card in it.

Just as Roy reached out to take the flash drive, Gwen grabbed the machine gun of the guard on her right and yanked hard, pointing the muzzle at the guard standing on her left. The gun released a volley of bullets into its target, and everyone in the room turned in her direction. Gwen yelled at John, "Kill them!"

In a deafening burst of firepower, John and his men opened fire on the stunned guards, but not before Roy took aim at Gwen. Annika caught a split-second glare of final defiance on the face of Gwen Riley before two bullets entered her skull. Annika gasped in disbelief as she watched Gwen fall lifeless to the floor. John emptied a double round into Roy's shoulder. Roy screamed in pain, dropping his gun. John grabbed Roy's wounded shoulder with a powerful grip that made Roy shriek in agony. The armed guards all lay dead on the floor. John held Roy up to the screen and put a gun to his head. He took back Lindell's hard drive and held it up.

"The information Lindell recovered on The Trust will stay safe with me, until the minute any of us die. Do you understand?"

"This is not over," Smoke scowled back.

"Not by any means," John said. He took aim at the camera over the big screen and blew it to pieces with one shot.

Annika and Peter followed John and his men back up the spiral stone stairwell, through the castle, and out into the circular driveway. John held Roy at gunpoint the entire time. The handful of armed guards that stood along their path all lowered their weapons at Roy's command. They piled into the largest van and Matt took the wheel, driving out and quickly hitting top speed.

"Do you know where we're going?" John asked Matt.

"Not really!" Matt said.

John jabbed his gun into Roy's shoulder wound and twisted the barrel back and forth. Roy screamed in pain.

"The faster you get us to the airstrip, the faster you stop losing blood," John said.

Roy guided them over the next ten minutes to the deserted airstrip. The Global Express sat waiting for them, the door still open. John motioned for Ken and Matt to secure the aircraft. With guns pointed first, they entered and soon gave the all clear. Ken began preparations for flight. John waited outside, guarding Roy. But before the plane was ready, the sound of vehicles approaching grew louder and louder. Two SUVs came to a rapid stop fifty meters away from the plane and a dozen guards jumped out, their rifles aimed at John.

John held his gun up to Roy's head and positioned Roy directly between him and the gunmen. "If we go, he goes!" John shouted.

Matt popped his head out of the aircraft door. "We're all good."

"Fire it up!" John yelled back. Seconds later, the whine of jet engines starting up filled the air. John motioned for Annika and Peter to get into the plane. John followed up the stairs backward, carrying Roy with him. Matt secured the door while John threw Roy down into one of the seats.

Ken shouted back from the cockpit, "Takeoff in twenty seconds!" The jet engines screamed and the plane jumped forward, gaining speed. Annika was pressed hard back into her seat as the plane tilted near vertically into the sky and banked hard to the right. She didn't even want to look out the window at what she was leaving behind.

John turned to Matt. "Call the police. Get them down to that house." John reached into Roy's pocket and pulled out his cell phone, handing it to Matt. "Use this."

Matt nodded, took the phone, and quickly walked to the back of the plane.

Roy gave a sickly laugh and shook his head. "You think that will stop us? The house is already emptied and sanitized. And you're already dead."

"I've heard that one before," John said.

"The Trust will continue. It always will, in one form or another."

John held up Lindell's hard drive with the information on The Trust. "It won't if this gets out."

Roy sneered back, "I promise you, when I'm Overseer of The Trust, I'll hunt you down and kill you all."

At those words, John grabbed Roy's bad shoulder and hauled him up. He looked at Matt and motioned to the airplane door.

"Are you serious?" Matt said.

"Ken, where are we?" John shouted to the cockpit.

"Five thousand feet over the middle of Long Island Sound. Why?"

"We're going to lose some pressure," John yelled back. He looked at Matt. "Do it!"

Matt yanked open the door and a rush of cold wind blew forcefully into the plane. Roy turned pale as John pushed him to the open door.

"I've got my own promise for you," John said. He pushed Roy until he was right at the doorway, the wind blowing on their clothes and hair violently. Outside was pitch-black. "You'll never have the chance." John pushed Roy with all his strength. Annika buried her face in her hands at the sight of Roy falling into the night sky, flailing like a madman to grab hold of something that wasn't there. She was certain she heard Roy's distant, sickening scream just before Matt closed the aircraft door. As Matt and John walked to the cockpit, Annika caught a glimpse of John's face. There was something horrifying about the face of a man who has just killed out of anger. She couldn't describe what it was. She just knew she would never forget it.

Annika felt Peter's hand come to rest on hers. "It's going to be OK now."

"How can this ever be OK?" Annika said, fighting off the tears.

"Get some rest. You need it."

The plane leveled off. Annika leaned on Peter and looked out the window. The first rays of daylight were breaking over the horizon. But now it was time to rest. She closed her eyes. She could still see Gwen Riley's defiant but almost peaceful face, just before she so willingly died. Even that image soon faded, and Annika drifted into a deep sleep.

CHAPTER TWENTY-SIX

———

Tuesday, June 21
Strathmore Mews
Downtown Vancouver, B.C.

Annika jumped at the sound of the door buzzer. She wasn't expecting anyone at seven a.m. and was in a rush to finish breakfast before her big meeting at Mitogenica. She opened the door and laughed in delight. Peter stood there with a dozen red roses in his hand and an envelope.

"I was supposed to pick you up at Vancouver General later his morning!" Annika said. After hearing about Peter's near death from the neurotoxin, the doctors had insisted he spend all day and night under observation in the hospital.

"Come on, I was going stir-crazy."

"And you're fine?"

"Of course. Except this little hole in my heart." Peter pointed to where Matt had injected the antidote two days earlier.

"How did you get here?"

"Uncle Alex. He just dropped me off down below."

Annika looked at the time. "I really need to get going."

"I know. That's why I'm here!" Peter put the roses and the envelope down on the table and grabbed the car keys. Annika took the keys out of his hand.

"I'll be driving today," she said.

Twenty minutes later, they arrived at Mitogenica and were promptly shown to the office of the new CEO, Li Wong. He politely greeted them, and without further discussion handed Annika a letter with his own signature and that of the head of human resources. It was a job offer.

Annika looked at the paper in front of her and the number written on it. She read the number again to be sure she wasn't misreading it. Peter's jaw dropped when he read it. The starting salary of one hundred and fifty thousand dollars was far higher than what Chromogen had offered Annika months ago. She looked back at Dr. Wong, who sat in the desk previously occupied by Gwen Riley. Vancouver's morning skyline filled the wall of glass behind him.

"There must be some mistake here," Annika said. She read the job description again. If she accepted the offer, she would become head of a new division of research within Mitogenica. The new Natural Products Division.

"Gwen Riley left very specific instructions about this, Annika," said Dr. Wong. "As acting CEO of Mitogenica, I will carry them out." He sat back in his chair and smiled.

"But this isn't like Gwen at all."

Dr. Wong stood up from Gwen's old desk. He brought the video screen up and turned to Annika. "There's something Gwen wanted you to see. She sent it to me from her hotel in New York not long before she died."

The screen lit up. Gwen's somber face appeared with the typical graininess and slightly jerky motion of webcam movies. In the background, the opulent furniture and decorations of her hotel suite could be seen. Gwen spoke.

"Annika, believe it or not, you and I have been fighting on the same side. I met Elliott Lindell many years ago when I was a master's student like you. I spent my childhood watching my father waste a brilliant scientific mind peddling his man-made, patented pharmaceuticals to the public. He cared far more about finding a patentable treatment than the best treatment. When Elliott showed me his computer model and told me of his ambitions for a natural cancer treatment, I decided to join his noble fight. But it soon became obvious to me that even he could never finish the model in his lifetime. He needed help. The kind of help only a company like Mitogenica could give. I created Mitogenica at all costs just for that purpose. I designed the Eden Project for no other reason than to help Elliott complete his model. And complete it he did. But, Elliott is now dead and the only copy of his model we have is encrypted. If I don't survive this, you have to continue the work, Annika. I need someone with your drive and integrity. Please take the job, even if you're not a Wistar rat yet." Gwen's arm reached over to the side of the camera, and the screen went dark.

The parting humor made Annika smile. But the smile soon vanished in the wonder of how she could have misjudged Gwen's intentions and motivations so badly. Gwen had given her life quite on purpose to save the model.

Peter grabbed Annika's hand. "What are you thinking?"

"I can never replace Dr. Lindell. His encrypted model will take twenty years to decode, won't it?"

Dr. Wong walked to the door and motioned for Annika and Peter to follow. "Please, come."

He led them into the elevator around the corner from the office, and after all three got in, he took out a key and inserted it into a lock in the elevator control panel. A numberless button below the underground parking level lit up. The elevator went straight down without stopping. When the doors opened, Annika and Peter found themselves standing in front of a large steel door that looked like that of a bank vault.

Dr. Wong nodded toward the panel and then at Annika. "Try it out."

Annika walked up and let Dr. Wong press her hand on the screen. She felt a flash of warmth on her hand as a bar of bright green light scanned up and down her hand. The entire panel then turned bright green, and the steel door opened with a heavy metallic clang. They walked inside a large, dark room of solid concrete. It felt cool and dry inside, and a constant humming sound filled the room. Three massive computers stood in a tight semicircle, each with a tall rack of multiple panels stacked up taller than Peter. A complex mesh of wires ran between the panels. Hundreds of LEDs on the front faces rhythmically flashed on and off. In the center was a large, black cylindrical object with small lenses arranged in clusters all over its surface. Exactly the same as the one Annika had seen in Dr. Lindell's office, and in Nolan's New York penthouse.

"Wow!" Peter gasped.

"You're already decrypting Dr. Lindell's model?" Annika asked.

Wong nodded. "Our cryptology specialists tell us it should take five years or less. When we do, you could be heading the team that puts it all together. And proves it with clinical trials."

Peter spoke up. "But the FDA still hasn't approved Mitogenica's new drug, so you don't have enough cash to last that long. What if someone else buys you out in the meantime and changes their mind on this?"

Dr. Wong smiled politely and looked at his watch. "That will be resolved very, very quickly."

Annika stared at the setup in awe. This was possible. She looked at Wong. "Let me sleep on it. I'll let you know."

Annika was in deep thought as they walked out of Mitogenica and got into the car.

"So what's there to think about? Isn't this your dream?" Peter asked, as they drove out of Mitogenica's parking lot. "And a salary like that is a no-brainer."

"Something just doesn't add up," Annika said.

"Like what?"

"All that hardware. That's not exactly the kind of equipment you just order online and get the next day in the mail."

"You're right. But what's your point?"

"She must have ordered it long before this thing with Dr. Lindell went so wrong. So the question is, what did she originally intend on using it for?"

Peter shook his head. "I guess it's too late to ask her."

"I still need some time," Annika said.

"Well, you're in luck. We have plenty of that, now."

"What does that mean?" Annika asked.

Peter didn't answer the question until they got back to the apartment. Annika set her purse down on the table and eyed the envelope Peter had left next to the roses.

"So what's that all about?" Annika asked.

"We've been through so much mayhem since getting married, I thought a real honeymoon would be in order. Go ahead."

Annika opened the envelope. It contained two first-class airline tickets to Paris. "We can't afford that!"

"Alex had a ton of air miles to get rid of."

Annika shook her head. "It always comes back to—"

The ringing phone cut her off. Peter picked up. He smiled and raised his eyebrows. "Hi, Alex." Then he nodded, grabbed the TV remote and turned it on.

Peter's favorite financial news station showed a reporter with a large red "Breaking News" banner across the bottom. The reporter stood in front of a large building.

Peter read the news ticker running across the screen at the bottom. "Look! Both Mitogenica and Avarus had their stocks halted from trading! Something big is happening!"

The reporter started talking. "I'm standing here outside the FDA offices in Rockville, Maryland. Last week, the FDA surprised many when it granted approval for Avarus's Phase Three prostate cancer drug Chrotophorib while effectively blocking Mitogenica by issuing an 'approvable' letter for its competing drug Mitasmolin—a drug many market players considered to be superior to Avarus's. But in a stunning turn of events, the FDA announced just this morning that it has received compelling and substantial evidence of fraud in Avarus's clinical trial data which affected not only Chrotophorib's efficacy but also covered up major liver toxicity issues. The irregularities stemmed from Chromogen Biotech, the company which Avarus bought out in April. In a rare move, the FDA is rescinding its approval of Chrotophorib, effective immediately. Much more troubling is that the fraud in the Avarus trial was linked to internal corruption within the FDA itself, involving suspect consulting fees, research grants, and outright bribes. Earlier this morning at these very offices in Rockville, the FBI conducted a so-called 'dawn raid,' removing computers, files, and in some cases leading people away into custody."

The scene shifted, showing several people in handcuffs being escorted out of the building by FBI agents. Some held their jackets over their faces. The scene shifted back to the reporter. "Coordinated raids were carried out this morning at the original offices of Chromogen and its new parent company, Avarus Pharmaceuticals. Several high-level arrests were made; however, spokespersons for Avarus have not answered our calls. Several analysts I spoke to this morning said this will essentially destroy any value Chromogen could have brought to Avarus. At the same time, investigations during the last two weeks have revealed the FDA wrongly blocked Mitogenica's drug Mitasmolin, and the FDA has this morning announced full approval of the drug for prostate cancer. Reporting for Finance World News, this is Dan Remick. Vince, over to you."

The scene switched to a reporter standing in the middle of the trading floor at the NYSE, with traders going about their business all around.

"Dan, I'm standing at the booth where Avarus is traded here on the NYSE. We are just about to resume trading on Avarus stock as well as on Mitogenica, which trades on the NASDAQ. Over the last two days, unusually large short positions have been building up on Avarus—enough to get the rumor mill grinding full-tilt. Many floor traders were wondering if something negative was around the corner. Well, we just found out. I sure hope the SEC will be busy following up on some of those trades." He pressed his earpiece into his ear. "OK! That's it, trading has resumed. Wow! Avarus has dropped twenty percent at the starting gate! Volume is huge! Not only does this drop wipe out all the value of Chromogen and its now dead cancer drug Chrotophorib, but the market is taking a sizeable bite into the value of Avarus itself. Talk about punitive! Meanwhile, my colleagues tell me that Mitogenica stock is up over forty-seven percent so far on the NASDAQ. It looks like Mitogenica is back in the game, folks!"

Annika motioned for Peter to switch off the TV.

"Well, what do you think?" Peter asked. His tone was leading. Annika knew where to. She smiled.

"I think I'll say yes to Mitogenica."

"Great!" Peter said, clapping his hands together and almost jumping up from the sofa. "We can have a celebration dinner in Paris."

"When do we fly?"

"The tickets are open-ended." Peter picked up the phone again. "Should I see if they have seats available today?"

Annika smiled and nodded. "Sure, give it a try."

Peter dialed and was put on hold to wait for the next agent. Before he got through, Annika's cell phone gave the short, shrill tone that denoted a text message had just come in. She got up to get her phone from the desk in the office.

Peter cupped his hand over the mouthpiece. "You better start packing!"

Annika laughed as she went to the office. This was the old Peter she loved so much. It was so good to have him back.

New York

Neil Perry Volger stood in the bright morning sun just outside his new home and office. He watched nervously, wondering if it would be finished on time. Crews of workers inside were installing the furniture, putting the finishing touches on the ceiling moldings, and hanging the artwork. Others installed state-of-the-art security systems and the main servers, with a dedicated fiber-optic link to Central Operations. Neil wanted to get inside and get things started. This was the big break he had been waiting for, after all. But now he had so much to do and so little time to do it. He walked over to the stone guardrail and looked down at the breathtaking view. Central Park from forty stories up never looked better. The table next to him held an antique sterling silver tea service. Apparently from Russia. Neil picked up the silver pitcher and poured himself a cup of Japanese green tea. He was never much one for antiques, but couldn't refuse a gift from his new boss. Speaking of, Neil glanced at his watch. It was time to report in to the new boss he had never seen. The man nobody sees if they want to keep living. The man they called Smoke. He dialed and waited for the answer. A slight cough sounded on the line, and then the sound of a throat clearing.

"Neil, how is the new office coming?" The voice was strong and clear, with only the slightest hint of raspiness. Apparently a great improvement from last month.

"Very well, sir," Neil responded. "Everything is on schedule."

"Excellent. And the money from Nolan's accounts?"

"The last of it will be routed through Barbados by next week."

"And how is the new team?" Smoke asked.

Neil balked slightly at that one. "They are doing well."

"Just well?"

"Everyone's still wondering exactly what happened to Nolan and the others," Neil said, as he looked far across Central Park. With his naked eye he could just make out the construction crew working where Nolan's penthouse used to be, before the explosion.

"They got careless and made some big mistakes. I know you won't."

"No, sir. I understand, sir," Neil said.

Smoke changed topics. "What about Lindell's model?"

"We'll keep working on the fragments we recovered from London. But we're better off monitoring Mitogenica. They have the full model."

"Encrypted," added Smoke. "Any news on it?"

"No. They just started. But if they break Lindell's encryption, we will know about it. I have two moles inside already."

"Where are they placed?"

"They're close. One in purchasing. One in IT services."

"Very good. But I have someone much closer," Smoke said.

Neil was surprised. "Really? Can I ask who?"

"No, you can't. Now if that's all…" Smoke paused as if ready to sever the connection.

Neil filled the void quickly. "Sir, may I ask a question?"

"Yes," Smoke said impatiently.

"Lindell may be gone, but I keep seeing more clinical trials using natural treatments against cancer. Vitamin D. Green tea. Pomegranates. Herbal cocktails. Even intravenous vitamin C is back. Are we really winning?"

Bellows of laughter erupted. "You're obviously too young to understand the strategy of delaying, my boy."

"You're right, I don't understand."

"We kept vitamin D at bay for a quarter century and now they're just scratching the surface. Serious trials on IV vitamin C still haven't started thirty-five years after Pauling. Herbs? They're considered healthy snacks, nothing more."

"And when their trials start going right?"

"We'll bury them in the press as yesterday's trivia. We'll question the methods. Discredit the researchers. Then we'll sponsor our own trials with our own results."

"They're going to figure it out sometime."

Smoke's angry voice snapped back. "Let them! We're lobbying with the Codex Alimentarius and the FDA for sweeping regulations as we speak. When we're through, you won't be able to take so much as a vitamin C pill without getting a doctor's prescription and paying ten times today's prices. High doses of vitamin E will be banned as dangerous. If the public wants a cure for cancer, they'll come to us, and us alone. And they'll pay with everything they've got."

Neil felt relieved. "So we'll still win this one?"

Smoke laughed again. "Of course we will. We always win."

THE END

SELECTED BIBLIOGRAPHY

Research for *The Eden Prescription* drew upon the articles and books listed below, as well as numerous other sources. Please note that the disclaimer at the beginning of the book also covers any comments made in this portion. For more information and discussion on these and other resources, as well as breaking news on current research and trials in natural medicine for cancer, please visit www.edenprescription.com.

Nonfiction Accounts of What Big Pharma Is Capable Of

Angell, M. *The Truth About the Drug Companies: How They Deceive Us and What to Do About It.* New York: Random House, 2005.
The author, Dr. Marcia Angell, was formerly the editor in chief of the prestigious New England Journal of Medicine.

Hawthorne, F. *Inside the FDA: The Business and Politics Behind the Drugs We Take and the Food We Eat.* New Jersey: John Wiley & Sons, Inc., 2005.

Kassirer, J. P. *On the Take: How Medicine's Complicity with Big Business Can Endanger Your Health.* New York: Oxford University Press, 2005.

Moynihan, R., and A. Cassels. *Selling Sickness: How the World's Biggest Pharmaceutical Companies Are Turning Us All Into Patients.* New York: National Books, 2005.

Rost, P. *The Whistleblower: Confessions of a Healthcare Hit Man.* New York: Soft Skull Press, 2006.

The Science of Natural Medicine in Preventing and Treating Cancer

Bagchi, D., and H. G. Preuss. *Phytopharmaceuticals in Cancer Chemoprevention.* Boca Raton: CRC Press, 2005.

Beuth, J., R. W. Moss, et al. *Complementary Oncology: Adjunctive Methods in the Treatment of Cancer.* New York: Thieme, 2006.

Halstead, B. W., and T. L. Holcomb-Halstead. *The Scientific Basis of Chinese Integrative Cancer Therapy.* Berkeley: North Atlantic Books, 2002.

Murray, Michael, et al. *How to Prevent and Treat Cancer with Natural Medicine.* New York: Riverhead Books, 2002.

Vitamin D: History and Current Status

Early breakthrough research on Vitamin D that was ignored.
Garland, C. F., and F. C. Garland. "Do Sunlight and Vitamin D Reduce the Likelihood of Colon Cancer?" *International Journal of Epidemiology* 9 (1980): 227–31.

Second try by the Garlands. Still no dice.
Garland, C. F., F. C. Garland, and E. D. Gorham. "Can Colon Cancer Incidence and Death Rates Be Reduced with Calcium and Vitamin D?" *American Journal of Clinical Nutrition* 54 (1991): 193S–201S.

People are beginning to listen. Too much evidence has piled up.
Garland, C. F., F. C. Garland, E. D. Gorham, M. Lipkin, H. Newmark, S. B. Mohr, and M. F. Holick. "The Role of Vitamin D in Cancer Prevention." *American Journal of Public Health* 96, no. 2 (February 2006): 252–61.

Michael Holick discovered the active form of vitamin D. In one of his own studies, he found that 42 percent of patients were vitamin D deficient. He showed it to be impossible to cover our vitamin D needs with food sources alone. Exposure to sunlight (UVB) is also needed. This was greatly resisted. This book summarizes the findings at the time.
Holick, Michael F., and M. Jenkins. *The UV Advantage: The Medical Breakthrough That Shows How to Harness the Power of the Sun for Your Health.* New York: iBooks, 2003.

Seven years later, vitamin D made great strides in recognition as the most important nutrient in preventing and/or treating cancer. Increased sun exposure could result in one hundred eighty-five thousand fewer cases of internal cancers (and thirty thousand deaths) per year in the USA alone. Sensible sun exposure, that is. Details, and all the latest references to research, are in this excellent book.
Holick, Michael F. *The Vitamin D Solution: A 3-Step Strategy to Cure Our Most Common Health Problem.* New York: Hudson Street Press, 2010.

The acceptance of vitamin D is not universal. But currently ongoing trials will prove the science one way or the other. Under the National Institutes of Health, there are now at least forty-seven active clinical trials with vitamin D (or an analog), either alone or in combination with chemo drugs, being tested on at least ten different cancers. Vitamin D is not just about cancer prevention. Many of these trials are using vitamin D as treatment. This is just the beginning.

Vitamin C: History and Current Status

The breakthrough trials by Linus Pauling on terminal cancer patients that started it all. Ten grams of intravenous ascorbic acid per day were enough to triple the survival time of terminal cancer patients, for 90 percent of the vitamin C group. The results were hotly debated, the main complaint being that the vitamin C group was healthier to begin with than the control group.

Cameron, Ewan, and Linus Pauling. "Supplemental Ascorbate in the Supportive Treatment of Cancer: Prolongation of Survival Times in Terminal Human Cancer." *Proceedings of the National Academy of Sciences* 73, no. 10 (October 1976): 3685–3689.

Cameron, Ewan, and Linus Pauling. "Supplemental Ascorbate in the Supportive Treatment of Cancer: Reevaluation of Prolongation of Survival Times in Terminal Human Cancer." *Proceedings of the National Academy of Sciences* 75, no. 9 (September 1978): 4538–4542.

Then, the two well-known Mayo Clinic trials which showed no benefit at all from vitamin C. Just one problem: they never injected any, but gave it orally.

Creagan, E. T., C. G. Moertel, J. R. O'Fallon, et al. "Failure of High-Dose Vitamin C (Ascorbic Acid) Therapy to Benefit Patients with Advanced Cancer: A Controlled Trial." *New England Journal of Medicine* 301 (1979): 687–90.

Moertel, C. G., T. R. Fleming, E. T. Creagan, et al. "High-Dose Vitamin C versus Placebo in the Treatment of Patients with Advanced Cancer Who Have Had No Prior Chemotherapy: A Randomized Double-Blind Comparison." *New England Journal of Medicine* 312 (1985): 137–41.

In defense of Moertel, Creagan, et al., and the Mayo Clinic, there may have been insufficient scientific grounds at the time for them to inject the vitamin C, rather than give it orally. I likely would have opted for oral administration given that, from a clinical perspective, injection is more costly, time-consuming, and painful. But in the meantime, science has demonstrated that injection of vitamin C yields blood levels up to 5000 μmol/L, compared to about 100 μmol/L obtained with oral dosing. See this reference for details.

Padayatty, Sebastian J., and Mark Levine. "New Insights into the Physiology and Pharmacology of Vitamin C." *Canadian Medical Association Journal* 164, no. 3 (February 6, 2001): 353–355.

Once such high blood levels of vitamin C are obtained, how does it kill cancer cells? Using cultured cancer cell lines, Chen et al. demonstrated nicely that it produces hydrogen peroxide in the tissues, and not in the blood.

Chen, Q., M. G. Espey, M. C. Krishna, J. B. Mitchell, C. P. Corpe, G. R. Buettner, E. Shacter, and M. Levine. "Pharmacologic Ascorbic Acid Concentrations Selectively Kill Cancer Cells: Action as a Pro-Drug to Deliver Hydrogen Peroxide to

Tissues." *Proceedings of the National Academy of Sciences* 102, no. 38 (September 20, 2005): 13604–9.

Chen et al. then successfully demonstrated this principle on mice.
Chen, Q, M. G. Espey, A. Y. Sun, C. Pooput, K. L. Kirk, M. C. Krishna, D. B. Khosh, J. Drisko, and M. Levine. "Pharmacologic Doses Of Ascorbate Act as a Prooxidant and Decrease Growth of Aggressive Tumor Xenografts in Mice." *Proceedings of the National Academy of Sciences* 105, no. 32 (August 12, 2008): 11105–9.

The next logical step was human trials. Here, Padayatty reports on high-dose, intravenous vitamin C therapy administered to three cancer patients who showed remarkable results.
Padayatty, Sebastian J., Hugh D. Riordan, Stephen M. Hewitt, Arie Katz, L. John Hoffer, and Mark Levine. "Intravenously Administered Vitamin C as Cancer Therapy: Three Cases." *Canadian Medical Association Journal* 174, no. 7 (March 28, 2006): 937–942

Frei and Lawson summarized all of the above in a review and called for further human trials.
Frei, Balz, and Stephen Lawson. "Vitamin C and Cancer Revisited." *Proceedings of the National Academy of Sciences* 105, no. 32 (August 12, 2008): 11037–11038.

Frei and Lawson, and many others, have gotten their wish. At the time of this writing, there are currently six active clinical trials registered with the National Institutes of Health using intravenous vitamin C against cancer, sometimes together with standard chemotherapy. Go to www.clinicaltrials.gov and find trials by searching for "vitamin C cancer." One, on solid tumors, started in August 2007 and is still active, but not recruiting. Three others which are currently recruiting started in July 2009 (general advanced cancer), December 2009 (pancreatic neoplasms), and January 2010 (metastatic pancreatic cancer). Two are so new that they are not yet recruiting, with start dates of March 2010 (prostatic neoplasms) and June 2010 (sarcoma, adenocarcinoma, carcinoma, multiple myeloma, desmoplastic small round cell tumor). Yes, vitamin C is back.

Green Tea

The research base on green tea and cancer is massive. A search on PubMed using "green tea cancer" yields 1,388 articles, starting from 1975 and accelerating rapidly in recent years.

Of all the papers on green tea I have read, the following two are the most impressive, reporting on a trial that has had remarkable success in suppressing prostate cancer. Sixty patients with pre-malignant prostate lesions were given green tea extract. After one year, 3 percent of those getting green tea extract had prostate cancer, compared to 30 percent in the placebo group. Two years later (the second paper), 10 percent of the green tea group had prostate cancer, compared to 50 percent of the placebo group. Wow.

Bettuzzi, S., M. Brausi, F. Rizzi, G. Castagnetti, G. Peracchia, and A. Corti. "Chemoprevention of Human Prostate Cancer by Oral Administration of Green Tea Catechins in Volunteers with High-Grade Prostate Intraepithelial Neoplasia: A Preliminary Report from a One-Year Proof-Of-Principle Study." *Cancer Research* 66 (2006): 1234–1240.

Brausi, M., F. Rizzi, and S, Bettuzzi. "Chemoprevention of Human Prostate Cancer by Green Tea Catechins: Two Years Later: A Follow-Up Update." *European Urology* 54 (2008): 472–473.

Although somewhat outdated, this is one good book.

Hara, Y. *Green Tea: Health Benefits and Applications.* Location needed: CRC Press, 2001.

There are currently twenty-six clinical trials currently registered with the National Institutes of Health for green tea extracts against cancer, either alone or combined with other natural supplements or with chemo drugs. These are recent. Of these studies, twenty-two are recruiting at the time of this writing. Go to www. clinicaltrials.gov and find trials by searching for "green tea cancer." The cancers being tested include: prostate, lung, bladder, breast, non-small-cell lung, head, and neck; multiple myeloma, plasma cell neoplasm, ovarian carcinoma, skin, non-melanomatous skin, follicular lymphoma, and leukemia.

Pomegranate

A good review of the latest evidence.

Adhami, V. M., N. Khan, and H. Mukhtar. "Cancer Chemoprevention by Pomegranate: Laboratory and Clinical Evidence." *Nutrition and Cancer* 61, no. 6 (November 2009): 811–5.

This is the landmark study that put pomegranates on the anti-cancer map, a Phase II trial that showed a statistically significant prolongation of PSA doubling time in prostate cancer patients after primary therapy, if they consumed eight ounces of pomegranate juice daily.

Pantuck, A. J., J. T. Leppert, N. Zomorodian, W. Aronson, J. Hong, R. J. Barnard, N. Seeram, H. Liker, H. Wang, R. Elashoff, D. Heber, M. Aviram, L. Ignarro, and A. Belldegrun. "Phase II Study of Pomegranate Juice for Men with Rising Prostate-Specific Antigen Following Surgery or Radiation for Prostate Cancer." *Clinical Cancer Research* 12, no. 13 (July 1, 2006): 4018–26.

A general review of pomegranates including the latest research up to its publication.

Seeram, Navindra P., Risa N. Schulman, and David Heber. *Pomegranates: Ancient Roots to Modern Medicine.* Boca Raton: CRC Taylor and Francis, 2006.

Pomegranate extracts have inhibited the growth of breast, prostate, colon, and lung cancer cells in cultured cell lines. In animal studies, pomegranate extract inhibited the growth of lung, skin, colon, and prostate tumors. The next logical phase is human trials, which is why there are now nine active clinical trials with pomegranate extract/juice. Search for "pomegranate cancer" on www.clinicaltrials.gov. All trials but one concern prostate cancer; it concerns follicular lymphoma.

Vitamin E

A general review of vitamin E against cancer is given here, with 163 references cited.

Constantinou, C, A. Papas, and A. I. Constantinou. "Vitamin E and cancer: An insight into the anticancer activities of vitamin E isomers and analogs." *International Journal of Cancer* 123, no. 4 (August 15, 2008): 739–52.

The research showing that alpha-tocopherol succinate is highly active against cancer cells was done in 1982 by Prasad et al. Sadly, after almost thirty years, no significant trials have been funded to test this cheap treatment on human patients. Follow-ups and recent findings are shown here, by Prasad.

Prasad, K. N., B. Kumar, X. D. Yan, A. J. Hanson, and W. C. Cole. "Alpha-Tocopheryl Succinate, the Most Effective Form of Vitamin E for Adjuvant Cancer Treatment: A Review." *Journal of the American College of Nutrition* 22, no. 2 (April 2003): 108–17.

There are scores of trials involving vitamin E and cancer. The tocotrienols have demonstrated outstanding properties. Note that anti-cancer activity is not linked to anti-oxidant power. More information and updates will be provided on www.edenprescription.com.

Ginger

This paper is the background for the fictional scene of Dr. Lindell going to Thailand for ginger. Research on zerumbone (from ginger) against cancer is accelerating. Twenty-nine articles can be found on PubMed: eight articles published from 2001 to 2004, and twenty-one from 2005 to 2010, and counting. No clinical trials yet on zerumbone, but watch this space.

Murakami, A., D. Takahashi, T. Kinoshita, K. Koshimizu, H. W. Kim, A. Yoshihiro, Y. Nakamura, S. Jiwajinda, J. Terao, and H. Ohigashi. "Zerumbone, a Southeast Asian Ginger Sesquiterpene, Markedly Suppresses Free Radical Generation, Pro-inflammatory Protein Production, and Cancer Cell Proliferation Accompanied by Apoptosis: The Alpha, Beta-Unsaturated Carbonyl Group Is a Prerequisite." *Carcinogenesis* 23, no. 5 (May 2002): 795–802.

Synergism in Natural Cancer Treatments

Synergism occurs if the effect of two things combined is greater than the sum of their effects when given separately. This is the principle of Lindell's cure for cancer, and is demonstrated in research that is ongoing.

This is a good example, with 50 mg of vitamin K3 given together with 5,000 mg of vitamin C to prostate cancer patients. PSA doubling time increased in thirteen of seventeen patients.

Tareen, B., J. L. Summers, J. M. Jamison, D. R. Neal, K. McGuire, L. Gerson, and A. Diokno. "A 12 Week, Open Label, Phase I/IIa Study Using Apatone for the Treatment of Prostate Cancer Patients Who Have Failed Standard Therapy." *International Journal of Medical Sciences* 5, no. 2 (March 24, 2008): 62–7.

This study takes it a step further, combining vitamin E with vitamin C and vitamin K3. When given together, they magnify each other's anti-cancer effects. Recall that alpha-tocopheryl succinate was identified as the best candidate of the vitamin E group to kill cancer cells.

Tomasetti, M., E. Strafella, S. Staffolani, L. Santarelli, J. Neuzil, and R. Guerrieri. "Alpha-Tocopheryl Succinate Promotes Selective Cell Death Induced by Vitamin K3 in Combination with Ascorbate." *British Journal of Cancer* 102, no. 8 (April 13, 2010): 1224–34.

Recall that high-dose vitamin C administered intravenously delivers hydrogen peroxide (H_2O_2) to tissues. The below paper shows that vitamin D sensitizes breast cancer cells to H_2O_2 as demonstrated in tissue cultures. Researchers running a trial with intravenous vitamin C against cancer might want to test their patients' vitamin D levels and cross-reference to the efficacy of the vitamin C treatment. Notice also the reference to the mitochondria here.

Weitsman, G. E., R. Koren, E. Zuck, C. Rotem, U. A. Liberman, and A. Ravid. "Vitamin D Sensitizes Breast Cancer Cells to the Action of H2O2: Mitochondria as a Convergence Point in the Death Pathway." *Free Radical Biology and Medicine* 39, no. 2 (July 15, 2005): 266–78.

If the current trials on intravenous vitamin C go well, the next step may be to *combine injected alpha-tocopherol succinate and high-dose vitamin C, together with vitamin K3 and vitamin D (either from UVB exposure or oral intake), assuming no dangerous interactions are found. Other ingredients such as curcumin, ginger, green tea, maitake, etc., may also be added.*

Other Specific Plants/Herbs/Supplements, Their Chemistry, and Anti-Cancer Potential

Eitenmiller, R., and J. Lee. *Vitamin E: Food Chemistry, Composition and Analysis.* New York: Marcel Dekker, Inc., 2004.

Hoffman, E. J. *Cancer and the Search for Selective Biochemical Inhibitors.* Boca Raton: CRC Press, 2007.

Kintzios, S. E., and M. G. Barberaki. *Plants That Fight Cancer.* Boca Raton: CRC Press, 2004.

Packer, L., M. Hiramatsu, and T. Yoshikawa. *Antioxidant Food Supplements in Human Health.* San Diego: Academic Press, 1999.

Preedy, V. R., and R. R. Watson. *The Encyclopedia of Vitamin E.* Trowbridge, United Kingdom: CAB International, 2007.

Ravindran, P. N., K. N. Babu, and K. Sivaranman. *Turmeric: The Genus Curcuma.* Boca Raton: CRC Press, 2007.

The Role of Mitochondria in Cancer

Why center on the mitochondria for killing cancer cells? This extensive review summarizes the current state of understanding, drawing on 866 citations. Virtually all apoptosis is mitochondrial mediated apoptosis. Targeting cancer cells' mitochondria is a quickly growing trend in chemo drug research and development.
Kroemer, G., L. Galluzzi, and C. Brenner. "Mitochondrial Membrane Permeabilization in Cell Death." *Physiological Reviews* 87, no. 1 (January 2007): 99–163.

Vitamin E and Heart Disease: A Case Study in Confusing Statistical Methods

The Shute brothers' original work on vitamin E, showing well-documented, near-miraculous results on many patients with various conditions. The Shutes treated more than thirty-five thousand patients at the Shute Clinic in London, Ontario, Canada.
Shute, W. E., E. V. Shute, et al. *Alpha Tocopherol [Vitamin E] in Cardiovascular Disease.* Toronto: The Ryerson Press, 1954.

A later work by the Shutes, with updates confirming the benefits of Vitamin E.
Shute, W. E. *Dr. Wilfrid E. Shute's Complete...Updated Vitamin E Book.* New Canaan, CT: Keats Publishing, Inc., 1978.

The science is confirmed: a survey of more than eighty thousand women starting in 1980, which showed that those taking vitamin E supplements for at least two years had a 41 percent risk reduction of coronary disease. Reported in the New England Journal of Medicine, *no less, but so quickly ignored later.*
Stampfer, M. J., C. H. Hennekens, J. E. Manson, G. A. Colditz, B. Rosner, and W. C. Willett. "Vitamin E Consumption and the Risk of Coronary Disease in Women." *New England Journal of Medicine* 328, no. 20 (May 20, 1993): 1444–9.

Then the meta-study which implied that Vitamin E increases death rate, and was loudly reported by the media.

Miller III, E. R., R. Pastor-Barriuso, D. Dalal, R. A. Riemersma, L. J. Appel, and E. Guallar. "Meta-Analysis: High-Dosage Vitamin E Supplementation May Increase All-Cause Mortality." *Annals of Internal Medicine* 142, no. 1 (January 4, 2005): 37–46.

This paper shows the complaints from members of the scientific community about major shortcomings of the above meta-study (these, sadly, were underreported by the media).

Blatt, D. H., and W. A. Pryor. Comment on "Meta-Analysis: High-Dosage Vitamin E Supplementation May Increase All-Cause Mortality." *Annals of Internal Medicine* 142, no. 1 (January 4, 2005): 37–46; Author Reply *Annals of Internal Medicine* 143, no. 2 (July 19, 2005): 150–1; 156–8.

Then a study showing that Vitamin E is safe across a wide range of doses (again, underreported by the media).

Hathcock, J. N., A. Azzi, J. Blumberg, T. Bray, A. Dickinson, B. Frei, I. Jialal, C. S. Johnston, F. J. Kelly, K. Kraemer, L. Packer, S. Parthasarathy, H. Sies, and M. G. Traber. "Vitamins E and C Are Safe Across a Broad Range of Intakes." *American Journal of Clinical Nutrition* 81, no. 4 (April 2005): 736–45.

This more recent study showed that 600 IU of Vitamin E every other day leads to a 23 percent reduction in myocardial infarction, stroke, or CVD death in women at increased risk of CVD, once the data was censored for compliance. For a safe and cheap drug with no side effects like liver toxicity, that was huge news. Why did our free and unbiased press barely report this? The confusion was that a large portion of the vitamin E group did not, in fact, take their vitamin E pills as they were supposed to. Using the intent to treat methodology, they were included in statistical analysis nonetheless, and their lack of compliance masked any significant benefit of vitamin E for the group overall. In line with this, the abstract said there were "no overall effects of Vitamin E on cardiovascular events." *But the positive effects were clear once the data was censored for compliance (i.e., analyzing the benefit only for those who really did take their vitamin E pills; see note on page 1614 of the study).*

Cook, N. R., C. M. Albert, J. M. Gaziano, E. Zaharris, J. MacFadyen, E. Danielson, J. E. Buring, and J. E. Manson. "A Randomized Factorial Trial of Vitamins C and E and Beta Carotene in the Secondary Prevention of Cardiovascular Events in Women: Results from the Women's Antioxidant Cardiovascular Study." *Archives of Internal Medicine* 167, no. 15 (August 13–27, 2007): 1610–8.

Will the anti-cancer potential of Vitamin E be equally ignored by the media?

Other Historical Materials

Estep, William R. *The Anabaptist Story: An Introduction to Sixteenth-Century Anabaptism.* 3rd ed. Grand Rapids: Eerdman's, 1996.

Goodman, Jordan, and Walsh, Vivien. *The Story of Taxol: Nature and Politics in the Pursuit of an Anti-Cancer Drug.* New York: Cambridge University Press, 2001.
A fascinating account of the development of Taxol and a good overview of the birth and untimely demise of the National Cancer Institute's Plant Screening Program.

Strouse, Jean. *Morgan, American Financier.* New York: Perennial, 2000.
A thorough biography on J. P. Morgan.
Note: J. P. Morgan was cast as an enemy of The Trust in the novel. This is consistent with Morgan's stabilization of world stock markets during the panic of 1907, at the risk of his own wealth. The concept of Fabergé secretly creating a copy of his original Russian Imperial tea service for J. P. Morgan is complete fiction.

Quotations from Sun Tzu's *The Art of War* were taken from the 1910 Lionel Giles translation.

ABOUT THE AUTHOR

———

Ethan Evers has a PhD in Applied Science and received his MBA from the Kellogg School of Management. Working for over ten years in Product Development in a Fortune Global 500 company, he is the inventor of technologies covered by over thirty patents granted internationally. Ethan became intrigued by natural medicine when a family member used it to hold her cancer at bay for years before finally succumbing to the terrible disease. After years of researching the subject, he became appalled at how the cancer industry and a very complicit mass media appear to be underreporting—if not ignoring—an ever increasing mass of bona-fide science which supports alternative and natural medicine, even when that science is published in peer-reviewed medical journals. Ethan has worked and lived in the United States, Japan, and Canada, and currently lives in Europe with his family. *The Eden Prescription* is his first book.